PINNED DOWN

As I was getting into Abed's Jeep for a drive back to Freetown, I heard the too familiar sound of an AK-47 spitting rounds. When a bullet hit the rear window, there was no mistake: we were the target. I jumped into the Jeep with the driver. Abed pushed him to the back and hit the gas.

"Go, go!" I shouted.

He frenetically drove the Jeep on the dusty road at high speed, but the shots continued and bullets hit the Jeep's body.

"If they hit the gas tank, we're toast," I yelled. "Let me have your gun."

Without waiting for Abed's answer as he maneuvered the Jeep, I bent forward and grabbed it from his lap, turned around, and shot in the general direction of the fire. But whoever was shooting at us flattened two tires and made us stop. We jumped out of the Jeep and crouched behind a hill. . . .

Other *Leisure* books by Haggai Carmon:

THE CHAMELEON CONSPIRACY
THE RED SYNDROME
TRIPLE IDENTITY

TRIANGLE OF DECEPTION

HAGGAI CARMON

LEISURE BOOKS NEW YORK CITY

To Rakeffet my Cyclamen flower.

A LEISURE BOOK®

November 2009

Published by

Dorchester Publishing Co., Inc.
200 Madison Avenue
New York, NY 10016

ISBN 10: 0-8439-6192-9
ISBN 13: 978-0-8439-6192-8
E-ISBN: 978-1-4285-0761-6

Visit us online at www.dorchesterpub.com.

TRIANGLE OF
DECEPTION

INTRODUCTION

You and me, my family and yours—we are all targets. My house and yours, your bus terminal and my train station, our children's schools—all of them and all of us are on a terrorist hit list.

Some people are starting to realize just how great—how imminent—the threat of terrorism is to life as we know it. September 11th brought a glimpse of that reality to the Western world. Haggai Carmon's novels—more than anything else I have read—are what will, if you care to find out, give you the most realistic glimpse into the intricate machinations of a secret world of fighting terrorism. Secret because it has to be if it has any hope of succeeding. Its sole purpose? Security. And right now, that means security against the threat of terrorism.

Terror, death and injury, destruction and mayhem are the tools terrorists use to make clear their hatred of our culture, of our religion—be it Christian, Muslim, or Jewish—and to infect it with a poisonous zeal that knows no rest. Israel, the United States, and the rest of the free world are now more committed than ever to facing the challenge of defeating the evildoers in our midst.

The role of any intelligence organization is to be one step ahead of the enemy. Discover his plans, identify his capabilities, and know his weaknesses. Then comes the frustration of their sinister plans, the attack—whether by combat or by deceit.

Hezbollah, an internationally recognized terrorist group harbored in Lebanon, is one of the world's most closely knit and secretive organizations. It is also one of Israel's arch enemies . . . and biggest challenges. Most of Hezbollah's members have known each other since childhood, have grown up together, and no new kid on the block can infiltrate their inner circle.

Reading Haggai Carmon's *Triangle of Deception*, I was in awe of how accurately he depicts the methods intelligence services employ to penetrate secretive hostile organizations. Haggai has assured me that the book is largely fictional, but still, I find instances where his word weaving is so vivid, so realistic, that I have to remind myself that it is not reality that captivates me. Haggai is a master of the tradecraft and with each twist and turn of this, his fourth thriller, my appreciation for his fictionalized reality has grown.

Apart from the riveting read, Haggai is doing a great public service. His novels may be fiction, but the threat of terrorism is more real than ever, and we can't alert the world enough to the perils terrorist organizations pose; they have no borders, no morals, and no code of ethics, and we are not safe until they are stopped in this battle for survival, fought largely undercover and by deception.

Jacob Perry
Tel Aviv, Israel, 2009

Jacob Perry joined the Israeli SHABAK (Internal Security Service, commonly known as the Shin Bet) in 1966 as a field agent operating undercover in the Arab sector. In 1978 he became chief of the Service's Northern Command and in 1981 he was appointed the Service's chief of the Jerusalem, Judea, and Samaria command. In 1988 Israel's Prime Minister appointed Perry the Director of the Service, a position he successfully held until he retired in 1995. The SHABAK uses human intelligence to gather information on planned attacks and the location of terrorists; at the same time, it's assigned with counterintelligence duties to foil foreign attempts to spy on Israel or incite sedition. The Service enjoyed overwhelming success under the directorship of Jacob Perry, during which time his agents penetrated and destroyed Palestinian terrorist cells and captured or killed their leaders.

ACKNOWLEDGMENTS

For nearly two decades I led a double life. I had "a day job" and "a night job," but only one wife and family. Since 1985, my publicly known "daytime" activity has been to represent the United States government in its Israeli civil litigation, appearing in Israeli courts in lawsuits to which the U.S. is a party. However, away from the public eye, I had a "nighttime" covert activity. I was engaged by the U.S. government to perform intelligence gathering in multimillion dollar, white-collar crime cases that required sensitive undercover work in more than thirty countries.

Obviously, in my years of working for the U.S. Department of Justice and other federal agencies, I could not share the hair-raising aspects of my work with anyone but my supervisors, and some adventures not even with them. Sadly, these events, which are sometimes more breathtaking and imaginative than the best thrillers I have ever read, will never see the light of day. Dan Gordon's battle against the elusive and ruthless FOE—forces of evil—is my idea of the next best thing.

Triangle of Deception is the fourth installment in the Dan Gordon Intelligence Thriller® series, preceded by *Triple Identity*, *The Red Syndrome*, and *The Chameleon Conspiracy*. More thrillers in the series will follow. In my professional life, first in Israel and then working for the United States government, I have had enough adventures, frequently dangerous, to fill at least ten books, and those are just the ones I can talk about, the others I can't even fictionalize.

With this novel, many helped me to avoid the pitfalls which loom when fiction and reality intertwine; unfortunately they cannot be named. Although *Triangle of Deception* was inspired by my work, it is not autobiographical, but rather a work of fiction. Apart from historical events, all names, characters, personal history, and events described in this book never existed. Nonetheless, *Triangle of Deception* is fiction brought closer to reality with every passing day.

Many of my friends—after reading the barrage of my literary-related announcements and realizing I had written four books in recent years—asked me whether I'd switched careers, again. My answer is always the same: my love for the law and my passion for writing intelligence thrillers exist side by side. My novels, though fictional, carry a real-life message: *read the writing on the wall!* Terror, terrorists, and their State sponsors threaten the free world and must be stopped. Unless we learn from the mistakes of others, we are doomed to repeat them.

To the readers in the United States and around the world, who wrote to me asking about the next Dan Gordon thriller, I offer my deepest thanks. I cherish each correspondence.

My former supervisor and mentor David Epstein is now retired. But in eighteen years of guidance he helped me to achieve that which inspires my novels, and I am forever grateful to him for that.

My anonymous Mossad friend used his computer to apply more "cut" than "paste" in his comments, and Jo Anne Shaw put an order into my otherwise erratic writing. My former colleagues in South America helped me steer away from trouble, and Isadora Levi reminded me just how beautiful Bulgaria is.

My journalist daughter Irin spent endless hours reading

drafts and making suggestions. She applied to the manuscript her excellent editorial skills, and I'm thankful to her for that.

My wife endured the nonfictional tension of my long absences. Many of the hours I spent writing this book were taken away from my family, and my gratitude for their sacrifice is eternal.

Haggai Carmon
New York, 2009

CHAPTER ONE

Istanbul, Turkey
January 5, 2007

I held my breath and clutched a worn-out brown leather briefcase to my chest. I was alone in an unadorned hotel room at the heart of Istanbul, not far from the six-minaret structure of the Blue Mosque. Although a magnificent panoramic view of the Bosporus and the Sea of Marmara was visible from the window, the room itself was quite ordinary. One king-size bed; a mahogany-veneered desk; a television mounted on a wall unit; a cheap, machine-painted, framed landscape printed somewhere in Asia to make it appear like an original oil painting; and a carpet that had seen better days but reeked as if it never had. A sweet smell of yogurt mixed with honey seeped underneath my door from the breakfast that hotel guests were having in the dining room just down the hall of this three-star hotel. A blinking red light on the bulky telephone on the night table indicated a message was waiting, but I didn't give a damn. I was deliberately doing the opposite of what Alex, my Mossad Academy instructor, had taught our class of cadets years before I ended up working for the United States government. I was hoping to attract attention, not avoid it.

When you check into a hotel, be aware that the receptionist and the bellman report anything unusual to the

*assistant manager on duty, or the night manager. Always
rent a room for a period longer than your intended stay.
But take caution: if your room is reserved for a few days,
and you come with only a small bag, an entry of "light
luggage" is made on the room rack folio. If asked, you
can concoct some story why you have no, or very little,
luggage. However, you can simply avoid the problem. If
the reservations are for a week, carry a larger suitcase,
even if you have to fill it with old newspapers.*

At this very moment, completing my "active measures"
mission, to use a KGB term that stuck in my head, was my
only priority. I was about to leave behind a briefcase filled
with top-secret documents. Leave behind? Well, how about
"abandon"? Just an oversight of an overworked, burned-
out, senior investigative attorney of the Office of International Asset Recovery and Money Laundering at the U.S.
Department of Justice, temporarily co-opted to the CIA
for this case. I had no idea why I had thought of *active measures*, a term usually used to label a media-related disinformation campaign, when in fact I was engaged in a
covert action of deceit, subterfuge, and espionage. A huge
difference.

I was going to do something I'd never done before—
intentionally desert documents of the United States government marked *Top Secret*, intending that they end up in
the hands of FOE, or forces of evil, enemies of the United
States and the free world: Iran, and Hezbollah, their terrorist subsidiary.

I wiped my wet forehead off with the back of my hand,
surprised I was sweating, although the air-conditioning unit
was noisily blowing cool air. My inner heat was blowing my
mind and wetting my shirt. Why the excitement? I was
working under orders. Were my instructions in writing? No.
Given over the telephone: "There's a box left for you at the
hotel's reception. Bring it up to your room. Inside, there's a

briefcase with files. Discreetly discard the box outside the hotel and leave the briefcase in plain view in your room when you go out to dine or run errands. We want it to be stolen."

Are the documents really faked? What if they also contain genuine secrets? How much genuine valuable information would the CIA give away to establish a credible deception scheme?

What if I'm disavowed? The voice of the person who gave me the instruction was unfamiliar, although he used the correct code words to identify himself, and I was told to expect his call and follow the caller's verbal instructions. Had that been an entrapment planned by my homegrown rivals?

I had to admit that over the years I had collected several enemies, some of them within the bureaucracy. I had learned that friends come and go, but enemies accumulate. I knew I had stepped on sensitive toes of cunning people with elephantine memories and a strong determination to retaliate. "Ruthless," they called me, although I'd just been doing my job. "I'll be there to see you fall," one of them had sworn to me in ominous anger.

What if hell breaks loose and some ageless, balding, and chubby bureaucrat wearing rimless spectacles reads out a statement to a platoon of news-hungry journalists in a crowded press room in Washington, DC? "The United States denies any suggestion that Dan Gordon's questionable acts were part of any purported government assignment. The investigation surrounding this matter is ongoing, and Gordon will be brought to justice if the allegations warrant indictment."

The bureaucrat would be asked, "Is it true that Dan Gordon previously used the alias of Peter Wooten while on different U.S. government assignments overseas?" and would ignore the question.

"Is Dan Gordon an operative of the CIA, who betrayed

us?" another reporter would shout from the back of the room.

"Dan Gordon previously served in the Mossad, Israel's foreign-intelligence service. Do you suspect that he never left their service, but forgot to tell you?" a young female reporter in a red suit, standing close by, waving her pencil, would ask.

"Dan Gordon is an expert in hunting money launderers and white-collar criminals who absconded from the United States. Why was he assigned a mission involving U.S. national security?" would yell a sweating, overweight reporter in a crumpled, cheap suit, holding up his notebook to attract attention.

The bureaucrat would ignore all the questions, fold the single sheet of paper into his jacket pocket, and walk out of the news-conference room escorted by an aide while a dozen journalists in a feeding frenzy shouted more questions as he disappeared behind a closed door.

I touched my forehead again. It was still wet.

I opened the briefcase to give it another look. Inside was a brown government stock file fastened with a white rubber band. The file contained seven FBI counterintelligence memos and other documents with various degrees of classification: *Top Secret, Limited Distribution–Controlled Dissemination,* sometimes together with *Eyes Only,* underlined. There were also three CIA memos. At the bottom part of some of the documents was a notation in boldface:

WARNING: This material contains information affecting the National Defense of the United States within the meaning of the espionage Act 18 USC Secs. 793 and 794, the transmission or revelation of which in any manner to an unauthorized person is prohibited.

Documents carrying such warnings are a real treasure trove to anyone who understands the meaning of knowing your enemy's most guarded secrets and uses it as a sword or a shield. I slowly put the briefcase on the carpet at the left side of the wall unit, just next to the desk. It felt like giving up a baby for adoption. I gave the room a last look and exited to the hallway, closing the door behind me.

The corridor was empty. I took the elevator down and went out to the street through the main lobby door. Istanbul was bustling, cold, and windy. I hailed a beat-up cab. "To Taksim," I said. I liked being in the Taksim section of Istanbul, where some of the best restaurants, tourist shops, and cafés can be found. I looked at the street through the window as the cabbie swerved in heavy traffic. Present-day Istanbul is a bland mixture of architectural styles of East and West with the drabness of commercial areas. But I wasn't a tourist in need of a city tour.

I knew I was being watched. I didn't know by whom, or how. My training at the Israeli Mossad Academy, and later by U.S. federal agencies I've worked for, enhanced by years of experience as an investigative attorney for the Justice Department, helped me focus on my mission. However, this time, maybe for the first time ever, being under FOE's surveillance was exactly what I wanted. I didn't look back or around; I just pretended to be minding my own business, and acted naturally.

Suddenly, I changed my mind. I had to know who was after me. That was against my orders, but old habits die hard. When we stopped in traffic, I told my cabbie to make a sharp right turn, handed him a bill for approximately twice the fare, and slipped out without waiting for my change. I entered a café and went directly to the men's room. Twenty minutes later, I came out but saw only a hopelessly angry and cursing man whose persistent knocking I'd ignored waiting outside. I mumbled something to sound apologetic and went out to the parking lot through the kitchen door. I took another cab and returned to my hotel.

I saw him in the hallway, just a short distance from my

room. A young man, not more than twenty-five, was clad in blue jeans and a white T-shirt. He was carrying my briefcase under his right arm, making his way out. A change of circumstances called for a change of compliance with my orders. The files had to be stolen, but I couldn't see the thief and ignore him, not if he could identify me. That would arouse suspicion, in him and anyone else who might be watching.

The bloodhound in me would never let prey escape. This time I'd let him go at the end, but he'd have to work for it. I ran down the hall and pushed him against the wall. With the extra thirty pounds I carried and my six-feet-four height against his slim body, he had no chance. There was a startled look on his face. He *knew* he'd been caught red-handed. There was no need to point a finger. I held his neck and pushed him toward my room. He showed little resistance. I inserted the key card into the door lock's slot and pushed the man into my room. I quickly frisked him; he had no weapon. I found and removed a screwdriver he'd probably used to enter my room. Although I'd last practiced martial arts when the Beatles were at their height, some things never leave you. I could do what was needed, if it was needed.

"Who are you?" I asked in English.

"No English," he groaned. "Turkish."

"Name?" I repeated, tightening my grip on his throat. That did wonders for his understanding of English.

"Mehmet."

"Last name?"

He didn't respond. I tried again. "Family name?"

"Kemal."

"What where you looking for?"

He didn't seem to understand, although I asked the question several times. When his face changed color, I let out the grip to allow him to breathe a little, but made it clear I'd give him even rougher treatment if he acted foolishly. Then

I did something I would have never done under different circumstances. I turned my head toward the window. Even professionals make mistakes, and they're even easier if you plan them. He quickly pushed my hands away, grabbed my briefcase, and ran out through the door. I chased him down the hall and yelled at him to stop, but he had already disappeared. I angrily reported the burglary to the hotel management, who called the police. Two hours later, when the bureaucracy ended and a police report had been written, I checked out of the hotel and took a cab to the airport. Thirty minutes after my arrival at the terminal building in Istanbul Ataturk International Airport, I dialed a local number, punched in the nine-digit pass code, and left a message on the answering machine: "Seeds planted successfully."

I boarded the next flight to New York. Only when I saw the departing views of the Turkish shores at the horizon and we were over the azure blue of the Mediterranean Sea did I let out a deep breath. The flight attendant served me a mimosa, but the champagne was flat. It didn't matter. I'd had enough fizz that day, and I could still feel my insides bubbling.

Manhattan
January 13, 2006

I was sitting behind the desk in my office on the twenty-fourth floor of a stylish midtown Manhattan office building. Not bad for a government office: wall-to-wall carpets; huge windows in the outer offices, with East River views; soft black leather sofas; and a decor that could mislead people into thinking we were a successful law firm, or management consultants. In fact, this was the Office of International Asset Recovery and Money Laundering, a covert section of the U.S. Department of Justice that battles money launderers who have absconded from the United

States with their loot. What's so secretive about chasing money launderers that actually induced the bean counters in Washington to budget this lavish office? We had to be undercover, because some of the money launderers are also the world's most vile and dangerous terrorists. Some were in Afghanistan and Iraq, but others could be roaming freely in our streets.

Getting them by following their money trail had seemed like a good idea at the time. When I started working for that office as a senior investigative attorney, it became an even better idea, according to the reports the office director at the time, David Stone, and his successor, Bob Holliday, were sending to the front office. Coincidence? Or did I have something to do with it? If only I were modest, I would be perfect. . . . Bottom line: the multifigure dollar amounts that the government collected from my cases and the letters of recognition from the attorney general said it all.

I thought that part of my success resulted from what I'd brought with me when I hopped on that covert U.S. government wagon. My Israeli upbringing and my three-year service in the Mossad equipped me with the conniving chutzpa to succeed in this outrageously interesting but also highly dangerous job. Why was that background important? Because I was trained to think differently—never to take things at their face value, and to question the validity of information others claimed to be facts. Single-source information was treated with suspicion. *Oops*, my Mossad instructor called it in English, an acronym for "only one person saw, only one person said."

I still fondly remember my final admission interview to the Mossad before a panel of three stern-looking veterans. They presented me with a dilemma. "You're driving your two-seater car on a deserted road in a stormy night. You see a bus stop with three people waiting: a frail old lady who looks as if she is about to collapse, a good friend who once saved you, and a woman you have been dreaming about.

Whom do you offer a ride, knowing that only one passenger can fit in your car?"

I answered without hesitation. "I would give the car keys to my old friend and ask him to take the old lady to the hospital, and I would join the woman of my dreams in waiting for the bus."

Although they had said nothing, their facial expressions sent me the message that they'd liked my answer. One of the panel members confided with the two others, wrote something on a sheet of paper, folded it into an envelope, sealed it, and said, "That's our decision regarding your moving to the next level of the recruitment process. Take it to Human Resources down the hall." I went out to the corridor. I was alone and unescorted in this building for the first time. I couldn't resist the temptation or the opportunity. I stopped at the men's bathroom, locked the door, and opened the hot-water tap until the room was full of steam. I carefully opened the envelope and read the note.

> You've proven that you think outside the box. And since you've opened the envelope, then we must have read you correctly as a curious and resourceful person. Welcome to the next level of recruitment. If the formalities are cleared, you'll hear from Michael.

I went to Human Resources with the resealed and slightly damp envelope, although I'd done my best to dry it. A woman sitting behind a desk smiled when I handed her the envelope. "Keep it as a souvenir," she said. "Michael will get in touch with you regarding admission formalities, but that could take several months." That experience gave me a lifetime lesson: ignore any stubborn thought limitations and think outside the box.

Unlike my co-workers at DOJ, who were trained by the FBI or CIA, I was a free spirit. They were products of the assembly lines of Quantico or of "the Farm," making them fine investigators or case officers in the Clandestine Service who were hardworking and honest. I found out the hard way that being a lone wolf in a bureaucratic organization is a sure prescription for conflicts and friction with your boss and co-workers. Add my big mouth and disdain of arbitrary orders, and you may start to wonder why I stayed on, or question the judgment of my supervisors, who didn't show me the door, with or without a boosting kick in the butt.

But for fighting devious minds of the century's most treacherous terrorists, who laundered money on their way to murder civilians, whose cause is chaos, you needed more than what the CIA's Farm delivered. You sometimes needed operatives who could be just a step behind them, or sometimes even one step ahead, waiting for their arrival, and bang! Sometimes, I was lucky to be one of those waiting there. Admittedly, there were other occasions, when they were waiting for *me*. I touched my forehead, remembering the blow it had taken from a bat on one such occasion, when I'd exited through the service entrance of a German bank with a bunch of documents the opposition didn't want me to have.

I looked at my desk in a moment of despair. As if I didn't already have a huge pile of files on it, another one had just landed on top, exactly when my boss, Bob Holliday, called from Washington.

"Dan, there's a new matter I'm sure you're going to like."

With such an overture, I always run for cover and prepare for the worst. What follows usually turns out to be a case of a money launderer who has absconded to someplace where the mosquitoes are bigger than birds, and Mrs. Mosquito loves, just loves, to suck you dry at two o'clock in the morning. Alas, she's just an insect—not the real thing. Or maybe this new case was about a banker who took off with a small fortune and thought that hiding in a country where the waiter at a local restaurant wipes the plate clean with his soiled sleeve before serving you food from the trolley would shield him from my prying eyes.

"Dan, are you there?" asked Bob when I failed to offer the expected jovial expression, "Great," or "Fantastic."

"Yes, I'm here." I was cool.

"Read the new file I sent you yesterday, and talk to me."

"It's just been dropped on my desk," I said, looking at its bar-coded cover name, "Operation Pinocchio." I'd wanted to say "dumped," but I took a deep breath first. I already had more cases than I could handle.

"Super—then go over it, and we'll talk," he said, ignoring my weary, uninterested tone.

Two hours later I had to concede that Bob was right. I liked what I saw. It was different from the routine international-money-laundering cases I investigated for the Justice Department. I called him back.

"OK, I read it."

"And?"

"You were right; it's intriguing. What's next?"

"Come down to Washington on Monday. Be at my office at nine A.M. Leave the file behind—don't let it leave your office."

That day I entered the conference room adjacent to Bob Holliday's office on the eleventh floor in a modern Washington office building. Esther, the office admin, welcomed me. She was a pleasant-looking African-American in her early fifties with streaks of gray hair.

"Wait until you hear the rest of it," she suggested in a low voice. She knew me well and understood my temperament. I liked listening to Esther, who always knew how to insert sense and reason into a conversation when none was immediately available.

Inside, Bob welcomed me. "Dan," he said ceremoniously, "I'm sure you remember Eric Henderson of the CIA." He pointed to a tall man, once blond but now balding, who stood next to the window, looking over the red-brick buildings of east Washington. "He heads a CIA special task force," Bob added.

"Of course," I said coolly. There went my day. I thought of the heartburn Eric had given me during my chase of the man with triple identities and in another case during my combat against the perpetrators of the Red Syndrome. Conveniently, I didn't think about the palpitations I'd given him. Although to err is human, blaming others for your mistakes was something Eric had perfected. Having participated in several covert operations with Eric, in my mind I classified him as the quintessential CIA top dog: long and sleek, with a bite that can sever your arm. Was it just a coincidence that the description also fit an electric ray of the torpedo type? As suggested by the Latin origin of that ray's name, Eric could "*torpēre*" his rivals, cause them to be stiffened or paralyzed, as if they'd touched a live power line. Eric might head a task force, but his conduct was of an autocrat nonpareil.

"Dan," he said with equal enthusiasm.

"And this is Paul McGregor from the Agency's Directorate of Operations' CAS subdivision, the Covert Action Staff, handling political and economic covert action." He was a burly man in his early fifties with raven-dark hair and blue eyes. He looked like my favorite high-school teacher.

I shook Paul's hand.

Bob closed the door as we sat down. "Eric and Paul are here to discuss a case that needs our cooperation. Have you read the file?"

"You mean Operation Pinocchio? Yes, I have." I looked at Bob, who sat at the head of the table. His three years as the head of the Office had given him extra confidence. It had also grayed the hair of his mustache and hastened the loss of hair on his scalp. He had clever eyes behind rimless spectacles, which reflected a sharp and quick but careful mind.

Bob turned to Eric. "The floor is yours." Eric started talking, at great length, about geopolitical changes in the world. Country-against-country wars are diminishing, while state-less terror is increasing. Staring at him, I thought, what the hell is he talking about? Is this why I was brought here from New York? To hear *this*? I tried not to sigh and patiently waited for the overview to end. I knew there was something they wanted me to do, but my patience was running thin. I might have managed to keep a straight face, but my de-meanor sent different signals. Eric recognized my body lan-guage and seemed annoyed. Five minutes later, he finished his review and asked Paul to continue.

Paul spoke with the authority of a man who is listened to, but as I quickly discovered, one had to have patience and lots of time to do that listening. He spoke very slowly.

"We're increasing our intelligence-collection efforts throughout the world, particularly in HUMINT, human in-telligence gathering, rather than relying solely on SIGINT, technical communication gathering. I'm here to discuss one segment of that effort: terror financing. Since Iran never sends its soldiers to fight the dirty terrorist war, pre-ferring proxies to dipping its hands into the mud, one way of thwarting the master and proxy's plans is by following the money trail and cutting it. Otherwise, when money flows in, terrorists act."

Finally.

"Hezbollah's financing comes from Iran, approximately one hundred million dollars per year. With mounting fi-nancial difficulties caused by sanctions imposed by the U.S., a lagging local economy, and the need to modernize its aging oil industry, Iran just can't supply Hezbollah with all the money they need. Therefore, Iran tells Hezbollah to raise more money independently. Iranian funding, even when traced, doesn't tell us much. It's a transfer from point A to point B. However, Hezbollah independently raises money from thousands of sources, small and big. That gives us the opportunity to follow the money trail until it reaches their growing network of terrorists in and out of Lebanon and their preparations to attack Israeli and American targets under Iranian orders. Although Iran created Hezbollah in 1982 and exercises enormous influence over them, Hezbollah is nobody's puppet." He paused for a drink of water. "Analyzed money movements tell about plans, and when plans are known, they can be averted. Hence the need for intelligence before they move."

I took a deep breath. Iran was very much on my mind. Although already long safe at home, I still had many sleepless nights remembering what I'd been through just a few years ago. I'd ventured into Iran in a covert operation accompanied by an unwitting Austrian woman to look for an Iranian sleeper agent coded "Chameleon" operating in the U.S. I had barely escaped capture by VEVAK, the Iranian security services, and made it safely through the mountains to Turkey. Since then, just discussing operations relating to Iran sent my heart racing.

Eric continued. "During the past three or four years we've been closely watching Hezbollah's illicit finance network in one particular area: the Triple Frontier region of Paraguay, Argentina, and Brazil." He paused.

"Are you familiar with the area?" asked Paul, looking at me.

"Just generally," I answered. "I know that Ciudad del Este, Paraguay's second largest city located in the Triple Frontier, has long been known as a cesspool for bad people of the worst kind—money launderers, arms and drug traffickers, contraband smugglers, and other hoodlums."

"Right," confirmed Paul. "On top of these activities, the Triple Frontier region is also used by terrorists who can blend into a population of more than thirty thousand Middle Eastern and Iranian immigrants. Islamic terrorist groups including Hezbollah, Al-Qaeda, and Hamas use the Triple Frontier region to raise and launder money, recruit followers, even train and hide operatives."

"Successfully?" I asked.

"Bringing in tens of millions of dollars every year since the late 1990s seems successful to me. We were well rooted in the Triple Frontier region, but in a relatively small town. Everyone knows everyone. Our local guy's identity was recently exposed, and he's since been made a pariah. People stay away. We need a new face there, one with moneylaundering investigation experience."

"Dan is the man," said Bob, putting me up for sale.

"What am I expected to do?" I asked, accepting the task.

Eric looked me in the eye. "Recently, Hezbollah got worried about increased pressure by local authorities, who in turn were pressured by the U.S.—that this would decrease their cash flow from these operations. So they began shifting efforts toward another lucrative source of financing: the diamond trade in West Africa. Here's where you come in as well."

"I'm listening," I said.

"Your mission is to identify the new trails from the Triple Frontier region to West Africa. See who the players are and follow them to their new location. Get to know their methods and intentions. Find out whether the new location is scheduled to become a moneymaking source, for money laundering for other profit centers. Maybe they have a whole other idea there. The key is tracking down money that finances terror organizations."

For the next two hours, I listened to Eric and Paul outline the plan for a covert operation to follow my stay. It would get my attention, curiosity, and time for the next year and a half. I had no reason to doubt Eric's or Paul's description of my mission, but I suspected they were keeping out a major part of the picture. It was just a hunch. But boy, how accurate can hunches sometimes be. I didn't know it then, didn't realize what I was getting myself into. Had I known that then, would I still have done it?

Of course.

CHAPTER TWO

Under instructions from Bob, my meticulous and careful boss, I continued using my Manhattan office, but transferred all my pending cases to others in the department. My time was exclusively dedicated to Operation Pinocchio.

I sat at my computer desk and read the posting on the LebaneseDate Web site on the Internet:

> Hi! My name is Anthon Shammas. I'm from Lebanon, precisely from Kana. I plan to coming to Lebanon soon. I was borned there thirty-three years ago but moved with my family to Sierra Leone when I was three years old. My dad stablished here his own business, and now he has more than ten companies with his brothers. Our main major is Import & Export. Can we correspond? I really wish it. I speak French, English, and Arabic. Take care of you and answer me! I attach my picture. Je parle Le Francais l'Anglais et l'arabe. ECRIVEZ MOI!! Et Salut à tous les Libanais et Libanaises où qu'ils soient au Monde!!

"Look at that," I told Eric, who was standing behind me looking at the monitor. "Do you think he will do?" This posting was number three hundred forty-four on my short list. Three hundred forty-three postings hadn't quite qualified. I was tiring from the tedious process and from sitting at the computer all day. I missed the action and excitement of field operations. If I were content with a desk job, I would have stayed at the Mossad. Of course, I hadn't left by choice. My identity had unexpectedly been exposed during a European operation, and my cover blown. A man that had accompanied a potential source turned out to be a Palestinian who had previously worked as a landscaper at my parents' garden in Tel Aviv. He knew me well, and seeing him come to the rendezvous had placed him as member of the opposition. Apparently, he'd left Israel and joined a terrorist organization; that didn't stop him from selling information on his associates for quick cash payments. When he saw me, he realized we were Israelis, and not Europeans, as we'd said we were during the earlier recruiting process through third parties he trusted. He said something to the man next to him, and they quickly turned around and left. His willingness to sell out his comrades was apparently limited to European intel buyers, not to Israelis. In that case our "hooking points," which had led to the rendezvous, were only financial, not sexual or other pressure points, and that enabled them to quickly forgo the cash—staying away from Israelis was incentive enough. That incident doomed my professional fate and future at the Mossad. I was trained to be an enigma and turned out to be an open book. I could no longer participate in covert Mossad operations.

"Thanks but no thanks," I'd told my boss when I told him I was leaving. A desk job for the rest of my professional life? It had become my only option at the Mossad, and pushing paper at headquarters wasn't my idea of combating terror. It took him by surprise, since a Mossad job is usually a lifetime career, not just a few lines in a long résumé. I went to law school, divorced my wife, and after graduation and several years of practice in my father's law firm, relocated to the United States to work for the Justice Department. The rest is, well, not history but an ongoing series of adventures.

My life not only turned around, it actually turned upside

down—in a positive sense, not counting the times I was attacked, taken hostage, or shot at. And now at the DOJ? There were some desk-job aspects, but the field activities that followed made all the difference. Whenever I was tired of reviewing bulky office files, I reminded myself that I was about to move to the next step. All I had to do was set the trap, lace it with honey, and go for the kill. Sometimes I just couldn't wait.

Eric read the posting. "I'll get back to you," he said as he walked out of my office. On the following day, he called.

"OK, we checked him out. He has some good 'starters.' He's an ethnic Lebanese, a Catholic Maronite from the South. He comes from Kana, where in 1995 the Israeli army mounted 'Operation Grapes of Wrath' to halt Hezbollah's bombardment of Israel's northern frontier, and its artillery mistakenly hit a UN base, killing nearly one hundred Lebanese civilians. Since Kana is a small place, I suspect many of the dead were members of his close or distant family. Therefore, he could harbor rage at Israel. We estimate that he would support whoever fights Israel, particularly the Hezbollah. Yes, they're mostly Shiite, but they have many Maronite supporters. His immediate family is well rooted in Sierra Leone and is known to support Hezbollah through big-money donations. They have about eleven clothing and souvenir stores, two gas stations, a movie theater, and a flea market. Let's try him out."

Finally.

Dear Anthon,
My sister told me about your posting on the Internet and I saw your picture, so I decided to write, although I'm not Lebanese. I hope you don't mind. I'm Erin Mitchell; I'm twenty-five years of age and live in Dublin, Ireland. I work as a shop assistant in a grocery not far from where I live with my mother and older sister. I like going to the cinema and read romance books. I've never been outside

*of Ireland, but I hope to save up enough money to travel
one day. Please tell me more about you.*
Sincerely, Erin
*P.S. I don't have a current photo of me, but I'll get one
soon and e-mail you.*

Eric quickly read on my monitor the response I'd prepared. "Good, send it."

I pressed the send button. I didn't need to worry about
an attempt to trace my computer's IP address or my e-mail
address. A CIA computer technician had taken care of
that. "It's mirrored," he had explained as he installed my
new dedicated desktop. A trace would lead to a computer in
an Internet café in Dublin.

Five hours later, a response appeared in my mailbox.

"He took the bait," I reported to Eric over a secure telephone. "Given his enthusiasm, I suspect Erin was the only
one to respond."

"Keep on it," suggested Eric. "I'm e-mailing you a photo
to attach. Keep him simmering. Nothing practical, such as
a personal meeting or anything of that sort. Just chat, and
trickle personal information according to the legend. Try
to get info on Anthon and his family from him, but don't be
too inquisitive."

For the next two months Erin—that is, I—and Anthon
became the best of friends. We e-mailed each other about
everything . . . well, almost. Very quickly, Anthon wanted
to know if Erin had a boyfriend.

"I used to, but we broke up," wrote Erin. "What about
you?"

"No. I never had a chance for serious relationship. My
family is very conservative. I must see only Christian girls
from respectable families like mine. But those in Sierra Leone are either respectable or nice. I couldn't find anyone
who is both."

* * *

"Take it up a notch," suggested Eric when I reported that Anthon wrote that he returned to Sierra Leone from a family visit to Lebanon.

"There's something that bothers me," I said.

"What?"

"His English is all of a sudden much better. You've seen his original posting. It was ridiculous, and two months later he perfected the language?"

"You're paranoid," said Eric. "There no chance in hell that he knows we're behind it. He probably found local help to make him look good."

Anthon,
Please tell me about Lebanon. I'm curious.
Erin

Dear Erin,
Lebanon is the most beautiful country in the world. I never realized how much I missed Lebanon. Now we have pride because my hero brothers of Hezbollah drove the Israelis out of southern Lebanon several years ago. I loved looking at the hills and the valleys that were carpeted with olive groves. The Lebanese people have been growing up the tree for centuries. Olive and olive-oil production is an important part of the Lebanese village society and culture, exactly as our seafaring Phoenician ancestors did before us.
Anthon

Erin waited three days without answering.

Hi Erin I have been waiting to hear from you, are you OK?
Anthon

I let him simmer for two more days.

Thanks, Anthon. Yes, I'm fine. I was busy at the grocery and I'm all excited that my father, whom I've not seen for a long time, is coming to Dublin to visit. I'm glad you enjoyed visiting Lebanon. Frankly, I don't like politics and seldom watch the television. And when I do, I see only violence all around. Why can't the world have some peace?
Erin

Anthon was quick to respond.

We're tired of violence as well, but I can't betray my Leb-anese brethren in their struggle. Someday I hope to marry and raise my children in a peaceful society. Until then I'm a soldier for the cause.
Anthon

Erin waited two days and replied.

I'm sorry I didn't write earlier. My father came for a visit. I was so excited. He is a mining engineer and has just re-tired from a long service for the United Nations. Must run, I'll write later.

Another two days passed and an anxious Anthon sent two messages, which we ignored. On the third day, Erin responded.

I'm having great fun with my father. He's home for a while but I'm afraid he'll leave soon. He's been asked to do some consultancy job in Paraguay that's in South America. I don't think he wants to go there because he doesn't speak Spanish and doesn't know anything or anyone in Paraguay. On the other hand I think he'll be miserable doing nothing, so he's torn.

A response came a few hours later.

Dear Erin,
It so happens that my father has a cousin who lives in South East Paraguay, if your father's job is in that area perhaps my relative could help.

Erin answered.

Hi Anthon,
Thank you very much; my father's job offer is in Ciudad del Este. I have no idea where it is, but my father says it's on the banks of the River Paraná, close to the Brazilian border.

Anthon's reply came almost immediately.

Dear Erin,
What a coincidence, that's the city my relative lives in. Tell your father I'll be happy to make the connection.

I reported progress to Eric.

Hi Anthon,
Thank you very much. I told my father about your kind offer and he thanked you. However in the meantime, he has additional job offers in other countries, which he is also considering.

The e-mail exchange went on for additional ten days, but we let the topic stray from Erin's father's job plans. Then Erin wrote.

Dear Anthon,
Remember your kind offer to introduce my father to your relative in Paraguay? I think my father is ready to use it.

*Last night he signed with the Paraguayan government a
short-term consultancy contract—something about diamond drilling. So, if you can give me your relative's name
and address I'll give it to my father. It'd be nice if you told
your relative to expect my father's call. Oh, I forgot to ask
for his name and telephone number. My father's name is
Patrick Sean Mitchell.*

On that evening Anthon responded:

*Dear Erin,
My father's cousin's name in Ciudad del Este is Jacques
Shammas. He is expecting your father's call and said
he'd be happy to help. He owns a big electronics shop
and knows everyone in town. His number at the shop is
(595 61) 12 2121.*

CHAPTER THREE

Bob called me. "Time to move. I've just forwarded you
instructions to report within twenty-four hours to
Camp Peary, Virginia." I went home, packed my bag, and
headed south. When I passed Williamsburg, I saw the
sign:

DEPARTMENT OF DEFENSE
ARMED FORCES EXPERIMENTAL TRAINING ACTIVITY

It was the Farm, a ten-thousand-acre site where CIA career trainees undergo an eighteen-week course in "operational intelligence." The graduates are assigned to CIA's
Clandestine Service and become intelligence and case of-

ficers. Given the type of mission I was assigned to do, and in particular my personal résumé of service in Israel's Special Forces and then at the Mossad, I didn't have to do any PM, or paramilitary training, which is no picnic. Instead, I had four days of briefing, and an additional six days of training, which included escape and communication procedures, and a code-use-refreshment course.

I was introduced to cryptonyms again. A young brunette was all business. I wondered if she ever smiled.

"Just so you're aware," she said patiently, "we use only code words, not even aliases in intra-agency communications."

I didn't want to interrupt to tell her I already knew that, and let her continue.

"The cryptonym we use usually has a two-letter prefix—a digraph—which identifies a geographical location or a particular section of the Agency. Most of the time, for security reasons the cryptonym is an arbitrary English word. If the cryptonym relates to a group, then the generic cryptonym will describe the group, and if particular members of the group are referenced, then the cryptonym will be followed by a number, where each member of the group has a pre-designated number."*

I also got half a dozen vaccines that made it difficult for me to sit for two days. I received a new identity as Patrick Sean Mitchell, an Irish-born and South African–educated mining engineer. In a travel folder, I found airline tickets, a passport with many entry and exit stamps from six countries, two credit cards, family photos, a genuine vaccination card, and pocket debris. I went home to New York to see and kiss good-bye Karen and Tom, my real-life children, and Snap, my playful golden retriever. At JFK airport, I gave my Dan Gordon U.S. passport to an Agency represen-

---

* To ease reading, I did not use the cryptonym attached to each character in the novel.

tative and became Patrick Sean Mitchell. I flew with American Airlines to Asunción and continued with TAM Mercosur to Guarani International Airport serving Ciudad del Este, Paraguay. My airline ticket showed that my flight originated in Dublin, Ireland.

I got off the plane feeling every bone and muscle in my aching body and went to the arrival hall to rent a car. A forty-five minute drive through endless traffic jams told me the story of this dusty, hot, and fairly new city of two hundred fifty thousand. Old-model cars sputtered black exhaust, forcing me to shut my car windows. Boys on mopeds were weaving through traffic. I was in the midst of a shopping extravaganza. It started on the highway, where vendors were standing or sitting in the outer lanes selling bread, fruit, but mostly CD/DVD players and other home electronics. Four- and five-story air-conditioned malls with names like "Monalisa," "America," and "China" were full of shoppers. Fake Gucci and Coach goods were displayed next to watches and soccer-jersey knockoffs. In front of some stores, I saw fierce-looking armed guards with sawed-off shotguns and even machine guns. It seemed as if I could buy these killing toys at a street vendor's stand with no questions asked or ID required. I knew I wasn't watching a movie about lawless California or Alaska during the gold rush. Ciudad del Este was a real twenty-first-century story. I even expected to see a speeding car with passengers spewing a spray of bullets. But there was no gunfire—and besides, how could a car speed in these congested roads?

I drove to Casablanca Iguazu Falls Resort, a twenty-room, Spanish-style, old mansion hotel with great views of the Iguaçu Falls. I had dinner on the veranda overlooking the river and enjoyed the local specialty, Surubi, a river fish served cordon bleu style.

Within a few days, I had more "friends" than there are in a Quaker school. Sadly, they weren't a bit as nice or as honest as the Quakers. I went right to work seeking good sources of information. Under the pretext of locating service providers for my soon-to-follow engineering survey team, I searched for security consultants, telling them I wanted to assess the risks and provide physical protection for me and my future staff while on location. I easily found self-proclaimed former intelligence operatives vying to sell me compelling information about anything. Very quickly, though, I discovered that verifying the credibility of their stories—or their identities—was an exercise in futility. One thing for sure: the money they wanted for their services and information was the only valuable thing offered in the exchange.

In my search for suppliers, I happened onto Alberto, a jack-of-all-trades. I inquired about food and fuel supplies for "the expedition that would follow." After a two-hour negotiation over five bottles of beer and half a bottle of wine, most of which he consumed, and an advance of two hundred fifty dollars, which he also consumed, I became his best friend of the day. I realized that his price quotes for the goods were higher than the cost of similar goods if I purchased them independently, even when I included his commission. I asked him for the reason. "Is it taxes?" I played the fool.

"No taxes," he said, "but I must pay . . ."

He didn't say "protection," but the insinuation was clear, and *that* was my main interest.

"You mean you have to pay some guy just for the right to do business here?" I asked, hoping I sounded surprised.

He looked at me with disbelief. "Mister, were you born yesterday? Of course I have to pay, unless I want to die early, Santa Maria."

"I didn't realize the Mafia was here," I said with my best naïveté.

"They're just like the Mafia, but they are from the Middle East, and they have guns and a short fuse."

"I read stories about that in the media, but I thought they had left."

He gulped beer directly from the bottle. "There were many more here. Some left."

"I thought you just said they were extorting you."

"They do, the *hijos de putas*. The big-time guys moved out but left violent 'tax collectors' behind. They come and say I must contribute money to the Orphans of Martyrs Program run by Hezbollah in southern Lebanon to support families of persons killed in Hezbollah attacks and other operations."

He had just corroborated the intel that Hezbollah extorted money from mom-and-pop operations. He had also confirmed what I'd heard back home, that the main show—Hezbollah's massive presence here—was over for some reason, but not for the purpose of my assignment.

I went to see the local chief of police. Thankfully, he spoke English. "I'm a mining engineer on a fact-finding tour heading a soon-to-arrive group of diamond-exploration surveyors. We're concerned with the personal safety of our staff. Can you tell me what we should expect? I was encouraged, hearing about your great success in driving some bad guys out of town."

With such a kiss-ass introduction, he was all smiles. But it wasn't enough to answer my questions, because he looked at his watch and said, "It's lunchtime. Can you come back later?"

"I'm hungry, too," I said jumping on the opportunity to have an uninterrupted conversation with him. "Why don't you join me for lunch. I'm on a generous expense account."

He offered me another broad smile that stretched his narrow mustache. "I'd be happy to."

"I must compliment you on your excellent English," I said, buttering him up again.

"I lived for nine years in Michigan," he said. "I was married to an American woman, and very few people spoke Spanish in our town. I had to pick up English quickly."

We went to his beat-up squad car and drove to a restaurant just outside the city center. Ignoring traffic and parking rules, he parked right outside the restaurant's entrance. The owner rushed to greet him and gave us the best table.

After food and drinks were ordered ("Order the best wine," I suggested), I resumed our conversation. I reminded him that my company was concerned about local bad guys.

"Which bad guys? There were many," he asked, drinking a glass of Chilean wine.

"Hezbollah, Hamas, and similar organizations."

"Yes," he said in satisfaction. "We, together with the antiterrorist police, known as SEPRINTE, the Secretariat for the Prevention of International Terrorism, raided local Hezbollah supporters. We have uncovered records showing that millions of dollars were illegally transferred to Hezbollah. We arrested most of them."

"Most?"

"Well, one managed to get away to Brazil. Assad Ahmad Barakat. He was Hezbollah's leading operative in the region."

"So he's at large?" I asked. "Should we consider him a threat to our operation?" I didn't mention, of course, that I knew that Barakat was declared by the U.S. government as a SDGT, a specially designated global terrorist.

"No. He was nabbed by the Brazilian police on tax evasion and criminal association charges and was extradited to Paraguay. Here he was convicted on charges of tax evasion and sentenced to six and a half years."

"How was he caught?" I asked politely. "It sounds like a good thriller movie."

"He was arrested in Brazil because he had a big mouth. Can you imagine a terrorist giving interviews to journalists using his own name?"

"An idiot," I said in agreement.

"No. Worse," he chuckled. "He thought he was invincible. Barakat lived only a few miles from the Paraguayan border." The police chief leaned toward me and said in a lowered voice, as if he were telling me a secret. "There's some evidence that he was linked to the bombings in Argentina. You know, the Israeli Embassy, the community center." I knew well. In 1992, at the embassy, twenty-eight people were killed; in 1994, the AMIA community center was blown up, with eighty-six dead.

"So why didn't you prosecute him in Paraguay before he fled to Brazil?"

"At the time, we didn't have antiterrorism or money-laundering laws. We were only able to prosecute suspected terrorist financiers for tax evasion or other similar white-collar crimes, and had actively prosecuted other suspected terrorist fundraisers. Hezbollah fundraisers Sobhi Fayyad and Ali Near were sentenced to lengthy prison terms for tax evasion. We have also brought charges of document fraud against Barakat's brother Hatem Barakat, also a suspected terrorist financier."

"So we should be safe, since Hezbollah's leaders are no longer here?" I asked.

"Yes, you'll be safe from them. Many other operatives left as well. Until a while ago, this city became so popular with terrorists that every foreign-intelligence service on earth sent its representatives here as if this were the United Nations general assembly. After 9/11, the FBI sent forty agents. Forty! That's almost as big as the city's entire police force. There were too many hunters around," he muttered, "so the prey escaped."

"And it's not anymore?" I asked. "I mean, a hornet's nest of bad guys? I want to be sure, before I recommend sending over the expedition. You know, diamond exploration can attract unwanted attention."

"Oh, we still have a lot of mean guys around, but they're not as dangerous."

"Doing what?" I asked.

"Think of anything illegal, and they're doing it. Arms sale, drug and immigrant trafficking, identity theft, bank fraud, and money laundering. Recently we caught three people from the Middle East who sold tens of thousands of fake Viagra pills. They confessed that a cut of the profits went to Hezbollah—and to families of Lebanese 'martyrs' who died in terrorist attacks against Israel."

"But the gun-holding terrorists have left?" I repeated the question. "I want to make sure."

"Mostly, although they developed new business products. Those who stayed here started offering 'security services' to their Lebanese countrymen doing business here."

"Security services?" I repeated the words.

"Yes, just like the wise guys of New York and Chicago. Protection and extortion, plain and simple."

"Run by a Mafia-type local don?"

He nodded. "We suspected at the time that it was Barakat. Now there could be another one in his place. But as I said, too many hunters made the serious terrorists move out to more hospitable countries."

"Where to?"

"Colón Free Trade Zone in Panama; Iquique, Chile; Maicao, Colombia; and Chui, Brazil."

"Didn't you say that some are still here?" I tried to sound confused.

"Yes." He sounded apologetic. "They're making money here, so why should the moneymakers leave? The weather is good, the booze is even better, and the women . . ." He left the sentence open. "The training camps they had here were shut down."

I couldn't tell whether he was credible, but I suspected that the bottle of wine in his veins made it more difficult to lie.

I went out to the street. The air was hot and humid, and passing cars polluted the little air I could breathe with fumes and dust. I returned to my hotel. The concierge greeted me. "Señor, there were some people asking for you."

"Oh, did they leave a message?" I wasn't expecting anyone. My senses went on alert.

"No, señor, they just left."

"How many were here?"

"Three."

"OK, thanks." I gave him two dollars and proceeded to my room. On second thought, I went outside to the yard, approached my room's window, and peeped inside. Unexpected guests in this part of the world could be very unfriendly. The light on the night table was on. When I left my room in the morning, I had turned off all the lights. I slowly surveyed the room. Nothing was suspicious. I opened the window and climbed inside, locking the window after me and closing the curtain. I checked the room again. Nothing.

The following morning, while I was having breakfast, two Hispanic-looking men approached my table.

"Mr. Mitchell?"

"Yes," I said, looking at them and wondering what I had done to deserve the honor. One was in his late thirties, short and muscular with dark eyeglasses and a black mustache. The other man was tall and in his midtwenties, dressed casually.

"I'm Abdul Shammas. My father has asked us to look you up," said the younger man as he shook my hand, while I tried to look surprised. He didn't introduce the muscle, who I assumed was his bodyguard.

"Mr. Shammas? Oh yes, nice of you to come by. Please sit down." So Anthon was as good as his word when he promised "Erin" (aka me) a contact person in Paraguay for her "father" (aka me).

"Mr. Shammas is expecting you for dinner tonight at his home—that is, if you're available."

"I'd be honored," I said.

He stood up briskly. "Good. We'll pick you up at nine forty-five P.M."

Dinner at ten P.M.? I'd forgotten for a moment the Latin custom of late dinners.

At nine forty-five, a white Mercedes was waiting at the hotel's entrance, and the man I'd seen earlier, this time dressed in a dark suit, approached me with a smile.

"Hello. My father is expecting you."

I noticed a black Mercedes with four men parked right behind us. When we left, they shadowed us. His driver, who looked as if he was also a bodyguard, drove me to a posh neighborhood northeast of the city.

"Where are we going?" I asked Abdul.

"To my father's home at Paraná Country Club. It's about half the way between Ciudad del Este and Itaipu Dam."

As we entered the neighborhood, the change of landscape was dramatic. I looked, amazed at this enclosed and exclusive neighborhood built on a peninsula with gorgeous views of the Paraná and Acaray rivers.

We arrived at a three-story, white-walled palatial villa with a wide wrought-iron gate. High-beam projectors illuminated the house, and guards carrying short-barrel machine guns were standing at the gate. As our car approached the gate, it slowly opened wide, and the driver didn't even have to stop. The black Mercedes stayed outside the gate. A man in his late fifties with a white trimmed beard, dressed in a white linen suit, stood on the marble stairs leading to the main entrance.

"That's my father," said Abdul as we exited the car.

"Welcome to my house," said the man, "I'm Jacques Shammas. I'm glad you could come." He shook my hand with his right hand and held my shoulder with his left hand as if he were going to embrace me. He didn't, although he came really close to my body. Was he checking whether I was armed? The thought crossed my mind, but I brushed it aside. In the foyer, his formally dressed wife and four children stood in line.

"This is my family—and my pride," he said. "Abdul you have already met."

He spoke good English with a strong hint of Arabic and French. Financial success was visible anywhere I looked. Deep Persian carpets, marble floors, expensive paintings on the walls, and at least half a dozen housemaids in white uniform, and other male helpers standing by. A quick calculation I made brought the number of security men to at least twelve. We walked through a spacious living room to a porch overlooking a garden with a huge illuminated swimming pool. We sat on cushioned rattan chairs around a small round table. Servants in tuxedos brought small crystal plates with nuts and dates, and a cart full of the world's choice liquors. Shammas's sons joined us, but none of the women of the family did.

"Anthon urged me to offer you any help you might need," said Jacques with a smile, as he poured arak in my glass, mixing it with water and ice, giving the clear white liquor an opaque milky white color. The aroma of anise was rather strong. "Welcome to our home," he said, raising his glass, then gulping the drink in one shot while looking at me. I followed suit. Thanks to my Israeli military service, I had already been exposed to that drink, which can start a small fire in your stomach.

"It's really good," I lied. "What is it?"

"Arak Zahlaoi, from the Zahlé region in the Bekaa Valley in Lebanon." He poured us another round. "I understand Anthon is interested in your daughter." His face lit with a smile. "These are modern times," he said. "In my time we married only within the religion. We're Maronite, members of one of the Eastern Catholic Churches."

"Well, Erin recently told me that she'd been in contact

with Anthon for a few months now, and I think talking about marriage is premature. Erin is Roman Catholic, so in any case they are not that far apart, religiously speaking." I paused. "These days, the kids are more independent than we were at their age." Too late I realized that I sounded more like a Jewish mother than an Irish father, but Jacques just nodded in accord.

We had chatted for a few more minutes when Jacques moved the conversation toward the purpose of my visit. He very politely asked general-interest questions, but I had no illusions as to their motivation. He was checking me out. Why did he need to check out a mining engineer recommended by his cousin? Had my cover and legend been compromised?

We moved to the dinner table set with English china, plated gold silverware, and crystal goblets and candleholders. Jacques did most of the talking, while his wife, a beautiful blonde in her early forties who'd just joined us, barely said a word. None of the children spoke.

"Tell me about your work," he said smoothly.

"I'm on a contract to advise the government on diamond prospecting in this area and the suitability of rotary diamond drilling, which was recommended by engineers years ago. A very boring subject, I must assure you."

"No, really, I'd like to know." He actually seemed to be telling the truth, and I couldn't quite tell why he was so interested. "Are there diamonds in Paraguay?" he asked. "I'm surprised."

"Well, the government hopes that there are. There is enough solid evidence to warrant experimental drilling."

"How is it done?"

I recited the technical explanation I'd received during CIA briefing.

"Very interesting indeed," concluded Jacques. The questions that followed gave me the impression that he knew more about the topic than he cared to reveal.

"I must tell you that one of the reasons I agreed to take this job was the knowledge that I could meet people here," I said. "On many previous occasions when I did drilling surveys in remote places on earth, I used to return to my hotel or to my tent after a day's work without talking to anyone. I decided not to take on any future assignments in locations where I'd be alone all the time."

"You must consider us as family," said Jacques. "You're welcome here at any time."

"Thank you. I already feel at home. Please tell me about your family," I said. "Have you always lived in Paraguay?" I played dumb.

"No. We're originally Lebanese, but had to leave during the civil war in 1975. We first went to Sierra Leone to join my cousin, Anthon's father, and then moved here."

"I hear you're in the electronics business."

He smiled. "Yes, we have stores and other businesses. Life in Paraguay has been good to us, but we miss our homeland, Lebanon. There's no substitute for home."

"I know the feeling," I said. "I've been away from my country most of my adult life, so I don't even have one place I can call home."

We kept on chatting for an hour or so, until I felt it was time to leave. I thanked him and his wife for their hospitality.

"My son Pierre will drive you back to your hotel. I'll call you soon. Perhaps we can talk again."

"I'd like that," I said.

Back at the hotel, I used the encrypted-communication device built into my laptop computer to send Eric my report, together with an e-mail to forward to Anthon using Erin's e-mail address as sender. If I sent it to Anthon directly from Paraguay, security would be reduced and tracing and cracking abilities increased.

Dear Anthon,
My father called to tell me how much he had enjoyed

meeting your relatives in Ciudad del Este. Thank you
very much for the introduction.
Erin
P.S. Did you get the photos I sent? My father takes great
pictures.

Hours later, Anthon responded.

Dear Erin,
I received the photos they are very nice. I wish I could
meet you soon. You look so happy. I know my father
spoke with Jacques Shammas after the meeting and said
your father was great. I was pleased to help.
Anthon

Three days later, Jacques Shammas called. "Mr. Mitchell,
hello."

I cut in. "Just call me Patrick."

"OK, Patrick—call me Jacques. Are you free for lunch?"

Of course I was free. All I did was sit next to the phone
and wait for him to ring, like a teenage girl after a first date,
wondering, Will he call again?

We met inside Vendôme Mall, and Jacques told me he'd
selected the best restaurant. Judging from the decor, it
didn't look like much.

"I'm glad you could come," said Jacques as we sat at the
half-empty restaurant. He went on talking about anything
except the one thing I could only assume was on his mind—
though I couldn't yet say what that thing was. I sensed it.
Otherwise, why he was all smiles in the midst of a busy business day, wasting his time on a stranger? Just to talk about
nothing? There *had* to be a reason. After beating around
the bush for ten more minutes, he finally got to what I
thought was the point. He wanted to talk about diamonds,
drilling, mining, prospecting . . . everything.

We continued to meet once or twice a week, though I

was deliberately inaccessible several days at a time, saying upon my return that I had been busy working. I took trips to areas surrounding Ciudad del Este and made sure I wasn't followed. I remembered the warning our Mossad Academy instructors gave us: The probability of being successfully watched is directly proportional to the stupidity of your act. So don't act stupidly.

At midday, Jacques called me and invited me to his home.

"I told my cousin in Sierra Leone about your visit, and he was very interested to hear about your professional activities."

"Is he in the diamond business?" I asked politely.

"Yes, in retail sales and in many other areas as well. Do you have any plans to go to Africa anytime? He'd be happy to meet you."

Now, that was an odd way of extending an invitation, sort of "drop by whenever you're in the neighborhood"— only the neighborhood is four thousand miles away. On further consideration, it seemed like the Middle Eastern custom of avoiding direct talk. Never ask anything directly, and when asked, never give a straight answer, making your answer open to multiple interpretations.

"I'm here for another week or so and have no travel plans after that," I said carefully.

"I think I mentioned that my cousin has interests in several diamond-jewelry stores in West Africa. Anyway, I really don't know what he has in mind concerning you. But let me know if you'll be working in West Africa so you can meet him."

I reported to Eric in an encrypted e-mail.

"We'll place you in a nearby country," Eric responded. "Sending you to Sierra Leone will be too obvious and may raise suspicion."

I sent him another e-mail. "Perhaps we can tie it in with the growing friendship between Erin and Anthon.

Maybe Erin will finally accept Anthon's invitations to visit him, and I can visit her immediately afterward, because I'm working someplace not too far away—say in South Africa?"

Eric's response came moments later. "Let me run this idea by some people here. In the meantime continue to build up your relationship with Jacques."

A day later Erin replied. I received an encrypted copy.

Dear Anthon,
I have great news. I won the first prize in my Church raffle: a trip to Israel to visit the Holy places. I've always dreamed of walking in the footsteps of Jesus. I'm so excited. Have you ever been to Bethlehem? I understand it is not far from Lebanon, just a few hours' drive. Perhaps we could tour the holy sights together.
Erin

Clever, I thought, trying to lure Anthon to Israel, where monitoring or even recruiting him would be easier, and at the same time pretending to be ignorant of geography. If a meeting were held in a foreign country other than Israel, then CIA agents would have to watch Anthon, but also their own back. Governments don't like agents of foreign countries playing cops and robbers in their territory, breaching their sovereignty, violating laws regarding eavesdropping, and endangering the innocent locals. However, while in Israel, things would be much simpler for the CIA. Since Operation Pinocchio was a U.S.-Israeli joint venture, they could get help from Israel's Shin Beth, the internal security service.

Anthon sent his response, which wasn't what we'd hoped.

Dear Erin,
Unfortunately I haven't been to occupied Palestine, and

*I don't think I can go there as long as the Zionists occupy
that land. Maybe one day when we'll again be the masters I could go.*
Anthon

Good to the legend we built for Erin, the response sent
reflected Erin's lack of interest in politics.

Dear Anthon,
*I understand you don't like the Israelis, to say the least,
but my Priest told us that Bethlehem is in the Palestinian
Authority, not Israel. Anyway, I don't care who rules the
area, I just want to fulfill a dream. I wish you could come
too.*
Erin

Anthon still refused the bait.

Dear Erin,
*I also wish I could join you, but to enter the Palestinian
Authority I must pass first through Israel. Although I
have a Sierra Leonean passport, it shows I was born in
Lebanon, and the Israelis might give me problems. So,
although I really want to meet you, I can't join you on
this trip. Why don't you arrange your ticket to include
Sierra Leone as well, maybe on your way back?*
Anthon

I composed the next e-mail with the solution Eric suggested.

Dear Anthon,
*That's a great idea to return through Sierra Leone. I
spoke to my travel agent and he said it could be done, but
the ticket would be more expensive. I talked to my father
and he agreed to give me the extra money necessary to*

*change my ticket. I'll make travel arrangements and will
let you know. Anyway, the grocery building where I
worked was condemned and the grocery had to close,
and so I'm not working. I'm excited to see you soon.
Erin*

It worked.

*Dear Erin,
I'm so happy to hear that you're coming. Tell me when
your flight arrives and I will prepare the red carpet for
you.
Anthon*

"He took the bait," I reported to Eric as I forwarded him
Anthon's last e-mail. Eric responded, "Technically, Israel
would have been a better place for a first meeting, but we'll
settle for Sierra Leone. We'd hoped it would be used only at
a later stage."

I didn't limit my reconnaissance tour into Ciudad del
Este to Jacques Shammas. Through the nonstop talker,
Alberto, I managed to obtain interesting intel on Hezbollah, Al-Qaeda, and Hamas activities. I was still in the dark
regarding the identity of the local leaders of these groups,
but I was able to collect significant intelligence about
Hezbollah's fundraising in the area. And it wasn't done
by Scrabble tournaments or solicitation by mail. I also
watched Jacques Shammas's businesses. But I had no success there. Maybe he was just a respectable businessman
with no connection to Hezbollah? Just because he was ethnic Lebanese, a cousin of a Hezbollah supporter, did it also
necessarily mean that he had ties to terror or terror financing? Of course not.

CHAPTER FOUR

Eric instructed me to leave Ciudad del Este and tell Jacques that I was going back to Ireland, and then to Liberia for a short job assignment.

"*Au revoir*, my friend," said Jacques as he escorted me to his car. "It was a pleasure knowing you, and I hope we will meet again. I'll tell my cousin that you'll be in Liberia. Maybe he could meet you there."

I flew to Sao Paulo and continued on to London and Dublin. Three airlines and almost two days later, I had made the switch from a fresh Patrick Sean Mitchell departing to an exhausted Dan Gordon arriving.

I checked into the Clarence Hotel in Dublin city center, practically on the banks of the Liffey River. Eric came to see me on the following day, accompanied by a young woman dressed in a tweed skirt and a beige blouse that offset her red hair and blue eyes. She looked very Irish and very familiar.

Eric introduced her. "This is Erin Mitchell," he said with a rare smile. "Your daughter."

Of course she looked familiar; I had sent her photo to Anthon.

Erin looked at me curiously. "I'm pleased to meet you, Dad," she said, with a slight Irish accent.

We sat in the Tea Room Restaurant on the ground level. The waiter came to our table. I ordered *terrine gourmande* with apple and pear chutney as appetizer and roasted mallard duck, braised white cabbage, and caramelized leg confit in apple and juniper berry *jus* for the entrée, and these were the *simple* dishes on the menu. Erin ordered just two appetizers, and Eric passed.

"Erin is fresh from the Farm," said Eric after the waiter left our table. "This is her first assignment. I suggest that the two of you spend some time together, kind of 'father-daughter bonding,' and I'll see you here in three days." Then he just got up and left.

Typical Eric behavior, I thought. *There's nothing wrong with him that a personality transplant won't cure.*

"Tell me about yourself," I said while finishing my dinner.

"Let's take a drive to the country," she suggested. "I have a car outside."

Erin was driving the Nissan Primera on the left side of the road as if she were a native. Or maybe she was. She didn't say.

"How old is my daughter?" I asked her. She looked a bit older than my own daughter, Karen.

"Twenty-six."

"Where were you born?"

"Erin Mitchell was born in Dublin," she said, signaling that I could only ask her questions about Erin.

For three days we toured Ireland, enjoyed the beautiful countryside, the hospitality of the people, and the great dark beer. By the time we returned to the Clarence Hotel, we each had the other's life story, family tree, and small details about our CIA-designed family legend. This was the easy part, almost like a vacation, with no looking over your shoulder.

There was a message waiting from Eric. "Meet me tonight at 7:00 in room 112."

I was there on time. Eric opened the door. Inside the spacious room were seated Erin and a medium-built man in his early thirties with a crew cut, wearing a tweed jacket and jeans.

"This is Eddie," said Eric. "He'll brief you on the mission ahead."

I sat on the couch; Erin and Eric sat on the sofa opposite. Eddie sat behind the desk and worked on his notebook computer. He projected images on the wall, with maps of West Africa and Sierra Leone.

"Sierra Leone is a likely destination for terrorists because of its demographics, corruption, and unregulated territories. Terrorists discovered that they could operate there with almost total impunity. Although the vast majority of the population is African, the communities of ethnic Lebanese, Pakistani, and Indians are substantial in size and influence. Sixty percent of the population is Sunni Muslim, thirty percent follow indigenous religions, and the remaining ten percent are Christians and Shiite Muslims of Lebanese descent. The Lebanese merchants have served as a link between Sierra Leone and radical Islamist movements. Hezbollah and now Al-Qaeda have used their contacts within this community to obtain documentation, travel certificates, and financing for terrorist operations. That was easy, because Sierra Leone suffers from endemic government corruption. The diamond industry has long been a source of revenue for Hezbollah and more recently Al-Qaeda. While Hezbollah entered Sierra Leone in the 1980s, Al-Qaeda is a restive newcomer. Hezbollah targeted Lebanese diamond traders of Sierra Leone who have a lot to hide. We estimate that one hundred million dollars' worth of raw diamonds are illegally exported from Sierra Leone each year. That's a big chunk of the country's total diamond exports."

He paused to gulp water from his glass. "After winning a power struggle over the more moderate Amal movement, Hezbollah has had a free hand in tapping into this revenue flow. Their first steps in Sierra Leone involved collecting voluntary contributions from ethnic Lebanese. Those who refused were reminded of their close family and business connections in Lebanon. You know the kind: 'You had better donate money to support our struggle, or there'll be midnight visits to your family in Lebanon.' Since much of the diamond trade in Sierra Leone is illegal—the revenues are kept away from the government's tax collectors, and sometimes even the mining is without a license—you can understand why victims of Hezbollah extortion don't complain."

"Did this Hezbollah money-raising operation go unnoticed?" I asked.

"In general terms, yes, until the plane crash. In December 2003, a Union des Transports Africains airliner loaded with Lebanese passengers crashed off the coast of Benin in West Africa. On board was a Hezbollah courier carrying two million dollars in cash. That got our attention."

"And that was only one shipment," added Erin, signaling that she was already in the loop.

"But fundraising wasn't enough. Hezbollah decided to take a piece of the action, and in Sierra Leone the action is in diamonds. Hezbollah's next step was to force the weak government to give them mining licenses, which increased their profits substantially. You all know what Hezbollah would do if they struck it rich."

"Their dependence on Iran would be reduced. They wouldn't need Iran for terror financing," I commented.

"Right," said Eddie.

"Alarmingly, there's a new kid in the block. Al-Qaeda. They have quickly identified the potential in Sierra Leone and have stepped in."

His overview took a step forward toward confirming my earlier hunch. I hadn't been told why the legend of my cover was selected. Now I suspected that posing as a mining engineer was probably designed to ease my way into Hezbollah's operations in Sierra Leone. My visit to Ciudad del Este was just a detour before planting me in Sierra Leone—suspicion free. Somehow, I wasn't completely comfortable with this conclusion. However, I didn't rule out additional goals that they'd neglected to tell me. Something was still missing in the jigsaw puzzle. I didn't know what it was, but I was determined to find out what would happen after I was temporarily placed in Sierra Leone.

"After 9/11, Al-Qaeda bought twenty million dollars' worth of diamonds from Samih Osailly, who shipped them from Sierra Leone through Liberia. Although Al-Qaeda and Hezbollah are usually mentioned in the same breath when terrorist links to the diamond trade are discussed, their involvement is very different. Al-Qaeda buys diamonds as a way of *hiding* money, because their source is difficult to trace, while Hezbollah is involved in the trade to *make* money."

"Does it also create friction between the two organizations?" I asked.

"That's a likely scenario, but we have no country-specific intel on that."

We continued discussing various contingencies concerning the next move, and then Eric put Erin and me to work. Eric told us he needed to be convinced that Erin and I could pass as father and daughter. He asked us approximately two hundred questions regarding our family habits and relatives, reading them from a booklet intended for people preparing for their green card interviews at the immigration service. He left out the questions that were supposed to prove a marriage of an alien and a U.S. citizen was legitimate, but even without them, there were plenty of detailed puzzlers. What did you do on the last birthday of your relative? Were there presents given? A card? Eric remained impassive throughout, but I think we passed.

Dear Anthon,
Sometimes dreams can become a reality. I'm traveling in Jerusalem! I'm e-mailing you from an Internet café on

*Jaffa Street. I plan on going to Bethlehem tomorrow. I'm
so excited.
Erin*

Anthon responded later on that day.

*Dear Erin,
I am so pleased that you're having a good time, even if it is
in the occupied land. I can't wait until we meet.
Anthon*

I drafted the final e-mail Anthon must have been waiting for.

*Dear Anthon,
Arriving in Freetown, Sierra Leone, on Tuesday afternoon. You already have my flight details. Can you please
make a reservation at a youth hostel? As you know, I'm
on a limited budget.
Erin*

Anthon was quick to respond.

*Dear Erin,
There is no need to stay at a youth hostel. My parents
are inviting you to stay with us. We have a big house
and you could use my sister's room. Nadia who is
twenty-two will soon travel to Paris with our aunt to
help her during a medical procedure. I will meet you at
the airport.
Anthon*

Three days after Erin's arrival in Freetown, I flew to Monrovia, Liberia. I made my way through the airport, hailing a
cab to my hotel. It was in suburban Monrovia, the Africa
Hotel on Organization of African Unity Island, at the

Unity Conference Center. After check-in, several beautiful and well-dressed women who made no secret of their deep desire to get to know me better immediately approached me. And when I say "me," I mean, well, my wallet and every valuable I had. Although my Mossad training and current service with the U.S. government had given me plenty of experience with such things, my cabbie was only too willing to help out and even act as a go-between in the transaction. I told him I wouldn't need his help, in polite but firm terms. I certainly wasn't looking for trouble, not this time, and not with them. I sent Erin an e-mail from the hotel's business center.

> My dear Erin,
> I'm settled in Monrovia now. The hotel is clean, the staff is hospitable, and my hosts are doing anything they can to make my stay pleasant. We're going into the jungle tomorrow to do some work. I'll be in touch. Take care of yourself.
> Love, Dad

Erin responded.

> Hi Father,
> It's soooo good to hear from you. I'm having great time. Anthon and his family are so nice and hospitable that I just can't even begin to describe. I use his sister's room and computer, so I can e-mail you anytime. I'm sure that won't change when she returns in a week or so. Is there any chance you'd come visit? It's not far from where you are. I'd love that.
> Love, Erin

On the following morning, I put on my work gear, rented a Jeep, and drove into the jungles with two locals I'd hired to escort me. I *had* to make sure that if I was being watched, I'd appear to be a bona fide mining engineer. Since the road was almost vacant, verifying that I had no followers was easy. Upon return, I sent Erin my next e-mail.

Dear Erin,
I've just got back from my jungle tour. Next weekend is a holiday here, so I suppose I could come over to Freetown for a few days, if the invitation is still open. Let me know.
Love, Dad

Erin answered immediately.

Dear Dad,
Are you kidding? Of course I want you to come and meet Anthon and his family. Ramzi, Anthon's dad, told me that he's also looking forward to your visit.
Love, Erin

Later on in the evening, I answered.

Dear Erin,
I'll see you on Thursday. I've made reservations at the Hotel Kimbima. Can you meet me there at 7:00 P.M. and we could have dinner?
Love, Dad

I landed in Freetown's airport and walked into the painfully modest air terminal. A thuggish-looking, unshaved, middle-aged man met me at the gate.

"I'm Abed, Ramzi Shammas's younger brother." He then introduced a medium-height younger man who was standing next to him. "This is Anthon Shammas, my nephew." We shook hands.

Diametrically opposed to Abed, Anthon was a clean-shaved, wiry man dressed in fashionable clothes. He had a thin mustache and black eyes and hair. "We are here to welcome you. Erin is waiting for you," said Anthon in a heavily accented English.

I made a great show of thanks and got in his car. Everything was going according to plan. They drove me to Hotel Kimbima, Freetown's best hotel, on the shore of the Atlantic Ocean, along Bintumani Drive.

It was impossible to ignore how this country, the size of South Carolina, had been ravaged by a civil war that had only just left it. Burnt-down buildings, trash-strewn streets, destroyed neighborhoods, and countless displaced refugees, many missing arms and legs, carrying all of their possessions, with no place to go. The hills around the capital were covered with shanties made of corrugated iron and junkyard material. Despite being rich in diamonds, titanium ore, bauxite, iron ore, gold, and chromites, the country ranked 173rd out of 173 countries in the U.N. quality-of-life index. It was tragic.

I settled into my hotel, as commodious as could be expected under the circumstances. Two hours later, as I was about to leave to meet Erin, Ramzi and Abed Shammas came to my hotel unannounced. We sat in the lobby, and they discussed diamond-exploration options. Ramzi mentioned that they wouldn't stop at diamonds. They had a big appetite for other minerals as well.

"What other mineral deposits are you referring to?" I asked.

"Sierra Leone has bauxite and rutile deposits. The government had plans to reopen abandoned mines that were shut down during the eleven-year civil war, but these efforts led nowhere."

"Why?"

"The government is corrupt and broke, and no foreign investments are coming in. So diamond mining remains the major source of exports here."

"And what do you want to do?" I asked the obvious question.

"Control the entire local diamond market," Abed laughed, exposing his uneven teeth. Somehow, I didn't think it was funny, but I showed him my appreciation and support of the idea by raising up my thumb.

As planned, on the following day, Abed came to my hotel with a driver who spoke with Abed in Krio, an English-based dialect that I barely understood.

He drove us, mostly off-road, in a late model SUV to Kono, Sierra Leone's northern region and the heart of the diamond-mining region.

"Diamonds mined here were the center of and may be the reason for the civil war that ruined the country," said Abed. "It was also very bad for business."

I knew the history. The civil war was brutal and had devastated the country. After the peace accords were signed, this area was again available with its tens of thousands of free-for-all diamond mines and muddy puddles of stagnating, bloodsucking-insect-infested water. The workers that we saw, many of them children, had dug up the dry river beds. The nearby forests were logged.

"It looks terrible," I said.

"What did you expect? We're not in Canada. Can we start digging here?" Abed was impatient.

"It's not that simple. These areas of Northern Sierra Leone are marked by kimberlite pipes that millions of years ago were pushed from the earth's core toward the surface." I proceeded to give him a short technical lecture that I'd learned earlier from my CIA instructors.

"Can it be done?" He was persistent and impatient.

"Generally speaking, yes, but with a massive capital investment. Anyway, before you start pouring tons of money you must conduct a survey."

"Money is not a problem." He was dismissive.

"I hope you understand you're talking millions here. On

the other hand, the return could be huge. My earlier calculations showed that if past history means anything where diamond mining is concerned, in addition to geological surveys I've seen, you could probably export about one billion dollars a year."

Abed was speechless for a moment. Then he said, "That's more than Congo's diamond export, and Congo's territory is several times bigger."

"I guess you've got the numbers right," I said. "How are you going to get a nationwide exclusive mining and marketing license? The government failed to do it independently, because miners were bypassing it and exporting directly."

He smiled exposing again his teeth. "Trust me." He touched his assault rifle.

"You think you can succeed in controlling the market where the government failed?"

"I'm sure we can be very persuasive. Few people will dare to cheat us," he said with a sinister grin. Again, I didn't find it funny. In fact, the AK-47 he was holding on his lap made me nervous. "I want you to do the job," he said, "manage the whole thing." I felt a little chill. It was too sudden to get a job offer just like that, after only a few conversations. After all, he knew nothing about me. Or did he?

"I don't think the government would listen to you, even with this," I said and pointed at his gun, "unless you come up with a plan, well backed geologically and supported financially." I ducked the direct job offer. I needed to play this game for as long as I could, yet keep him at bay.

"Good. You take care of the science, and we'll worry about the money. How's that for a start?" There was an unpleasant tone to it. Manners were not his field.

"Before I'd even be willing to consider your offer, I've got to know what I'm getting myself into. This commitment involves high professional and other risks. I also need to know where the money is coming from."

"From Lebanon."

"The government of Lebanon?" I played dumb again.

"No. From our brothers."

"Can you be more specific?"

"Why is it your business?" He was losing his patience, a bad start for a disagreement when the person you're confronting is holding a gun. "We're willing to consider you for the engineering part. Everything else should be none of your damn business."

He couldn't have been blunter. Under different circumstances, I'd give way to my temper, but not here. The fact that he wanted to keep the source of the money and the identity of the investors in the dark meant that he thought that bringing up their names wouldn't help, or more likely might even hurt. But obviously it wasn't De Beers or Citibank that he had in mind.

"Well, will you take my offer?" he asked.

I paused. "You know, I really and truly appreciate the offer. But I'm just an engineer. I've only ever managed two secretaries," I said.

He seemed on the verge of rolling his eyes. "Tell me what you can do, not what you can't."

"I'm willing to be your consultant in selecting the best company to do the job, and help them start operations, provided I can complete my assignment in three months. I can't commit to a long-term relationship. I have other plans. My fee is ten thousand dollars a month plus all out-of-pocket expenses, including my hotel and transportation." I was hoping that my wages would be paid from a different bank account, broadening my information horizon.

"*D'accord*," he said, using the French word for OK. He was agreeing to my terms without so much as a moment of thought. For a moment, I wished I could keep the money. Too bad the CIA was going to pocket it.

As I was getting into his Jeep for a drive back to Freetown, I heard the too-familiar sound of an AK-47 spitting rounds. When a bullet hit the rear window, there was no mistake: we were the target. I jumped into the Jeep with the driver. Abed pushed him to the back and hit the gas. "Go, go!" I shouted. He frenetically drove the Jeep on the dusty road at high speed, but the shots continued, and bullets hit the Jeep's body.

"If they hit the gas tank, we're toast," I yelled. "Let me have your gun." Without waiting for Abed's answer as he maneuvered the Jeep, I bent forward and grabbed it from his lap, turned around, and shot in the general direction of the fire. But whoever was shooting at us flattened two tires and made us lose speed until we had to stop. We jumped out of the Jeep and crouched behind a hill.

"Who are these bastards?" I asked. I had no desire or intention of getting involved in somebody else's war.

"They could be from the Revolutionary United Front. Or diamond smugglers or diggers trying to keep us away." A rebel group, I assumed.

We heard more shooting. "How much ammunition do we have?" I asked trying to calculate our next move.

Abed didn't answer and tried his cell phone, but there was no reception. "I'll try to get back to the Jeep after dark," he said. "I have a radio transmitter—we could call for help."

We just sat there behind the red soil hill. Night was coming. No lights to be seen anywhere. The dead silence, interrupted by the nocturnal sounds of animals and birds, was giving me a feeling of being entirely alone out on the prairie of this godforsaken country. When it was dark enough, Abed quietly approached his Jeep and radioed for help. He signaled me and the driver to join him. "They must have gone," he said, referring to the shooters. "We should stay in the Jeep; there are some vicious animals out here you don't want to meet." I didn't know if he meant four or two legged, but I wasn't about to ask.

"Where did you learn to use a gun?" Abed asked, but I couldn't identify whether he was curious or suspicious.

"Oh, I'm an experienced wildlife hunter from my days in South Africa."

In the wee hours of the morning, two Jeeps with eight armed men came over. Abed snapped a few commands in Arabic, and our Jeep was fixed in no time.

After spending time with Erin, as a loving father should, I found an opportunity to ask her why I wasn't seeing more of Anthon, other than at occasional family dinners.

"He's avoiding you for some reason," said Erin. "He said he's not ready yet to spend time with you, because he's shy."

"Do you buy that?" I asked.

"Of course not. There must be another reason," she answered.

"Look for it," I suggested. I wasn't comfortable with his behavior. The little devil in me opened one eye. *It's not right,* he told me, and I don't think he meant etiquette.

A few days later, Abed took me to the airport for my flight to New York. "I'm sure we'll be talking soon," he said seriously, and I didn't know if it was a promise or a threat.

I arranged for a survey company to do the initial report. That took three weeks and $250,000 wired to their London office from Switzerland.

The survey report, bound in a clear-top, black-back, spiral binder was professional. It included charts and diagrams, spreadsheets and financial analysis. The bottom line was that an initial investment of ten million dollars was necessary before the first diamond would be excavated.

I returned to Sierra Leone to meet with Abed, a meeting I wasn't looking forward to.

"What's next?" he asked, puffing his cigarette smoke. "We've got the ten million dollars available."

"You need to hire a company to do the actual prospecting. I'd make sure you have a government license first."

"Don't worry about that." He was confident and indifferent.

"Good," I said, waiting for him to ask the next question. In these instances, silence is golden. He was quiet for a moment and then said, "I want you to recommend a company to do it."

"The drilling market is small, and you have to be very careful."

"Just find a drilling company," he said, sounding annoyed.

"If I put my name on this, I must be assured that you have all the necessary funding available. I can't afford to approach major drilling and prospecting companies and ask them to put time and effort in preparing a prospectus and then begin with contract negotiation, only to realize later that you don't have the funds readily available. I've had some embarrassments in the past. I hope you understand. I have a reputation to protect."

"Is the financial proof you require for your eyes only?" he asked circumspectly.

"No. Any drilling company would probably ask to see bank statements and other financial documents proving you have the money. That's standard procedure." The moment had come, the one that would give me a clue as to where the money was coming from, if not where it was going.

"Is that all?"

"Yes, for now."

Abed didn't blink. An envelope with bank statements arrived at my hotel three days later. I sent Eric an encrypted e-mail.

Eric,
I made some progress. Subject seems to be ready to move
forward. I have full details of their substantial bank ac-
counts, including a copy of last month's statement. I rec-

ommend we introduce a company that would hire employees we recommend. I should get him a short list of potential companies soon. Three Middle Eastern men arrived here two days ago, probably Lebanese. The Shammas brothers are treating them with awe and shield them from any contact with people outside the family. I'll try to identify them.
Dan

Eric answered a day later.

Dan,
I append names of three companies for the drilling bid. The first company on the list will decline; the third one will quote the lowest price. Go for that one. As for the new guests, I instructed Erin to investigate. She's an insider now.
Eric

I called Ramzi to wrap things up. "Can I see you and Abed tonight? I have the list for you."

"I'm listening."

"Flanagan Jones, Aquatic Drilling, and Nesmore Terra-Research. We need to go over the list together. Can we have lunch or dinner?" In other words, would he let me see his Lebanese guests?

"I'm really sorry, but I have family visiting and it'll be too difficult. But let's talk now. Are the companies serious?"

"They are the best. Feel free to talk to any number of other companies. We shouldn't be limited to these three."

"No. Let's try them out first. Send them a request. We talk more later." He hung up.

He had sounded impatient and disturbed, even more than usual. Whoever the three men I'd seen were, Ramzi was definitely disturbed by their visit. I took Erin for a walk near my hotel.

"Without doubt, they are not family," she said. "Anthon was evasive when I asked him who they were. He said, 'When you become family, you'll know.'" She didn't need to say it, but it was another indication of Anthon's intentions towards her.

"Any idea who they are?"

"All I know is that they're Lebanese, and that their visit worried the family. I can't get more without arousing suspicion, but I'll keep my eyes and ears open."

I left Freetown the next morning and returned to New York. Eric came to my office unannounced, as usual. *What the hell*, I thought. *Why doesn't he ever call first? What? Does he expect to surprise me making out with the copy machine down the hall?*

I handed him a bulky envelope with bank statements and balance sheets of the Shammas brothers' business, including incoming and outgoing wire transfers to Lebanon.

"Here, you can start from this."

Such complete financial information on the Shammas brothers would enable CIA analysts to trace money transfers, identify recipients, and help monitor potential terror financing.

"Good."

I had known better than to expect more than just a dry *good* for my achievements. Even that was a word he rarely used.

Two weeks later, it was time to return to Sierra Leone. I was getting tired of these journeys, exhausting and with more exhaustion at the end of them, but it was all part of the job. This time, Ramzi met me at the Freetown airport.

"Welcome back!"

"I'm glad to be back," I said as he helped me into his car. He drove me to my hotel.

"Let's have dinner later and we can talk," he said as he

dropped me off. His previous nervousness had disappeared. I waited for him to leave, checked into my room, and went directly to the business center with my notebook computer. I sent Eric an urgent encrypted e-mail. I decided to go immediately into a higher degree of alert. The adrenaline had kicked in. What was alarming me?

Well, for one thing, I had never told Ramzi on what date I was returning to Freetown and definitely didn't give him my flight details. I quickly searched my memory. Did Erin know and mention it? No. He must have found it out independently. That showed he had the means to do it, and—what was most alarming—the intent.

Over dinner, I showed Ramzi the bids of the three drilling companies, and the two finalists. This was the time to repeat my earlier suggestion that he ask directly additional companies to bid. I didn't want to look as if I were pushing one particular bidder.

"No, we shouldn't waste any more time," he said. "Who do you recommend?"

"Both finalists have good reputations. If you go for the lower bidder, then Nesmore should get it."

"Fine," he said. "Let's do it. Ask their representatives to come over with a draft agreement."

"The draft agreement is already here. It's one of the attachments to their proposal. I think your lawyers should study it before we move on."

He gave me a long look, wiped his mouth with a cloth napkin, drank water from his glass, burped, and uttered, "*D'accord.*"

The rest was easy, or so I thought. Ramzi submitted a comfort letter from the International Commerce Bank of Freetown confirming that Shammas brothers "have sufficient funds on the account and a sufficient line of credit with our bank to complete the above $20 million project."

Nesmore's representative arrived in Freetown a week later, and the agreement was signed. Teams arrived, machinery was shipped, and very often I found myself needing to urgently communicate with the Agency to get technical assistance when questions were raised. Eric told me to remind the Shammas brothers that my three-month contract would soon expire. "Tell them you got a job offer in China. Don't give out any details."

Erin drove me in Anthon's car to the airport; we didn't talk about anything of substance, as the car could have been bugged. Only when she pecked my cheek at the gate did she say, "I'll see you in New York next week." That was a surprise, but I said nothing and walked to the gate.

When I entered my New York office, I ran the decryption software on my computer. The first message that popped up on my monitor came from Erin.

To: Eric Henderson
CC: Dan Gordon
Further to Dan's report. The visit of the three young men from Lebanon created immediate tension within the Shammas family. They left three days later, and the men of the family have been holding lengthy discussions behind closed doors. As is customary here, none of the women in the family participated or were even allowed to be present or even see them. From pieces of information I was able to collect, the issue discussed was the amount of influence expat Lebanese have over Hezbollah in Lebanon. Thus far, the six-thousand-person Lebanese community in Sierra Leone has been providing Hezbollah with money and occasional logistical support. I overheard that now "they" no longer regard operational and financial support as separate. At this time, I don't know who "they" are. Is it Hezbollah, which wants to recruit Sierra Leoneans of Lebanese origin to actively work for Hezbollah? Or do the locals wish to have a stronger say in Hezbollah's policy in Lebanon because it ultimately affects their life in Sierra Leone? I suspect the visitors de-

manded active participation in a planned operation. Anthon confirmed that the visitors were from Hezbollah and
that they came over concerning "an operation." I think
Anthon's remark wasn't inadvertent, because he was
boasting of the family's ties to Hezbollah, that his father
was an important figure, and that Hezbollah consults
him before there's a major move. Although I have no
names of the visitors, I'm attaching the pictures I surreptitiously took of them with the remote-control camera I
left in the dining room. On the personal level, I find it is
becoming more difficult to rebuff Anthon, who's been
talking of marriage. We must find a quick solution. I suggest we move to the next level.
Erin

I received a copy of an e-mail sent by Eric.

From: *Eric Henderson*
To: *Erin Mitchell*
CC: *Dan Gordon, Paul McGregor, Robert Holliday*
You're authorized to commence to Level II.

I called Eric on a secure phone. "What the hell is Level
II? Why am I out of the loop here?"

"We're coming to New York next week," said Eric. Cryp-
tic as usual. Eric probably demanded his wife identify herself with a pass code before she was allowed into bed. "Didn't
you see the operational memo?"

"No."

"OK, I thought I sent you a copy," he said unapologeti-
cally. "We'll talk about it at the meeting."

From: *Erin Mitchell*
To: *Eric Henderson*
CC: *Dan Gordon, Robert Holliday*
I participated in a family dinner last night where Middle

Eastern politics were discussed. I asked for a permission to speak and commented very briefly that my three-month stay with the family opened my eyes to the truth concerning the Israeli-Lebanese conflict and wondered why the public in the West doesn't hear that truth. When Ramzi Shammas asked me how I thought it could be done, I said that I didn't know, but there must be a way to do it. Later in private, Anthon didn't seem to like the fact that I ventured to express myself on a matter that, in his words, "belongs to men only." I told him I merely answered his father's question. "He was being polite," said Anthon. "In our society women don't intervene in these matters." Nonetheless, Anthon conceded that he and his father thought that perhaps Hezbollah should "do something" to improve its image in the United States. I didn't pursue the matter any further.
Erin

CHAPTER FIVE

Manhattan
March 20, 2006

As I walked into my office, Eric called. "The meeting will be held at your office today at one P.M. I have already alerted the security officer to make the necessary arrangements." Although our entire office was well protected physically and electronically, on certain occasions the level of security was raised, and unauthorized staff weren't allowed in the corridor leading to the conference room on the day of the meeting.

At one, Bob, Paul, and Eric were sitting around the conference table.

Paul started. His voice was low, and he spoke slowly, after the bare-minimum niceties were exchanged. "We plan to plant with the Shammas brothers the idea of hiring an agent of influence for Hezbollah. The goal will be to sway world public opinion and to lobby the U.S. Congress to be more aware of the political and economic aspects of Hezbollah, urging it to balance its unequivocal support of Israel by developing a direct dialogue with Hezbollah. The Shammas brothers' selling point to Nasserallah, Hezbollah's leader, would be that there would be no need for Hezbollah to actually change its ways, but only to let the American public and Congress have the impression that there is a chance for it."

Eric turned to me. "What do you know about black actions?"

I wasn't going to tell him that during my Mossad service we actively practiced it.

"Well . . . ," I said, feeling a bit odd that I was being put on the spot. Was I being sent back in time to my school days to be tested? Eric's tone certainly mimicked my teachers'. I went on anyway. "Black actions, or dirty tricks, are an array of offensive covert operations, such as use of forgeries, spread of rumors, guerilla warfare, kidnapping, sabotage, and assassination—all without attribution. Following the successful practice employed by the Soviet Union and the United States during the Cold War, that type of warfare continued to be heavily used through agents of influence and covert operatives."

"Let's talk about the nonviolent aspects of black actions," he said.

"Spread of disinformation?" I asked.

Eric looked at Paul, who nodded in accord.

"Agents leak false information and rumors and plant them with the media. They also manufacture documents shedding false light on foreign leaders or countries, and generally try to influence politics and public opinion in foreign countries. I think we should also include in this category agents of influence who use covert but sometimes also overt methods to influence foreign governments and their public."

"Right," said Eric, and Bob scribbled something on his pad.

"Well?" I said with a touch of sarcasm. "Did I pass the test?"

"Not just yet," Eric said with a serious tone, ignoring my attitude. "Our next move is more complex and urgent, given recent developments." I sensed the tension in his voice, but he didn't elaborate as to what developments he meant.

"We need to cause your new rich Lebanese friends to lobby Hezbollah to hire Constantin Badescu."

"Who is he?" asked Bob while Eric distributed a two-page résumé of Badescu. I quickly read the sheets. Badescu was a disinformation expert who had headed the Romanian Department D of State Security (DSS), dubbed the Securitate, which was responsible for the spread of disinformation until the downfall and execution of Nicolae Ceausescu, the Romanian president, in December 1989. At the time, in addition to ensuring the internal security of Romania, the Securitate was used by Ceausescu to spy on his own people through a massive network of informants. I sat up in my chair. This is the type of work that made my heart pump more blood.

"What is he expected to do for Hezbollah?" asked Bob.

"According to the legend we created, supporters of Hezbollah in Sierra Leone want to bring Lebanon back to its golden days when it was the 'Switzerland of the Middle East.' The civil war in the 1970s, the subsequent Palestinian struggles against the Christians, and finally Hezbollah's attacks on Israel and Israel's resulting invasion which ended in 2000 ruined Lebanon, made Lebanon a crony of Syria, and caused the departure of talent and capital. Although Israel withdrew from southern Lebanon six years later, Hezbollah's frequent attacks on Israel's northern villages and other provocations ignited Israel's massive response that caused substantial damage to parts of Beirut and south Lebanon. That, in turn, compelled Hezbollah to exert pressure on its supporters outside Lebanon to donate significant amounts of money to rebuild the villages Israel had destroyed because they had been used to launch rockets on Israeli civilians. Without the promise of a rebuild, Hezbollah was risking the loss of the villagers' support. The Shammas brothers felt it was time to cause Hezbollah to change course, which, they hoped, might ease the financial burden on their supporters overseas."

Although Eric never said it, I suspected that he intended Badescu to become a double agent. The pathway Eric used was transparent. He first identified the need of the Shammas brothers to cause a change, then he offered them a solution to satisfy their need. Where did the CIA come into play? He was choosing a suitable agent of influence that could be acceptable to the Shammas brothers and to Hezbollah, and yet guaranteeing his loyalty to CIA in a manner that wouldn't arouse any suspicion. He didn't say whether Badescu was in the loop concerning Eric's plan. I decided not to ask.

"How can you be sure that he could fool them?" I asked.

"Because from their perspective, he'd be providing them with a service, not intelligence. We're not launching something to mislead sophisticated intelligence analysts. We know it wouldn't fly, if we used Badescu for that. The Hezbollah know that Badescu couldn't have plausible access to classified information. He isn't expected to be *their* spy. Even if he did come up with anything that could be of interest to Hezbollah, the credibility of the information would undergo extremely close scrutiny. We want Hezbollah to let Badescu do the job he'd be hired to do. We'll do the rest."

I thought of the instructions I'd had at the Mossad on how to cultivate a double agent. We learned how to provoke an Arab country's intelligence service to attempt recruiting a particular Israeli—in some cases, an Israeli of Arab origin. Just to be on the safe side, these decoys didn't have access to classified information. Once a recruiting approach was made, we'd receive a signal letting us know. Then the recruiting process by the Arab country's intelligence service would commence under our watchful eyes. These double agents helped us determine how an Arab country's intelligence service communicated with their operatives inside Israel; this was a crucial counterintelligence goal.

Sometimes the plan was even more sinister. An Israeli was unwittingly targeted to be offered as bait to an Arab intelligence service. He was put under a watch. If he took the bait and agreed to work for the Arab intelligence service, he was arrested, and during his interrogation was given the opportunity to be a double agent. Sometimes, these people were involved in some form of organized but known underground opposition to the state of Israel. Through that maneuver, Israel killed two birds with one stone. Herd a potentially dangerous individual into the mainstream and gain intelligence benefits. In that respect, Israel wasn't an innovator. Most counterintelligence services infiltrate dissident groups to put them under their own control and recruit informers. Israel perfected it by using the informers as double agents.

"And the Shammas brothers would agree to persuade Hezbollah to hire Constantin Badescu just because we asked them nicely?" queried Bob. This was the first time I'd heard Bob use sarcasm.

Knowing Eric, I suspected that his reasoning for whatever they were going to do was little more than claptrap. I didn't know whether his reasoning was faulty or that he wasn't telling the whole truth in the meeting. I decided to wait until more details were given.

Eric was just as patient. "The Shammas brothers, as Lebanese patriots, can't refuse Hezbollah's demands for help at times of conflict. Rockets are expensive. If Hezbollah becomes just a political party, and with peace in Lebanon, the pressure Hezbollah is putting on Lebanese expats to finance future military operations or the reconstruction after the war will diminish or be eliminated altogether." Eric drank water from his cup. "Although the Shammas brothers and other expats genuinely support Hezbollah, in fact they support only the social programs and the political agenda of Hezbollah, rather than its military and terrorist activity as a local thug and an Iranian proxy. Therefore, they see no contradiction in an attempt to bring peace to the region and support Hezbollah at the same time, particularly if they won't have to contribute as much as they do now, willingly and maybe unwillingly."

Obviously, if we failed to plan, we planned to fail. But it had to be a plan, not gibberish. Even after hearing Eric's explanation, I thought that the plan he suggested sounded superficial and naive. I didn't believe a word he said. That is to say, the legend of the operation was plausible, but I was suspicious of the explanation he gave us concerning its purported goal. The United States is far from being so gullible as to believe that by dedicating nonmilitary resources to Hezbollah they could sway the political direction of a declared terrorist organization that takes orders from Iran. There had to be another motive, but I had to concede that it was within Eric and Paul's right to keep it from us at this time.

"Eric, you said 'legend.' Does that mean you don't believe this is Badescu's true job description?"

I took Eric by surprise. "Did I say that?"

"Yes, sort of, but leave formalities aside." I was holding Badescu's résumé.

"I see that Badescu was born and educated in Communist Romania. As far as I remember, Communist-era intelligence services followed a motto coined by Lenin: 'We repudiate all morality that proceeds from supernatural ideas that are outside class conceptions.' In other words, everything that serves the Communist doctrine is permissible. Ethics and moral considerations that don't serve the workers are intended for others."

"Why are you mentioning it?"

"Because I find it hard to believe that Badescu would be shoved down Hezbollah's throat just to teach them to spread rumors or forgeries. Under the Soviet system, of which I gather Badescu was a loyal student, black operations included paramilitary activities such as terrorism. Aren't we playing with fire here? We're sending Badescu to do one thing, while he could do more than just spread rumors. If I find it hard to believe, what will Hezbollah think?"

"It's all under control," said Eric mysteriously, thereby supporting my previous hunch that the rest of the story had yet to be told.

"Is Badescu in the loop?" asked Bob.

"Hell, no," said Paul. "During the past decade he's been for sale to anyone who agreed to pay him."

"You mean he's already been recruited?" I asked.

"A week ago," said Eric. "False-flagged."

During my Mossad Academy training, we'd actually planned recruitment schemes where a target was unwittingly made to believe that he was asked to work for a European country's intelligence service, while in fact he was recruited to spy for Israel. I remembered the instructor asking us in our small classroom, "Can you recruit an average citizen of an enemy Arab country who lives outside Israel to work for Israel?" He was quick to answer. "Yes, sometimes, but with great difficulty and extra care and cost. If he betrayed his country and worked for its enemy, do you suppose he'd think twice before he betrayed you as well? But if he thought that he was working for Poland, Greece, or China, which needed the information he was asked to provide to protect their local interests, recruitment options would become much wider."

False-flag tactics were used by the Mossad in two distinct manners—for recruitment and operations purposes. I thought of a typical false-flag operation that Bitzur, a Mossad unit designed to help Jews in distress in foreign countries, helped unveil years after I left the service. In 1988 two Arab hostels in Cannes and Nice, France, were bombed. One person died in Nice and sixteen people were injured. French police found at the scene leaflets signed by the Mouvement d'Action et Defense Masada (Masada Action and Defense Movement). The leaflets carried a Star of David and included hate slogans against Muslims. The Israeli government was alarmed because riots against French Jews as retaliation could erupt. Bitzur was instructed to help the French investigation, which discovered in 1989 that the culprit was a homegrown French neo-Nazi group that assumed the name and insignia of Jewish organizations to make the attacks appear to have been carried out by Zionist militants. As the Mossad suspected, the French neo-Nazis' goal was to instigate conflicts between Arabs and Jews in France. False-flag operations are just a notch up in the scale of attribution. At the bottom, there were of course black operations for which nobody claimed responsibility. These are instances where the damage from taking credit outweighs the benefit, which is usually deterrence of the enemy or satisfying local political needs and regional public relations.

Eric continued. "Badescu was befriended by a Mossad operative posing as Mahmoud, a Palestinian Arab. Badescu was unemployed, unable to sustain himself on his meager Romanian government pension. After several meetings where Mahmoud hinted he was associated with a 'Middle Eastern organization,' Badescu asked his help to find him a job where he could use his talents and experience. Weeks later Badescu was approached by Ali, a 'friend of Mahmoud,' who told him about a limited-time job opening with an organization that could use Badescu's talents—one that helps Hezbollah."

"You described Badescu as an old hand in intelligence operations," I said. "Wouldn't he become wary?"

"Know what was behind it? Sure. But be suspicious? No. Why should he care? He wasn't working for any government and maintained no current secrets. Besides, he was so desperate that he couldn't care less. The only thing he had to sell was his cunning skills and experience, and at this point in time he was willing to sell it to Satan, if the price was earthly."

In the Mossad Academy, we'd learned the basics of the handler-asset relationship:

> First you spot the potential target, assess him or her to identify weaknesses and vulnerabilities, and based on that assessment develop a relationship until you feel comfortable to make the approach. That's the recruitment cycle. You, as the case officer, become the asset's father and mother, teacher, social worker, Imam, minister, or priest. You must listen to your asset, support him emotionally, flatter him, reward him, but at the same time forget all empathy and suspect him to the core. If the asset is intended to become a double agent, your responsibilities are significantly more complex. You teach an asset how to double-cross, you train him to work in the twilight zone and become a sly fox. So how do you supervise him to make sure he doesn't betray you?

I remembered my answer: *Keep him on a short leash, hold a reward in one hand and a whip in the other. Give him what he deserves from either hand.*

"What's the next move?" asked Bob, who had become as impatient as I. "Are you saying that Badescu won't be in direct touch with Hezbollah? What happens if the connection with the other organization fails?"

Eric smiled slyly. "Don't worry. We don't know what qualifications Ali has. The Mossad zealously protects his identity, but according to our plan, and as assured by the Mossad, Badescu will end up being introduced to Hezbollah. In fact, I believe he has already made contact. Although this is an agreed-upon joint operation with the Mossad, individual tasks are carried out separately by each agency. We have long realized that the Mossad has a habit of keeping us in the dark during each phase of their part of the joint operation until they move to the next one."

"Meaning . . . ?" asked Bob.

"When they promise to do something for us, or when we mutually allocate tasks in a joint operation, we know that in some cases they've already done their part, although they keep telling us it's still in the making."

I knew the routine. There were two reasons for that procedure: security—to protect Mossad's methods and sources—and they also wanted to make a difficult assignment look even more difficult by letting it seem to take longer to carry out.

"Bottom line?" asked Bob.

"Badescu is on board," confirmed Eric, "and he believes he works for an organization that supports Hezbollah."

"Who is his handler?"

"Ali. No last name."

"Also a Mossad operative?" I wondered.

"Apparently, most likely unwittingly, but what's most important, Badescu trusts him."

I wanted to say that there are no trust relationships in this business, only suspicions of varying degrees, but I was sure they knew that, and I didn't want to delay any further the already-slow pace of the conversation. Since Eric had just said that Mossad was protecting its operatives' identities, I had a hunch that the CIA was watching the operation from a distance, including the identification of the men involved, but neglecting to tell the Mossad about it. A kind of a protect-your-back insurance policy. As I'd witnessed from the Mossad's perspective while still working there, that was exactly the reason why operations that had ended were represented to the CIA as ongoing, thereby making detection difficult or impossible. It wasn't an earthshaking discovery that even friendly intelligence services snoop on each other, even during close cooperation. In these circumstances, there are no friendships, just interests.

"So what is Badescu doing now?" I asked.

"He is widowed, lives alone, and spends the extra money he just earned on better tsuica—Romanian plum brandy— until we get him to work for the real Hezbollah."

"I don't get it," said Bob, sounding embarrassed. "If he thinks he'd already been working for them, won't his association with the real Hezbollah label his previous connection as bogus? And another question: if he's already in, why ask the Shammas brothers to push Hezbollah to hire him?"

These questions made sense to me. Eric was quick on his feet.

"Hezbollah is heavily compartmentalized. It is one of the most secretive and guarded organizations in the world. If you work for one faction, others in different factions don't know you or even know about your existence. Badescu was told that he was working for a group supporting Hezbollah in Rome, not for the Lebanon-based organization itself. We must have an insider to vouch for him to step up the ladder. The Shammas brothers are our best bet."

Eric's tendency to give us the information piecemeal was annoying. Bob looked at me and quietly shared my frustration.

Eric continued. "Badescu was given a onetime assignment, believing that if he performed well, he could end up working for Hezbollah directly."

"What was his job assignment?" asked Bob in an obvious effort to move things faster.

"Imaginary, just something we concocted, and Ali pretended he was representing that organization. Badescu doesn't even know the purported organization's name. He was told that his assignment was top secret and that nobody within Hezbollah even knew about his existence or identity, a true statement." He grinned. "What Badescu was asked to do had no value whatsoever, other than making him happy to be paid in cash."

That kind of recruitment is well known in the clandestine world of intelligence. The quality of the work results performed by the new recruit has no importance. The first job assignment is meant to examine the recruit's commitment and for the recruiter to provide his superiors with proof that he has in fact recruited a new asset.

"There was no fallback plan in case he did his own checking? You're talking about an experienced high-ranking veteran of an intelligence service." Bob sounded skeptical.

"We did. There is such an organization affiliated with Hezbollah. The Mossad is surreptitiously controlling, but the Mossad didn't want to expose the organization's identity to Badescu unless absolutely necessary."

"Now Badescu is ripe for the next assignment," said Eric matter-of-factly.

"Which is what?" asked Bob. "I lost you."

"Getting the endorsement of Hezbollah supporters in Sierra Leone so that he'd be hired, this time for real, by Hezbollah."

"Why the runaround through Sierra Leone?" asked Bob.

"For several reasons. First, to assess Badescu's corruptibility. We wanted to make sure he'd have no qualms working for a terrorist organization. He passed that test."

"And the second reason?" I asked. As usual, Eric wouldn't

volunteer information even within his close circle unless asked.

"Security, distancing us and the Mossad from Badescu, who would emerge as an expert pushed by Lebanese expats in a legitimate effort to help Hezbollah in a nonmilitary manner."

"Why did you take the trouble to get him to do the work for the Rome group?"

"For two other reasons." Eric paused.

Here we go again, I thought.

"We wanted to see if Badescu was still capable of delivering the goods. It'd been fifteen years or so since he was a powerful general in the Romanian Securitate."

"And the second reason?" I asked wearily.

"To prepare a dossier about his contacts with CIA and Mossad, if he turns bad."

"I thought you said he never knew he'd be working for the U.S. and Israel," I shot back, as if Eric was on the stand in court being cross-examined, reminding myself of the days when I did that.

He remained calm. "Of course Badescu doesn't know that. If he went bad, he'd find out, and he'd also realize what Hezbollah's likely reaction would be if they discovered whom he really worked for." He paused and smiled. "Because we'd let them know."

"Badescu could say he didn't know," I said faintly, never believing it.

"He could try. If he were lucky, he'd be dead before their torture became really bad. Can you think of the pain a tightened vice could give your balls?" Eric was dead serious.

I cringed just at the thought, as Bob turned pale.

"Badescu will be asked to travel to Sierra Leone to meet with Ramzi Shammas," said Eric.

"Under what legend?" asked Bob.

"At the request of Ali," answered Eric, "Badescu will

meet Hezbollah supporters and move them to recommend him to Hezbollah. That part of the legend is truthful."

"What's Ali's connection there?" I asked. "What justification would he have to suggest Badescu's service to the Shammas brothers, and even more important, why would the brothers bother to listen?"

"Ali buys stuff commercially from the Shammas brothers, and they know he is a freelance supporter of Hezbollah who occasionally raises some money for their cause."

"I still don't get it," I said. "If Ali helps the Hezbollah and they know him, why does he have to use the Shammas brothers as a conduit to introduce Badescu directly to Hezbollah?"

"Because the Shammas brothers carry weight with the Hezbollah leadership, while Ali is just a line supporter," said Eric.

"Isn't Ali an Israeli?" asked Bob in surprise.

"No, he's a Palestinian Arab who is unaware that he is in fact working for Israel. He thinks he's employed by France through Mahmoud, his handler."

"And who's Mahmoud again?" asked Bob, trying to fit everyone into a mold.

"A Mossad case officer who handles Ali."

"Does Ali know that he works for Israel? Or maybe his legend is that he works for France, but he knows that Israel is the ultimate client?" I asked. I'd seen that happen before.

"We're not sure, but can't rule it out. There's a limit to the layers you can put on an asset before it starts to confuse and hurt you."

"So we have a double false flag here," I said. "Ali, an unwitting operative for the Israeli Mossad who thinks he works for France, is handled by Mahmoud, also a Mossad operative, who obviously knows his true affiliation. Ali is handling a Romanian national and recruits him to work for Hezbollah, while in fact he'll be working for the United States?"

Eric nodded.

"Forgive me, but how can anyone manage that without making life-threatening mistakes, by forgetting who's against whom?" asked Bob.

"Don't worry," said Eric in his low, flat voice. "Everything is being taken care of. Don't forget that the Mossad is handling Ali, and we have no contact with Mahmoud, so they're off our worry list. We only need to make sure at this point in time that Badescu meets the Shammas brothers and that they introduce him to Hezbollah."

"And it's not certain yet?"

"I'm pretty sure the meeting will take place, because Ali is a good business client of the Shammas brothers and shares their admiration for Hezbollah. They can talk shop and trust each other," he said with a spark twinkling in his eyes.

That brought me to my feet. "If you already had direct access through Ali to the Shammas brothers, why the hell did I have to endure Paraguay and Sierra Leone?" I thought in frustration of the bad weather and questionable food, not to mention dubious characters snooping around me like a pack of hyenas as if I were already dead, although I was still breathing. I was annoyed.

Eric was calm. "Well, how else could we get such detailed financial information of major Hezbollah supporters?" He reminded me what I'd almost forgotten—the bulky envelope I'd brought with me from Sierra Leone. "Also, your operation there was also meant to create a different opportunity for us."

Which one? I wanted to ask, but I'd already gathered the answer fairly early in the game: to plant Agency operatives in the drilling company who could report on the Shammas brothers' diamond trade and affiliations as well as on their Hezbollah connection even when Erin was around, and definitely when she left. I was appreciative of the lengths the CIA was going to, just to be in a position to attempt covert penetration into Hezbollah, and we were not even there yet.

"Say the Shammas brothers agree to introduce Badescu to Hezbollah. When will we know if Ali actually met the Shammas brothers, and the brothers' response?" I asked.

"Benny Friedman of the Mossad will be here soon. He'll tell us. We have no direct contact with Ali or Mahmoud; they're highly protected by the Mossad. Erin is joining us as well."

Twenty minutes later Erin entered the office while I was in the small kitchen, making tea. She apologized for being late due to traffic, and immediately after her, Benny entered, escorted by his aide. The four of us went to the conference room.

Eric rose from his chair and greeted them. "I'm sure you know Mr. Benjamin Friedman of the Israeli Mossad." Benny winked at me.

"We've met," I said. I put on my Sphinx face. Eric was just being ceremonial, since the three of us had worked together in previous operations.

"Really?" asked Erin.

"I know Benny. We've worked together in the past," I said nonchalantly, leaving out the exact period. This wasn't the place to discuss my Mossad background, which was buried in my file, accessible only on a NTK, or need-to-know, basis—and Erin didn't need to know. I was surprised at myself for invoking that attitude. Usually I was annoyed when faced with claims of NTK, which delayed or even hindered my progress in various investigations. Who is to judge when my NTK becomes relevant and imminent? What if the withholding of information caused investigative damage or even risked human lives, just because its release was belated? I've seen too many cases when NTK was unnecessarily used just to cover up failures, or worse.

Just minutes earlier, when I'd greeted Benny in the hallway, I asked him for the purpose of his visit. All I got were two words in Hebrew: *something big*, uttered with Benny's proverbial "cat that ate the canary" smile. You don't get that smile unless Benny is about to share a secret—a plan still on the drawing board, or maybe one that has already been carried out successfully.

Moreover, when Benjamin Friedman, the head of the Israeli Mossad International Division, was about to be hush-hush with you, you'd better listen carefully. Benny rarely shared anything professionally important with anyone outside the Mossad, unless on mutually important matters during an official joint operation with another foreign-intelligence service. Otherwise, even if you were a member of Benny's close-knit professional circle or had served with him in the Mossad, as I did years ago, he'd still be mostly tightlipped and would measure his words. Having won Benny's trust, my experience has shown that in Benny's terminology, "something big" was of the kind that would send Israel's enemies into hiding, occasionally extending only their tentacles out to sense whether the category-five hurricane force of Israeli wrath is over.

I smiled in anticipation. I tried to discern what he was up to this time by glancing at his brown eyes through his rimless spectacles. Nearing sixty, Benny was the indefatigable life and soul of the foreign relations of the Mossad, but he looked more like your pharmacist than a top executive in the Israeli foreign-intelligence service. He had gray thinning hair and a belt that had recently been punched up with a few extra holes to accommodate his growing belly.

Benny and I had joined the Mossad at the same time and gone through its academy training together. We became good friends in a class of twelve cadets. Many differences should have kept us apart, but in an odd way they fostered our friendship. He was an Orthodox Jew, while I was a liberal who only kept the traditional Jewish values in the loosest sense and celebrated the holidays. He came from a family of Holocaust survivors who managed to escape from the horrors of Europe in their midlife when Benny was a baby, and who owned a small grocery in central Tel Aviv. My parents had come to the land of Israel as young pioneers in the early 1920s. I grew up among children of similar background. Benny went to a boys-only, very strict and dogmatic religious school. Yet we found inroads to each other's heart and mind.

To me Benny was the smartest cadet in our class, who was never condescending and had a healthy no-nonsense attitude. I was happy to be his friend. I don't know what he saw in me, but whatever it was, we maintained our friendship for many years, a kind of friendship that survived the erosion of passing time. While I decided to leave the Mossad after three years, Benny stayed on. Now, since I lived in the U.S. and shuttled around the world, while Benny lived in Israel and also traveled extensively, we saw each other only once or twice a year, but could immediately continue with a conversation we'd begun when we met last. Our personal friendship became the basis for professional cooperation with the blessing of our respective superiors. However, our "off the books" relationship was never a reciprocal quid pro quo, scratch my back and I'll scratch yours. While I decided to leave the Mossad after three years, Benny stayed on and climbed the ranks to become head of the international division, which liaises with foreign governments and intelligence services and trades intelligence data.

Cooperation with foreign-intelligence services has a flip side—reciprocity—when the other side misbehaves. Although there were times when the U.S.-Israeli intelligence relationship strained, it never came even close to the tensions that frequently built between U.S. and Russian intelligence services. If a Russian diplomat was caught performing undiplomatic espionage in the U.S., he would be PNG'd (declared persona non grata). The next step likely to follow would be the expulsion of an American intelligence officer from Russia.

However, things didn't have to be brought to that extreme. If the FBI's Counterintelligence Division believed that the Russian undercover operative "exaggerated," they could send him a tacit warning by breaking his car's taillights or slash its tires. Then FSB, the Russian counterpart agency, or the KGB in the Soviet era, would likely retaliate against an American case officer in Moscow. That principle of reciprocity could go as far as assassinations—if you kill one of ours, we'll kill one of yours. In contrast, even during times of tension, the U.S.-Israel intelligence relationship and cooperation never ended in taking retaliatory acts against operatives. In reality, tension did and would continue to appear occasionally in these relationships because of conflicting priorities, though conflicts of interest rarely occurred.

Benny had always been helpful whenever I asked for assistance or advice, and I did my best to help him out, making sure my superiors knew and approved. Benny knew how to break bread with heads of intelligence services, provided the meal was kosher, or he just drank water, giving the impression he'd already eaten. Benny knew how to function anytime, anywhere and still maintain his Jewish identity and his observance of the Jewish laws.

"First stage of the mission is accomplished," said Benny. "Ali introduced Badescu to the Shammas brothers. They interviewed him for several hours and later told Ali that they liked the idea of suggesting Badescu's services to Hezbollah's Council in Beirut."

"To do what?" ask Bob. He wanted to make sure.

"Black propaganda," said Benny. "Deception and disinformation. Hezbollah needed wartime assistance of the kind that Badescu could provide."

"Who's going to teach whom?" I asked. "Nasserallah knows a thing or two about these things. In fact, he might be a master."

Benny smiled. "Indeed, Nasserallah knows how to maneuver the world with his confidence-building talk and bazaar-merchant negotiation tactics. However, his methods are transparent, and after a while he becomes predictable. I think Badescu could impress Nasserallah with his expertise in applying positive and negative black propaganda."

"Can you give an example?" said Erin.

Benny was unhurried. "Once a victim for negative black propaganda is identified, a smear campaign is planned. Slanderous rumors are spread, libel is printed and distributed, false accusations are sent to the media, supported by forged documents, and inflammatory or embarrassing gossip items are inserted into legitimate and illegitimate publications. Obviously, in the Internet era it's extremely easy and effective. The negative campaign intentionally distorts facts and doesn't distinguish between the victim's personal and professional lives. No ethics are even considered; everything is allowed to disparage the victim, if it's a person, or to vilify a government or an organization. That's the public side of the campaign. There could also be private campaigns more focused at the victim's friends, family, or business partners."

Most of the operations of intelligence agencies use disinformation and deception, sometimes using mainstream media to manufacture "facts." I thought of my Mossad Academy classes, in which we had rehearsed these tactics, and became temporarily overtaken by a memory flashback. I had been younger, slimmer, and full of the enthusiasm that filled all new Mossad recruits right after the Mossad Academy graduation. Over time, enthusiasm had been tempered by experience, a healthy appetite, and better judgment. My stroll down Memory Lane was interrupted when Benny continued.

"On the other end of the spectrum is positive black propaganda intended to promote a cause or a person. The same methods are used, with the necessary changes."

"Sounds pretty powerful," said Erin matter-of-factly, almost dismissively, supporting my earlier impression that she was very familiar with these tactics and just wanted to hear Benny out.

"It's a potent weapon," agreed Benny. "Therefore, we can't lose control and let things get out of hand."

Benny had a favorite story about these things, one that he told that day. I'd heard him tell it before. It was a seventeenth-century story about the Jewish rabbi the Maharal of Prague and the golem, the animated creature created from clay. As legend has it, the Maharal created the golem to defend the Jews in the Prague Ghetto from racial attacks and false blood libels. Jewish kabalistic legends describe the golem as a completely loyal robot. One legend tells of a golem that grew bigger and bigger until the rabbi who created it was unable to control it. The golem fell upon its creator and crushed him.

"It sounds like the monster of Frankenstein," said Eric.

"Exactly. We need to make sure that Badescu, the golem we're building, doesn't crush us." Benny's eyes flickered to his audience, making sure his point had been made. It had.

"How do you do that?" asked Bob. "I mean, control him?"

Benny gave Bob a pondering look, as if trying to decide whether to level with him. "We supervise him and apply corrective measures if he misbehaves," he finally said with a twinkle in his eye. There was no need to elaborate here, I thought.

"When is Badescu's meeting with a Hezbollah decision maker?" asked Bob.

"We don't know. The Shammas brothers gave their blessing, and told that to Hezbollah. Now we wait for Beirut to decide."

"And we sit idly?" asked Eric.

"Not at all," said Benny, with his cunning smile. "Beirut is running a background check on Badescu. They are extremely cautious and mistrust even their own family members, let alone an infidel that came out of nowhere. We have no doubt that their operatives are currently running a neighborhood check going back to the 1980s to see what Badescu did then, and more importantly, to see what he did since the collapse of Communism in Romania and determine if Badescu was recruited by any foreign-intelligence service." Benny didn't elaborate, but I knew he was "helping" the background checking process with "facts" to get the results he wanted.

"Would they discover Mahmoud's existence?" asked Bob.

"Maybe just by name, if Badescu talked before leaving Bucharest. I'm sure Mahmoud's legend will hold water. He met Badescu only on a few occasions, and never spoke 'business' with him. Mahmoud was what we call in Hebrew an *oter*—a talent spotter."

"Did he meet him in Romania?" I asked.

"No, in Germany. After Mahmoud identified Badescu's talents, he suggested him for potential recruitment. We told Mahmoud we wanted to pull Badescu out of his safe environment. A journalist called Badescu and suggested an interview about his past. Badescu loved the idea of receiving free advertisement of his skills. The journalist suggested an interview in Cologne, Germany. However, Badescu complained that he couldn't afford the trip. The journalist, a Mossad loyal contact, mailed him train tickets and hotel vouchers. While drinking in his hotel's bar, Badescu was befriended by Mahmoud. They met two or three times for dinner and a soccer game Mahmoud happened to have tickets for."

"Were they supervised?" asked Eric.

"Only by us. We made sure they were not shadowed or controlled from a distance. We wanted to make sure Badescu severed his relationship with any branch of the Romanian intelligence services. We have enough players on the field as it is. However, it's still possible that others were watching the rendezvous without us noticing it."

"Where is Mahmoud now?" I ventured to ask.

"Away from the scene. He talks to Ali only by phone. We don't want to take any chances."

I thought of Baruch Cohen, a Mossad operative killed in Madrid in 1973 by a young Palestinian source he intended to interview at the Café de la Gran Via. Cohen, who had previously been successful in recruiting assets from terrorist organizations, posed as Moshe Hanan Yeshay, a businessman. Unfortunately, Black September exposed his identity and affiliation. He was shot at close range; another Mossad operative, Zadock Ophir, was wounded.

Based on the facts, I wasn't as confident as Benny—or else he wasn't giving us the whole story, a more likely scenario. If Badescu was asked in an interrogation how he was introduced to Hezbollah, the road to Ali would be wide open and maybe even lead to Mahmoud. He should go underground, once Badescu's contacts were investigated. What about Ali? He couldn't disappear without raising suspicions and confirming them, because he was the one to introduce Badescu to the Shammas brothers. Something was missing in Benny's account; I didn't know what. But knowing Benny and his shrewdness, I was sure there was a hidden twist to his story.

"When do you expect to find out what Hezbollah decided?" asked Bob.

"Their council met last night, and if all went well, Badescu will soon know if they want to hire him."

"Benny," I said. "You sound so confident that your plan will succeed. Don't you have any doubts?"

Benny was surprised. "I'm optimistic. The Shammas brothers are hoping to ease the increasing pressure to contribute more money. They told Ali that they would pay Badescu's fees if Hezbollah hired him. Therefore, unless Hezbollah's background check of Badescu brought up negative findings, I think they'll take him. He's a gift horse."

We were continuing to discuss contingencies when Benny's aide's cell phone rang. He listened for a moment and handed Benny the phone. Benny walked away from the room, talking quietly, and when he returned he said, "Here is the story. Badescu just told Ali that he was asked to meet a Hezbollah operative in Tiranë, Albania. The meeting is scheduled for tomorrow, but I'm not sure if Badescu can make it on such a short notice."

"Why?" I asked. "I thought he was unemployed, and Tiranë isn't that far from Bucharest."

"Oh, technically he could make it, but we can't. We need to make arrangements." Benny left the sentence unexplained.

A week later, we all met again at 26 Federal Plaza in Manhattan, across from the federal court. Benny was all smiles. "It worked," he said.

"The meeting had been postponed for two days, and Badescu met at Qesarake Linze Komuna Dajtit in Tiranë with Ismail Nabulsi, who presented himself as a supporter of Hezbollah."

"Presented himself?" asked Eric in a cynical tone.

"Yes," nodded Benny. "He's in fact Ahmed Bin Jalal, a member of Hezbollah's council."

"What's that place, anyway?" asked Bob.

"A castle on the outskirts of Tiranë, in the Dajti Mountains," answered Benny with a grin. After knowing Benny for so many years, I knew that when he had that special grin, he'd planned something diabolical.

Even Eric was losing his patience. "Well, come on, Benny," he said. "Spit it out."

"Badescu was natural," said Benny. "From his perspective he was just selling his skills and had nothing to worry about. On the other hand, Ismail Nabulsi, aka Ahmed Bin Jalal, was edgy, nervous, and extremely suspicious."

"Of Badescu?"

"Yes, he had other reasons to be cautious. We gave him reasons in the past to watch his back. He must have figured out the other reasons independently by reading the reality map and recognizing he was wanted in many countries."

"What are you talking about?" asked Bob.

"Bin Jalal knew we were after him, as were many other Western intelligence services. He was planning and commanding terrorist attacks in Europe and South America. His hands are soiled with blood, although no legal proof is available. Usually, we don't need the 'beyond a reasonable doubt' shit to get even, particularly when scumbags like him boast of their murderous achievements. How do you lawyers call it? 'Confession'?" He smiled at me. "Nonetheless, this time, under the circumstances, we let him live." He paused and added, "For now."

I was amazed. It was very much unlike Benny to be so blunt, or to use such language.

"What about the substance of the conversation?" asked Paul.

"Badescu did most of the talking, answering Bin Jalal's questions."

"Did Bin Jalal offer him a job?"

"No. In fact, Bin Jalal said nothing of substance."

"Which means he suspected Badescu," concluded Bob.

"Sure, the meeting was held before Hezbollah completed Badescu's background check. I think they wanted to interview Badescu first, before they spent the time and effort of a thorough background investigation."

"Did you learn of Badescu's potential role from the questions Bin Jalal asked him?"

"It was really hard to tell, because Bin Jalal wasn't saying much, but it is likely that Hezbollah is not adopting the hopeful thinking of the Shammas brothers concerning the role of Badescu. We estimate that Hezbollah needs him for a completely different role."

"Which is . . . ?" I asked, without adding the obvious "I told you so."

"As we previously anticipated. Black propaganda. Not only denying any connection to terrorist activities, but at the same time covertly distributing earlier-manufactured 'evidence' proving that the real perpetrators were the U.S. and Israel in a joint conspiracy to disparage God-fearing Muslims around the world."

Benny had just confirmed our earlier estimates. Nobody was buying the bullshit argument that Badescu had been introduced to Hezbollah to steer them toward political activities. Maybe that ploy had been sold to the Shammas brothers, and they'd agreed with it, but it seemed that the CIA and Mossad had a completely different agenda regarding Badescu that they had kept from me thus far.

I remembered how Alex had taught us the difference between the three types of propaganda.

> Contrary to common thinking, the distinction is not made with reference to the content of the propaganda distributed, but according to its attribution. White propaganda is issued by a source that correctly identifies itself. Gray propaganda blurs its source. Black propaganda creates the impression that it came from a source other than the true one, preferably from the victim himself.

"Needless to say, that indicates that Hezbollah isn't thinking of abandoning terror and becoming a political movement," said Paul. "You don't hire a professional to clean up for you if you have no plans to act dirty."

"Anybody who believes that Hezbollah would abandon terror to achieve political goals should be awarded with the 'Sucker of the Millennium' award, courtesy of Hezbollah and their Iranian patrons," said Benny mockingly.

"Do you know when a decision regarding Badescu's hiring is expected?" asked Paul. All business, always, expressing his engineer-like mind—although a slow-moving engineer.

"No," answered Benny simply.

CHAPTER SIX

Manhattan
June 23, 2006

Days went by, and I returned to my routine work, sifting through files, identifying the culprits that perpetrated megafrauds in the United States and absconded with their loot to more welcoming jurisdictions, and chasing them in their financial hideouts in offshore locations.

I went to another meeting in the federal building in New York. The participants were the usual group: Paul, Eric, Erin, and Bob. "Is Benny coming as well?" I asked when I entered the small conference room.

"He's on his way. Security is giving him a hard time," said Paul with a chuckle. I was annoyed. Benny participated in far more dangerous missions than Paul, whose riskiest mission ever was probably the missionary position.

Benny entered a few moments later and said nothing about having had to stand in line in the lobby and go through a metal detector, a treatment all but federal-badge-holding employees must endure.

"I hear you have news," said Eric. "Let's hear it."

So typical of Eric, I thought. *He has the emotional intelligence of an eel.*

Benny was well above these matters. He only looked at Eric with patience.

"Badescu was asked to go to Beirut. He went there ten days ago and has just returned. The bottom line is that they wanted his services, but avoided giving him any confidential information. They are trying to make him work, but are withholding the essential details of their operations. That is a very difficult thing to do—difficult to avoid failure, and dangerous, given the fact that your client is known to be a ruthless, trigger-happy thug."

"Wasn't that expected?" asked Bob.

"It was. However, feeding Badescu to them was the best we could do under the circumstances. They'll get used to him over time, and he knows how to build confidence."

"What's the chain of command?" I asked. "I gather from your presentation that Badescu was recruited by Ali. Does Badescu know that Ali must be in the loop at all times?"

"Of course," said Benny. "Badescu only knows that the money for his services comes from the Shammas brothers and several other Lebanese expats in Sierra Leone and that Ali is his only connection to them. Ali told Badescu he must provide him with full details of his work so that the sponsoring expats can receive regular reports and issue payments to Badescu."

"And Badescu is complying?" asked Erin.

"So far," said Benny. "I think he'll behave himself as long as he doesn't feel a threat to his life is imminent, and payments are made regularly."

Eric looked at Paul, who nodded lightly in approval. "We need to move forward with this operation. There's a limit to the extent of time Erin can remain in Sierra Leone without making further personal sacrifices. Therefore," said Eric, turning to Erin, "we're pulling you out of the scene. You will notify Anthon that you aren't returning to Freetown." I looked at Erin. She appeared surprised but composed.

"Is my relationship with Anthon over?" she asked. "I told him I was going to Dublin to visit my mother in a hospital and that I'd return to Freetown soon."

Paul confirmed it. "Pretty much."

Eric intervened. "To make myself clear, we want to avoid the good-bye ceremonies and the emotional pressure, among other more significant risks."

"What if Anthon follows me to Ireland and persists with his marriage proposals?" asked Erin.

"It won't happen," Eric said conclusively.

Paul smiled pleasantly to soften the surprise as he spoke. "Your withdrawal from Anthon's life will seem honorable. He'll be convinced that your relationship began and ended on purely personal grounds and that you never had any ulterior motives for the relationship. He won't even guess that you were connected to Ali or Badescu in any way. Therefore, while already out of Freetown, you'll start a gradual withdrawal from Anthon's life. First, e-mail him that your mom's illness was more serious than previously thought, and so you must stay in Dublin longer than earlier anticipated. Next, you'll ignore his e-mails and reply only after his fourth message with a short e-mail telling him you must attend to your mother's growing medical needs, as her condition worsens, and therefore you can't travel to the Internet café to answer his e-mails. Finally, you'll ignore the next five messages and answer the sixth telling him your mom has passed away and that you are devastated. Next, ignore his e-mails for two weeks until you send him a Dear John letter telling him you have decided to go back to your old boyfriend, who's been very supportive during your difficult days caring for your mother, and after her death. You have decided to accept his marriage proposal, and will soon be accompanying your fiancé to London, where he just got a new job."

"What happens if Anthon calls?" she asked.

"At the beginning, before he's been told your relationship is over, the calls will be answered by an Agency person posing as your sister. She'll tell him that you're out, or with your mom at the hospital. Then the phone will be disconnected."

"That will break his heart," said Erin. She was kind, but businesslike. "Do I have to return the diamond ring he gave me?" There was a note of hope there. It was there, glinting on her finger.

"Wait," said Eric in surprise. "Were you engaged?"

"No, he just gave it to me while we were in his family jewelry store."

"Suggest returning the ring in your final e-mail. Let him decide," said Eric. "But don't get your hopes up. Even if he tells you to keep the ring, you know the federal rules concerning gifts to government employees. Does the ring cost more than twenty dollars?" There was no need for her to answer. "Then you must return it. Or better yet, surrender it to the Agency."

Erin glanced at the shiny ring on her finger, as if she was saying good-bye.

"Well, before I find the real prince charming, I'll have to keep kissing frogs." She turned serious and asked, "Will my legend hold water if he becomes suspicious and starts digging around?"

"Yes," assured Eric. "We've made the necessary arrangements. After all, you've stepped into the life of a real family that is now faced with the health crisis of the mother."

"Real?" she asked.

"Well," he said with a smirk, "we made it look real. That's one of the reasons we want you out of Freetown. If your cover is blown, I don't think it'd be advisable for you to be in the neighborhood. We dubbed you into a real family that matched your legend. It so happens that the family's mother very recently died, this time for real, so we're using it as well. The family house was just sold, and tracing anyone from the surviving family members will be difficult, or even impossible, trust me."

We interrupted for coffee and tea. I approached Erin, who was standing next to the window with a cup of coffee in her hand.

"I'm puzzled by one thing regarding Anthon. His first posting on the LebaneseDate Web site was written in very poor English, but his subsequent responses used much better language. Is there an explanation?"

Erin chuckled. "He made the first posting without telling anyone. His French and Arabic are good, but his English . . . Well, you saw it. He was expecting a response from Lebanese women who he thought would answer in French or Arabic, although his post used a mix of French and English. When he heard from an Irish woman, he realized he must write better English or risk looking silly. He asked for his sister's help. She spent three years in a boarding school in England and speaks very good English. Even when his sister was away, he e-mailed her his proposed answers, and she corrected them and sent them back."

"Did he tell you that?" I was a bit doubtful; maybe we were being duped by FOE.

"No, he was too proud to concede inferiority in anything. During most of my stay, after his sister returned from Paris, I shared a room with her, and she told me."

"And you believed her?"

"I guess so," said Erin. "I had no reason not to."

The session resumed. "Bottom line," said Eric, going back to the major issue, "if Badescu performs as expected, we may have another early warning on any terrorist attack or violent intervention in Lebanese politics planned by Hezbollah, subcontracting for Syria or Iran."

"Assuming Badescu is asked to prepare a black-propaganda campaign putting the blame on the United States or on Israel for these attacks," said Paul.

"That's true only in theory," said Benny. "Sorry, Eric.

Given the compartmentalization of Hezbollah's operations, and particularly since Badescu is not a Muslim or even a Christian Arab, I think he'd be kept away from vital information concerning the place and time of any attack. We would only know that something was forthcoming because his services would be required after the fact." Benny was uncharacteristically direct.

Eric just sidestepped the comment. "Where will he be living?" he asked.

"The way things seem now, back home in Bucharest," answered Benny. "But that could change."

"Monitored?" asked Paul.

"Obviously, budget constraints allowing," said Benny matter-of-factly, "so we hope he operates out of Bucharest and not from Beirut, where watching him would be more difficult. At any rate, I think we should plan an offensive action, rather than sit tight and wait for Hezbollah to move. It could be too late for us to identify their intentions if they pull the trigger and all we can do is identify bodies."

"What do you have in mind?" asked Paul. Knowing Benny, I was sure he already had a plan.

Benny looked around and said, "As you know, Badescu was asked to perform a nonsense job as his initial assignment for a group supporting Hezbollah. That's an organization started by supporters of Hezbollah in Rome for overt and innocuous charity purposes. In fact, it was secretly financing terror. Over time, Mossad operatives infiltrated it and slowly took control."

"So Israel was supporting Hezbollah?" Paul laughed quietly.

"In a manner of speaking, yes. Sometimes, when you go fishing you use small fish as bait to catch the bigger ones. Bear in mind that the sole purpose of that group was to raise money. The Mossad chipped in small sums to become involved. Then its confidants started raising small amounts of money themselves, volunteered to help, and finally took over the financial management. That gave them unfettered access to the lists of their much bigger donors, and most importantly, how and to whom the money was transferred. Of course, if donors were willing to contribute money, maybe they'd provide additional help to Hezbollah that Israel wanted to know about."

Benny continued. "There are additional similar organizations that collect considerable amounts of money anywhere they can. Their activities are coordinated with other Hezbollah-affiliated organizations, such as the Building Fund (*jihad al-bina'*), the Fund for the Wounded, and the Martyrs' Fund (*muasasat al-shaheed*). These organizations operate in Lebanese Shiite communities around the world. Although they pose as innocent charitable organizations, the money collected supports Hezbollah's terrorist attacks, self-initiated or under orders from Iran. I think we should engage Hezbollah by creating chaos, rifts, and mistrust among their governing body. Let them spend time suspecting each other rather than planning more attacks. Here is where we could use CIA assistance." Benny paused. "Although Israel's reach goes beyond its borders to fight terrorism, in that particular operation, I'm suggesting you could take the lead."

Was that Benny's subtle way of hinting that in Operation Pinocchio, Mossad was in the front seat? Or simply a suggestion it was CIA's turn to flex a muscle? I knew that under an agreement, each intelligence service contributed its fair share. Hezbollah is not only Israel's enemy; it killed two hundred forty-one U.S. marines in Beirut, caused close to six hundred civilian casualties in more than two hundred attacks, and serves as a proxy for Iran for dirty jobs. No question the U.S. has a well-deserved score to settle.

"Do you have a plan?" asked Bob, who was unfamiliar with Benny's cunning ways.

"Of course he does," said Eric. "Don't you know Benny yet?"

"This is the plan," said Benny. "We need genuine CIA and FBI documents marked *top secret* to be 'forgotten' someplace, ending up in the hands of Hezbollah. The documents will be evidence that the U.S. managed to infiltrate Hezbollah Council. American operatives will soon support with money, and if necessary with military equipment, several militant members of the council to encourage them to take a tougher stance against 'the decadent West and its infidel leaders.' Under the plan described in the specially prepared CIA and FBI documents, these council members would challenge Nasserallah's leadership, label him as a wimp, a puppet of Iran who is reluctant to take on a much tougher attitude against the U.S., fearing U.S. sanctions, but ignoring Hezbollah and Lebanese interests. Once the renegade council members manage to overthrow Nasserallah from the helm, they take control. CIA would then blackmail them, threatening to expose their unwitting connection to the U.S. before they gained power. The discovery of these documents, once they're proven authentic, would likely cause an immediate internal investigation by Nasserallah's security detail to judge their validity and the reliability of their contents. Just the internal investigation would cause mistrust and a rift between the various factions of Hezbollah, especially if they discovered the culprits within their organization."

"Do you think that a bunch of documents, as incriminating as they could be, could drive a wedge in that close-knit organization?" asked Bob. "Most of the council members have known each other from childhood."

"If we support them with other facts," said Benny and gave us more details of his plan. "I suggest we discuss the preferred location for the drop-off," he concluded.

"One option is to drop them in Dahieh, the Shiite suburb of Beirut," said Eric.

"And when you lose the documents, how can you be sure

they'll end up in the hands of Hezbollah rather than in a Dumpster, or turned in to the police by an honest citizen?" I asked.

"Anything looking American found in Beirut would end up in no time in the hands of Hezbollah. I think Dahieh is a good location," said Eric.

I looked around to see the reaction on everyone's faces. It was a mixture of surprise and "are you nuts?" looks.

"Too obvious," said Paul dismissively. "It's too eager."

"Then what do you suggest?" Benny asked Paul patiently, while giving me a friendly, quizzical look. I became convinced that the idea of using Beirut was deliberately floated as a test balloon.

"I like Benny's plan," said Paul. "However, I think Hezbollah should be forced to make an effort to get these documents. A windfall dropped in their backyard is too obvious. They need to sweat before they get the documents. Let's think about it some more."

"Benny . . . ," I said after a long silence. "That's not black propaganda, that's winning by deceit."

Benny smiled and nodded. The Mossad's motto at the time we served together was adapted from Proverbs: "By deceit thou shalt make thy war."

A few days later Eric walked unannounced into my office. "I think you should be the one to drop the documents in Beirut." He was nonchalant about it, as if we were discussing whose turn it was to drop off the laundry at the dry cleaner's. Apparently, when he made the crazy suggestion about Beirut he wasn't testing the waters, he was swimming in them, or must have had another agenda.

"Why? I thought that the Beirut part of the plan was shelved."

"If you land in Beirut, you will be followed by Hezbollah, who will try to figure out what you are up to. Then you 'forget' the documents and leave, letting your followers pick up the booty."

"Go to Beirut?" I asked, trying to make sure he wasn't joking, although I was hoping he was. Was that Eric's idea of getting rid of me?

"What's the matter?" he asked, squinting his eyes in contempt when he sensed my hesitation. "Are you afraid? Are you a man or a mouse?"

I wanted to say that in that instance I'd rather be a mouse than a senseless gung ho macho man who walked into a sure death trap, but I thought he wouldn't appreciate my candor. To be afraid is human, but to let it overcome you is a bad policy in this profession, and doubly so if you're unlucky enough to be sent to Beirut.

Lebanon had been compared to Switzerland in part because its banks had hosted the huge coffers of Persian Gulf oil millionaires who wanted to keep their money secret and away from any tax-collecting countries, just like some depositors in Switzerland in the pre-money-laundering-laws era. Nowadays, there was nothing Swiss about a society that was busy killing its neighbors across the street, across town, and across its southern border. Beirut was continually torn by civil wars between the Christians and the Muslims and between various warring factions within the Muslim population.

I couldn't hold it in anymore. "Eric, I don't think I should have to prove my mettle here. You may think I'm a mouse for thinking twice about Beirut, but refresh your memory about operations you and I participated in, or read my résumé again and judge for yourself. I think the plan is stupid and unnecessarily dangerous. It's stupid because it's so obvious. What would a CIA agent be doing in the lion's den with top-secret documents? Taking them for a walk for a breath of fresh air? Beirut stinks."

Eric wasn't deterred or offended. "You heard only part of the plan. Be patient. You'd go to Beirut as a rogue agent trying to sell the documents to Hezbollah. That's how you'd attract attention, but you'd leave them in your room while you go out to dinner or shopping or what have you and ease their removal from your hotel room."

"And if I'm lucky, I'll end up with a bullet in my head—or if I'm not, I'll be held hostage. I think whoever thought of this plan should go back to the drawing board and start by learning the ABCs of intelligence-operations planning."

"Do you think you know better?" asked Eric.

"Better than this crazy plan? Sure I do."

"Fine, then why don't you come up with a better one?" He got up and left the room. I knew Eric would finally do the right thing, but first he'd try all other options.

CHAPTER SEVEN

Manhattan
July 12, 2006

Bob called my office. "Turn on the news," he said.

I pressed the TV remote control and saw the breaking news. Israel had launched an aerial attack on strategic installations in Lebanon following a Hezbollah attack on an Israeli military convoy on the Israeli side of the border. That attack had killed eight Israeli soldiers, and two had been taken hostage.

"There goes the Beirut plan," said Bob.

"It was dead on arrival," I said. "Somebody at Langley needs a reality check. This is the Middle East, not Nebraska. People suspect each other."

"We'll have to move the location," said Bob. "If the plan was bad before the war, now it looks even more . . ." He paused looking for the right word.

"Brainless?" I suggested.

"You could call it that," he agreed. Bob was always choosing his words carefully, and when criticism he wanted to make was made by someone else first, it was even better.

"Is the general plan Benny suggested still viable? There's a war going on. Do you think anyone would pay attention to our little rift-creating games now?" I was skeptical.

"I haven't heard anything to the contrary from Eric or Paul, so the plan must still be considered alive and kicking.

"Anyway, wars in the Middle East don't take long. We should wait and see if the conflict is limited to a day or two, as always, or is prolonged. I think everyone in Israel has just had it with Hezbollah. Israel will probably strike disproportionately hard this time."

My occasional inquiries during the following month were met with the same reaction: the war has reshuffled our cards; we'll have to wait. I called Benny. For lack of a secure line, I used hints to hear if Badescu was actually working for Hezbollah.

"Yes," said Benny. "My aunt's maid is working hard, but my aunt is still nervous and doesn't let her polish the silverware yet. Maybe over time."

I went with my children to an ocean resort. Karen was growing up so quickly. Tom, a towering six four, was sleeping during the day and partying at night. College was over, and he had a reason to celebrate with loud music. When I complained, he countered, "Dad, in forty years rap music will be the golden oldies. Be ahead of the curve and enjoy it now."

We bonded again. I saw him talking to a bunch of glary-eyed girls with minimal bathing suits, and I quietly reminisced about my own adolescence, when all you needed to get a girl was a guitar and long hair.

By the end of August, I started to notice a sudden increase in the volume of encrypted messages over our office intranet. I remembered Mossad Academy instructors giving us the basics.

> Generally, an increase in intelligence "chatter" could indicate imminent enemy activity. When our SIGINT units monitor chatter, what counts is the volume—in other words, increase or decrease in the number of messages sent and received over enemy networks. Measured individually, a fluctuation in the number of messages doesn't reveal much. But when we chart it, put together with other communication intercepts, we can find a pattern and issue a warning that something is brewing.

Something was indeed brewing in my own backyard. Hours later, I was called for a meeting. "Benny is coming too," added Esther, the office administrator, who knew I wanted to know.

Benny looked very tired, with dark bags under his eyes. "Are you OK?" I asked him in Hebrew. "Yes," he answered wearily. "Just dead tired." When Eric, Paul, and Bob joined us, Benny started.

He knew we were about to ask him about the results of the month-long Second Lebanon War. "Forget the estimates that we won the war by points, not by a knockout," said Benny. "We killed approximately 700 Hezbollah terrorists. We have the names of 440 of them. All their military installations in southern Lebanon are destroyed. Our civilian population in northern Israel suffered 2,950 rockets, about 50 people killed and hundreds injured.

"However, I'm here on a different mission. We suffered an intelligence blow last week, and we need to rearrange our plans. Hezbollah arrested several of our local Lebanese agents." The gloom on his face was giving him a bassethound look. "They got two separate networks. A Beirut network, which managed to penetrate the Hezbollah command in Beirut's Shiite district of Dahieh. That network installed listening devices and other intelligence-gathering equipment at Hezbollah's headquarters. The results gave us a strategic overview of Hezbollah's plans.

"A second network operated in southern Lebanon and gave us battlefield intelligence. They identified and marked targets for our aerial attacks. Both networks are gone now. Badescu, in Hezbollah's service, is getting results, the kind we need now. I think the knockout punch Hezbollah just took from us makes the time for a revival of our plan crucial. And the time is now, because Nasserallah will soon be accused by his own people of making the wrong decisions, and if we add the documents drop-off as a means to create another rift, then we could expedite his fall through forces coming from within."

"I agree that now is the time to revive our plan," said Paul. "Langley still believes that the plan should be seriously considered. This is a low-budget, low-risk operation."

Ha! Low risk? Maybe when you were sending somebody else to Beirut and not risking your own ass. True, I needed some kind of diet, but not the one served by Hezbollah to its foreign prisoners before they disappeared en route to Damascus or Tehran in exchange for one hundred rockets. OK, make that three hundred.

Eric wanted to send me to Beirut, rather than an enthusiastic young recruit eager to get off the Farm into the real thing. I was never too bashful about voicing my opinion, but timing is everything, so I decided to stay silent. Two hours later, when the second round of kosher corned-beef sandwiches, courtesy of Benny, was consumed, and a plethora of new ideas was discussed, I thought it was time.

"Let's get back to Benny's initial idea," I suggested. "I've given it some thought, and even after the war, or rather because of it, when Hezbollah is trying to do damage control and regroup, it's time to wreak some havoc and make them look over their shoulder. They know that Israel has a score to settle with Nasserallah and other Hezbollah leaders for targeting Israeli towns for their daily rocket attacks. Israel usually settles these accounts using its special forces in personal retaliation against those deemed responsible. The rate of success is usually very high. Now, if on the top of this, Hezbollah leaders have to look over their other shoulder, they'll have less time to look forward. The idea of leaving the documents in Beirut is, well . . ." I paused.

"Shitty," said Benny. "We know that. Any suggestions?"

"Istanbul," I said. "It's close, and the Turkish government has been historically friendly with Arabs."

"Go on," said Benny. He seemed open to the idea.

"Paul said earlier that we can't just abandon the documents, we have to make them sweat trying to get them. I agree." I looked around and felt the silent support. I continued for ten more minutes.

"The best way to disseminate the plan to the enemy is to make it appear secretive and protected. If my plan is adopted, I agree to drop the files." Benny seemed surprised, but he said nothing. I had expected some reaction to my plan or to my willingness to take the lead, but nothing was said. Was it because my ideas had been tacitly rejected? I couldn't tell. Paul made some closing remarks that the boys at Langley would consider all options, and we left.

True to my word, when the plan was later adopted the following January, albeit revised, I went to Istanbul, left the documents in my room, and "allowed" them to be stolen.

CHAPTER EIGHT

Manhattan
August 18, 2006

Bob sent me a brief note to attend a plenary meeting at the Main Justice Building in Washington, DC, mentioning that Benny would attend as well. I had no idea whether it was connected to Operation Pinocchio—maybe there was something new. In the past, Benny came to us to talk about some crazy-sounding but well-planned joint operation of CIA and Mossad that needed our professional skills. Usually they were joint ventures where my expertise was needed to trace yet another group of terrorists by following the money used to finance their terrorist activity. Or maybe this time they wanted to use my impersonation capabilities to trap con men? This was something I'd been doing routinely for DOJ but also during joint operations with CIA and friendly foreign-intelligence services. This time, the location of the meeting was unusual. I assumed something different must be brewing.

I flew to Washington, and after going through thorough security in the lobby, I was directed to a windowless auditorium where about forty men and women were already seated. Eric, dressed in a dark blue suit and red tie, addressed the audience.

"Thank you for coming." Eric was standing on the podium behind a lectern. He referred to a sheet of paper and said, "We have here representatives from the FBI, CIA, NSA, the Department of Defense, the Department of State, and the Department of Homeland Security. Obviously we have several representatives of our host today, the Department of Justice, as well as counterterrorism experts, staff from the Chemical/Biological Quick Response Force, FEMA, and finally Military Intelligence." He raised his head. "Did I miss anyone? There are so many of you." Silence, so he went on. "We have asked Mr. Benny Friedman of the Israeli Mossad to share with you information vital to the national security of the United States." He looked at Benny and asked, "Ready?"

Benny started immediately.

"We have been cooperating with the Agency and Justice in a clandestine operation, code-named Pinocchio. Fortunately, our joint efforts have started to bear fruit," he said ceremoniously. "These plans concern Hezbollah and its master—Iran." Benny paused, took a deep breath, and said quietly, "Iran recognizes that it can't win a military war against the United States or even Israel. Any Iranian attack would result in a counterattack, sending it back to the Stone Age. In addition, Iranian history shows that they've never started a war against their enemies. I mean war in the usual sense—guns, soldiers, invasion, the works. The Iranians have either maneuvered others to do their fighting or launched clandestine warfare that could be blamed on others. Admittedly, they are masters of that art. Early intelligence gathered has indicated that they have decided to retaliate against the U.S. for economic and other sanctions that are causing Iran great harm. These sanctions are now felt by the people of Iran. For example, although it is one of the world's biggest producers of oil, Iran is rationing fuel to its citizens because the local refineries are old and spare parts are difficult to buy.

"We have intelligence showing that Iran, together with Hezbollah, is planning a new wave of terrorist attacks to retaliate against the Israeli massive bombing of Hezbollah's strongholds in Lebanon. There's a chorus of terror warnings around the country. Since the world has already recognized that Iran has outsourced its terrorist attacks to Hezbollah, they are now in the process of aligning themselves with different Islamic groups that couldn't, so they hope, be linked to Iran or Hezbollah. The intelligence we have thus far is limited and far from being sufficient to warrant peremptory action. There's a tacit and sometimes overt competition between Islamic terrorists who'd be recognized by the Islamic world as the leader and carrier of the torch of jihad. During the past two decades, it was Shiite Islam led by Iran and Hezbollah that was responsible for most of the terrorist attacks. But during the past few years, there has been a growing rivalry between Shiites and Sunni Muslims, not only for political power, but also for military dominance and prominence. You see that on a daily basis in Iraqi streets, and we both see it in the clandestine world of intelligence, where Al-Qaeda, which is mostly Sunni, is competing with Shiite Hezbollah over money and influence. There were times when the two organizations were collaborating in money laundering, gun running, and training, and when Hezbollah helped Al-Qaeda smuggle diamonds and gold through Africa.

"Since the war in Iraq, however, the relationship between the organizations has become tense as a result of the Shiite-Sunni violent civil war in Iraq. But common interests may turn yesterday's rivals into partners again. Look how Shiite Iran, which opposed Sunni-dominated Al-Qaeda, was accused by the U.S. of allowing Al-Qaeda operatives to escape Afghanistan through Iranian territory. Iran has also released Saad, Osama bin Laden's son, from an Iranian prison, and these are only two examples.

"On the other hand, Osama bin Laden criticized Hezbollah's leader, Nasserallah, for agreeing to the deployment of UNIFIL soldiers in Lebanon. There were exchanges stronger than words between these two groups away from the public eye. We have information, but no evidence that Lebanese security services have recently thwarted an Al-Qaeda assassination plan against Nasserallah. I'm sure we'll see more of that in the coming years in Lebanon, Iraq, and elsewhere. Our estimate is that Al-Qaeda and Hezbollah may share resources, but wouldn't join forces for overseas attacks. The bottom line is that these organizations know how to put aside their differences and cooperate against their perceived common enemies: the United States and its allies." Benny paused and asked, "Any questions?"

A person sitting in the front row asked, "Anything imminent?"

Benny nodded. "We're picking up chatter suggesting an impending terror attack, but now more than ever, attribution is difficult. Is it Iran-Hezbollah speaking on their own behalf, or is it Al-Qaeda, promising terror? Or maybe it is either one of them planning a heinous attack that would be considered monstrous even by their Muslim supporters, and therefore would leave traces to frame the rival organization for the act? We hear threats from Al-Qaeda, but also keep hearing statements from Iranian leaders that 'martyrdom is a holy phenomenon that is affirmed by the Islamic religion, which also views defending against aggression as a duty. Thus martyrdom is also a valuable tool for deterring attacks.' That means suicide bomb attacks against the U.S. We have seen that these human missiles are cheaper in terms of money, and far more accurate than ground-to-ground missiles. The risk is that the rivalry between Al-Qaeda and other extreme Islamic organizations will spill over beyond the operatives of the rival organization.

"We have seen that on multiple occasions in Israel. Whenever there was tension between Hamas and Islamic Jihad in Gaza, Israeli villages were attacked with missiles by both organizations in a monstrous competition for the public sympathy and support of the Palestinians, who would then have reason to decide which organization was more successful in fighting Israel and therefore worthy of being put in the driver's seat to lead all Palestinians. I suggest we seriously consider that eventuality when Al-Qaeda fights for attention and recognition as leader of jihad with other jihadist organizations.

"If you think Hezbollah is limiting itself to the Middle East, I draw your attention to the notice the FBI recently sent to eighteen thousand police agencies alerting them to a possible Hezbollah threat in this country. This is not the first time the FBI has placed Hezbollah in its sights. A few years ago, the FBI suspected that up to one hundred agents of Hezbollah and other radical Islamic organizations had infiltrated the United States for fundraising and intelligence gathering. We're told that the FBI has more than two hundred active cases involving Hezbollah operatives. In Israel, we've always treated Hezbollah's intelligence-gathering abilities as innovative and effective. In that respect they have capabilities superior to Al-Qaeda's."

Benny went on to describe what needed to be done, and a serious discussion followed with many participants offering their views. As usual in these multiparticipant events, nothing concrete was concluded or happened immediately after the conference. It was just a wake-up call. However, all future communications concerning Operation Pinocchio started to include Alec Station, a unit within CIA Counterterrorism Center that targets Al-Qaeda and bin Laden. I went back to work on my other cases.

Manhattan
February 6, 2007

I was immersed in another case when I received a sealed plastic envelope, hand-delivered by a special courier. Inside was another envelope with a red *Top Secret* seal stamped on both sides. I opened the envelope. It contained instructions to report to CIA station in Istanbul, Turkey. "Be prepared for ten to fourteen days of absence."

When I arrived in Istanbul, it was early evening. At the airport gate, a dark-skinned man came over, introduced himself as Ned, and verified his identity by giving me the correct current password. I followed him to his car, which was parked outside.

"You must exercise extra caution in this town," he said maneuvering his car in the rush-hour hectic traffic.

"What do you mean?" I asked when I realized he wasn't referring to the traffic.

"Istanbul is a world center of espionage, just like Tangier before World War II or Berlin during the Cold War. Agents of every major country are flooding the city."

"I know that, but have always wondered why," I said politely. Of course, I knew why, but I had to be courteous.

"Turkey is our strategic alley. Look at the map: it borders Iraq, Syria, and Iran, among other countries. It's just south of one of the world's greatest oil reserves. Additionally, it has a substantial Kurdish population, which is in a constant struggle for self-determination. It has an Islamic government in a country that is historically secular, although the population is religious. It has strong ties with Israel. Need I say more?"

"Where are we going?"

"You're staying in an apartment building in Cihangir, an upscale residential district of Beyoglu."

He dropped me next to a cab station. "Take a cab to this address," he said, giving me a handwritten note. "I shouldn't get any closer to your neighborhood and risk being seen with you. If the apartment were to be compromised, it would contaminate me, and if I am exposed, I could contaminate you. Use this while you're here." He gave me a mobile phone and the apartment keys.

"The mobile's number is written on the note I gave you.

Don't use the landline at the apartment, but if it rings, answer it—we may call you if for some reason your cell phone is dead. Communications infrastructure in Turkey needs more time to meet the European standards. On that note, there's also a number to call us. Ask to speak with Ata and hang up; we'll call you back immediately."

The apartment was comfortable but tiny. I was too tired to care. The next morning, my cell phone rang. "Please take a cab to the Conrad Hotel's driveway. You'll see a green taxi with a license plate ending with six zero eight. The cabbie will introduce himself as Berker. Please be there in one hour."

Berker brought me to an apartment overlooking the Bosporus, a strait that separates Rumeli, the European part of Turkey, and its Asian side. I was welcomed by Paul, Eric, and another man. "This is Mac, chief of station, CIA," said Paul. We shook hands. Mac looked to be in his late thirties, with a small and fragile looking frame and blond hair. Behind his eyeglasses were intelligent brown eyes.

Eric spoke first. "With the documents you dropped last month in Istanbul ending up in the hands of Hezbollah, we're moving into the next stage."

"Are you sure the thief was working for them?"

"We know for sure they have the documents now. There were discreet inquiries about your cover as Peter Wooten."

"Who made the inquiries?"

"No attribution or source. Our wire intercepts got it. We'd spread rumors in the streets of Beirut that we were looking for an operative that disappeared with top-secret documents and that we're not sure if he defected or was kidnapped. Circumstances of his disappearance suggested he was rogue."

My mouth became dry. I wasn't aware of that legend. That rumor suggested that the documents were intended to be sold by me rather than to be forcibly taken or stolen, as the original legend provided.

"You've just made me expendable," I said with mounting rage. "If I end up with a bullet in my head, some jerk could come forward for a reward: 'We killed a traitor.'"

"That's unlikely to happen," said Mac. "You're worth more alive than dead. If you went rogue, you would talk voluntarily, and you'd be kept alive to advise them on how to read our intentions. Don't worry, that legend bought you a life-insurance policy."

"For a week, in a cage," I said bitterly. At this point, there wasn't much I could say or do. We had designed a horse, but when it came off the drawing board of Langley, it had a hunchback, and had turned into a camel.

"The next move," said Paul, "is to contact the Hezbollah Council members mentioned in the documents, warn them that they could be exposed as American spies, and offer them our help in return for cooperation."

"Who are we?" I asked.

"BND, Bundesnachrichtendienst—German federal foreign-intelligence service."

"What's their motive?"

"To protect German soldiers in a United Nations UNIFIL mission deployed in southern Lebanon to help secure the ceasefire between Israel and Hezbollah. That will give the Germans an early warning if a Hezbollah attack is planned or forthcoming. Hezbollah already issued a warning that if German soldiers are deployed at the Lebanese ports or airports, rather than restricted to southern Lebanon, they would become fair game."

"We use a German cover as false flag?" I asked.

"Of course. The Germans don't know we use their name."

"Has Hezbollah broken the code?" I asked. The names of the three Hezbollah Council members that were purportedly American informers were coded to provide extra assurance that the documents would be treated as authentic. They were referred to only as Apple #1, Apple #2 and Apple #3.

"We don't know, although we planted in the documents several vague hints concerning their identities. At this time, we're not aware of any arrests. I think Hezbollah intelligence is still digesting the documents. Maybe they are already satisfied that they are authentic, but it doesn't mean of course that the information contained there is genuine." Mac smiled.

"Can they verify that?" I asked.

"Only if they have extrinsic proof."

"Such as . . . ?" I asked, but immediately guessed the answer. They'd need me to help them break the code, and if I refused or couldn't, then they'd break something else, probably my neck.

"We'll contact any of the three Apples we can locate while in Europe. We have brought Gerard here," said Eric.

"Who is Gerard?"

"An Agency veteran."

"Here he is," said Eric as a plump, brown-haired man in his midfifties dressed in a beige suit entered. "That's Gerard Coulter."

We shook hands and spent the next six hours going over the details, while having a good Turkish meal of fried fish and consuming endless cups of sweet apple tea. Apples— how appropriate.

"Where and how do I make the contact?" asked Gerard.

"The first contact will be with Apple #1. He is in Istanbul for a few days. His name is Sheik Wazir. We don't know for sure the exact reason for his visit, but there are fuzzy indications that he could be meeting Lorenzo, an arms dealer, to negotiate a weapons purchase."

"Will I carry a gun?" he asked.

"No," said Mac. "There could be complications with the Turkish government."

"What makes you sure he won't send someone to chitchat with me at the point of a gun?" asked Gerard. "Diplomatic incidents are hardly of any concern to Hezbollah."

"It won't happen." Eric was adamant.

"Why?"

"You'll meet him at a nonthreatening public place, and later use our incentive package, if it becomes necessary." Eric pulled a thick pack of documents out of his briefcase. "That'll convince him in the end."

"I hope so," said Gerard. "Let's not forget they're zealots, with burning inner conviction. They're difficult to corrupt."

"I agree," said Paul. "But when they go bad, they're rotten to the core."

"You assume he'll agree to meet. I'm not that convinced. Then what?" I was skeptical and was getting increasingly annoyed with Eric for only revealing part of the picture.

"Of course, if that fails, we'll go to Plan B and confront him in the street, but that could be complicated if he isn't alone." Eric gave us reading material on Apple #1 and further instructions to Gerard on how to conduct the conversation.

"Who is Lorenzo?" I asked Gerard.

"NSA ran a check on the sheik's incoming and outgoing calls. He received two calls from a mobile phone occasionally used by L," said Mac.

"L? Just L?" I asked.

"Yes, he used so many first and last names that we're not sure what his real name is, so we call him L, because many of his last-name aliases started with an L. He is a notorious sleazeball, a disbarred attorney from Seattle with a scientific education. He was caught molesting schoolboys and fled the U.S. just before he was indicted. He returned and plea-bargained a three-year sentence, served two years, then had the nerve to try to restore his license to practice law again. The amazing thing is that he managed to keep his disbarment and conviction from the media. There were suspicions he was involved in a sale of embargoed weapon systems to Iran."

"What's his demographic profile?" I asked.

"Caucasian, age fifty-eight."

"Why do you think the sheik intends to meet him? Is he in the neighborhood?" I was curious.

"We're checking, but he should be far away if he has general plans to meet the sheik. Wherever he is, we'll limit his ability to talk with the sheik, with you around," promised Eric.

"I'm sure he'll try. If there is a genuine transaction, it could be substantial, and no arms dealer would walk away from such bonanza that easily," said Gerard.

"NSA's communication experts are trying to locate the origin of the calls Lorenzo made. Europe is practically one country now. He could be calling the sheik from France or Austria, or from hell, as far as I'm concerned," concluded Eric. Turning to Gerard, he added, "All you need to do is get him to meet you. Mention the supplies."

At a late afternoon hour, I went back to another safe apartment to meet Mac, Eric, Paul, and Gerard. Mac dialed Apple #1's apartment's number from a cell phone he'd brought with him, and when it was answered, he handed Gerard the phone. We put on our earphones to listen in through a relay device.

"Hello, is this Sheik Wazir?" Gerard asked.

"Yes, who are you?"

"My name is Gerard Coulter. This is a private call for your ears only. Am I on a speaker?"

"No. What do you want with me?"

"I want to talk to you about a sensitive matter." Gerard paused.

"I think you have the wrong number," said Wazir.

"Please don't hang up. It's about the supplies."

"Monsieur, I still think you have a wrong number. I'm a man of God."

"With all due respect, Sheik, we should talk because it involves the supplies you're interested in purchasing," said Gerard.

"What are you talking about?" There was suddenly no tension in his voice.

"Please, Sheik Wazir, I'm sure you don't want to discuss this over the phone. Let's meet."

"Monsieur, we have nothing to talk about unless I hear from Mr. Lorenzo first." He hung up the phone.

"One down," I said. "He sounded very polite but firm. He didn't feel Gerard had anything interesting to tell him."

"He'll change his mind tomorrow," said Paul. "He also confirmed a connection to Lorenzo when supplies were mentioned. That's a good sign."

In the morning, Gerard dialed again. The sheik's apartment phone rang only once before he picked it up.

"It's me again," Gerard said apologetically. "I thought maybe you'd reconsidered."

"Monsieur, I don't know who you are and why you are calling. Unless you stop bothering me, I'll call the police."

My immediate thought was that the sheik feared an entrapment, exactly the sort of thing Gerard was attempting.

"That's fine with me," Gerard said nonchalantly. "Did you talk to your banker lately? Perhaps a visit to the bank would help."

Gerard quickly continued. "Can we meet, at a public place? We'll talk about it. I don't feel comfortable discussing it over the phone."

"Call me back in one hour," said Wazir, and hung up.

An hour and a half later, deliberately delaying his wait time to let the sheik simmer, Gerard called.

"When?" Wazir asked. Something had made him change his mind.

"This afternoon at five P.M. at Café Istanbul, at Saray Mah Guzelyali Cad, in Alanya section." Gerard hung up before the sheik could say anything.

"Very good," said Mac, who'd listened in. "I'll make arrangements. It's a nice area not far from the sea."

Three hours before the meeting, a technician carrying a small suitcase came over to the safe apartment. "Sit down," Mac told Gerard. "Joe will fit you with a Hollywood-style makeup mask."

I remembered hearing about the highly secretive method of changing appearances developed by the CIA together with top-level Hollywood makeup artists. In 1980, a group of American diplomats escaped from the captured U.S. embassy in Tehran and went into hiding at the Canadian ambassador's home. Their appearance was changed, and they were extricated back home. This time, it also worked beautifully: Gerard looked like a sixty-year-old man with gray hair and thick glasses. His own mother wouldn't have recognized him.

"Security on location?" Gerard asked.

"Two of our men will be sitting at the café near the windows overlooking the street. A much bigger detail will be close by." He showed us a floor chart marked with the exact location of the operatives.

At four forty-five, I was sitting two tables away from Gerard at the café, sipping a long drink and munching on the excellent mezes. People came in and left, but no Sheik Wazir. At five thirty-five, I heard in my earpiece an order to Gerard. "Leave, he stood you up. A white cab is approaching you now. Go outside, hail it, and leave." Gerard left a ten-euro bill on the table and walked out to the approaching cab. I waited ten more minutes, stopped another cab, and jumped in.

My earpiece came to life again. "OK, we've identified one of their operatives surreptitiously taking pictures of all men in the café. He just left."

When I entered the safe apartment, I asked Eric, "What was going on? Did you know there'd be a no-show? Did you want Gerard's and my pictures taken?"

"Nothing in particular happened," said Eric coolly. "He didn't show up. We'll give him one more chance." Eric didn't answer my question regarding the pictures, and that increased my frustration that something was brewing without my knowledge.

"Where do we go from here?" Gerard asked Paul as he stretched on the sofa, munching on an apple he'd dug from the fruit bowl on the table.

"We'll call again after Gerard catches his breath," said Paul.

Gerard protested, "I'm ready now."

Paul dialed.

"Sheik Wazir?" Gerard said as he heard the deep, Arabic-accented voice. "I was disappointed not to meet you today. Was there a misunderstanding?"

"Look, I know who you are, and I've had enough of your dirty tricks. Nothing will sway us from our position; we're not buying your toys. They are too expensive, and your delivery dates are unacceptable. If you think you can bribe me by depositing money into my bank account, then you're wrong! Tell Mr. Lorenzo that unless we get a better deal, we'll take our business elsewhere."

Quick thinking was the key here. Gerard had barely enough time to blink before Wazir was ready to hang up. "Fine," Gerard said, trying to figure out how to respond. "Please accept my apology if we hurt your feelings. Mr. Lorenzo thought that you'd find a good use for the money. He is aware of the important charity and welfare work you do." Gerard was a real professional.

"Take back your money," said Sheik Wazir in a menacing tone.

"If that is your wish, Sheik. I'll call you soon with wiring instructions to return the money, and again, our apologies. As to the transaction, please tell me what your terms are, but please be reasonable—you know our limitations. Everybody is watching us."

"We can't do it over the phone," said Sheik Wazir. "Come to . . ." He paused, muffling his mouthpiece.

"Write it down." He gave Gerard an Istanbul address. "Be there tonight at seven o'clock and be sure to bring details of your bank account. And one more thing: if you or Mr. Lorenzo try to bribe me again, there will be consequences more serious than just a refusal to do business with you."

"It won't happen again, I promise." Gerard hung up.

"Here are the money-wiring instructions." Paul gave Gerard a printed page he tore off from a document in his file. "We can use the money for petty cash in our office. You know, for coffee and muffins. But seriously, we'll also have written proof that Sheik Wazir was paying *us* money. . . ."

At that time I had no idea how we could use the newly created opportunity. If we tried and failed to blackmail him by depositing money into his account, then maybe it'd work the other way when he returned the money, because he would need to do a lot of explaining about why he was paying us. Only later did I discover that it was more complicated than I'd thought.

"Can you imagine what'd happen if Lorenzo, whoever he is, calls Wazir and they discover that Gerard is not working for that Lorenzo?" I asked. "Have you made arrangements?"

"We're sabotaging Wazir's communications, mobile and landline," said Mac.

We dedicated the few hours we had to explore potential contingencies with Gerard, Mac, and Paul. Eric had left the apartment immediately after our recent conversation and had yet to return. Joe, the CIA technician, gave Gerard a pair of black shoes. "Put them on."

"My magic shoes?" he asked.

"Sort of," said Joe. "We planted a GPS device inside them. Just press this button on the shoe to activate. The shoe will transmit your location until the battery runs out.

But if you walk for ten minutes, the batteries will recharge by a small generator propelled by the foot's movements."

"Where is the chip?" I asked.

"Built into the bottom of the shoe."

Joe handed Gerard a black shirt. "Put it on."

"More magic?"

He nodded.

"What is it this time?"

"An invisible RFID tag is sewn into the shirt. The radio frequency ID tag will communicate information by radio waves through a microantenna mounted on a small computer chip. If you're under duress in certain indoor locations, such as airports, the RFID can track you down."

Eric returned to the apartment. "Here is the deal. All landline communications to Wazir's apartment are monitored. If a call comes in or goes out to Lorenzo, we'll jam it. We don't want to physically cut off the telephone lines. That might arouse suspicion when the telephone company tries to fix the problem."

"What about mobile phones?"

"We don't know who is in the apartment with him, or how many mobile phones they have. We have identified only one number, and we jammed it by sending it a virus, but there could be more."

"So what are you going to do?"

"In one hour"—Eric looked at his watch—"a small white Dodge truck will be parked around the corner from Wazir's apartment and will jam all cellular phones in his building, just in case. Temporary wireless communication shutdown is fairly common here."

Gerard nodded. "Got you."

"As to security, I hear that Joe has already fitted you with a bug. The battery will hold for five hours, and the signals will be sent to our truck in encryption."

"What do I do if they search me or scan me with a bug detector?" asked Gerard.

"A manual search won't discover it; the bug is built into a nonmetallic pin that supports your hairpiece. A standard bug detector won't identity it either; the bug uses frequency beyond the range of the standard detection instruments. Two teams are being sent to the location as we speak. If you feel you're in danger that we're unaware of, such as if for some reason we can't hear you or the threat is nonaudible, go to a window overlooking the street and cover your mouth as if yawning."

It's not the best solution, I thought. We wouldn't hear a gun barrel shoved to Gerard's back unless he said "Ouch."

"Will I be armed?" Gerard asked "This time the meeting is not in a public place."

"We considered and discarded that option. I'm sure they'll search you and could find the gun. It might have a chilling affect on a budding friendship," said Paul grinning. I didn't think it was funny, and judging by Gerard's facial expression, neither did he.

"How do I get there?" asked Gerard.

"Take a cab to meet Wazir," said Eric. "I don't want to use an Agency car that may already have been compromised. When you're done with the meeting, take a cab to the Hilton hotel and get a key from the reception for room 1131, registered to Gerard Coulter. Joe will be waiting in the adjoining room, 1132. Knock three times on the connecting inside door, and Joe will open it and arrange for your safe departure from the hotel. If Wazir or his aides offer you a ride back, avoid it. We don't want to start a car chase in the streets of Istanbul, if our tailing vehicles discover you're not being taken to the Hilton." Gerard nodded in understanding.

The additional security required that Joe wait in an adjoining room, so if Gerard was forcibly brought to his hotel room, it'd be empty. Although I was scheduled to monitor the meeting from our van parked outside Wazir's apartment, Gerard was the one to face the heat. To say I felt comfortable with the arrangements would be an exaggeration. Normally, during my Mossad days and even during DOJ-CIA-Mossad joint operations, preparatory time was measured in days or weeks, not hours and minutes, and still there were "hiccups" and a frequent need to improvise as events developed.

And now? This was an operation whose existence and dynamics were dictated by Wazir's apparent failure to take precautionary measures before discussing anything over the phone with a stranger. Was it a bona fide carelessness? Wazir was known to be a crafty son of a bitch. First, he mentioned Lorenzo's name in a conversation with a complete stranger. Next, he avoided meeting Gerard in a location previously set, and now he was dragging him to his den in an unfamiliar territory—and Gerard was going there voluntarily without a gun? Had I lost all my instincts and defenses when I didn't protest that the planning was faulty? Could Gerard rely solely on half a dozen Special Forces men to save his neck if things really did go awry? It was too late to change things. After all, the improvisation was Gerard's. He'd led the conversation toward a meeting when he realized Wazir had failed to verify his identity. Whether the meeting was his mistake or Gerard's would be discovered very soon.

An hour before the scheduled meeting, we went to the van and drove to the location, a mixed residential and commercial neighborhood in southern Istanbul. We heard in our earpieces Gerard taking a cab and telling the cabbie to stop. He told us he was approaching the entrance of a two-story building and was ringing the bell on a green wooden door. We saw a young unshaven man open the door. Paul took his picture with a telephoto lens. The man let Gerard in, but before he allowed him to continue, we heard the noises of a quick frisk he performed on Gerard. He told Gerard to follow him up the stairs to the second floor. We heard a door open and Gerard's steps following him inside. We heard Gerard say, "Hello, I'm Gerard Coulter." There was no audio to indicate that the sheik answered, but we heard a man saying, "Sit down, you can't get any closer to the sheik." It seemed that there wasn't going to be a handshake or exchange of cordialities.

We heard Gerard say, "Sheik, thank you for agreeing to see me. Please tell me, what would be your terms? I understand that Mr. Lorenzo's previous quote was unacceptable."

"As I told Mr. Lorenzo earlier, we need twenty-five hundred units of Strela 3 portable missile system, including five hundred launchers, tech support, and spare parts. Delivery in sixty days, and the price you're asking is exaggerated," he said with authority.

My heart accelerated its pace. The Ukrainian-made Strela 3 is a guided missile that can overcome countermeasures, and has a longer range and greater flight altitude than many other similar missiles. Strela 3 is very effective against low-flying aircraft and helicopters. Hezbollah had quickly learned its lesson from the success of Israeli helicopters in roaming freely through southern Lebanon.

"Where would you wish it delivered? The Israelis are blockading the shores of Lebanon," Gerard said.

"We'll let you know."

"It'd help if you told me now; it has an immediate effect on the price quote."

"Then calculate it as if it were to be delivered to Damascus."

"How will you pay?"

"We can pay cash, but only if you come to Beirut, or by wire transfer to a bank account anywhere."

"Please excuse my saying so, but we can't accept wire transfers from Lebanon. I hope you understand. The Americans are closely monitoring the international wire transfers looking for transactions such as this." Gerard knew his stuff.

"We're aware of that. You can get a wire from a European bank."

"What would be an acceptable price?" Gerard asked.

We heard a pause and the sheik said, "We'll pay ten thousand dollars per unit delivered."

"Sheik, you know we can't do that," Gerard said, probably remembering Mac's quick tutorial that these missiles cost anywhere from twenty-five thousand to one hundred thousand dollars. I had no idea how much the Ukrainians were selling them for to whoever was willing to transship them to Hezbollah for a quick coupon cutting, through the intermediary services of Lorenzo. Obviously, Gerard couldn't ask Wazir and bring the meeting—and himself—to an abrupt end.

"You're making too much money on this. We think you can do it for ten thousand dollars and still make a profit," we heard the sheik say.

"Sheik, as you know, the decision isn't mine. I simply follow instructions." Gerard handed him the note with the banking information. "Here are the details, if you still want to return Mr. Lorenzo's charitable contribution."

The aide said, "The money will be in your account tomorrow. Don't try that again." His voice was calm, but its intensity froze my blood. "We need proof of your ability to deliver," he said suddenly.

"I thought Mr. Lorenzo already gave you that proof." Gerard was shooting in the dark. We still were not sure who Lorenzo was, although his name showed up on many of the CIA lists. There was always the possibility that he was new in the business or an old hand using an alias, a wise choice in a profession where sudden accidents make room for new bold and forgetful players.

"No, he didn't."

"Then what kind of proof do you require?"

"I want to send my men to physically inspect the missiles

to make sure we're getting operable missiles, not junkyard rejects."

"I'll convey to Mr. Lorenzo your terms," Gerard said. I thought he should leave. There was only so much he could pull out of his imagination until he stepped on a land mine—or maybe he already had.

"Let me give you my mobile-phone number," Gerard said, "for future communications. I think Mr. Lorenzo has immediate travel plans, so I will continue the negotiations for him."

We heard steps; the aide was escorting Gerard out.

We saw Gerard emerge from the green door, walk one block, and hail a cab.

We made a circle around town until we were certain that we were not shadowed, and drove to the Hilton hotel.

"Well?" asked Mac, as we all sat around. "What do you guys think?"

"I don't think we got anything from this meeting," said Gerard. "I even think that the story about the missile trans-action was a sham perpetrated by the sheik to expose our hoax."

"I agree," I said. "He didn't believe a word Gerard said."

"Why?" asked Mac.

"No reason, just a hunch. It was all too easy. I think they were like two dogs sniffing each other's butt at the same time. He was reading Gerard, and Gerard was reading him." I was sure the sheik knew it was a scam, but I couldn't say why he hadn't said or done anything.

Late that night, while we were drinking beer and wine at the hotel bar, trying to relax even just for a moment, Gerard's mobile phone rang.

"Mr. Gerard Coulter?" We heard a thick Arabic accent after quickly hooking up the phone to the relay device and to our earpieces.

"Speaking," Gerard said. I was sitting not far from him, sipping a glass of mediocre-tasting red wine.

"I'm Sheik Wazir's assistant. We met earlier." He paused.

"I'm listening," Gerard answered.

"The money was wired into the account you gave us."

"Thanks."

"Do you have answers for us?"

"I'm sorry, but I was unable to call Mr. Lorenzo, who, as I told you earlier, is traveling. Perhaps he has contacted you directly?"

"He has."

"And?" asked Gerard, and I felt a bombshell was about to be dropped on us.

"He says he has no idea who you are. In fact, he told us you're probably a CIA or Mossad operative. Would you like to comment on that?" He was so polite, as if they were in a news conference regarding the future of modern architecture.

"If he said that, it means he's held against his will someplace or he believes his conversations are recorded. Did he leave you with a number to call him back? If he's in danger, I must find him."

"Mr. Gerard Coulter, if that is your real name, which I doubt, I want you to know that we take very seriously enemy attempts to infiltrate our Resistance. You'd better not be found." He hung up.

I marveled at how cool Gerard was. My stomach was churning on his behalf. But he shrugged and said that he could never again use the face Joe had fitted him with. It had just become popular among terrorists with a bear, a gun, and a surfeit of zeal. A genuine toxic combination. Mac walked in just then, so Gerard filled him in quickly.

"I'll pass on the word," Mac said. "Stay put until we fit you with a new face, so you can leave the hotel."

"What about our little money ploy?" Gerard asked. "He said the money was wired. Can you verify that?"

"We already did. The sheik was true to his word; the money is in the account we gave them."

"Why did he return it?" Gerard asked.

I wondered about that move. I knew the Hezbollah was working very hard to collect donations, voluntarily or through extortion, and now they were giving away two hundred thousand dollars without a blink or an argument? That was strange.

"There could be two reasons," said Mac. "One is to clear himself from any potential accusations of graft, if it turned out to be a sting operation by law enforcement of an intelligence service."

"And the second?" I humbly followed the ritual.

"They are not sure that Gerard is in fact a Mossad or CIA operative. Perhaps Gerard was telling the truth and Lorenzo was coerced to deny any knowledge of him. There are things you say on the phone if you have to, or if you think other, unintended parties are listening in, and then you say different things face-to-face."

I tried to figure out what the purpose of the call Gerard got was. To tell him to raise his alert level from "hide" to "run"? To tell Gerard about the deposit of the money, as a courtesy, before they tried to catch him? I had no answers, but I was certainly going to work on getting them.

"Paul," I suddenly said when it dawned on me. "How did Lorenzo call the sheik if we jammed the communication to his phones?"

"We wondered about that," said Paul. "Either the caller was bluffing, or they have additional locations in the city, and the call was made to that location."

CHAPTER NINE

Washington, DC
March 7, 2007

I flew to Washington, DC, to participate in a briefing session evaluating the most recent Istanbul encounters. When the session ended, and as I was about to leave, Benny grabbed my hand. "We need to talk." Eric joined us. We entered a vacant conference room. Eric closed the door.

"There's something we wanted to talk to you about," said Eric in an uncharacteristically pleasant voice. It dawned on me that when Eric wants something, he becomes nice all of a sudden. On all other occasions, Eric usually reserved his kindness for women over eighty. Since I got the honor now, I was giving him the benefit of the doubt.

"Yes?"

"We need you back in the field."

I sat down. "Doing what?"

"Allowing Badescu to recruit you."

"In Beirut? Have any more crazy ideas?" I muttered.

"No. He's expected back in Bucharest for Christmas. We want you to become available for him." Eric was calm.

"In what guise?" I was becoming more interested.

"As Peter Wooten. You have defected after your indictment for the documents fiasco. Badescu will have instructions to recruit you, hoping you'll agree to retaliate against the U.S. for what it has done to you."

"How can I explain the approach to him? How do I know that he'd be interested in what I have to say?"

Eric looked at Benny. "Why don't you answer that question."

"You don't know that," said Benny. "Your details will be given to Badescu by Ali, his handler, who heard the news about you and located you in Paris, suggesting you meet Badescu. Ali will tell you he acts as an intermediary for Hezbollah."

"Badescu would be rewarded nicely by Hezbollah if he brought valuable information, and recruiting you is a good example of that," added Eric.

"You mean Badescu will tell Hezbollah about me, and they will instruct him to get me on board?" I asked, trying to get to the bottom of the plan.

"No," said Benny. "The initial flow will be in the opposite direction. Ali will tell Badescu about you but instruct him not to tell Hezbollah anything, because this is a matter exclusively handled by DGSE." He was referring to the Directorate-General for External Security, France's foreign-intelligence agency. "Badescu will be asked to report to Ali."

"What will Ali tell him about me?"

"The legend, in general, is that DGSE has identified Peter Wooten as an American rogue operative who is trying to sell some documents to Hezbollah." Benny looked at me to see if I got the picture.

"And . . . ?" I asked.

"The legend Badescu will be told is that DGSE wants to use him to elicit from you—or rather, from Peter Wooten—CIA plans regarding Hezbollah. Don't forget that Ali thinks he works for France. Ali will tell Badescu that Wooten believes that Ali worked as an intermediary for Hezbollah, but only Badescu is qualified to negotiate because, as an expert, he can examine the value of the documents." Benny seemed to have all the ducks lined up.

"Why wouldn't DGSE approach Wooten directly? Why the merry-go-round to have Badescu talk to him?" I asked.

"Because France is a U.S. ally and Wooten would be reluctant to talk to the French, but he'd talk to a Hezbollah representative. That's the story Ali told Badescu, who was likely to ask the same question," said Eric.

"I see," I said. "The plot thickens."

"You've heard nothing yet," said Benny. "Obviously, Badescu won't tell Peter Wooten that he actually works for the French. He'll probably only reveal his affiliation with Hezbollah and suggest acting as a go-between, facilitating the sale of information by Wooten to Hezbollah. However, from Peter Wooten's perspective, using Badescu as a liaison to Hezbollah will make sense particularly when Wooten doesn't need to risk his neck and travel to Beirut. From Ali's perspective the move is natural, because again, Ali thinks he is working for France, an American ally, and by directing Wooten toward Badescu—his asset—the transfer of information to Hezbollah will be averted because Badescu, under Ali's orders, won't tell Hezbollah anything about his meeting with Wooten until further notice 'due to internal complications.'"

"Complicated," I said, trying to keep it all straight in my head, who was against whom.

"It's a perfect plan," said Benny.

"It sounds to me more like a Shakespearean drama, with multiple people double-crossing each other as a result of mistaken identities. One door on stage is opened, and another one is slammed." I took a deep breath. This was no play. "What is the purpose of this?"

"There are several independent objectives," said Eric. "First, we want to test Badescu's own credibility and see if he reports to Ali everything he hears from you. You record your conversations with Badescu. We'd check him out this way. The second objective is to use you, as Peter Wooten, to feed Hezbollah disinformation through Badescu, in case

Badescu violates Ali's instruction to withhold the information from Hezbollah. Under these circumstances the value of the documents and the tendency to believe their authenticity will increase."

"That's funny," I said. "First we recruit Badescu to allegedly help Hezbollah feed us with disinformation, and in fact we use him to feed Hezbollah crap?"

"Exactly. You've got it perfectly," said Eric in a flattering tone, which immediately led me to suspect that there was more to it than that.

"Any additional objectives?"

"Yes, but you'll soon find them out. Are you willing to do it?"

"Where do I sign?" I asked. I hadn't joined CIA, even on temporary assignment, to be a paper pusher. I needed to be in the field. What other excitements was I left with? It was hard to concede that as time went by, the list was shrinking.

"I knew you'd agree." Eric smiled at me.

A smile? Something was definitely wrong here, the little suspicious devil in me told me. *Is something wrong? Has Eric undergone a secret CIA-sponsored experimental character change?* I hadn't gotten the memo on that.

"You'll get your marching orders soon," he promised.

Three days later, I was instructed to attend a three-day briefing session at the Farm. I packed a duffel bag, called my children, and arranged a dog sitter for Snap, who gave me the sad puppy-eyes look when he understood I was leaving him again. A car was sent to drive me to Williamsburg, Virginia. It was a long and boring ride. At two gas stations where we stopped, the bathrooms were locked. What? They're afraid someone will clean them? After about six hours of driving from New York, we got there. Although this was my third stay at the Farm, I had to be fingerprinted and photographed again, let a nurse draw my blood, and allow a technician to take my measurements for biometric identification. I was directed to a different building, where I met Donna, a middle-aged woman with short blonde hair, friendly gray eyes, and a pleasant smile.

"Welcome to Camp Peary," she said with a tone matching her demeanor. "I'll be your instructor and liaison for the three days of your briefing. I know you've been here before, but I must repeat the security instructions." She commenced with a ten-minute instruction on the things I must do or avoid doing, such as not being allowed to leave the camp or communicate with the outside world, including a total ban on phone calls and e-mails. I had to leave my mobile phone with her. For the next three days I had a crash course in matters, topics, tools, and tactics I had either already forgotten or didn't know existed. The use of technology was impressive. Unfortunately, I signed an oath of total secrecy, effective forever, hence the lack of detail.

Donna put a special emphasis on communications and emergency procedures, and I listened attentively and re-hearsed the use of the technology. The final day was devoted to paperwork, and once completed, I was taken to Dulles airport near Washington, DC. An Agency representative gave me an envelope with my Peter Wooten passport, credit cards, and pocket debris. I left with him all signs of my Dan Gordon identity. I boarded British Airways flight BA0292 to Charles de Gaulle airport in France. Upon arrival, I took a cab to a small hotel not far from the Opéra and quickly went out to a bistro in the corner to have a simple but good French dinner.

On the following day, an Agency representative came over to my hotel and told me that Ali was in town. He'd received my name and description from Mahmoud, who Ali believed was his handler for DGSE, but who was actually a Mossad operative. I received additional instructions, and the Agency representative left my hotel two hours later. I took a walk in the streets, enjoying the special beauty of

Paris, and when I returned to my hotel the concierge told me I had a guest waiting for me in the lobby.

I walked over to the only person sitting in the lobby. A dark-skinned man in his midthirties with close-cropped hair and dressed casually was reading a newspaper and calmly raised his eyes when I approached him.

"*Bonjour monsieur,*" I said. "*Je suis Peter. Etes-vous à la recherché pour moi?*"

My accent must have revealed the fact that French wasn't my native language.

"Indeed," he answered in English with a French accent. "I think you'd be more comfortable in English, Mr. Wooten."

"And you are . . . ?" I asked.

"I'm Ali, and I'm happy to meet you."

I put on a surprised and suspicious face. "Do we know each other? How did you know I was staying here?" I took a step back to show I was intimidated.

"Please Mr. Wooten, please don't be alarmed. I want to talk to you about your plans. Perhaps I could help. Please sit down." He pointed at the couch next to him. Showing signs of reluctance and curiosity, I sat down.

"Please tell me who you are," I insisted.

"The word is that you have some merchandise to sell, and I think I can help you do just that without assuming any unnecessary personal risk." He smiled, exposing perfect white teeth.

"I still need to know who you are." I just couldn't give in that easily.

"I'm in the information business. I buy and sell. If you have goods to sell, I can find you a buyer."

"Monsieur, please tell me exactly how you found me here."

"I told you I'm in the information business. Therefore, I had information that you were here. The fact is that a brief-case was stolen from you, and you filed a complaint with the police. My brothers, therefore, knew who you were. Then they heard you were fired and were angry. But why is that important?"

"I want to make sure I'm not walking into a trap. I don't want to be accused of something I didn't do," I said hesitantly.

"You're not, and you said nothing and gave me nothing, so where is the trap?"

He waited for my continued defiance, and when it failed to come, he continued. "Here is what I suggest. Don't tell me anything you have or can get. Just confirm your willingness to meet outside of France, at a place of your choosing, with people who are connected to those who'd be interested in your stuff. If you agree, I'll give you the name and address of a person to contact. I will then be out of the picture and will collect my commission from those who buy the information, if they find your merchandise interesting and valuable."

I got up. "Monsieur, I think there's some kind of a mistake. I'm here as a tourist, and I have nothing to sell." I had to play hard to get, because there could be others around, with or without Ali's knowledge.

"Please sit down," he said calmly. "The brothers in Lebanon want to hear you out. We know you were ousted from the CIA after the files were lost in Istanbul. You're out of a job; we can help."

"Are you from Lebanon?" I asked, relenting a tad.

He nodded. "I'm a Palestinian living in Lebanon. The Resistance to the Israelis will know how to show their gratitude for your help."

"How do I know I'm not walking into a trap, assuming you are who you say you are? It's true I'm out of a job, but that doesn't mean I want to sell myself." I tried to sound bitter.

"I don't know what other assurances I can give you. Think logically. For the Resistance you could be a goose laying golden eggs. Why would they want to hurt you?"

I wanted to say that once my well of knowledge dried up, I'd be a cooked goose, but I didn't; it wasn't in the script. "And how do I know you work for them, and not for my previous employer?"

Ali smiled. "Make your own security arrangements and build around you any security wall that would make you comfortable. We'll meet then, as long as we both understand that we need to move forward and strike a deal."

"Let me think about it," I said, and got up to leave.

"Here is my number," said Ali and handed me a small piece of paper. "It's my mobile phone. You can call me at any time." He walked out without much ado.

I thought the situation was rather comic. I knew who Ali was, and I knew he was working for the Mossad, but *he* didn't know that. Ali didn't know whether I was really defecting or selling anything. Ali told me he was working for Hezbollah, when we both knew it wasn't true. So why the charade? Because we had to maintain a certain degree of plausible deniability and security. What if Ali was doubled and was betraying the Mossad? Maybe he'd discovered that he wasn't working for the French foreign-intelligence services after all? What if DGSE was eavesdropping on our conversations and decided to step in and arrest us for conspiracy? I didn't even want to think about the magnitude of the scandal that could erupt if the French discovered that the Mossad, with the CIA, was using their name in a false-flag legend by telling an operative he was working for France and that clandestine activities were held in French territory, of all places. No wonder Ali suggested a meeting with someone working for his "brothers" outside France. A meeting in French territory attended by a Hezbollah operative was likely to attract the attention of DGSE and increase the likelihood that the legend would be blown.

I reported the meeting to Eric and Benny using an encrypted e-mail. Since Benny was out of our loop and obviously didn't have our encryption program—at least not legally—I asked Eric to forward Benny a copy of my report. I asked for instructions.

A day later, I received a one-word e-mail from Eric. "Proceed."

I called Ali. "OK, we can proceed. Here are my terms: I want to meet your contacts in Europe. I'm not going to Lebanon. In addition, I need to know the full name of anyone I'm expected to meet, at least three days before the meeting. Rest assured that although I'm out of the Agency, I still have friends, and I can check out anyone to make sure there'll be no surprises. The third condition is that I get five thousand dollars in cash, left in an envelope at this hotel. I need the money to pay for my local expenses. I expect to get the money before I make any move."

Ali paused. "Five thousand dollars is a lot of money, and I don't know if the brothers will authorize that."

"No bargaining," I said. "Once I get the money, I'll call you to arrange the rendezvous with your brothers' representatives." I hung up. Hilarious, I concluded—the idea of demanding five thousand dollars for the meeting occurred to me at the last moment. If authorized, Ali would get the money from Mahmoud, who would get it from Benny. CIA accounting people would laugh all the way to the bank. I didn't think about what Benny would say when he heard about it. However, my demand was justified as a precautionary measure, if any layer of security failed, because the money demand made my appearance on the scene look more credible.

I enjoyed Paris by day and by night for two more days—it sure beat Sierra Leone—until the hotel receptionist handed me a thick envelope. "This came in for you."

I went up to my room and put on plastic gloves that I

pulled from the emergency kit I'd received at the Farm. I carefully opened the envelope. It contained fifty one-hundred-dollar bills. I went to the nearest bank and handed the envelope to the teller. "Please convert it to euros," I requested. Just in case there was some snafu along the line with this almost ridiculous arrangement of layer upon layer of operatives, double operatives, double-crossers, and the like, I didn't want to touch the money with my bare hands and couldn't enter the bank with plastic gloves without causing a commotion. If an invisible powder marked the dollar bills, it would leave marks on me as well. I was also certain that the notes' serial numbers were recorded. I took the euros from the teller, went to the nearest pharmacy, and purchased nail-polish remover, hoping it would remove from my hands any powder residue, in case it was applied to the bills. I returned to my hotel, cleaned my hands with the chemical, reported to Eric, paid the hotel bill with cash, and checked out.

I took the train to London, not before routinely making sure I wasn't followed. I met an Agency representative in London who gave me an unregistered mobile phone. I checked into a hotel near Marble Arch and called Ali from my mobile phone.

"The goods were delivered—thanks. You may arrange for a meeting now, but remember I must have the name of the person or persons at least three days in advance."

"I can give you the name right now," said Ali. "It's just one person; he lives in Bucharest, Romania. Are you willing to travel?"

"Give me the address."

I wrote it down and hung up.

I called Eric. "The coast is clear," he said. "Go ahead and schedule a meeting not earlier than a week from today—we need to make arrangements."

I placed the call to Constantin Badescu in Romania.

After three rings a man answered in Romanian. "This is Constantin Badescu."

"Mr. Badescu, my name is Wooten. Do you speak English?"

"Enough to understand you," he said. He sounded like a man in his late sixties with a grouchy voice. "Are you in Bucharest?"

"No, I plan to arrive in eight days."

"Good, meet me at a café on 112 Calea Mosilor in Bucharest on the twelfth of this month at eleven o'clock in the morning. Can you make it?"

"I'll be there," I said and hung up.

I reported to Eric. He called me an hour later. "The location is good, but the café and the adjacent Armonia Hotel need improvement. Anyway, we're booking you at the Armonia Hotel."

I returned to New York, only to be told to pack again. "Where are we going?" I asked Eric.

"To Rome, but separately. Apple #3 will be there as of tomorrow."

I went from the Rome airport to a safe apartment not far from the Spanish Steps. On the following day, Eric, Gerard, and Paul came over with muffins and orange juice. A genuine surprise.

"Apple #3 is already here," said Eric as we were muncing on the muffins. "We don't know what his plans are, so we'd rather talk to him now. We can't expose Gerard again."

Paul added, "We're sending Chris instead, but you need to stay put. We may still need you here."

Before I managed to ask who Chris was, a young red-haired man came in. He was in his midforties and dressed in blue jeans and a black shirt. They handed him a mobile phone and gave him instructions regarding the background and the goal of the call to Sheik Naboulsi, Apple #3. Chris seemed to be in the loop already.

"A tourist in a restaurant forgot this phone," Paul added. "One of my men picked it up. That's an unregistered pre-paid phone. It's perfect for us."

Eric said, "Naboulsi is much younger than Wazir and junior to him in the Council, but he's gaining greater influence fast. He has the same background as Hasan Nasserallah. They went to the same schools, and their families have social ties."

"Here is the legend," said Paul and distributed a printed page with a faded black-and-white photo. "It's all here." He turned to Chris. "Get him to meet you regarding the stolen briefcase."

"Don't you think Wazir reported his encounter with Gerard Coulter, thereby increasing the chance I'll get a slammed phone in response to my call?" asked Chris.

"You never mentioned the stolen documents to Wazir, right?" Paul asked Gerard, to make sure. Gerard shook his head.

"Then, Chris, you shouldn't worry. You're coming with a different name, a different face, and a new legend. Besides, Wazir didn't report the meeting with Gerard Coulter or his suspicion. That's not how they operate. There is no bureaucratic or military hierarchy or set procedures or channels of reporting. Each member of the Council is like a medieval feudal prince responsible for his own principality. They convene and exchange views and make strategic decisions only. Anyway, unless Wazir alerted Hezbollah by messenger, he didn't report the meeting."

So, they were eavesdropping on Wazir. Chris dialed. We put on our earphones to listen in.

"Sheik Naboulsi?"

"Yes?" His voice was sharp.

"My name is Brian Ness. I'm calling about the contents of a stolen briefcase in Istanbul."

There was no answer. Chris waited ten seconds and asked, "Are you there?"

"What about it?" he finally responded. That was a better answer than I'd expected.

"There were names and clues in the documents. Maybe we can discuss it."

"Who are you?"

"A friend told me about the documents. I'm a supporter of your Resistance against the Israelis. I think there is a conspiracy by the Americans to destroy you. I can help."

"How?"

"Finding out who the Apples are."

A pause again. "Let me have a number where I can call you."

Chris gave him his Italian mobile-phone number.

"Good," said Paul after the conversation ended. "At least he didn't deny knowing about the briefcase, or pretend to be just a member of the clergy without any earthly involvements."

Two hours later Chris's mobile phone rang. He glanced at the display—it was Naboulsi's number. He hooked the phone to the relay and recording box and answered. We listened in.

"Yes?"

"Mr. Ness?"

"Yes."

"Tell me what you can do for me." The caller didn't identify himself, but I recognized the voice: Naboulsi, if it was indeed Naboulsi who'd spoken with Chris when Chris first called him.

Chris lowered his voice. "Sheik Naboulsi, I'm taking a huge personal risk by talking to you. We must meet in person. It has to be secretive and quick."

Mossad training had taught me that people are more likely to believe things you whisper in their ear.

The sheik got right down to business. "Where and when?"

"Café Antonio opposite Banca di Europa on via Capo la

Casa, just off the Spanish Steps, this afternoon at five thirty." Chris was cool and professional.

"I'll be there," Naboulsi said decisively.

I looked at Joe with his magic box as he approached Chris. "After you're done working on Chris, can you take twenty pounds off of me?" I asked.

Joe didn't think it was funny. "I have my orders," he said. I gave up. People who don't have a sense of humor probably don't have any sense at all.

"Don't look around to identify our men," said Paul as Chris stood at the door. "They know who and where you are. Have you memorized your instructions?"

Chris returned his five-page instruction sheet to Paul. "By heart."

At five P.M., Chris took a cab. We left in a van moments later and parked nearby. The technician turned on the listening devices Chris was carrying. We heard his steps and even his heartbeat. We saw Chris entering the café, but there was no sign of Naboulsi.

We've been had again, I thought.

My tiny earpiece came to life. I heard a voice instructing Chris over the network: "Stay put. We see you and the café, and we'll alert you to any hostile activity." This was central command located in another van parked not far from us. A minute later, a man came over to Chris's table. He was in his early forties, wearing a light suit without a tie, and dark eyeglasses.

"Mr. Ness?"

Chris said, "Yes?"

"Please follow me," said the man. He was skinny with slightly dark skin, and spoke English with an Arabic accent.

Chris didn't move. "Where to?" he asked.

"To meet the sheik."

"Where is he?"

"Not far."

Chris seemed to hesitate. Although an unknown number of CIA combatants were protecting him, he knew he shouldn't follow that man, even with a platoon of men.

"Refuse the offer." I heard the order to Chris through my earpiece.

Chris looked at the man standing next to his table, and I heard him say, "Sorry, I've taken a considerable risk by contacting the sheik. I suspect I could be followed by people who don't want me to say what I'm about to say. I can't risk myself any further. Please sit down." Chris pointed at the chair next to him.

"Are you being followed now?"

"No, I managed to lose them in another country," said Chris. "Please ask the sheik to come here; a meeting in a public place will protect us both. Please sit down—we're attracting attention."

Reluctantly the man sat down. "Who are you?" he asked.

"Never mind. I have important things to tell the sheik."

"Tell me."

"I can't," said Chris firmly. "I can discuss it only with the sheik."

From our position, we could see the man's face and could sense how his mind was weighing his options. "You said it had to do with the stolen documents. Tell me more."

"These things are for the sheik's ears only," Chris insisted.

Maybe he could corrupt the sheik, but to succeed at turning two people would be stretching it.

"The sheik is a holy man and doesn't meet with ordinary people. I'm his assistant. You can tell me, and I'll forward the message. I promise."

Chris didn't budge. "Well, in that case, we have nothing to talk about. Please tell the sheik that I gave him his chance. I may not be able to repeat it."

"Chance? What chance?" The man raised his voice.

"As I said, it concerns the stolen documents in Istanbul. I'm sure he knows what it's all about." Chris was nonchalant. "And you as his confidential assistant should also know, unless you're not who you say you are."

The man opposite Chris seemed to hesitate. To tighten the bolts, Chris started to get up to leave.

"Wait," the man said. "Sit down." He took off his sunglasses. "I'm Sheik Naboulsi. Now talk."

I inspected his face and tried to cull from my memory any resemblance to the photo we'd received. There were similarities, but I wasn't sure. Obviously, Chris couldn't pull out his instruction sheet with Naboulsi's photo. He couldn't carry it around and risk blowing his cover, if apprehended.

• "We think he could be the sheik," said the voice in my earpiece.

"Can you prove it? I must be sure I'm talking to the sheik," Chris insisted, looking at the man's face.

The sheik looked around and pulled out a burgundy-colored Lebanese passport.

Chris flipped through the passport and said, "OK."

It was either a fake passport, or the man was Naboulsi. I opted for the latter, and it seemed that Chris thought so too, probably due to a lack of choice, but also because in all likelihood he was talking to a Hezbollah insider whose exact identity we'd find out later on.

"What do you know about the stolen documents in Istanbul?" Chris asked.

"You tell me," he countered.

"I must be assured we're on the same page," Chris said.

"I heard there were some American documents," said the sheik. "Now tell me who you are."

"I'm a supporter of your Resistance against the Israelis," Chris said. "I'm unhappy with the U.S. policy toward the Arab world in general and toward Hezbollah in particular." He paused.

"I'm listening," Sheik Naboulsi said without a trace of expected impatience.

"This is a ploy," Chris said.

"A ploy . . . You mean the documents?"

"Yes. The fact of the matter is that the Americans don't know the identity of the three individuals code-named in the documents."

"Do they exist?"

"Yes, we were sure of that, but had no idea who they were."

"Then if they don't work for the Americans, whom do they work for?"

"CIA doesn't know; they think for an unknown rival organization. CIA wanted to sell the documents to Hezbollah, hoping to smoke out the moles and force an internal investigation and distrust among Council members until the three individuals are exposed. The plan was frustrated when the documents were stolen." Chris chuckled. "Now the CIA doesn't know who the moles are, and they don't have control over who has the documents."

"What you're telling me doesn't make sense," said Naboulsi. "You're telling me that the CIA planned to sell the documents to Hezbollah to start an investigation. Then the documents were stolen and ended up in the hands of Hezbollah, so they had their plans frustrated? Just because they never got the money for the documents?"

He wasn't stupid, I thought.

"Because the documents you have may not be the originals," said Chris.

"What do you mean?"

"Since they were stolen, the thief or his masters may have altered them. The U.S. is not your only enemy. I saw them in Washington, DC, and can tell you if you're holding the real ones. Either way, I want to make sure that the CIA plan is buried for good."

"How do you know all that?"

"I used to be an insider."

"Used to?"

"Yes. I was forced out after I grew more and more uncomfortable with U.S. policy and wasn't afraid to voice my opinion. So instead of allowing a dissenting voice, they showed me the door."

"What can you do for us?"

"Tell you if the documents you have are genuine, and help you in many other ways."

"Go on."

"That's it."

"Why are you doing it? For the money?"

"First for satisfaction. I want to get even. I also want to help your cause. And finally, yes, money is a consideration. I'm out of a job because I told a co-worker that I was supporting your struggle against the Israelis. I was assigned to another job, where my biggest responsibility was to arrange theater tickets for the assistants of visiting dignitaries. They stripped me of my security clearance, took away all my perks, and then told me to go. The bastards." Chris sounded bitter. I was impressed with his acting abilities.

"What was your position?"

"An analyst."

"Where?"

"Never mind. I'm in a position to help you if you meet my needs."

"What are they?"

"Modest," Chris said. "I need ten thousand dollars immediately and an additional five thousand dollars for each piece of information I bring."

"Why should we believe you?" The sheik had asked the most reasonable question. "Just because you know of the documents, we should pay you ten thousand dollars?" He said that in a polite tone, which didn't mask the dismissive nature of his answer.

"Suit yourself," Chris said. "You can ignore my offer of help. You're not the only player in the marketplace."

Naboulsi slanted his eyes. "Are you threatening me?"

"No need to get excited. Let's treat it as a proposal that was rejected. We'll go our separate ways." Chris was cool.

He gave Chris a long look, and said, *"Tayeb"*—*good*, in Arabic. "I'll call you later."

The sheik got up and left. We followed him with our eyes after he was out of the camera's angle. He made a turn at the street corner.

Chris left money on the table and took a cab driven by an Agency operative. It was too risky for him to remain there and become a sitting duck, in case someone had ideas. There was no question that the sheik, or whoever the person Chris had met was, wasn't alone. We started the van, circled the city for an hour, and then drove to the Hilton. First, we went downstairs, making sure we were alone, and then we went up the elevator to the third floor. We exited to the hallway and waited until an old woman entered her room, and took another elevator to the tenth floor. Joe was waiting for us. We knocked on Chris's adjoining door. There was no answer.

"Where is Chris?" I asked Joe.

"I took off his mask, and he went to the bar downstairs."

I went to the door. "I'm going to have a beer," I said.

"Please stay here," Paul asked. "I don't think you should be seen with Chris, even after Joe removed his mask. Use the minibar."

Mac entered the room. "Dan, you must leave Rome immediately. There are too many opposition operatives around us. We can't risk being connected with you if they identify you as the person who left the documents in Istanbul."

"So?" I asked, contemplating my next move. I don't run that easily.

"What if they nab you? What would you say when inter-rogated about the documents?"

"That I had to allow the documents to be stolen in case the CIA was watching me. I didn't want to sell and hand them over directly to Hezbollah and risk facing treason charges. Accused and punished for negligence was harsh enough."

"An interesting thought," said Mac, "but I have my or-ders. Langley said to bring you back in one piece."

I turned around and went to pack.

I flew to Bucharest's international airport, Aeroportul Internaţional in Otopeni, and upon arrival, took a cab to my hotel. The driver wasted no time in trying to sell me the usual stuff—tours and women. All suggestions met my polite rejection. The end result was a cab fare double the usual. I kept my mouth shut. The difference was less than ten dollars. If I could live with that, so could the bean counters in Washington. There was no point in arguing with the cabbie, which would help him to remember my face.

The street the hotel was on was under construction, and I had to walk a long block. The hotel's staff was friendly, but the hotel itself was painfully modest. Perfect for my image of a desperate man out of a job. I went out to the street for a walk. I strolled through Sfintilor Street and within ten min-utes found myself in University Square, where I couldn't avoid seeing the yellow arches of McDonald's. I continued down Balescu Street until I ended up in Piata Unirii, with its restaurants, cafés, and stores. I felt as if I was walking in a city past its time. It was dressed beautifully but gloomily—as people are at a funeral. Still, there were glimpses of the future here and there—a bright store, a new office building. I thought of Ilya Ehrenburg, the Russian writer, who said that you could cover the whole earth with asphalt, but eventually green grass would break through. Similarly, a new, better-looking Romania was slowly emerging from the ruins of the old.

But I wasn't on a tourist excursion. I needed to find out who was behind me. I applied the entire detect-your-follower manual, but I didn't identify anyone, although I knew that there were several pairs of eyes watching my movements.

I played it cool and returned to my hotel. I inserted the key card into the key slot on my door. A red light blinked, but the door didn't open. I tried again with no success. I stepped back and hid behind the service door, peeping through its round window to see if someone was exiting my room. After about twenty minutes, I gave up and went to the reception desk.

The receptionist issued me another card. "We always have problems with these keys," she said.

I returned to my room with a new key card. The door opened and the room was intact. An SMS message on my mobile phone confirmed that there were no problems ahead. Although I didn't see any of my support and security teams, I knew they were somewhere in my vicinity.

At ten o'clock, an hour before the meeting, I sat at the café reading a newspaper and having a cup of tea that tasted awful. At eleven five, a man fitting the description of Badescu came and sat at my table without a word. The first thing I noticed about him were his weary eyes and facial couperose, a skin disorder where the face shows diffused redness made visible by bright red around the nose, cheeks, and chin. Badescu was wearing a white shirt that badly needed a meeting with a hot iron, and a tweed jacket that was at least twenty-five years old. He was smoking a cheap, locally made cigarette, and I noticed a light tremor in his right hand. He was in terrible shape, that was clear. However, when my guest opened his mouth, after ten minutes I realized that I had misjudged him. The man was bright, even brilliant. He knew what he was talking about and handled himself professionally. I was chastened for jumping to conclusions before I had all the facts. That jumping was my physical exercise for the day, I consoled myself.

"What can I do for you?" he asked. He didn't even introduce himself.

"Mr. Badescu?" I asked.

He nodded.

"I don't know," I said. "You tell me. Ali suggested I meet you. So here I am."

"Tell me about the documents you lost."

"Are you recording this conversation?" I asked.

"No, are you?"

I shook my head. We were both lying. This could be the beginning of a beautiful untrusting friendship.

"There's nothing to tell," I said. "I had to meet an Agency operative at my hotel and deliver a briefcase to him. A burglar stole it from my room. I was fired. That's the whole story."

"Had you inspected the contents of the briefcase before it was stolen?"

I was walking into a quicksand area. The briefcase hadn't been locked or sealed, unlike all bona fide diplomatic pouches.

"Just briefly," I said, trying not to attribute any importance to the fact that I'd seen the documents. His swift verbal right-hook punch was all but expected.

"Why was the briefcase unsealed? Did you break the seal?"

I shook my head. "No. My instructions were to remove the seal before landing in Istanbul. I wasn't traveling under a diplomatic cover and had no diplomatic passport or immunity. A sealed briefcase could have attracted the attention of Turkish customs at the airport, or even worse, of others. The briefcase had to look like an ordinary businessman's briefcase."

He looked at me and I braced for the next verbal punch.

"I'm told that you picked up the briefcase only at your Istanbul hotel, and that you didn't travel to Turkey with it." His Romanian-accented English was clear, but so also was the acidity in his questions. Whoever it was at the agency who had constructed the legend hadn't thought it through. A simple detective job of asking hotel employees, coupled with a twenty-dollar-bill incentive, would have revealed that I'd received a box delivered to the hotel. Probably that's exactly what Hezbollah local operatives had done. Badescu must have gotten that information from somewhere, since I wasn't sure that Ali knew these details to give Badescu.

I shook my head. "No. Your information is inaccurate."

"Then what was in the box delivered to your Istanbul hotel?" Yes, he did his homework.

"Old magazines. It was a decoy. We wanted to see if anyone was observing me and tried to open the box before I arrived." I was pleased with my quickly thought of answer, which sounded plausible but was a flat lie. "Mr. Badescu, can we get to the point? Tell me what is it that you want, and I'll tell you if it's available and the price for it."

"I need to know if the documents are authentic, and if so, whether you can get additional documents."

"I have a quick answer for that. I don't volunteer information, I sell it."

"But you've just told me about the magazines in the box," he countered.

"Only to demonstrate my credibility."

"What do you want for your answers?"

"Not much. Thirty thousand dollars, plus ten thousand dollars for each future meeting."

"You must understand that I work as a middleman. I have no authority to offer you any payment."

"Fine," I said. "Then call me when you have answers." I got up.

"Sit down," he said in a commanding one. "We're not done yet." Obviously, he was accustomed to giving orders, but now the circumstances were different. He was no longer a high-ranking officer of the Securitate, the fearful Communist-era secret police, and I wasn't chained to a chair in their interrogation room, fearing for my life. Nevertheless, true to my legend of a nervous rogue operative looking for a quick deal, I didn't give him a sample of the usual Dan Gordon temper and instead sat down in obedience, demonstrating nervousness.

"My clients have a lot of incentives to offer you. Mostly, they are interested in research work on political trends in the U.S. Can you do that?"

Did I have to change my mind again about Badescu? Was he depriving a village somewhere of an idiot, or did he think I qualified? This was the most basic entry-level trick of the trade. Ask a potential asset to do a nonsense job just to bring him in. That's also the maneuver the Mossad had used on Badescu, although I was sure he'd known exactly what was behind the offer he received, but couldn't have cared less. He'd needed the money and was out of any government job anyway. But now? He thought that since I was a defecting analyst with the CIA, I'd lost the ability to recognize the recruiters' textbook advance tactics? In fact, Badescu left out one other request a recruiter should ask a walk-in—somebody who volunteers to serve—which is to incriminate himself, knowingly or unknowingly. Terrorist organizations request proof of integrity not by demanding that the recruit bring a police confirmation that he lacks any criminal record, but rather by ordering him to kill someone. Intelligence services could also ask for a signed receipt "for services" or to have classified documents brought to them before they'd agree to talk business.

True to my proclaimed image, I pretended to consider his offer.

"I'll think about it, but if you want to see me again, tell your clients they'd better deliver thirty thousand dollars, or there'll be no second meeting."

"I think you're exaggerating," said Badescu calmly. "Why would anyone pay you thirty thousand dollars? Just to see you? You'd better tell me first what they can expect for that kind of money. Then I'll tell you if we have a deal."

I thought for a moment. "I can help them with the documents in the files they already have, and also concerning future operations of the Agency regarding your client's finances. I can also help identify insiders within your client's organization who could be double agents."

His eyes lit briefly. "Tell me more."

"About what?" I played dumb.

"About the insiders. Do you have names?"

"No, but I can help an internal investigation, because I can identify names from the clues in the documents. I saw the raw material that came in, where only aliases and code names were used. A good counterintelligence investigator, who would work with me, could narrow down the list. I don't think thirty thousand dollars for my service is a lot of money."

Badescu gave me a long look. "Fine—where can I find you? I need to talk to my clients."

"I'll meet you here in seven days," I suggested.

Badescu hesitated for a moment.

"Or I can call you in a few days. I have your number," I added.

"That's better," he said.

I went up to my room, packed my bag, and checked out. I took a cab to Aeroportul Internaţional in Otopeni and boarded the first flight to Vienna. I met an Agency representative, gave him my Peter Wooten passport and other documents, received back my Dan Gordon identity, and took an El Al flight to Israel. Although it was the end of winter, Israel was sunny and mild. I called Benny's mobile phone.

"Dan, where are you?" came Benny's jovial voice.

"In a hotel in Tel Aviv, the usual place. Where are you?"

"In Europe, but I'll be back in a couple of days. Anything happening?"

"Nothing I didn't report already. Our friend is talking to his friends, and I need to get back there in a week or two. I decided to come here and see some friendly faces."

"Stick around. I'll call you when I get back," said Benny.

I called Gila, a longtime female friend I liked to spend time with. Indoors. Just the two of us. In the morning, I looked at her side of the bed. She was gone, leaving behind a light scent of her perfume. I felt guilty for limiting our meetings to my hotel room, reminding me that my conscience hurt only when all my other body parts felt so good.

I enjoyed Tel Aviv, a city that never stops, day or night, met friends and family, and waited for Eric's instructions. Benny called me at the same time I received Eric's encrypted message. "Meet Benny, he has updates." I guessed that the delay in Eric's instructional mail was caused by the need to coordinate with Benny.

Benny was driving us to Caesarea, an old Roman port on the Mediterranean Sea, twenty-eight miles north of Tel Aviv. After going through the excavated Roman town, we entered a fish restaurant overlooking the small bay. There was only a handful of diners in the restaurant on this sunny day. We sat at the corner, away from the other guests.

"Tell me about the meeting," said Benny, once we were done with the usual *how are you*s and inquiries about our respective families.

"Badescu is direct," I said. "He wasted no time in going for the jugular."

"He is definitely not what you call a pleasant person. His reputation is in different areas. I looked him up in our database. Before becoming the head of the black-propaganda division of the Securitate, he worked in an ultrasecret unit that assassinated opposition activists. Badescu was a favorite of Elena Ceausescu, the yellow-toothed, crazy wife of the

Romanian president. She was a fearful tyrant in her own right and was in many aspects more ruthless than President Ceausescu was. You'd better be careful with Badescu. He could be dangerous."

"Physically?" I asked, trying to figure out how this frail, sixty-nine-year-old man could endanger me when I was younger, bigger, experienced in martial arts, and surrounded by CIA security.

"No, he is very clever and could trap you in more than one way. Just be careful and measure what you say or do."

"Eric instructed me to get additional guidance from you. I want to get back to Bucharest soon to hear his responses. But I need to know first if he checked."

"We matched the transcript of the recording made during your meeting against his report to Ali."

"And?" I was anxious.

"Generally speaking, his report matched the recording."

"Generally?"

"Yes, and it's a good sign of regularity. We also verified that the man you met was indeed Badescu and not an imposter."

"How about the report of Ali to Mahmoud?"

"Same thing, both checked."

"What do you mean by 'both'?"

"The report Ali made to Mahmoud and the report Mahmoud made to us."

"I guess the only question left then is the report Badescu made to Hezbollah, if he broke his promise to Ali."

Benny didn't answer.

"I'm listening," I said. I expected him to tell me that Badescu didn't report it to Hezbollah. Therefore Benny's silence was worrisome.

"You'd have to talk to NSA about it," said Benny in a tone that conveyed the message that I shouldn't ask him that again. I made a mental note to find out, because there seemed to be a problem here.

"What are Eric's instructions?" asked Benny.

"Just to call Badescu and arrange a new meeting in Bucharest. Eric needs to know about the date and place a few days in advance."

We spent another hour schmoozing until it was time to go. I decided against calling Badescu from Israel using my mobile phone, and on the following day, I boarded an El Al flight to Vienna, changed my identity to Wooten, and flew to Bucharest. Learning from my Romanian food experience, I had a hearty Wiener schnitzel before boarding. Nothing could beat that. In Bucharest, I took a cab to the Armonia Hotel. A smiling receptionist welcomed me and checked me into that very modest hotel. She handed me a small white envelope. "This is for you," she said. Inside was a handwritten note on the hotel's stationery. "This is a telephonic message received today for you." It was signed, "The telephone operator." The body of the note read, "Mr. Wooten, in case you're looking for me, my home telephone is out of order. Please come to my home." The address was scribbled at the bottom.

I went out to the street and found an Internet café. I sent a coded urgent message to Eric, asking for instructions. Several hours later, I received an answer. It took me a while to decode it. "Go to his residence at five P.M.; security team will be behind you. Don't attempt to make contact with them. Put on your gear."

In the afternoon, I decided to call first—maybe they'd fixed his phone. I didn't want to travel to his house with the security detail behind me, only to realize he wasn't home. I dialed Badescu's number again. An answering machine came on. That was a good sign; at least the phone was working. I left a message that I'd come to his house on that evening at five P.M.

At four thirty, I put on the black shoes with the GPS device and the black shirt with the sewn-in RFID, and took a cab to Badescu's house. He lived in the outskirts of the city in a modest neighborhood, but the house itself, a single-family home, was rather nice. The lights inside the house were on. I opened the gate and walked to the wooden front door. I rang the bell and waited. There was no answer. I knocked on the door, and the unlocked door opened slightly. I pushed it open.

"Mr. Badescu?" I called several times. There was no response. I gingerly walked inside the house and called his name again, but to no avail. As I was about to turn back I saw behind a sofa a pair of legs on the floor. I walked over. Badescu was lying on the floor, a pool of blood dripping from his chest. I crouched and touched his neck. He had no pulse. His corpse was still lukewarm—he had been dead for no more than an hour. My stomach churned, and my heartbeat did overtime. I turned to the front door and closed it. I searched the body, but his pockets were empty. I didn't see the murder weapon, but it was probably a knife or another sharp object. I went to his desk and searched it. Old newspapers and bills were piled. I opened the drawers. On the top-right drawer was a .38 caliber pistol. I didn't touch it. I had no use for a gun in Romania, and being caught with it would double my problems. I opened the bottom drawer and pulled out the most valuable item I saw there. It was a fourteen-by-ten-inch white envelope filled with documents, some in Arabic, some in Romanian and English. At first glance, they seemed official or military.

I pushed back the drawer and was about to put the envelope under my coat and leave when I heard a very firm order in my earpiece. "Leave as quickly as you can. The police are here. We're out of here. Dump your electronics if you can." I didn't answer so as not to risk my backup team, if our communication was intercepted. I dropped the envelope to the floor and pushed it with my leg under the heavy credenza. I looked around to find an escape route through a back door, but I couldn't find any. I rushed to the bathroom and flushed down my receiver-transmitter earpiece. The front door to the house was burst open and three uniformed men holding guns shouted in Romanian that anyone could understand just by looking at their menacing gestures: "Stop where you are and raise your hands."

CHAPTER TEN

Shit. Deep shit. I raised my hands. I was going to hell in a handbasket. I thought of the no-win situation I'd heard of from Alex, who'd told us to always be prepared. "Your enemy will attack when you least expect it—or," he'd added with a chuckle, "when you're expecting it." I quickly assessed my situation. Under any circumstances, it ranged from bad to worse. I was inside a house whose owner had just been murdered. I was a stranger and couldn't speak Romanian to get myself out of it somehow. To make things even worse, I was a walking spy-electronics store.

One of the cops, probably the senior ranking officer, quickly searched me. I was handcuffed and led away to a squad car waiting outside, while curious neighbors gathered. I sat in the backseat trying to figure out what to do next. I had more than one thousand dollars in cash, but trying to bribe the cops at this time could be risky. As the car drove away, I tried to rearrange my thoughts. During all my training at the Mossad and then by the CIA, my instructors had paid a lot of attention to my conduct if I was apprehended inside a building or a facility without a good and plausible reason.

The first hours are the most important. Assess your situation and see if you can extricate yourself by force, maneuvering, or bribe. Under no circumstances do you

*identify yourself as a foreign agent. Most of the time the
arresting police are low-level cops who don't speak your
language and under the best circumstances might think
you are a burglar or a common thief. Don't correct their
mistake hoping to be treated better. The opposite is true.
Being identified as a foreign agent will make things much
more difficult, and might even cost your life. A sudden
move could trigger a nervous cop to shoot the "dangerous
spy" he has just caught. Keep your mouth shut until you
get to the police station. A closed mouth catches no flies.
If no means of escape are available, demand to see your
consul. Don't ask to see the American consul if you're
carrying the passport of a different country. Use your
legend to explain what you were doing when apprehended.*

I tried to figure out who had whacked Badescu, and why.
Was it Hezbollah, because they discovered that he was getting cozy with the Mossad, double-crossing them? Was it
the Mossad, who'd killed him after they finished extracting
everything he knew about Hezbollah but neglected to tell
Ali? If that assumption was true, then Benny had lied to me
when he said that Badescu reported in full the contents of
his conversation with me. Maybe there was additional information Badescu had withheld from the Mossad, and
when they discovered it, they didn't like to be fooled around
with? Benny knew I was going to meet Badescu, and killing
Badescu now could put me at risk—and indeed, I was in
danger. The assassin was unlikely to be a random burglar.
The first thing a burglar would take, other than cash, would
be a gun. Since the .38 was left untouched in the top drawer,
and the house looked tidy, I ruled out burglary. Was he
killed by any other enemy Badescu might have had? I had
no idea. Intelligence operatives working in the dark have
enemies who do the same. I also wondered who'd called the
police, who had very conveniently arrived exactly when I

was inside the house. After a twenty-minute ride the police car went through a metal gate near a street sign, 13-15, STEFAN CEL MARE STREET. The barrier was lifted, and we entered into a cobblestone-paved yard. I saw the sign: THE GENERAL INSPECTORATE OF ROMANIAN POLICE.

I was pulled roughly out of the car, banging my head against the door in the process. Inside the police station, I was photographed, fingerprinted, and ordered to empty my pockets. Their contents were put in a dirty plastic bag. I noticed how the cops eyed the cash I was carrying, but there was no way I could safely suggest they take it in exchange for my freedom. I was brought into a windowless interrogation room that had a strong odor of cigarettes. In the middle were a wooden table and three wooden chairs. Two cops pushed me in and signaled me to sit down. A young man in a blue uniform was holding my Peter Wooten American passport, "I am Agent Şef adjunct Iulian Dumitraşcu. You're under arrest for murder and burglary," he said in English with a strong Romanian accent.

I responded, "I am an American citizen, and I demand to see the American consul."

"I set the rules here, and you make no demands," he said in a cold tone, and then shouted, "Why did you kill Badescu?"

"I didn't kill anyone, and I demand to see the American consul," I repeated.

"Now, you talk and I listen, and then you sign a confession. American consul later, maybe yes, maybe no."

"I demand to see the American consul," I said again.

The blow to the left side of my face came hard. My eyes welled with tears from the blow, and my vision blurred. It hurt. I said nothing. I was handcuffed, chained to the chair, and couldn't avoid the next blow to my chest. That sucked the air out of my lungs. I fell panting to the floor with the chair hurting my back.

"Now you talk. Why did you kill Badescu?" Dumitraşcu

asked again and again while I was still on the floor with the chair, twisting my handcuffed hands.

"I want to see the American consul. I am an American citizen," I yelled, my face bleeding and my body suffering excruciating pain.

He kicked me hard in the groin and I blacked out. I came to after a bucket of dirty water was emptied on my face. I opened my eyes and was blinded by a severe headache. I closed my eyes again. I was in no hurry to resume the interrogation. Another officer came into the room. "The American consul says he's busy and will come to see you next week. Maybe."

The routine continued. They asked why I had killed Badescu and demanded a confession. I said I didn't and demanded to see the American consul, and they responded with more beating. Hours went by, and nobody from the embassy came over to see me. The cops kept telling me that the consul wasn't coming. Apparently, they believed that a hostile interrogation would succeed in breaking me, gaining a confession. It didn't.

Five hours later, I was dragged into a small and fetid cell and was locked inside. An hour later a guard pushed in a slice of white bread that tasted of nothing, a mug of water, and a sticky corn cereal that looked terrible and tasted even worse. I had no appetite, but ate it. My body was aching all over. I sat on the bed and leaned my head against the wall, shuddering in the cold. It was cold enough to freeze the balls off a brass monkey.

What do I do next?

Sleep wasn't an option. I was too cold, and the noise was unbearable—heavy metal doors slamming, yelling and shouting of prisoners and prison guards—and the smell was a combination of vomit, urine, and excrement. I wondered why no one had come for me.

On the following morning, they gave me half a hard-boiled egg with two slices of bread and tea. Moments later, I was taken to another interrogation room. A tall uniformed man with gray hair and black-rimmed eyeglasses was sitting next to a table. Another officer sat in the corner.

"Sit down," said the officer. "I am Comisar Meciul Paunescu."

I sat.

"What is your name?"

"Peter Wooten. I'm an American citizen—you have my passport. I want to see the American consul."

"We checked with the American Consulate. They say that your passport was reported stolen. They need proof that you're an American citizen as you claim, before a consul visits you. Who are you?"

I was caught by surprise, but quickly composed myself. Such a fast response, or any response, from the consulate was suspect, particularly when I was unaware that the passport CIA gave me was reported stolen. True, I wasn't Peter Wooten, but I was certain that my passport was issued by the State Department as part of my legend. An inquiry by the Romanian police would have been sent by the consulate to Washington to check the authenticity and validity of my passport. Washington would immediately take action to protect me one way or the other. The consulate was unaware of Operation Pinocchio, and therefore telling the Romanians, without checking with Washington, that my passport was stolen would sink me deeper, instead of doing something to pull me out. What the hell was going on?

"I'm Peter Wooten, and the passport is not stolen, it's mine. Let me talk to the consul and hear from him that the passport was reported stolen. It's absurd."

I was convinced that Comisar Paunescu was applying an old investigative trick on me to shake my self-confidence.

He moved on. "What were you doing in the house of Constantin Badescu when arrested?"

I had to decide quickly whether to answer the questions or insist upon seeing the consul first. Since my backup team knew I'd been arrested, I was confident that, whether the police were lying to me regarding the consul or not, another branch of the American government knew I'd been arrested, and therefore their representative would soon visit me.

"I had a meeting with Badescu. He left me a message at my hotel with his address and asked me to come over to his house."

"Where is the message?"

"You have it. It should be in the stuff taken from me by your officers last night."

"There was no such note in your belongings. I personally checked it."

I tried to figure out what I'd done with the note, but couldn't remember. My head was still aching from the treatment I'd received the night before.

"How did you call Badescu?"

"From my mobile phone. You have that, too."

"We checked your phone; no calls were incoming or outgoing."

I remembered why. The phone was a specially equipped phone with a button that erased the memory. I'd pressed it when arrested. The police couldn't check with the phone company, which was probably located outside Romania. Even if I'd wanted, I couldn't tell them, because I had no idea which company it was.

"Why did you kill Badescu?"

"Comisar, I swear that I didn't kill him. I came to the house, the door was open, I saw him on the floor, I checked to see if he had a pulse, and then the police came."

"Our lab found Badescu's blood on your coat."

"That's possible. When I crouched next to him to check his pulse, my coat might have touched the blood pool or the body."

"Your fingerprints were all over the house, not only on the front door, as you just described your entry. There were prints on the desk, on the drawers, everywhere. Can you explain that?"

"Yes, I was looking for a telephone directory to call the police. In the U.S. I dial nine one one, but here I don't know the number of your emergency services."

The interrogation went on and on for two hours with no end in sight, but without violence.

"I'm telling you I was wrongly accused. I had nothing to do with his murder. Why don't you check who called the police in the first place. It seems like the caller wanted the police to come when he or she saw me inside the house."

"The call came from one of the neighbors, who heard yelling and shouting from the house. Mr. Badescu lived alone, and a neighbor became suspicious when he heard loud noises."

I didn't buy that, but showed no expression of disbelief.

"What was the purpose of your meeting with Badescu?"

"Comisar Paunescu, I repeat my answer to the questions asked many times already—it won't change. I work for a research institute in Washington, DC. It is a not-for-profit organization, a think tank is what we call it. We're researching the political views of people, trying to understand their motivations and how they can be modified. Our reports are then offered to the general public to foster better understanding of political conflicts. Mr. Badescu was recommended to us as an expert on changing public opinions, and we were going to retain him as a consultant. That's the whole story."

"Nice story, Mr. Wooten," he said. "Bravo, bravo." His face became menacing. "Do you think I'm an idiot?" He raised his voice, his face becoming red. "Bullshit. Tell me the truth!" Now he was yelling.

I didn't answer, primarily because I wanted him to vent his rage first, but also because I had no better answer.

There was a knock on the door. A man walked in and whispered into the comisar's ear.

"The American consul is here," the comisar said. He opened the door, and a man in his midforties dressed in a blue suit and a yellow tie walked in.

"Hello, I'm Andrew Watson, deputy consul general." He gave me his card, with the embossed golden eagle. The police officers left the room.

"I'm Peter Wooten. Thanks for coming."

"Are they treating you well here? Do you have any complaints?" He didn't even ask me about my U.S. citizenship. He took it for granted.

"Just get me out of here," I said.

"Sorry, no can do. We have no jurisdiction here."

"Please tell me the things you can do for me, not what you can't." I was angry.

"I can communicate with the Romanian authorities to protect your legitimate interests and ensure you're not discriminated against. I can visit you and contact your family and friends in the U.S. The consulate can also transfer money, food, and clothing to the prison authorities from your family or friends. If you're treated inhumanely or under unhealthy conditions, we can intervene. That's about it."

"In both countries, there are protections for wrongly accused individuals. I expect the embassy to be on my side here," I said.

"You're in the hands of the Romanian law-enforcement and justice system. I must tell you that while in a foreign country a U.S. citizen is subject to that country's laws and regulations, which differ significantly from those in the United States. Forget about the protections available under U.S. law."

"Are you telling me I have no rights?" I knew the answer of course, but I had to sound like an ordinary American caught in a foreign web.

The consul ducked my comment. "I understand you're a murder suspect. Do you have an attorney? He could raise these issues with the courts here. If you're not represented yet, I can provide you with a list of local attorneys that registered with the consulate, though obviously we can't recommend any particular one."

"I don't have an attorney, and I don't think I need one. This whole thing is a huge mistake."

He smiled knowingly. "I understand."

"Anyway, I heard that the consulate told the police that my passport was stolen."

He nodded. "That's the report we received from the State Department. We have no further details."

I was speechless while trying to figure out what had happened. All I could say was that it must be a blunder, and that the passport was mine, valid and authentic.

"I'll forward Washington your response. If you have no complaints and they are treating you well, call me if you change your mind regarding an attorney. As I said earlier, we can notify any family member in the United States about your arrest. Would you like us to do that?"

I almost fell for it and asked him to contact my dear cousin Eric Henderson. On a quick second thought, I remembered the warning we'd received during Mossad training:

> *Never, and I mean never ever, when using an alias, under any circumstances admit or give away your identity to anyone, even if that person tells you he is your direct supervisor, because he is not expected to ask you that question, as he should already know. You should keep your mouth shut if you're arrested. Even if they bring in a person who says he is the ambassador, the consul, or any other person you think is on your side, keep your mouth shut. We have seen more than one case where they brought in someone pretending to be the ambassador or consul, and our poor schmuck gave out his name and assignment.*

If I gave this guy Eric's number and he was not a consul but an impersonator the police had brought in, then I'd be fucked, because Eric's name and number could be registered in some database as a CIA senior officer. That would raise unnecessary questions. I looked at Andrew Watson. He seemed legit, but I just couldn't risk it. Obviously, I couldn't give him my children's numbers. What would he say to the Gordon children? "Your father, Mr. Peter Wooten, was arrested in Romania"?

"Maybe I'll call you later, thanks," I said. He shook my hand and left. The entire visit lasted less than ten minutes.

"Your consul can't do much for you, huh?" said the comisar in contempt as he reentered the room. He was right, of course, but I wasn't going to concede defeat. My backup team knew I was arrested before they took off. Maybe a copy of the consul's report would end up on Eric's or Bob's desk telling them exactly where I was, and they would figure out a way to extricate me from this shit hole.

After one more day of futile efforts to get my confession for a murder I didn't commit, I was brought before a judge. A stern-looking woman in her late fifties dressed in a black robe, she didn't even let me talk. I had no interpreter. She appointed me a lawyer and adjourned the hearing for two hours to let me confer with him. I waited for an hour until he came to my holding cell carrying a file.

"The evidence against you is strong," said Ionel Illescu, the local lawyer the court appointed to represent me, as he flipped through the file. He was a slim man in his late fifties dressed in an outdated black suit.

"Under Article 178 of the Criminal Code, homicide of a person is punished by severe detention from fifteen to twenty-five years and the prohibition of certain rights."

"Shit," I said, reflecting what I felt like.

"Maybe I can strike a deal with the Parchetul—the Prosecutor General's Office. If you agree to admit your guilt, maybe they'll agree to reduce the charges to manslaughter, and you'll be out in ten years . . . maybe less, if we can show you have a good character."

As every criminal lawyer knows, when your case is bad and your arguments weak, you point to your client's good character. This wasn't the case here, and I needed to tell him that.

"I am not going to confess to anything I didn't do. Tell me what they've got."

"There's evidence that you met with the victim approximately one week before the murder. Then you were caught next to the body immediately after the murder. The victim's blood stained your coat. Your fingerprints were all over the house. The American Consulate says your passport was reported stolen. The prosecution believes you're a professional assassin hired to kill Badescu. They're trying through Interpol to find out your identity."

"All that is bullshit," I said dismissively.

"Maybe, but the court may not think as you do, and convict you of murder."

"My passport is authentic, and I told that to the consul as well. I have no idea why the U.S. government is claiming otherwise."

After a few more attempts to convince me to enter into a plea-bargain agreement with the prosecution, the slob left. I saw him again in the courtroom talking briefly to the judge. When I wanted to say something, she hushed me. She asked me in poor English if I'd killed Badescu, and after she heard me deny the charge, she cut me off and ordered me held without bail, pending trial. Andrew Watson, the consul, sat at the back taking notes, but said nothing. I was transferred to Bucharest-Jilava Prison, a maximum-security prison dedicated exclusively to pretrial prisoners.

"There are fourteen hundred prisoners here," said the assistant warden as I was processed, "and each and every one of them claims to be innocent and plans to escape. However, they are all still here. If you escape, we'll give you, once captured, a preview of what to expect later on in hell. We're overcrowded, and half the prisoners share beds." He looked at me as if expecting a reaction.

"I don't think you can give me half a bed. I spoke with the U.S. consul, and I know my rights." Being firm in these circumstances is the best way to avoid being stepped on.

"I'll see what I can do," he said. "As all other prisoners who enter this prison, you'll go through a twenty-one-day quarantined admission process during which you'll be interviewed and evaluated by our treatment staff. Once assigned to a cell, normal procedures will apply. All prisoners are able to take a shower at least once a week. You'll also receive a change of underwear once a week."

That explained the stench here, I thought.

"As a pretrial detainee you'll be given the opportunity of wearing your own clothes, if they're clean and suitable. You're allowed to be visited once a month. There is no restriction on the number of letters that you may send and receive. We don't open and read prisoners' letters. You're allowed one hour a day of walking in the yard. You're also allowed to speak with family and friends by telephone, with the approval of the prosecutor or a judge." An hour later, I was sent to the quarantine and was put in an eight-by-twelve cell with a bunk bed, but I was alone.

In the morning, I woke up from the cold. I had only one rough wool blanket, and it was snowing outside. The blanket smelled of urine and other human fluids, none of which was pleasant. Although my training and military service had prepared me for such a contingency, I wasn't patient. Why wasn't the Agency making contact? Did they expect me to dial 1-800-Send Help?

They should know where I am. I'm still wearing the shoes with the built-in GPS. Although it doesn't work while I'm indoors, I was also outdoors before I was locked here, so where are they? What are the plans to extricate me?

* * *

Three days passed. I was still alone in my cell, and even the screening process had not started yet. However, on that afternoon I was led into an office where a woman in her midthirties was sitting next to a metal desk. She was working on an obsolete-looking desktop computer. The office walls were covered with landscape photos cut from magazines, and framed professional diplomas were displayed on a shelf.

"Sit down," she said pointing at the chair and told the guard to wait outside.

"Hello, my name is Mikaela Grosaru, and I'm the prison's psychologist. I'll evaluate you for prison processing purposes."

I nodded. She went on to ask me bio questions, which I answered, being careful not to mix Dan Gordon's and Peter Wooten's résumés. Then she paused the routine questioning, raised her head, and looked at me with her deep and big blue eyes. She was slightly overweight, but the feminine outlines of a body were visible through the polka-dot dress she was wearing with a light blue wool sweater on top. She had short blonde hair and wore very little makeup. She surprised me when she began a friendly conversation. Was it because she sensed I wasn't another sample of her routine prison clientele, or a tactic to get me to talk freely? An hour later, she sent me back to my cell. I was no longer alone. There was another prisoner in my cell.

"Hello," he said.

"Hi," I answered.

"You American?"

"Yes," I said. "And who are you?"

"My name is Adrian Balan," he said slowly. He was chubby, in his midsixties, bald with ash black eyebrows and sunken cheeks. He smiled to expose just a few teeth, all crooked and stained.

"Hi, Adrian. I'm Peter Wooten."

"American?" he asked again with a spark in his otherwise bland eyes.

I nodded. "Are you Romanian?" I asked, hearing his accent.

"Half-Romanian, half-Hungarian." He chuckled for no apparent reason. "Why are you here?" he asked.

"Murder."

He recoiled for a second.

"And you?"

"Rape. But I didn't do it. She put a spell on me." He chuckled again, making me suspect he was deranged.

"Who put a spell on you?" I asked, trying to figure out what he meant.

"The girl. She has these black-magical powers; it wasn't my fault. She made me do it."

"How old was she?"

"Nine or ten. A Gypsy girl, the whore," he said in a mix of hatred and rage.

If this person were any more stupid, he'd have to be watered twice a week, I thought. I felt disgusted just to look at him, this pathetic creature, now my cell mate for who knew how long. Adrian tried to develop more conversation, but I had no patience or will to talk, definitely not with him. I was preoccupied with a plan that was starting to germinate in my mind.

On the following day, I was brought to Mikaela the prison psychologist's office again. She started from where we had ended the formal interview. She asked me about my childhood, marriage, and children. "I'm divorced now," I said when she kept asking about my wife. I had not seen Dahlia in several years.

"Why did you divorce her?"

"Perfectly matching pairs can be found only in shoe stores."

Mikaela grinned.

"Seriously, we had communication problems. The only

time my wife listened to me was when I talked in my sleep."

"Maybe she was hoping to hear things you wouldn't say otherwise," Mikaela chuckled. She shifted her questions to my dating other women, and I had a creeping suspicion that her interest went beyond the professional.

"Tell me about America," she asked, all of a sudden sounding like a little girl. I told her about New York and Washington, DC, cities I know well, and about New England, a region I like.

"Have you ever been to America?" I ventured.

"No, but I would love to one day." I knew that her dream was unlikely to become reality. The average monthly salary of a state employee in Romania is two hundred dollars.

"Once the misunderstanding concerning my arrest is cleared and I'm out of here, perhaps one day I could show you my beautiful country." A little kiss-up couldn't hurt here.

She sighed. "It's only a dream. I know I can't afford it, and I'm still supporting my ten-year-old son." She pointed at a framed photo on her desk of a blond boy on a bike.

"Where is his father?"

"Died in a mining accident soon after our son was born," she said. "But why are we talking about me, when I'm expected to do my job?" Her face turned serious again. She asked me questions about the murder, under the clear assumption that I'd done it. When I balked she said, "If you intend to negotiate any deal with the prosecution, you must show contrition."

"There will be no deal. I'm telling you I didn't do it. Under the best scenario, I was at the house at the wrong time, just after Badescu was murdered. And under a less-favorable scenario, someone who wanted both me and Badescu out of the way killed him and framed me."

"Why would anyone do that, frame you?" She looked at her notes. "You're a researcher in a think tank. Why would anyone want to harm you?" Was there a softness to her tone, or was I imagining things?

Remembering my Mossad training prior to an operation in Eastern Europe during the Soviet era—"Eastern European women enjoy an intelligent conversation with a man; they find an interesting man sexy, leading them to trust you"—I tried to steer the conversation to areas I thought would create an intellectual challenge for Mikaela. I looked at her bookshelves, spotting two psychology books and several criminology textbooks. On the corner shelf was a framed diploma issued by the University of Bucharest, conferring the degree of Bachelor of Arts in psychology to Mikaela Grosaru. Next to it, another diploma showed she had received a master's degree and a certificate of excellence from the Romanian National Institute of Criminology. I registered it in my mind. Later on in the afternoon, I asked to go to the prison's library. Just eight or ten men were sitting next to long tables, reading books in the big semidark hall. I searched information about the University of Bucharest Department of Psychology and jotted down its telephone number. On the next day, I took money from my deposit with the prison and "allowed" the guard to convert one hundred dollars to Romanian lei at double the official exchange rate. He was very pleased, and so was I.

"We can do it again," I suggested. "All I have is American dollars, and I'm so grateful that you agreed to help me change it."

The fifty-dollar-or-so profit he made from screwing me on the exchange rate—with my heartfelt blessing—turned him into my fan. It was probably more than his weekly wages.

"I could use a favor," I said. "There's this woman at the University of Bucharest, whom I promised to call. Can you help me?"

I knew he needed an approval of a prosecutor or a judge to allow me to use the phone. Nevertheless, little wonder what fifty dollars could do to cloud the guard's judgment. He took me to a pay phone in the hallway and walked back to his office.

Mossad training taught us how to use the five-step process to elicit information under a pretext: "First, identify the information you want to get. Identify who holds that information. Discover to whom the custodian of the information would release it, and under what circumstances. Impersonate that person."

I called the Department of Psychology at the University of Bucharest.

"This is Dr. Mansfield from the Psychology and Criminology Research Support Fund of the University of California. We received a grant application for research from"—I paused, rustling my notes—"yes, Ms. Grosaru. She listed your institution as her alma mater. Can I speak with the dean concerning the academic qualifications of Ms. Grosaru?"

Within ten seconds, I was talking with the assistant dean, who apologized that the dean was out of town, but promised to help me as best he could. When I hung up the phone, I had the story of Mikaela's academic life, her interests, her areas of expertise, and every detail contained in her university file. I returned to the library and spent the next two days reading anything I could find about Mikaela's areas of interests in psychology and criminology.

Two more days passed, and I found myself wondering why she'd stopped bringing me to her office. Had I been hallucinating when I'd thought I detected a personal interest? At night I couldn't sleep, because my cell mate Adrian, the child rapist, was snoring like a warthog with partially obstructed airways. To make things worse, he also smelled like one.

On a cloudy morning, when snow was falling, a warden came over to my cell.

"You have a visitor," he notified me. I was taken to the

visitors' area, where a well-dressed elderly man, probably in his seventies, was smiling at me.

"Hello, Peter," he said and hugged me. I had no idea who this person was until he whispered in my ear. "Show how happy you are to see me. Eric sent me. I'm your Uncle Joe." He then added the code word set for emergency communication: "Tempest." I confirmed with the matching code. He smiled.

At last.

CHAPTER ELEVEN

"Hi, Uncle Joe. Thank God you're here. I'm so happy to see a familiar face. How is everyone?" He had sharp blue eyes, and his hair was full and gray, giving him an appearance of a respectable doctor or a banker. He smelled of good aftershave, a nice change from the prison's stench.

There were ten other groups of prisoners visited by family members. Only two guards stood at the corners of the room. I felt it was reasonably safe to talk to Joe.

"When did you arrive?" I asked when I thought for a moment that a guard was listening in. He wasn't.

"Two days ago," he said with a smirk. "Sorry I didn't come yesterday—I had some action last night," he said with a broad smile, making me wonder if he meant that the prune juice he'd be gulping had finally started working.

Joe saw my expression and said quietly, "Peter, men my age never pass on a bathroom or an erection!"

"I'm glad to hear it," I said, trying to think of the last time I'd had the kind of action Joe probably meant.

"Well, I've retired from the Agency, you know. Everyone's booking their vacations on this Internet, so who needs a travel agent? I'm enjoying life, reading, fishing, and visiting my grandchildren. Are you OK?"

"I'm fine—physically, I mean. I've been here for almost two weeks, and your visit is my first family visit. Why am I still here?"

"Be patient. I know other family members are working on it. Keep low."

"For how long?"

"As long as it takes. You know the routine."

"What's this bullshit about my stolen passport?" Mark Twain once said that under certain circumstances, profanity provides a relief denied even to prayer. I hoped I'd find some relief here.

"I have no idea what you're talking about."

"The police told me that the consulate notified them that my passport was reported stolen and that they were inquiring with Interpol to discover my identity, suspecting I was a professional assassin. The consul who visited me confirmed that the State Department told him it was stolen."

"That's the first time I've heard about it. I'll check at home."

"So that there will be no doubt, tell my family that I arrived at the scene *after* the murder. Somebody very conveniently waited for my arrival, killed Badescu, and called the police."

"I'll convey the message. Do you need anything?"

"A one-way airline ticket."

Joe smiled. "Be well, keep low, and I'll keep in touch." He gave me another bear hug and left.

The visit was encouraging, but I was also unsettled by it. It was good to realize that I wasn't forgotten or lost in the bureaucratic maze. But why didn't Joe tell me about efforts to release me, and on the top of everything else, why did he tell me to lay low? In plain language it means "Keep your mouth shut, and don't say, 'Hey, I'm a CIA operative; I had nothing to do with the murder. Get me the hell out of here.'" True, even CIA operatives committing crimes overseas stand trial, but their affiliation attracts attention and expedites things. The U.S. government had to move faster. I was going to follow orders and not speak up, but I had a nagging feeling, because the little devil in me was saying something I refused to listen to: *You may have been designated as a sacrificial lamb—a pawn in a bigger game, who can be sacrificed to achieve a goal much more important than one operative's freedom.*

I braced myself for a long, cold, and lonely winter and perhaps additional seasons with my smelly cell mate. As the saying goes, he was sane approximately twice a week, but I could never tell which days those were.

Mikaela sent for me. She went through the routines, asked questions I'd already answered, and again I sensed there was more to it. Was it because I was an American from a world she had seen only on TV and in the movies? There was no doubt she was curious. I decided to test the reach of that curiosity. I steered our conversation to areas of her expertise. It was my turn to ask questions about the topics of her interest in psychology and criminology, nothing personal. I carefully, but not showily, let slide some of the terms and concepts I'd picked up at the prison's library.

It was clear she enjoyed carrying on an intelligent conversation. I was mostly listening. I asked a question or two about her interests and hobbies. I paid attention to the details to make a good conversation. Mikaela was very bright and open-minded, but with a limited knowledge of the world "out there." I sensed she was lonely, busy with her work and attending to the needs of her son. I didn't ask and she never said, but I felt that there was nothing much going on for her, socially or academically. I steered the conversation toward academia in the U.S., the existence of postgraduate degrees and research opportunities, without making any specific suggestions. At this early stage in our developing trust relationship, it would have been a bad move to insinuate that I could help her in the U.S. in return for small favors to ease my stay at the prison.

That was, of course, the goal, or one of them. Obviously, it was my ultimate intent—beyond just spending time in her company, as opposed to returning faster to my cell with Adrian—but it was way too early. Besides, I didn't know what Mikaela could do for me. She wasn't holding the key to my cell, and had no power to release me. I needed to discover first what she *could* do for me, without asking her.

One answer to that question came faster than I'd anticipated. In the morning, I was told to collect my things. "We're moving you to a different cell," said the guard. He took me to a bigger cell, also with a bunk bed. This time my cell mate was a younger man, maybe forty, accused of vandalizing his ex-wife's apartment. He told me he was a schoolteacher in a custody battle over their young children. "I did it," he confirmed. "I suffered throughout the marriage from that bitch, and finally, when she refused to let me visit my children, I broke a few things in her apartment."

"Why are you here?" I asked. "This is a maximum-security prison."

"Her uncle is a police comisar. He managed to put me here pending my trial." Rotten luck.

In the afternoon, when my session with Mikaela resumed, she asked whether I liked the new cell.

"Yes, it's much better."

"I instructed the warden to move you. I didn't think sharing a cell with a psychopath was the right thing." She smiled at me. I thanked her. She asked a few more questions about my failed marriage and whether I had ever been violent toward my ex. I hadn't been, although the thought had crossed my mind when things got really bad. I kept that to myself. I had to be evaluated as a docile poodle, not as a raging bear. Mikaela then asked politely if I could answer additional questions about obtaining a scholarship from American universities. Of course I could, and I did. I told her a few jokes when the atmosphere was shifting from professional to personal. She laughed a lot. It was Alex's advice when we learned how to recruit female assets: "Adding humor into a conversation can spice things up. Women prefer men who make them laugh, since laughter is the shortest distance between two people."

Two hours later, I was back in my cell. My new cell mate, Aurel, was very inquisitive. He wanted to know everything about American food, lifestyle, music, and women. We held an innocuous conversation, and I answered his questions. Then he asked me about the night at Badescu's house. When did I come there and why? What had I done there? That little suspicious devil in me opened up one eye. Did he have a reason for asking such pointed questions, other than curiosity? I had one version of the events that night, the one I'd given the police, and briefly offered it to Aurel. Obviously, I could duck his questions or simply tell him to go to hell. But I was immediately on guard. Aurel shifted the conversation to his case. He was looking for *my* advice on how to lie to the police and how to fabricate evidence for his benefit.

Something was definitely up. I shrugged. "How would I know? Ask a lawyer." I couldn't say anything that could be even remotely interpreted as aiding him or suggesting perjury or obstruction of justice. Although I was completely ignorant of Romanian law and couldn't help him even if I'd wanted to, the best policy was to say as little as possible. Aurel kept on hammering me in an attempt to get me to say something I hadn't told the police.

"I have friends outside," he said in a low secretive voice. "If you want, I can send them over to Badescu's house and remove any incriminating evidence you forgot to destroy, if the police haven't found it yet. But you haven't got much time."

Most law-enforcement agencies use snitches as an investigative tool. In the United States, incriminating statements made in a jail cell to a snitch who turns out to be a jailhouse informant can under certain terms be excluded as being obtained in violation of the prisoner's right to counsel, Miranda rights, and due process. I was doubtful whether the Romanian law afforded the same protections.

I remembered how once in the Mossad we were asked to help in the investigation of a suspect in Southeast Asia who'd shot several rounds at the Israeli Embassy. We had intel about his involvement, but no proof, and he claimed innocence. At our suggestion, the local police installed a snitch in his cell, who convinced the suspect that gunpowder residue on his hands could be removed if he wiped them with black coffee. The snitch was transferred from the cell, and the suspect was videotaped desperately trying to clean his hands with coffee. He later admitted his guilt.

If I needed any additional proof to my earlier suspicion that Aurel was a snitch, I needed to look no further. Why? Because I'd never told him that the victim's name was Badescu.

"Aurel, please listen to me. I have nothing to hide . . . there is nothing. I didn't kill Badescu, and I have no idea who did. You mustn't do anything for me in this matter—definitely not obstruct justice by hiding or destroying any evidence. On the contrary, I *want* the police to search the house and develop any evidence they can find. It will only help exonerate me."

Aurel was relentless. "I know that lawyer. He is very good, but he doesn't speak English. If you tell me how you did it, I'll ask him how you can craft your answers to the police. Just tell me. I won't tell anyone but him, I promise. I want to help you."

It was getting pathetic. I could have punched Aurel then and there, or yelled at him to shut the fuck up. I held myself not to ruin the charade. It was the only entertainment I had, and I didn't want to expose the fact that I was a trained intelligence officer and ate snitches like Aurel for breakfast. The only question remaining was whether Mikaela had been a part of the ploy when she moved me here. If she was, then I had misjudged her.

"Look," I finally said when it was clear Aurel wasn't letting up. "I'm tired, I'm going to sleep, and I don't want to talk about this anymore." I got into my bed and turned my head to the wall, although I'd just discovered that turning my back to him wasn't advisable.

A day later, I asked to see Mikaela. "Thanks for keeping me safe from Adrian. But I'm sure you know that Aurel also needs help."

"What seems to be the problem?" she asked.

"Well, I'm embarrassed to say."

"Go ahead. We're adults. Believe me, I've heard and seen it all."

"OK," I relented. "Aurel masturbates twice a night."

"That's not unusual," she said matter-of-factly. "Men, particularly while in prison, do that."

"And talk about the horrible things they want to do to sexy Mikaela the bitch, while they are at it? He is a sex maniac of the worst kind. I pretended to be asleep, but I heard him well. I don't think you want to be alone in a room with him. The things he said he wanted to do to you are sick, just sick and dangerous," I said in disgust. "The little I understand of Romanian was enough. In the morning, I talked to him about it, but he denied ever saying anything about you. He is in complete denial."

Mikaela frowned and wrote a note on a pad. "Thanks for telling me. I think he'll have to be moved to a different ward."

"You're so nice to me, I don't want anything bad happening to you." I was trying to kiss up again. Desperate times call for desperate measures.

"I'll be all right," she said.

When I got up to leave, she asked, "Is there anything I can do for you?"

"I'm fine, thank you," I said. "You've already done a lot. I enjoy our conversations. Can we continue with them, even after you're done with my evaluation?"

"Maybe," she said blushing. I left her office.

The next morning I went to her office again. I closed the door behind me, and she didn't protest. She just looked at me, waiting for me to say something.

I was hesitating. "You asked me if there was anything you could do for me. Well, there is something. I'm a stranger in Romania with no friends or family. The lawyer that the court appointed for me is no good."

She signaled for me to go on.

"I know everyone tells you they are innocent. I don't expect you to believe me when I say so, although I'd be happy if you did. Since I have nothing to hide, I want to help the police catch the person responsible for the Badescu's death; that will clear me. However, being locked up here prevents me from doing anything."

"What can I do?" she asked. "I can't release you. It's the decision of the prosecutor and the court."

"I'm not asking you to release me or help me escape, nothing of the sort. I could use different help though."

She seemed relieved to hear I wasn't trying to get escape help. "What do you need?"

I told her about the strange coincidence that the police arrived at the scene a few short minutes after I came into Badescu's house. It was too coincidentally perfect and convenient to be a coincidence. It was planned by someone, and that someone could be the killer or lead me to him.

She nodded, saying nothing.

"If you have access to the police file or to the arrest file, you could see who called the police. That could be a good start."

She finally spoke. "I'll see what I can do," she said. That was good enough for me. I'd managed to move her to make one step in my direction. She seemed deep in thought. I went even further. "The arrest file should be here, in central registration or whatever name you call it. Why don't you start from there?"

She shook her head. "There'll be nothing there that's of interest to you. Just the booking information, date, place, charges, and your personal details. The file will also contain the police warrant for your arrest and the court's decision to keep you here. That's all."

"Can you get the information from the police?"

"I'll see you tomorrow," she said cryptically. I hoped I'd done the right thing.

When I returned to my cell Aurel's stuff was gone. I was alone in the cell. I couldn't sleep all night contemplating my next move. Right after breakfast, I asked to see Mikaela.

"Nothing yet," she said as soon as she saw me. Was I that transparent? Had I sent the message that I was just using her? "Oh, I know it takes time," I said, trying to diffuse that impression. "I just came by to say hi, and to thank you for removing Aurel from my cell."

"It wasn't me at all. When I called the warden to instruct his transfer, I was informed he'd made bail and had been released."

First maximum-security prison, then out in the street in no time? No question he was a snitch, even if he wasn't any good at it.

Two days later, when I was about to give up on getting any help from Mikaela, I was called to her office. She closed the door, sat down, and said, "I finally got through to the police. Your file was transferred to the Romanian Intelligence Service."

"What the hell?" I said. "Do you have any idea why?"

"All I know is that the file was requested by the intelligence service. My contact had no further information. He seemed to be surprised too."

I didn't know what importance or relevance to attribute to the news. Did that mean they had uncovered me? Did that mean the Agency had made contact with them, identifying me as an operative? Did that mean that they'd discovered Badescu's connection to Hezbollah, and maybe even to the Mossad? Did it mean anything else I couldn't think of right now? All I had were questions but no answers, as well as new worries.

"One last question," I said when I pulled myself back to Mikaela. "Did your police contact tell you *when* my file was transferred?"

"Yes, four or five days ago."

"Thanks!" I returned to my cell still preoccupied with the news. Later on at night, just an hour before the lights usually went off, I was told I had visitors. This was unusual at this time of day. When I entered the visitors' hall, I saw three plainclothes men waiting for me.

"Peter Wooten?" asked a tall and freckled man wearing eyeglasses and a hat.

"Yes."

"I'm Neculae Fulda of SRI, Romanian Intelligence Service."

"Yes?" I said, hoping they wouldn't notice the light tremble in my voice.

"Go to your cell and pack your things. You're coming with us."

When I hesitated, he yelled, "Now!"

"May I ask why? I hope you came to tell me that I was arrested by mistake and that you're bringing me to the American Embassy."

"Go to your cell and get your things," Fulda barked. He told the guard to escort me.

All I had in my cell was a toothbrush and paste, a comb, and a few little items. Fulda and his men took me to prison central booking and signed me out. There was the plastic bag with the belongings I'd had to surrender when I was admitted. I peeked inside the bag: my money was still there.

Fulda took me, handcuffed, to the backyard, where a black car was idling. It was blistering cold. My coat was taken from me as evidence, and I was exposed to the elements, wearing a light shirt and a prison-supplied sweater. My relief at the car's heater was soon replaced with a deep concern. I looked out the window. It was completely dark, but I could see a foot of snow covering the ground. Visibility was bad because of the blowing snow, and the only light came from our car's headlights and the dim streetlights. I saw no other cars. It was eerie. I felt I was in deep shit, even deeper than the time I was first arrested by the police. Were they taking me to some remote snowy ditch to shoot me in the back of the neck? Horror stories of Communist-era torture and the death of foreign spies at the hands of the secret police came to my mind. How would my children be told? Would they ever find out what had really happened to me?

Ten seconds of self-pity was too much. I braced myself. No one spoke during the half-hour ride. We entered Beldiman Street and parked in a gated lot next to a five-story building guarded by soldiers. Fulda got out of the passenger seat and disappeared into the building. I waited in the car with the two other agents. Three soldiers walked over, talked to the driver, and peeked into the car to take a closer look at me.

Fulda quickly returned. "Get out," he said, while his two agents pushed me out of the car and toward the entrance. We entered a narrow elevator that took us to the third floor. I still hadn't been told anything about what I was doing here or why I'd been pulled out of prison. We entered a big room, empty but for a few chairs and a Formica-covered oblong table.

"Sit!" he ordered me.

There was no doubt they were trying to create an atmosphere of intimidation without actually doing or saying anything. The greatest fear a prisoner has under these circumstances is of the unknown. You don't know what to expect and how bad or painful it will be.

"We know you're an American spy," Fulda said.

I didn't respond.

"I'm talking to you!" he barked.

"I heard you. What do you expect me to say? First I was a murderer, now I'm a spy. I wonder what will come next. A rapist?" I spoke haltingly.

I closed my eyes, expecting him to hit me. But he didn't. He just yelled again, and it was as bad as the yelling spells of my ex-wife.

"We know you came to Romania to spy on us. Tell me exactly what your mission was!"

"I'm not a spy, or a murderer. I came to Romania as a tourist." I told him I worked for a think tank and the purported purpose of my visit—to meet Badescu and retain his professional services aiding our research.

"What is your name?"

"Peter Wooten."

"You're lying!" He yelled so hard that I instinctively recoiled. His bark was worse than his bite.

I didn't answer. There was no point, particularly when he was right.

"In response to our request, Interpol has distributed a Blue Notice to all one hundred eighty-six member countries. Do you know what a Blue Notice is?

"No."

"It's a request to collect additional information about a person's identity or activities in relation to a crime. We've received answers concerning you."

My heart raced, but I kept quiet.

He continued. "Turkey has informed us that a person named Peter Wooten entered Turkey through Istanbul's international airport on January 5, 2007. He later filed a complaint with the Istanbul police that a briefcase was stolen from his hotel room. What were you doing in Istanbul?"

I couldn't deny this. My visit was recent, and hotel staff, as well as the police sergeant who'd taken my complaint, could easily identify me. At the time, my instructions were to report the theft to the police to support the robbery story. The CIA wanted to remove any suspicion that the alleged theft was in fact an attempt to intentionally abandon the documents to obtain an intelligence objective.

"The same thing I intended to do here—meet with professionals about internal policies of Eastern Bloc countries during the 1970s and 1980s to help us with our research. If you go on the Internet, you can find my name on the think tank's Web site as the author or co-author of many research papers."

"You're lying," he yelled. "You told the police that you came to hire Badescu as an expert on changing public opinions."

"I was telling you and the police the truth. Our research is on methods for changing public opinion. Badescu had no current job, and there was nothing he could tell us about present-day Romania, which is anyway outside the scope of our research. But we heard that he was an expert on the subject during the Communist era, and we wanted to gain from his experience." I wanted to say that spies are not interested in historical events, which were the only matters Badescu could ostensibly have told me, but I discarded the idea. I didn't want to look too well versed in the subject.

He didn't seem to be impressed. "We have an additional report from the German police that a few years ago you were a suspect in a break-in into a German bank where Iranian financial documents were stolen. We believe it was a CIA operation. Are you working for the CIA?"

"I have no idea what you're talking about. I never broke into a bank, and I have no connection to the CIA. Listen, I'm not the only Peter Wooten in the world. There are several other people with that name. There could be a case of mistaken identity here."

"How do you know?"

"Sometimes I get mail or phone calls for other Peter Wootens. Try googling it, see for yourself."

He wasn't deterred. "Interpol's U.S. National Central Bureau says your Peter Wooten passport was reported stolen. We sent them your fingerprints, asking to investigate who you are. We expect their report soon."

What the hell was going on? Should I believe him? Or maybe the left hand of the U.S. didn't know what the right hand was doing? First, I was dispatched by the CIA with a supplied passport, and now the Justice Department liaison to Interpol was saying they didn't know who I was, and the State Department was saying that my passport had been reported stolen. Had some bureaucrat gone mad? Or maybe more than just one. Were they trying to bury me in a Romanian prison? Had I become expendable? Were they testing my nerves and endurance? Should I believe Joe's statement that he didn't know anything about a passport reported stolen? Should I believe the deputy consul, who said the State Department had told him the passport was stolen? Was he a genuine American consul?

I realized, and not for the first time, that I was alone in this battle. It was me against them, whoever they were. Just the Romanian police? The assholes that killed Badescu and framed me? Anyone in the U.S. bureaucracy whose toes I'd stepped on? There were so many of them, I didn't even know where to start counting. Even without a declared enemy, I needed to wage my own war the best I could, for whatever the price or consequences. Falling down isn't a failure unless you stay down. Stay put? Keep low? Not yours truly. Somebody out there hadn't read my résumé. I've always been a lone wolf. That's how I got the best sheep in the flock. I obey orders only if they pass my judgment test first. I've always been defiant, subversive, and demonstrated sedition against my teachers' attempts to rein me in.

I'm still surprised how I managed to stay out of Israeli military prison for disobedience or avoided being kicked out of the Mossad for being too independent. For a moment, I thought about how in 1972 the Soviets sacrificed one of their KGB officers in Egypt, to make their "active measures" operations appear credible. First, they had one of their operatives sell forged Egyptian documents to a CIA operative. Then they told President Sadat that a CIA operative bought top-secret Egyptian documents from a rogue KGB case officer working undercover in Egypt, and that the CIA gave them to Israel. The Egyptian police treated the CIA operative harshly and expelled him. The KGB officer was arrested and imprisoned. The maneuver worked. The Soviets got rid of an American operative who was probing their activities in Egypt, and at the same time smeared the United States' activities in Egypt. And their KGB operative who was never rogue? They couldn't have cared less. Was I being similarly sacrificed by the CIA?

I could almost hear a bureaucrat sitting in a government building in Washington, DC, reading a report about my arrest and thinking, *Is Dan Gordon still in a Romanian prison? I thought he was out already. Yeah, we should do something about it.* He would then turn the page of the report and move on to the next report, answer a phone call from his wife—"Yes, dear, I'll be home for dinner"—read the mail, and quickly go over two other reports nobody else had bothered to read, so he could generate a third report with a similar fate to glorify a minute thing he did, and remove a piece of food stuck between his teeth with a toothpick. Then he'd go home. *The Dan Gordon case can wait for another day. In fact, I never liked the guy.*

"You could make it easier for you and for us," Fulda said. Was there a subtle message?

"How?"

"We heard that the American government is after you. We heard rumors that you're a rogue agent who attempted to sell secret documents to Hezbollah."

I lowered my head. Let him think I was conceding. I needed to hear more before I'd concede to anything that could let me walk with impunity.

"Let's say we can help you," he said. "Let's say I could get you out of prison."

"Great. I'm happy that you've finally realized I had nothing to do with the murder."

"I didn't say that," he said immediately. "The prosecutor—*procurorul*—tells us he has enough evidence to convict you."

"So how can you release me?"

"Let us say just for the moment that I could persuade him to charge you for a lesser crime."

"I've already told anyone who cared to listen that I had nothing to do with the death of Badescu, and I'm not changing my mind now."

"Who said admit to murder? Let's say that the prosecutor will tell the court that he has insufficient evidence to convict you for homicide. However, you entered Badescu's house without permission."

"I'm listening."

"Let's say for a moment that you'll admit to a charge of criminal trespassing and be sentenced to time served. You'll be out in the street on the same day." I knew that under most countries' law I wasn't a trespasser but an invitee, but it wasn't the time to hold a learned legal debate.

"And you're offering it to me just because I'm a nice guy

and you like me?" I said hoping he wouldn't again say "Let's say for the moment," or I'd scream.

He didn't even smile. "Of course not, particularly when I *don't* think you're a nice guy and I *don't* like you. I'm offering you a business deal."

"What's the deal?"

"You work for me."

"Doing what?" I was cool as a cucumber.

"Anything I tell you."

"I need to know exactly. I can't type, for one thing, or make coffee, or file."

Getting your interrogator off balance is a known tactic to send the message that you're not a lapdog yet, but it can be dangerous if it backfires. Fulda was holding the key and could use the whip. But I couldn't resist the temptation of annoying my interrogator at the same time he was offering me a way out. I thought of a story I'd read about Niccolò Machiavelli when he was on his deathbed and had asked to see a priest to confess. "My son, are you willing to accept the Lord and renounce Satan?" asked the priest. Machiavelli didn't answer. The priest asked again and again, but no answer came, until Machiavelli finally answered, "I heard you, Padre. I'm considering whether it is the proper time to make new enemies." I knew some people attributed the story to Voltaire, but I found Machiavelli more fitting.

"Don't get smart with me. I'm offering you a deal that will save your unholy ass."

"You still haven't told me what I need to do." Of course, I was going to take the deal, but I had to stall and play hard to get a bit. I couldn't appear too eager. But boy, was I eager.

"The U.S. government is looking for you. You can't return to the U.S. unless you want to be arrested." I doubted whether he believed it.

"Based on what you're telling me, I'll be arrested anywhere I go, because if the U.S. reported my passport stolen,

I'll be stopped in all airports and most likely be extradited to the U.S."

"Exactly," he said. "Therefore, we'll get you a shiny and authentic passport with your photo and a new name."

"Won't I need a visa to go to the U.S.?" I was betraying too much knowledge. Romanian citizens, although coming from an EU member country, are not included in the U.S. visa-waiver program that allows tourists from some countries to enter the U.S. for ninety days without a visa.

"You seem to be knowledgeable," he said. "There are other EU countries that participate in the visa-waiver program that will agree to our friendly request to issue you their passport."

"OK, then I could travel to the U.S. and stay for three months. What do you expect me to do then?"

"A lot of things. We need a local representative who can assist our interests and inform us about developments in science and technology for civilian purposes."

Nothing had changed, I thought. Eastern Bloc countries during the Communist era had excelled in stealing Western companies' technology for use by their industries, royalty free. From a national-security point of view, theft of military-oriented technology was obviously the riskiest. However, who was to judge what is intended for military use? Some technology can be used for civil as well as for military purposes. High-technology American computers and programs can be used in research on ballistic missiles and in the operation of nuclear plants, but they can also be helpful in scientific research, weather forecasting, or astronomical research. The damage from the thefts can be in the billions, in addition to the national security risks. Many of the resources American science-based industries allocate to research and development will go down the drain if they fail to protect their technologies from theft by foreign competitors.

He read my facial expression. "Everybody is doing it—even your great America. Why do you think they invite foreign scientists to 'cooperate' with the U.S. in American research institutions? Don't play naive, because I know you're not."

"I think you're wrong here. It's the foreign countries who are sending their students and scientists to the U.S. to *steal* proprietary information, not to *offer* or *share* theirs."

"Whatever," he said, thereby confirming my earlier estimates. Industrial espionage was just the beginning. Then, once I was their puppy on a leash, they could tell me to do anything.

"I can tell you right now that I won't engage in theft of military technology. If I'm caught, I'll go to prison for life." I had to sound wary.

"So you're a virgin all of a sudden? Weren't you trying to sell secret documents to Hezbollah?"

I raised my head in defiance. "Never! I told you that these documents were stolen from me."

"And I told you that the word in the street was that you wanted to sell them."

"I can't be responsible for every oops—only one person said—information or rumor." I let out a deep sigh to sound relenting. "OK, the rumor was probably spread to hike the price on my head. I did jump bail and left the United States in violation of a court order. I'd been indicted for losing the files in Istanbul. So maybe that's why they're saying my passport was stolen—that's half the truth. It's my passport, and it was taken from me when I went back to the U.S. after the Istanbul fiasco and I was arrested. Later I was released on bail, and during one of my interrogations, I managed to remove the passport from the assistant U.S. attorney's desk without him noticing. The U.S. was too embarrassed to admit how the passport went missing." I took a deep breath. "Anyway, one way or another I'm wanted in the U.S. on more than just the theft of my own passport or jumping bail."

His eyes widened. That legend, he *did* buy. Of course, I'd made it up.

He took a verbal step back. "I said we're interested in civilian technology only."

Of course, if anyone were to believe him, then I had a bridge in Brooklyn to sell them. My face remained straight when I asked, as if I were yielding to his suggestion, "How can you be sure I won't betray you? Take your offer, get out of prison, disappear somewhere, and forget about you?"

"I am sure you won't do that. You see, the murder investigation will remain open. There's no statute of limitations for a murder charge in Romania. All of a sudden, we could discover new incriminating evidence and ask all Interpol member countries to put your known aliases and picture on the Red Notice list. Do you know what that means?"

I nodded. Red Notices, or international wanted-persons notices, are dispatches of Interpol to its member countries that an arrest warrant was issued by a court. Although there was no such thing as an "international arrest warrant," as the media likes to call it, under certain circumstances it is treated as such. Many member countries regard a Red Notice as a request for a provisional arrest. They usually arrest the suspect if the issuing country and the host country are parties to an extradition treaty. Since a Red Notice is just a notice, not a detailed extradition request, there's no way for the host country to know how strong the case against the wanted person is. I leave it to anyone's imagination what some countries are willing to do to have a person they want, guilty or not, arrested by a foreign country.

"Besides, I don't think we'd need it. We can get to you wherever you are. Remember what happened to Badescu."

So they'd croaked him? I didn't ask, because I knew I wouldn't get a truthful answer from this bully. Nevertheless, the insinuation was clear. The cold reality had finally dawned on me. Badescu's murder and my arrest might have been a clever and sinister scheme of the Romanian internal security service to recruit an American agent and at the same time get rid of Badescu, who'd probably appeared too often on their radar as connected to Hezbollah—a bedfellow nobody wanted in his country. Ceausescu had been very friendly toward Arafat, but the post-Communist Romania, with strong ties to the West, clearly distanced itself from terrorist organizations. They'd learned their lesson: if you lie down with dogs, don't be surprised to wake up with bloodsucking fleas.

"Let me sleep on it," I said. "But I can't get any sleep in prison; it's too noisy and distracting."

"We're putting you in a hotel," Fulda said. Surprise good news. "Your room is already booked." He removed my handcuffs.

I was wondering what additional plans they had in mind to induce me to agree. She'd better be a blonde. They drove me up to the center of town. The car stopped in a parking lot, and I was led into the back entrance of a four- or five-star hotel. We went up to a top floor, and Fulda opened the door of a spacious, clean, and quiet room. I rejoiced in seeing all the material things I'd missed in prison.

"This is a suite; your room's door to the hallway is locked. Don't even try to open it. My men will stay in the adjoining room, and the doors between the rooms will remain open at all times. You can ask my men to order room service. They will pick it up and sign for you. No hotel employee should see you. I'll be back in the morning." He left.

CHAPTER TWELVE

I felt like a kid in a candy store. What would I do first? Order decent food? Take a shower, or maybe a bath? I hoped I wasn't being groomed like a bride before her wedding night. I didn't feel like being screwed, albeit only metaphorically, by the Romanian security service.

In the morning, I ate a hearty Romanian breakfast—*ceai complet*—an omelet, salty cheese, and white tea.

Fulda walked in and went straight to business.

"Have you decided?"

"I need to understand exactly what is it that you want. In principle though, my answer is yes."

"Good," he said in satisfaction. "We'll go over the details with you later. You will have to undergo a few days of instruction before we send you back."

"How do you start the process?" I wanted to get rid of the murder charge and the risk of returning to prison, even for one more day.

"I already spoke with the prosecutor. He thinks he could go ahead with the plea agreement. I'll call him now to schedule a court session. Anyway, it'll be a few days before your new passport comes in."

He went to the night table and called the prosecutor. "He'll call me back," Fulda said as he returned to the corner where I was standing, looking out the window at the city views. Bucharest was covered with snow, giving the old buildings a newly gracious look.

An hour later, the phone rang. Fulda spoke for a few minutes and hung up. "Get ready. The judge can see us now."

We drove to the courthouse situated in the heart of Bucharest's Unirea area. We went straight to the judge's chambers. I had no interpreter and no idea what they were saying, but I wanted to make sure I wasn't admitting to murder, or *omucidere*, but only to trespassing—*trecerea*—and was being sentenced to time served. To my delight, this time the judge, a younger woman, spoke good English and assured me of that. I walked from the courthouse a free man. True, there were some "technicalities" I had to resolve first with the secret service, like releasing me from my sham consent to become their spy. I'd worry how to get rid of that overweight baggage when I got back to the U.S. and had a serious talk with Eric and Benny.

Back in Fulda's car, I was sitting in the backseat without my handcuffs. We were heading to the hotel. "What will you do if the American consul comes to visit me? What will they tell him?"

"Do you want to go back to prison and resolve the problem?" Fulda chuckled.

"No thanks."

"That will not be a problem. The prosecutor will call to inform him about the reduced-charges plea bargain and that you were released."

I was planning my next move. If only I could get to a phone without Fulda or his agents listening in. I wanted to call my children, but I couldn't expose their phone number to Fulda and his men. Besides, it had been less than a month, and they were accustomed to not hearing from me for weeks, knowing the nature of my work.

We returned to my hotel and went in, this time through the front entrance. As we entered my room, Fulda pulled out a two-page document, gave me a pen, and said, "Sign!"

"Can I read it first?" It was the attorney in me asking.

He nodded. It was written in English—poor English. It said that I agreed to work for the Romanian Intelligence Service (SRI) as well as for the Romanian Foreign Intelligence Service (SIE) in "research and fact-finding" outside Romania for a fee to be agreed upon from time to time; that I agreed to take orders from my supervisors and to strictly follow them; that I undertook to maintain strict confidentiality in the performance of my work and in my reporting; that I agreed not to disclose the fact that I was working for the Romanian intelligence agencies; and that if I violated any of the provisions, I would be subject to severe penalties under Romanian criminal and state security laws. The agreement further provided that it couldn't be rescinded except "by mutual consent." And I thought that slavery, peonage, and involuntary servitude were abolished long ago. In the U.S. it happened in 1865, but apparently for recruits caught in the Romanian security services' web, they were still in force.

I signed. "Do I get a copy?" I ventured to ask, although I knew the answer.

"No." He changed the subject brusquely. "We're going to the Beldiman Street facility for training. Get your things; you're checking out." The courtship period had just ended.

When we arrived at the building, I was taken through an underground corridor to an adjacent building used as a dormitory. The smell reminded me of my barrack during basic training in the Israeli army: dirty socks, and blankets that were probably laundered once every few months. An agent showed me to my room. A simple metal-framed bed with a foam mattress, a cotton sheet, and two heavy rough wool blankets. A side door led to a shower and a toilet that had no seat cover or toilet paper. He handed me a small bar of soap and one small towel. "Hot water only one hour in the morning," he said in a heavy accent and closed but did not lock the outside door. I peeked outside. There was no guard near my door.

On the following day, after a military-style breakfast, I was taken to a classroom in the main building. There were a dozen wooden chairs with an extension to rest your arm on and write notes. I found one designed for lefties and sat down. Throughout the day a variety of instructors taught me covert communication methods (they still had a way to go, compared to the CIA), recruiting informers (I learned a few new tricks), and garden-variety intelligence basics. Of course I was an enthusiastic student, asked the expected questions, never showed that I'd been through that kind of training at the Israeli Mossad, and then on several different occasions by the CIA. "One more day," said my instructor at the conclusion of the first day. A day later, which was dedicated to rehearsal, I was done.

Fulda met me at the door when we were finished for the day. He handed me an EU passport issued by . . . well, never mind; I don't want to ruin this country's image as a law-abiding country. And what's more important, it was a member of the exclusive club of countries included in the U.S. visa-waiver program.

"You're leaving tomorrow tonight."

That was bad news, because I still had plans in Bucharest.

"So soon?" I asked in disappointment. "I wanted to have a night out in Bucharest."

"That can be arranged," said Fulda. "My agents will take you out tonight."

I didn't like the idea of being chaperoned, particularly with what I had planned.

"Great, I'll pick up the tab," I said. They already knew I had money, and I wanted to make sure we'd go to a good restaurant.

At seven P.M., two agents drove me to Burebista restaurant, which serves game and meat dishes and is located very close to University Square, opposite the U.S. Embassy. I was amused by the location and wondered what I'd say if I bumped into the American vice consul. Stuffed fowl and animal skins adorned the walls, as well as carved wooden spoons and some masks. A band of musicians wearing traditional costumes was playing. I had the traditional *mititei* (ground meat) and *sarmale* (stuffed cabbage with meat and rice). The food was delicious. I ordered a bottle of Romanian wine and let the agents consume most of it, then ordered two additional bottles. My plan was one bottle, two bottles, three bottles, floor. But they defied my plan and ordered and also drank three beers each, gulping it as if there were no tomorrow. How often could they eat and drink in a fancy place and let someone else foot the bill? That notion probably kept them off the floor.

I tried to steer our conversation to my case, hoping to elicit some information. But their English was limited, and they took a greater interest in the alcohol than in chatting with me. Next, we went to a dark bar nearby, and they had four more beers. At midnight, it was time to go. My idea to let them stay drunk on the floor so that I could proceed with my plan was thwarted. I moved to Plan B and risked my life by agreeing, for lack of a better alternative, to let them drive me back to Beldiman Street SRI facility. The driver was completely drunk and swerved the car, hitting the curb several times. When we arrived, miraculously without incident, they just let me off at the entrance and drove away. That was my chance. Now or never—there was no Plan C.

During my military service, I learned that anyone could be a minesweeper. Once. I knew I was risking everything, particularly my freedom, but I thought I was qualified, and just couldn't resist the urge. I walked leisurely down the road until the soldiers guarding the facility couldn't see me, and hailed a passing cab. I went straight to Badescu's house. What I'd left there was too precious to leave behind. I told

the cabbie to stop a block away and wait. I walked to the
house, which was in complete darkness. A foot of snow was
on the ground. I went to the backyard and found the damn
back door. Where had it been when the police came? I
broke a window using my coat to muffle the sound of the
breaking glass. I hopped inside and went directly to the
study. I moved my foot underneath the credenza, seeking
the envelope of documents I had kicked there when arrested. My leg didn't reach it. I couldn't risk turning on the
light. I kneeled, while praying that the police hadn't
found—and removed—the envelope. I stretched my hand
underneath the credenza through spider webs and pulled
out the envelope. With complete darkness and without a
flashlight, I couldn't continue searching the house for more
treasures. Besides, I was certain that the intelligence services had already taken anything of value to them. I found
the answering machine on the desk, pulled out the microcassette, put it in the envelope, and stashed it under my
shirt on my lower back. I turned some bedroom closets and
drawers upside down as burglars would do. I wiped off the
glass fragments that stuck to my shoes when I'd entered the
house after breaking the window, wiped off my fingerprints
from anything I had touched, and left the house through
the back door. In fifteen minutes, I was back in the cab. I'd
beaten the old military rule: if your move into enemy territory is without incident, then you're probably walking into
a trap.

Sitting in the cab, I couldn't but wonder why the house
hadn't been thoroughly searched. It seemed intact. Why
weren't my shoes and shirt searched at the police station or
in prison? An oversight? Perhaps negligence, or a hidden
agenda I couldn't identify, although I really tried. So choose
one of the above.

I stopped the cab in a side street and walked a block
to the SRI facility. I showed the guards my temporary
ID, which allowed me entry to the ground floor only,

and crossed the semidark underground corridor to my room.

In the afternoon of the next day, an agent drove me to the airport, gave me a one-way ticket to JFK airport, and told me to make contact seven days later by calling the telephone number they'd given me earlier. He left without another word.

I was back in New York, feeling free again. I had an emotional meeting with my children. In family time, a month away is approximately five centuries. Particularly when spent in prison.

The next few days were dedicated to report writing and to debriefing with CIA and FBI agents—giving out the whole story of my "recruitment" and undergoing two polygraph tests. In my reports and debriefing, I detailed the events in Romania, my meeting with Badescu, the entrapment, the arrest, and again, my "recruitment." I attached the documents I'd retrieved from Badescu's house.

Two days later, I attended a quickly scheduled meeting with Bob, Eric, Paul, and Benny. Since I'd returned from Bucharest with a virtual feather in my cap—I was certain that the documents would prove to be a treasure trove—I was waiting for that meeting, as I also had baggage to unload. I had kept it in my stomach for too long. This was my opportunity to level with them. After describing my ordeals in Romania and the intelligence conclusions I'd drawn, I looked at Benny and noticed that he had lost some weight, something I could finally say about myself as well, after my short prison term during which the food was inedible.

After exchanging jokes about my escapades and the fact that I'd returned as a "recruited Romanian spy," I said, "Before we start discussing my report, there's something I must tell you. I'm disappointed that you were not honest with me regarding the true reasons for my mission. You knew the truth, but I was kept in the dark."

"Why does it matter to you?" asked Benny, tacitly confirming my accusation. I was sure he knew why I was upset.

"Because it put me in a greater danger. What the Romanian intelligence service probably knew, you also knew, but I didn't. There was no Mickey Mouse plan to sway Hezbollah from its military orientation to becoming a political party abandoning all acts of violence."

"Did you ever believe that?" Benny was amused.

"No. I knew we had to get the Shammas brothers to believe it. That part of the plan was fine with me. But you kept me in the dark by failing to tell me all the facts and what to expect. Badescu was at odds with the Romanian intelligence service, and his assassination raised the level of his importance, giving the intelligence services a perfect scapegoat, your humble servant. SRI probably found out, maybe even from Badescu, that he wasn't going to be an 'influence agent' advising Hezbollah on black-propaganda matters out of his home in Bucharest. That's bullshit—he was a spy planted in Beirut. Maybe that's the story you sold the Shammas brothers, and they told that to Hezbollah, but his genuine role was plain and simple: 'report anything you hear or see.' He must have attracted the attention of the Romanian security services.

"Consequently, I received no instructions regarding potential conflict with SRI, which was on his tail. When I first met him at the café, I was contaminated as well. The end result was that I was trapped, arrested, and interrogated—and I wasn't prepared for that. There was no legend to use, no contingency plan, no escape routes, nothing. I was led to believe I was going to a meeting with an old man whose career was behind him. Luckily I managed to maneuver myself out by improvising answers to their interrogation."

"Dan," said Bob, "these are exactly the qualifications that made us choose you for the assignment."

His conciliatory tone didn't calm my mounting rage. "That should serve as a lesson to whoever constructed these shitty legends. See what happened to the story about Badescu's role? Nobody believed it. Not Badescu, not SRI, not Hezbollah, and I'd be very surprised if the Shammas brothers ever believed it." There was an odd silence. Eric was busy reading his notes. Yeah, right. I continued. "And what about my assignment to abandon the documents in Istanbul? What did that have to do with Badescu? Letting me use the same Peter Wooten alias in both places turned me into dangling bait."

"It had a lot to do with Badescu," said Benny in an assuaging tone. "The Istanbul operation had two goals. First as decoy, to engage Hezbollah leadership to suspect their peers and council members. It's a small organization with limited resources, and they are not experts in multitasking. Keep them busy doing one thing, and they have less time to do other things and halt operations, fearing a leak. We need to tie them up and make them engage in fruitless activities. Look how Operation Pinocchio started. First by making the lovers' connection by e-mail with Anthon, then sending you to Paraguay, and later planting Erin at the home of the Shammas brothers. These steps were a part of a grand plan: to enable the placing of Badescu at the nerve center of Hezbollah in Beirut. And you're right, of course, regarding the true nature of his assignment. But look at the bottom line, and don't you forget it, the operation worked until Badescu was killed. So why are you angry?"

"Benny, I'm sorry, but please don't try to be cute with me. If you blindfold me when I'm on a mission and prevent me from getting vital information, you're increasing the likelihood that I'll bump into something, and that's exactly what happened."

Eric intervened. "Dan, I didn't want to tell you or say it, but you're forcing me. We had earlier intelligence, rather vague I must say, about a plan to kidnap you in Istanbul.

Therefore, we did two things: sent a bigger protective team to your hotel, and . . ." He hesitated.

"Go on," I said. "Spit it out."

He sighed. "We limited the information we gave you in case you were kidnapped and were made to talk."

Although I knew it to be standard procedure, I was still full of rage. I swallowed it for the moment. "What was the other goal you mentioned in sending me to Istanbul?" I asked.

"To map the chain of command and see how the information in the documents trickled down their organization. This was a joint CIA-NSA project. Right after the documents were taken at the hotel, NSA increased the monitoring on all major players of Hezbollah, including the local Iranian liaison officer. Since the Hezbollah organization has no ranks as a regular army does, we needed to know who reports to whom and how they digested the information. Dan, we're all small parts in a big machine. The days when a single operator brought the entire intelligence picture ended a while ago."

Benny added, "In fact, it was during biblical times, and even then when Moses sent spies to tour the country, there were a few in the party."

I wasn't ready to give up. "Why was I dumped in Bucharest? Why did it take two weeks to send over a visitor, and what's this crap about my stolen passport?"

"That was intentional," said Eric. "By claiming that your passport was stolen, we removed even a shadow of suspicion that you were a USG operative. We couldn't risk making any move that would have connected you with us and had to act slowly, so we waited before we sent Joe. A swift response from us would have indicated your importance. I'm sure you appreciate how sensitive the matter is for U.S. foreign relations. On the one hand, the U.S. is angry and vindictive when it uncovers foreign agents, even from friendly nations, snooping around, and at the same time, it sends its own operatives to foreign countries to do the exact same thing. There was also another reason. We suspected that the police's arrival at the scene was orchestrated, and therefore we assumed it was a ploy intended to recruit you. We wanted to give them a chance to do just that."

"Well, it worked," I said.

"Absolutely," he said.

"We can feed them crap from now to eternity," said Benny.

"Slow down," said Eric. "Not so fast. We need to consider a plan that will combine Dan's new assignment for the Romanians with our intelligence objectives."

"I'll think of something," said Benny, as he got up to go.

"I hate to let down Benny," said Eric after he was gone, "but the State Department is intervening, and he's not going to like the result."

"Are *we* going to like the result?" I asked.

"Maybe. We can always turn the tables," said Eric.

I was home in New York, and my life had returned to equilibrium. But I couldn't help but remember Mikaela and her kindness. I felt, as absurd as it was under the circumstances, that I had abandoned her, or at the very least that I owed her a call. So I broke down and called her at the prison.

"Mikaela? This is Peter Wooten. How are you?"

"Peter, are you still in Romania? I heard that you signed a plea agreement and were released. I'm happy for you."

I told her about the plea to admit to trespassing only, and that the homicide charge was dropped, enabling me to return to the U.S. "I felt bad for not calling you earlier to thank you for all your help. So here it is: thank you!"

"It was nothing," she said kindly. "I'm glad it's all over. Funny that you called though, because I was trying to figure out how to find you."

"Why?"

"Something very exciting happened a few days ago," she said. "I'm really happy for you."

"What happened?" I was a bit confused.

"Last week I interviewed a new prisoner during routine processing. You know, the same one you've been through."

"And?"

"He was arrested for murder. When I read his file and talked to him, I realized that he was accused of and confessed to the killing of Constantin Badescu. Isn't he the same person they accused you of murdering?"

"Yes, he was. Go on! Tell me more."

"The prisoner told the police that he heard that Badescu was living alone and kept a lot of money and jewelry at home. He broke into Badescu's house, but as he entered, he was surprised and confronted by Badescu, holding a gun. The burglar stabbed him with a kitchen knife he grabbed from the kitchen sink and ran out the door. He was certain that he only injured Badescu, because as he ran out, he heard Badescu yelling in pain and crying for help."

"Did he tell you what he did with the knife?" I remembered that I hadn't seen the murder weapon when I discovered the body.

"He didn't, but I read his arrest report. He said that he took both the knife and Badescu's gun and ran away. That means that you're cleared from the charge of murder. I believed you all the time."

"So nice of you say that." I'd known, of course, that I didn't kill Badescu, and now I was eager to hear more about the burglar-turned-murderer.

"What is the name of the prisoner?"

"Enver Kadare. An Albanian citizen."

"Do you believe his story?"

Mikaela hesitated. "Well, he confessed to killing Badescu, but insisted it was in self-defense."

"Do you have his file in front of you?"

"Yes."

"Please look at his background. What can you tell me?"

"Nothing special. Born in 1970 in Tiranë, Albania, as a Shiite Muslim. His father was a factory worker, his mother stayed at home, he has three siblings. After dropping out of high school after one year, he worked at odd jobs in Albania until becoming a shipmate on a freighter sailing in the Mediterranean. He later went to Lebanon, lived there for seven years, and returned to Albania for a few weeks. From Albania, he moved to Bucharest and worked in the fruit and vegetable wholesale market. He had no prior arrests in Romania. That's all."

"Did he tell you what he did in Lebanon?"

"He said there wasn't much to tell. He worked in several jobs. I don't have the names of his employers."

"Can you do me a favor?"

"Sure. You're not a prisoner anymore."

"Please ask the police to send you a copy of his passport."

"I have it here, actually."

"Please look at the stamps. Which countries did he visit?"

"There are only a few. I see Lebanon, three—no, four—entries, and two entries to Iran, and the rest are to Albania and Romania."

"Was his visit to Iran made during the seven-year period he lived in Lebanon?"

"Let me check. Yes, he went there twice, once for three months and once for six weeks. Why are you asking these questions?"

"I'm curious, that's all. He doesn't sound like a career criminal."

"I thought so too. He didn't fit the profile. But since he confessed to killing Badescu, even in self-defense, I don't think the police are continuing with the investigation."

"That's exactly my concern," I said. "Maybe his confes-

sion was coerced, and at the end of the day they will reac-
cuse me."

I sensed hesitation before she ventured, "When are you
coming for a visit?" Her tone was soft.

"After everything, I hope you understand that I'm not
eager to come back to Romania," I said gently. "But who
knows, things might change. Here is my e-mail address, in
case you want to communicate with me."

I gave her my Peter Wooten e-mail address. Soon I'd need
to find a way to avoid her or reveal my identity. I felt uncomfortable with either alternative.

I reported to Eric and Bob the substance of my conversation with Mikaela and the news she'd told me. The little
suspicious devil in me told me to look further. The story of
the Albanian prisoner confessing to killing Badescu in
self-defense just didn't sound convincing. Badescu was
poor as a church mouse, barely making ends meet on his
pension, which was wearing away as a result of increasing
inflation. Therefore, the story of cash and jewelry hidden
in Badescu's house didn't make sense. I'd seen a gun in the
drawer *after* the murder. Did Badescu have *two* guns at
home? When I came, the front door was open, probably
left open after the assassin fled. But how had he entered
the house? Enver told the police he thought Badescu was
out of the house. The body was on the floor of the study, in
the back end of the house. I saw no signs of forced entry,
not when I came through the front door the first time, and
not during my second visit when I used the back door. Had
the assassin rung the bell, and Badescu, who lived alone,
opened up and allowed a complete stranger to go with him
through the house to the home office at the back? It didn't
jibe with the suspicious personality of a former secret-po-
lice officer, or the confession Enver made to the police. Mikaela said that the murder weapon had been taken by
Enver from the kitchen sink, but the kitchen was on the
other side of the house, away from the study. Finally, the

confession was too simple. I was further troubled by Enver's two long visits to Iran. As a Shiite, did he have any ties to Hezbollah? Why had he traveled to Iran? These were the matters that I recommended be investigated further, while I did some homework on my own. But I suspected that either Enver was not the assassin or he lied about what really happened.

I kept to myself and didn't include in my report another possible twist to the developing story concerning Enver. If he was indeed the person who killed Badescu, and he did it in self-defense as he claimed, then my earlier estimate that the Romanian intelligence service killed him collapsed. Fulda insinuated SRI did it, but how could I verify that statement? Maybe Fulda just took a piggy-back ride on Badescu's assassination to frame me in order to recruit a valuable American asset and tacitly hinted that his service was responsible for it. Badescu was a former general at the Securitate who was under suspicion for some reason, so SRI was most likely following him. Since I'd met with him, I was probably under their watch as well. Therefore, Badescu's assassination could have been reported to SRI in real time. Once I'd entered Badescu's house, SRI could have dispatched the local police to arrest me. It was a golden opportunity well used by a shrewd intelligence officer. Fulda met that job description.

Now it was time to get my life back to normal. Bob told me he was coming to New York with a surprise.

"Here is the surprise," said Bob as he entered my office and handed me a letter. The letterhead read *Serviciul Roman de Informatii*. I read it quickly.

> *We have considered your request to terminate our agreement with respect to research work assigned to you. The Directorate has decided to accept your request and*

therefore our agreement is hereby rescinded, effective immediately.

It was signed by hand next to a round seal. I had a broad and surprised smile on my face.

"What is it? I never requested that. I've just ignored them, as we all agreed."

"After reviewing your debriefing and consulting with the Department of State, the FBI, and the CIA, we decided that we couldn't allow such an agreement to remain valid, albeit nonactive, obtained under false pretenses and coercion. However, since Romania is now an ally, we made a request through channels to give them the opportunity to put the lid on this matter without causing a diplomatic incident. I'm glad they got the message. We were further assured that the initiative was limited to low-level staff, who were counseled and reprimanded."

I put the letter in my pocket. I was amused. In the old days, Fulda would get a medal, not a reprimand.

I had trouble sleeping that night. Something was bothering me. Was it the news Mikaela had told me? I should have felt relieved, not sleepless. Was it the release letter from the Romanian Intelligence Service? Was it the sound of Mikaela's voice that made me think of her in more than one way? All of the above? Switching to reality, I ran through my mind the details of Enver the Albanian that she had given me, trying to figure out how to support or refute his story. I looked at the red digits of the clock radio. It was after two A.M. I got up and made tea.

As I poured the boiling water into the thin glass cup, it occurred to me. If Enver wasn't a burglar, but an assassin, whom did he work for? Identifying his affiliation could lead to the motive for the murder, and maybe even to the revival of Operation Pinocchio. Maybe, just maybe. The fact that he was a Shiite Muslim who worked in Lebanon and traveled to Iran was interesting, even important, but without any additional information, it was meaningless. Obviously, not all Shiite Muslims who travel to Lebanon and Iran are connected to terrorism. However, if Badescu was killed under orders from Hezbollah, then there must have been prior intelligence collection. They don't operate like a 1920s street gang in Chicago, when a nod was enough to flatten a victim with a barrage of bullets. Hezbollah is well versed in assassinations. Somebody had to follow Badescu, learn his routines and habits. When he leaves his home, and when he returns. Who he associates with and where. Where is the best location to assassinate him? With what weapon? If caught, what would be the legend? Who would be selected to do the job? Would he operate under a false flag, believing he was working it for somebody else? What about escape routes? Communications? There must have been people who asked these questions and provided answers. How could I get these answers while in the U.S. with no plans or desire to return to Romania? Besides, why should I care? My murder case was closed. I couldn't have cared less who had killed Badescu—or maybe I should have. Why? What did I have to do to find the assassin?

I had no answers and knew that they couldn't be found by searching on Google. I made all sorts of crazy plans. Obviously, anything is possible if you don't know what you're talking about. *That* reality calmed me down. Sitting in the dark, sipping my tea, it occurred to me that I'd left an item out of a jigsaw puzzle that still had many missing parts: the microcassette I'd removed from Badescu's answering machine. I jumped to my feet and pulled it from my travel bag, which I hadn't had time to unpack. I went to my answering machine and tried inserting the cassette. It didn't fit.

On the spur of the moment, I dressed up and went out onto the street. I couldn't sleep anyway, and this new direction sent new energies through my veins. I took a cab to a twenty-four-hour Walgreens drugstore in the East Village on Manhattan. For $24.95 I bought a small answering machine that took the same type of microcassettes and rushed back home. I plugged in the machine, inserted the cassette, and listened. The first two messages were from women over sixty, judging from their voices, probably family members or close friends. The third message came from a man. He spoke slowly for about thirty seconds. I played it again, trying to understand bits and pieces of this Romance language, recruiting my command of Spanish and French. All I could understand was that the man suggested a meeting to discuss payment. I ran it again and transcribed the message phonetically. It was three twenty-five A.M., and I couldn't call anyone who spoke Romanian to ask for a translation.

Mikaela? What the hell, I'd think of an excuse why I was asking her to translate the message. Before calling her, I ran the tape forward to hear any additional messages. Other than my own recorded message, there were none. It was ten thirty-five A.M. in Bucharest. Mikaela should be at work. I dialed her number.

"Peter! You must be around here if you're calling at this time."

"No, I'm in New York and I can't sleep. I have a small request. Can I play a thirty-second recording in Romanian for you to translate?"

"Sure."

I played the cassette into the phone's mouthpiece.

"Peter, this is a message from a person who didn't leave his name. Maybe the recipient recognized his voice. He says that he has not been paid yet, and unless payment is made when he comes to collect it today, there will be consequences."

I wrote down the translation. "What do you make of it?" I asked.

"He sounded very threatening," she said. "I thought the voice sounded a bit familiar, but maybe I'm wrong."

"Can you estimate the age of the speaker?"

"I'd say a man under forty who is not a native Romanian, although his Romanian was good."

I thanked her. I was too energetic to return to bed. I spent the remaining three hours in plotting and planning my next move. The problem was that I was treading water, because I had no idea what to do next.

On the following day, I was called to a meeting at a CIA safe house. I was driven for an hour to the north shore of Long Island, where turn-of-the-century horse-breeding farms were divided and converted into sites of million-dollar homes. We entered a long circular driveway leading to a red-brick house secluded among tall birch trees. The nearest neighboring house was at least one hundred yards away. Although the house was from a bygone era on the outside, the inside decor was modern. A stern-looking young man dressed in a dark blue suit guided me to the library. Bob, Paul, Eric, and Benny, who was chatting with his aide, were waiting for me.

Paul started. "We're here because Badescu's death and the refusal of the two Apples to cooperate made a shambles out of Operation Pinocchio. We need to go to Plan B—go after the Apples' wives, or choose just one of them. Each of the three women has a bank account in Rome, a leftover from the period their husbands served, at different times, in the Lebanese Embassy. They never closed the accounts and continue to use it for shopping during their visits to Italy, once or twice a year."

Was that all we had? I was disappointed. *That's crap*, I thought, but only let out an edited version of my thoughts. "Do you think they'd be afraid to be exposed for having a foreign bank account showing routine household expenses? Lebanon is not the Soviet Union circa 1980."

Paul wasn't deterred. "We can wait for their next visit and make a sizeable deposit into their account. Let them explain to Nasserallah when he questions their husbands how the cash deposits found their way into their wives' personal account exactly at the time they visited Rome." Was it a coincidence or maybe a payoff to their husbands?

"Have the deposits actually been made?" I became confused for a moment.

Paul shook his head. "No, but there's no limit to what computer hacking can do. We can transfer money from some other account at the same bank to theirs. We won't risk our money. That's what we did with the two hundred thousand dollars we made appear as a deposit into Sheik Wazir's account."

Aha, that's what they did. At the time I'd been surprised that the bean counters in Washington had agreed to risk USG money.

"Since the women know they never made the deposits, why should they mind if all of a sudden there's more money in their account?" I wasn't convinced.

"They should mind. You will soon see why."

"Who'd stop them from withdrawing the money?" asked Eric.

"We'll put it in high-interest-bearing accounts requiring a thirty-day prior notice. We'll have a month to reverse the transfer before they withdraw."

"What about the owners of the account you plan to hack and transfer the funds from to the women? Won't they cry foul?"

"We have identified several accounts that have been idle for years. Either their owners don't have a current need for the money, or they may have died. Can you imagine the amount of persuasion the women will have to use to explain that fortune, when additional incriminating evidence could appear all of a sudden on the desk of the chief of Hezbollah's internal security?"

"Such as what?"

"Photos of clandestine meetings with foreigners. You

know, Photoshop is excellent software. There could be encrypted messages appearing as they were sent from their home computers to some strangers. When you see the package of 'incentives' for cooperation, you'll be convinced too."

"How will they discover the unexpected high balance?"

"They'll get a call from us, purporting to be a manager at their bank, telling them that the bank is asking if they want to extend their interest-bearing deposit, this time for an additional six months."

"And . . . ?"

"We'll refuse to discuss it over the phone. They'll rush to the bank, and we'll get them on video."

"Paul, if their husbands become aware of the deposit, they'll immediately make a connection to the meeting they had with our men. We already used that ploy with one of them."

I thought the plan might have potential, but it was far from being operative. Judging from Benny's face, he didn't have much enthusiasm for the plan either.

"While we're considering Paul's ideas, which I think are in the right direction, let me run another idea by you," said Benny diplomatically, meaning "Paul's plan sucks." "We have assets in Lebanon that gave us a new direction concerning Badescu's murder and consequently made us think how to revive Operation Pinocchio without Badescu. These assets, although Hezbollah members, are at a low level and without access to the leadership. Therefore, we still need to find a better solution to the problem created when Badescu was removed from the scene.

"Our assets told us that they heard about an Albanian Muslim, Enver—we only had his first name—who worked on a freighter in the Mediterranean, spoke with admiration about Hezbollah, and left the ship to join the organization when it docked in Beirut. We ran a system-wide computer check and discovered that a man with the same first name was arrested in Bucharest for the murder of Badescu. If they are the same person, then we may tentatively assume that Badescu was assassinated by Hezbollah, or at least by a sympathizer. Again, this is just an assumption, not evidence, and definitely not proof. We continued working in that direction, though." Benny paused and looked around. "As a result we had to pull out Mahmoud, and he in turn put Ali on a back burner. We can't allow a ripple effect on our assets because we don't know what FOE knows about our operation. The rule is," he said with half a smile, "if you see a bomb technician running, don't ask questions, just start running too. Here Badescu's fall was the run of the bomb technician."

I was surprised that Benny had been kept out of the loop and hadn't been told that my report corroborated his intelligence, that the confessed assassin was Enver.

Eric quickly corrected it. "Yes, we have the same information and also a last name: Enver Kadare, an Albanian citizen."

Benny gave him that "now you're telling me?" look. But his lips remained tight. He wrote down the name. I could feel the tension in the air.

I was mulling over whether to tell them about my discovery of last night when I'd listened to the voice message left on Badescu's answering machine, but decided against it for now, because the information was too raw. My best source to get further information on Enver was Mikaela. Did I reach that conclusion for additional reasons, more personal ones? Whatever the reason, I couldn't just call her again as Peter Wooten. Revealing my identity could be risky. I couldn't forget she was a part of the Romanian security apparatus. Letting the Romanian intelligence service discover my identity could lead to a backlash against the CIA for maintaining double standards. Without a better alternative, I decided to keep things as they were and continue my contact with Mikaela as Peter Wooten. I wasn't sure, though, what to tell her and what legend to use. Mikaela wasn't stupid, far from it, and if I slipped here and aroused her suspicion, then instead of solving a case, I'd create a new problem. First, I had to define what I wanted from her, and determine whether I thought she could get it. That was a reasonable question that could be answered objectively: did she have access to the information? That was something I had no control over. Would she get it for me? was a question to be answered along subjective and personal lines. How willing, determined, and motivated was Mikaela to help me out? In that department, there were things I *could* do.

I called Mikaela. "I hate to bother you again," I said hesitantly, not knowing how she'd react if I continued calling her with questions regarding Enver. If she was annoyed, there wasn't any sign of it. She was glad to talk to me. I told her that I had continued "looking into the matter"—I didn't want to say "investigating"—and asked if she would help me with it.

"Maybe I'll write a book about it one day," I joked.

"That's not a bad idea at all, and then they'll make a movie . . . ," she responded.

"Yes, and you'll be the star," I continued with the fantasy.

"Only if I could use the money to give a better future to my son." All of a sudden, there was a sad tone to her voice.

"When is his birthday?" I asked. She had just given me an idea.

"Next month. Why do you ask?"

"I'll send him a present, for his luck in having you as his mother."

"That's very kind of you, but you don't have to."

But I did have to. That was my way of getting her home address. She gave me his name and their Bucharest address. I wrote it down. I took her home phone number as well.

"Anyway, I continue to be puzzled by Enver. I have several difficulties with his version of the murder, and I wonder whether you could ask him a few questions that would help me clarify the matter and put it behind me. Maybe he, like me, was wrongly accused, and if he is exonerated, the police might come back to me with their ridiculous accusations."

"But he confessed," she said, sounding surprised.

"You know how the police work, and you understand prisoner psychology. Isn't it possible for an alien from a foreign country with a different ethnic culture and religion to be manipulated into signing a confession for doing things he had never done? Look at my case. I barely escaped a similar steamroller attempt to get me to confess."

"I think you may be right, although I'm not sure about that particular case. But OK, if it'll help you sleep better, tell me what you want me to ask him."

I told Mikaela about my concerns, and she promised to question Enver.

Three days later, I received an e-mail from Mikaela: "Call me."

I dialed her number. This time she wasn't friendly, but concerned, or maybe angry. I couldn't tell.

"I hope you had good reasons for asking me to question Enver," she said.

"Of course, I gave you the reasons. What happened?"

"He was found dead in his cell last night."

I paused to digest the news. "Do you know the cause of death?"

"Not yet. There were no physical marks on his body. The police think he died of natural causes or by poisoning. We'll know better after the autopsy."

"Do they suspect suicide or foul play?"

"He wasn't the type to commit suicide, although I could be wrong."

"Are you angry at me?" I asked, a bit subdued.

"I want you to tell me that you know nothing about Enver's death and that you were not involved in it in any way. You mentioned in our previous conversation that if Enver was exonerated, then you could become a suspect again. That tells me you could have an interest in him being killed to prevent his exoneration, or at least make it more difficult, if not irrelevant."

"I swear that I heard about his death just now, and that I had absolutely no connection to his death. From my perspective, it only complicates things. With Enver alive and confessing, I'm clearly exonerated—and now? There are questions."

I heard a sigh of relief. "I want to believe you," she said, "but now I don't know what to believe."

"Trust me, I'm clean as a whistle. I have a suggestion. Let's continue with our interest in the case. Maybe the findings will help you believe me." I didn't say, "Let's continue with our interest in each other," although that message was subtly conveyed.

"I'll do that," she agreed.

A report with the recent news was encrypted and sent to Eric, Paul, and Bob immediately:

If we rule out death by natural causes, because Enver was a young man, then we have to assume that somebody got to Enver. Although it was still remotely possible, I find it hard to believe that Enver was able to commit suicide with poison smuggled from the outside. This is a maximum-security prison. There are sudden unannounced searches in the cells when the prisoner is out in the yard, and the searches of anyone entering the prison are thorough. On the other hand, they missed the hidden stuff in my shirt and my shoes when they searched me, so maybe they missed again. My theory is that someone wanted Enver silenced for good. Hezbollah?

The next day, I knew it was too soon to call Mikaela, but I did anyway.

"Peter," she said in a low voice. "Check your e-mail." She hung up.

I logged onto my e-mail and there was nothing from Mikaela. Just as I was about to call her again, I realized that of course she could have sent it only to my covert e-mail address of Peter Wooten. Even I was having trouble keeping up with my identities. I found her e-mail message: "Bizarre things are happening; I can't talk to you over my work phone. Call my cell after hours, but be very careful of what you say. M."

There was no cell-phone number given. I refreshed my inbox just in case and found another e-mail sent from some Internet café in Bucharest. The only text was a telephone number. That mail wasn't signed. I waited until it was nine P.M. in Bucharest and called her.

"Peter, I'm glad you called. We need to talk, but we can't do it over the phone. Can we meet?"

"Where?"

"In Bucharest."

Eric, Paul, and Bob would be perplexed to hear that I wanted to return to Bucharest and rekindle the ire of SRI after the U.S. government had rubbed their face in the mud.

"I'd love to meet you, but I'm hesitant whether a meeting in Bucharest is a good idea. I may still be a suspect, and I've gotten used to my freedom." I couldn't suggest a meeting in the U.S. That would complicate things, for now. "We can meet in any close-by location—Istanbul, Belgrade, Sofia, you decide."

I sensed her hesitation and quickly added, "I'll pay all your expenses of course."

She pondered for a moment and said, "OK, I can come to Bulgaria. I'll meet you in Sofia—is Friday OK? On that weekend my son is going away on a class trip, so I must be back in Bucharest by Monday morning."

"Perfect, I'll call or e-mail you the travel details."

Saying that was the easy part. Now I needed travel authorization not only for me but for Mikaela as well, and not only from Bob, my Department of Justice boss, but also from Eric and his accounting department at the CIA. After jumping through several hoops, some of which were on fire, I answered their repetitive questions and swore to stay out of more trouble. *If the State Department gets another complaint about you cutting corners in your assignment, we will refuse to be your pooper scoopers again. . . .*

But I prevailed. I called Mikaela and told her to pick up her prepaid ticket at the airport. I rushed to prepare for my trip. There were things I needed to know about Sofia, things I needed to ask Mikaela, and things I could not do and still keep the flames low—the Bulgarian government's, not mine—in my fervent drive to get results.

I made sure I had my Peter Wooten passport and that no remnants of my Dan Gordon identity could be found on my person or in my luggage.

I flew two days ahead of the meeting to Sofia international airport and took a cab for the six-mile ride to the Sheraton hotel at Sveta Nedelya Square. The majestic building, worthy of a king's palace, was illuminated. I walked through its archways and across the marble floor to the reception-desk area, which was defined by a dark blue carpet with golden stars, while scanning the people in the lobby. I didn't notice anything out of the ordinary, but with my background, I just couldn't avoid doing the ABC of counterintelligence surveillance: identify your opponent but don't let him know you did.

CHAPTER THIRTEEN

I still wasn't sure how to treat Mikaela. Did the fact that she was employed by the Romanian justice system mean I had to be on guard with her? Did she suggest our meeting on her own initiative, or had she been asked to arrange it to lure me outside the protective environment of the U.S.?

"Welcome, Mr. Wooten. We have a specially reserved room for you on the fourth floor. Our manager has upgraded your room reservation in appreciation of your continued patronage of our hotels."

When I entered the room, I was surprised to see how spacious and luxurious it was. I went back to the lobby and asked to move to another room.

"There's a smell of detergent from the carpet which makes me sneeze. I think I'm allergic to it," I said. The receptionist looked at me in amazement but gave me another room. Had I sneezed? Of course not. I'd employed an old habit from my Mossad days. While on assignment, if you get a preassigned room, go to the room and return to the desk asking to move to another room. "This one has a queen bed; I need a king-size," or "I feel lost in a king bed; let me have a smaller one." The reason? If they put a fruit basket or flowers in your room, expecting you to enjoy them, they might have also put in your room things you didn't ask for, such as a microphone or a video camera.

You'd be surprised what a hotel clerk will do if you only ask and slip him a banknote to jump-start his willingness to help you, particularly if you confide in him on something that he is expected to keep secret. "My older brother was just released from the hospital, and the doctor suggested that he be monitored because he suffers from sudden fainting spells. He's too proud to allow a 'babysitter' to watch him, so this is a safety precaution for his health." Of course, in most instances we never ask for permission and just break into the room.

I took additional precautionary measures. I also locked my luggage, which was packed in a very particular fashion, so that any attempt to search it would be noticed. I ordered room service and was dead asleep even before the food arrived.

On Friday evening, I left a note for Mikaela at the desk: "Welcome. I'm in room 306. Please call me." An hour before her expected arrival I sat in the lobby in a black leather armchair that I'd dragged to an area behind a white column, blocking me from people standing near the check-in desk and at the same time giving me a good view of the incoming traffic. I felt embarrassed for taking these precautions, but I wasn't going to let my personal affection cloud my judgment. Mikaela was actually an asset unwittingly recruited to perform intelligence work on my behalf. Period. Since she was, I had to employ all the "must add" bells and whistles that go with the territory. Too many recruiters have ended up in a coffin for being too lax on security. I had to see if Mikaela was alone, whether she was being shadowed, and whether she came by cab or with someone who drove a private vehicle and dropped her off.

About thirty minutes after what I'd roughly calculated as her expected arrival time, I saw Mikaela through the window walking toward the hotel carrying a duffel bag. I didn't see her being dropped off from a vehicle. She entered the hotel's reception area gingerly, and with unconcealed amazement, looked around at the expensive decor, a strong contrast to the overall grayness of the city. She talked with the receptionist, picked up her key, and went to the elevator. I bought a newspaper at the store and went up to my room. The message light was blinking. "Hi, Peter." I heard her soft voice. "I'm here in room 411."

I waited an hour to let her freshen up and called her. After greeting her, I asked, "Your room or mine?"

"Mine," she said. "If you don't mind."

She opened the door dressed in dark blue jeans and a yellow cotton blouse. She wore little makeup, but her blonde hair seemed professionally styled. She shook my hand and I sat on a chair next to her desk.

After finishing with cordialities and questions about her trip, I asked her why she'd insisted on a personal meeting.

"Peter, you must promise me never to reveal who gave you this information, or tell anyone that we even met after your release."

"Of course," I said solemnly.

She took a deep breath. "The death of Enver was determined by the coroner to be unnatural, probably homicide. Suicide was ruled out."

"Go on," I said in a bland voice that masked my deep interest.

"The point is that the man who died in prison wasn't Enver."

"But who?"

"I don't know. The police are investigating, but they know for sure that the corpse in the coroner's refrigerator is not of Enver Kadare, an Albanian citizen."

"How can they be so sure?"

"The Albanian police sent the Bucharest police a sample of Enver's fingerprints. They didn't match the dead man's prints."

As I was trying to figure out how this news affected our interests, Mikaela dropped the bomb. "The police think the Americans are behind it."

I swallowed. "What do you mean? Behind what?"

"The assassination of Badescu and maybe even the assassination of Enver—or whoever that man was."

"Is there a basis for this madness? They think the American government did all that? Why?"

"My contact at the police gets his information from SRI. That's what they told him."

"Mikaela, you'll have to forgive me. I'm just an academic researcher of past political events, and what you're telling me goes beyond my experience, even beyond stories I read in the media or in the intelligence thrillers I like to read when I find the time. What's going on?"

"The bad part is that the police think that they let you go free too quickly and that perhaps you're not an innocent researcher as you persuaded everyone you were, that maybe you're the one behind all this." All of a sudden, there was a suspicious tone to her words.

"That's absolutely false," I said vehemently, trying to figure out whether the classification I'd given Mikaela as a harmless and unwitting asset was too rushed. Although one sentence didn't label her a member of FOE, it certainly didn't put her in line with innocent, disinterested third parties that had just happened to pass by.

I decided to play the personal card. "What else can I say to convince you I had nothing to do with all this? I was hoping the stupid accusation was behind me and that now I could pay more attention to you."

Alas, as far as Mikaela was concerned, this was solitaire, and I was the only player. She seemed to have other things on her mind. She still hadn't been put on my FOE list, although she had just become a candidate.

She didn't answer my question and just looked at me. Maybe it wasn't all lost. I tried again. "What do you want me to say? And if you think I'm guilty of something, why did you ask to see me?"

"I don't know what or who to believe," she finally said. "When I interviewed you in prison, I believed in your innocence. Now, when I hear all sorts of stories, I'm confused again. I wanted to give you the opportunity to explain." I expected her demeanor to be one of a woman wanting to believe me, but what I heard sounded cold, and maybe even a calculated attempt to get me to offer another, possibly contradictory version. My alerts went up, and the little dormant devil inside me opened one eye again and told me to watch out.

"Nothing has changed. Everything I told you in prison is the same thing I told the police and SRI and is also the same thing I'm telling you right now. There's no connection to me whatsoever. Period."

"Then how come you never gave me your phone number in the U.S? I called several people listed in the telephone directory on the Internet under Peter Wooten, and none of them were you."

This raised more red flags. What accounted for her persistence? Was it a suspicious woman checking out a man talking here or what?

"There's a simple explanation," I said. "My number is unlisted. I've had too many prank and sales calls."

"Can I get your number now?"

I was prepared for that. "Of course, it's (212) 555-6591." She wrote it down. "Just so you know," I added, "since I live alone, I have an answering service that takes my calls when I'm not at home, so don't be surprised if you call and a woman answers. Sometimes it will be a different woman answering, because they work shifts."

We have always had ready-made background cover stories, including a fake office and a fake home. The number I gave her rings at a center somewhere in the Midwest, and the computer tells the operator to whom the call is directed and what, if any, background noise to add: children crying, planes taking off, train-station announcements, or sea waves, among thousands of other possibilities. They could even play the mechanical sound of an answering machine, and if the caller is on the "approved callers" list, the recorded message is automatically transferred to the agent, who can return the call with a push of a button.

"Do you believe me now?" I asked in a sulky tone that showed my impatience to get this thing over with.

I didn't feel that Mikaela was overly impressed with my act. As a prison psychologist, she must have seen better actors, pretenders, and crackpots. I'm sure she had met a few Napoleons and people with a direct link to God too. No matter how good or bad I was, I still had to pass the wall of professionalism that surrounded her. Though I wasn't completely relaxed, I tried hard to appear nonchalant. After our short conversation, I became convinced that there must have been another reason for Mikaela's initiative to meet me in person. I ruled out romance, given her demeanor. To be nice to me? She could have sent me the information by e-mail from that Internet café from which she had sent me her cell-phone number. I decided to play it cool and give her the opportunity to do what she had on her mind, whatever that was.

I excused myself and went to the bathroom. I pulled out my microsized bug detector and directed it toward the door. The device was sensitive enough to detect any electronic activity thirty feet away. The results were mixed. There were signals, but they could have come from the hotel's Wi-Fi network. So the question remained: was she recording me? Between the two of us, who was the paranoid? Was it me, who suspected her motives in flying in from Romania to tell me things she could have e-mailed and then tell me she didn't believe what I'd said? It just didn't make sense. Or maybe that really was all it was. Even psychologists aren't exempt from strange behavior. Of course, there was room here for two paranoids, but it was becoming crowded.

"Let's go out to dinner," I suggested. At the very least it would reduce the tension, and at the most it could allow me to discover the real reason for her visit.

The hotel's restaurant matched the lavishness of the lobby. I wanted Mikaela to feel pampered. She drank wine, smiled, and laughed but said nothing to satisfy my curiosity regarding the true motives for the meeting. After dinner we went to the elevator, and I pressed two buttons, the third floor for me and the fourth for her, to show her I had no intention of going to her room. Would I have changed my mind if she had suggested that? I didn't know, and was glad I didn't have to decide whether to mix business with pleasure. We went to our respective rooms.

The next morning, we met for brunch in the dining room. Again, there was no substance to our conversation, and she didn't demonstrate any impatience. After brunch, she suggested having coffee in her room.

"Maybe in mine? It's bigger," I asked testing her.

"No, let's go to mine."

My dear, is there something in your room that can't be found in mine? the little devil in me asked inaudibly.

"Sure."

We went to her room. Mikaela removed an envelope from her duffel bag and handed it to me.

"Here are some documents that could help you. A copy of the coroner's report on the prisoner's autopsy and a copy of his police files, which includes a copy of Enver's confession. I'm sorry it's all in Romanian, but you can get it translated. Is there anything else you need?"

I was confused. She had just given me precious documents, but the tone of voice was businesslike, if not hostile.

"Thank you very much. I do appreciate it. Let me go over it. Maybe I'll ask for clarifications. Can I do it now?"

She nodded and pointed to her desk. I turned on the desk lamp and read the bulky file. Not only was everything written in Romanian, most of it was in longhand. There was no chance in hell I could read, let alone understand it.

"Tell me what it says," I asked, realizing I couldn't do anything with the file until it was translated.

"You already know." She was impatient.

"Meaning . . . ?"

"I've already told you. The coroner's autopsy determined it was homicide, not suicide, and the prisoner's confession."

"Let me ask you about the police report. Does it say how they discovered him as a suspect?"

She took the police file and read for a few minutes, flipping through the pages.

"Here it is. An anonymous phone call to the police identified him as the assassin and gave his address."

"Anything else on that?"

"Nothing that I can see, other then the name of the man found dead in the prison cell. His name is Dhimitër Daci, also an Albanian citizen."

"Who is he?"

"A foreign worker in Romania. He came from Albania just three weeks before Badescu's murder. He lived in a cabin with six other workers, in a field of a Romanian farmer just outside Bucharest."

"Any idea why Dhimitër Daci claimed to be Enver Kadare and confessed to a murder he probably didn't commit?" I asked.

"I have no idea," she responded. "The police think he killed Badescu and are about to close the file."

"You said earlier that they suspected the Americans," I said.

"True, but all I know is that the murder file is closed now."

"Does the coroner's file include a toxicology report?" I wanted to know if poisoning was the cause of death.

She nodded. My little devil stirred again. *Don't believe what the report says,* he suggested. A toxicology report takes two weeks to develop, and it'd been hardly a week since Dhimitër died. Should I suspect the report? I asked my little devil, and he said, *Don't believe anything here.* I agreed with my little devil; the information was too convenient, too easily fed to me. First, an anonymous phone call identifying Dhimitër impersonating Enver, sending the police over to him, arresting him, getting a confession, then killing him, hoping to put a lid on the matter. I just couldn't accept it. It was a series of events planned by someone, and it wasn't Dhimitër Daci.

I stared at Mikaela and figured out what was bothering me. Why did the anonymous informer finger Dhimitër Daci, telling the police he was Enver Kadare, and then why had Dhimitër Daci cooperated in claiming he was Enver Kadare? There were two possibilities. One was that Dhimitër Daci, unless suicidal, didn't know he was about to die, and the second—although I wanted to reject the idea because for me and for others they were the epitome of evil—somebody *wanted* it to appear as if Hezbollah was behind it all. Enver's connection to Hezbollah wasn't front-page news, but not a huge secret either. Therefore, his involvement in Badescu's assassination would have implicated Hezbollah. But apparently, Enver Kadare had no plans for an early death, and Dhimitër Daci had been sent in his stead. Who was behind it? A rival group? A foreign-intelligence service? That also meant that the real Enver Kadare was still alive and kicking, unless he too had been sent to a reunion with his ancestors.

"What are you going to do with it?" asked Mikaela, breaking my train of thought.

"I don't know," I said candidly. "It seems stranger by the moment. Maybe there's a screenplay in it."

"Seriously, what's next?"

"Is SRI or the Romanian police continuing with their investigation?"

"I don't know about SRI, but my contact at the police told me they'd lost interest, and as far as they are concerned the case is closed, unless new evidence or suspects surface." She raised her head to look me in the eye. When I didn't move a muscle, she added, "Since you started investigating it, I think you should continue." She was encouraging me, and there was a trusting tone in her words. I found that odd. Why would she encourage me to continue with the investigation? The murder wasn't my problem anymore, so there was no reason for me to solve the case, unless Mikaela knew something that I didn't, or wanted something that I was unaware of.

I excused myself and went to the hotel's business center, scanned all the documents, and e-mailed them to Bob. "Please have the attached documents translated. Please confirm receipt ASAP." Six minutes later, the ever-efficient Esther mailed back, "Received." I shredded the originals, which were in fact just photocopies, took the confetti-like shreds, and threw them into the fireplace in the back lobby. I returned to Mikaela's room.

"Where are the documents?" she asked when she saw me returning without them.

"I mailed them to my home in the U.S. I didn't think it'd be wise to carry them around." I didn't tell her how I'd mailed them. NTK basis.

CHAPTER FOURTEEN

As if on cue, someone banged on the door loudly. "Open up!"

Mikaela became pale and looked at me. "Who can that be?"

Who, indeed? I went to the door and opened it. Two men in Bulgarian police blue-gray uniforms were standing there with the hotel's assistant manager.

"Mikaela Grosaru?" asked a mustached officer.

"Yes," she said.

"You have to come with us." The assistant manager was translating.

"Why?" She didn't lose her composure. Facing the law was routine for her, though she was usually on their side of the fence.

"You'll soon find out. There is a request from the Romanian police concerning stolen classified police documents."

He turned to me. "Your ID?"

"I don't have it here; my passport is in my room." In fact, I'd put it in the hotel's safe.

"What is your name?"

"Peter Wooten."

He looked at his note. "You too, come with us!"

Not again.

"I'm not going anywhere until you show me a warrant for my arrest or the American consul sees me first."

The officer looked confused.

"Call the consul!" I demanded.

He exchanged looks with the other officer, who also looked confused.

"I need to go to the bathroom," I said and entered the bathroom without waiting for his approval. I pulled out the tissue-paper box from the sink's front panel, removed most of the tissues, and stomped on the box to flatten it to half an inch thick. I returned to the room. The officer was standing at the far end of the room next to the window, talking into his cell phone, and the other officer was standing next to him. I took the opportunity. I rushed to the door three feet away, closed it behind me, and inserted the flattened tissue box underneath the door. They would need a few minutes to push open the door, giving me enough time to disappear. I ran down the stairs and could hear yelling in Bulgarian coming from the direction of Mikaela's room. I went to the basement, "borrowed" an employee's coat and hat from a coatrack, and went out the back of the hotel.

In the middle of an empty square, I saw an early-era red-brick rotunda. I passed the square and found myself on a busy boulevard where a big garbage truck was being loaded. I had some Bulgarian money and more than one thousand dollars, but no passport. I was breathing heavily, thinking about what to do next. I considered commandeering the garbage truck, but I realized it wouldn't get me far, not only because it was slow, but also because it was easily spotted. I crossed the boulevard and entered one of the back streets. A man was clearing the snow from his car's back window, its engine running. I came from the front, jumped inside, and drove away. I looked in the mirror; he was yelling at me and waving his hands in despair. The car was very small and dirty. I drove through Sofia, following the signs to the E80 highway to take me to Serbia. I knew well that I couldn't keep the car for long—it'd be reported stolen very soon.

I located a block of high-end apartments and parked the car a block away, taking the keys with me. I entered the building complex. It was dark and snowing. The parking lot was full of cars, but I saw no people. I tried the doors of several cars—not those on the driver's side, as one would think, but the back doors. Unless the car has a central locking system, sometimes people don't pay attention and forget to lock the back doors, particularly if they have children who exit and leave the car door unlocked. The third car of an unknown Eastern European make had its back door unlocked. I entered, crossed the wires, and in a few minutes I was on my way. I even thought of passing near the car I had abandoned earlier, to be nice to the owner and leave the keys, but I scrapped the idea. I wanted the police to think I was hiding nearby. But if the keys were left in or near the car, it could signal I'd gone away and wouldn't be returning to the car.

I checked the gas gauge. It was almost full. I turned on the heater and cruised on the empty road. I feared that due to the poor visibility caused by darkness and the weather, I'd see police roadblocks too late to turn around. I parked the car near a highway exit and waited for a few hours. Just before daylight I started the car, and within one hour, I was in Kalotina, one of the busiest Bulgarian border check-points, situated near a very small Bulgarian village on the Serbian border.

It was very cold outside. I parked the car on a side street. All five shops on the village's main street were still closed. It was six A.M., and I entered the only place that had lights on, St. Nicolas Church. It was empty but warm inside, and I saw just one parishioner. I stretched out on a bench and looked around. It was quite small and slightly neglected, with the marks of a gorgeous past, as evidenced by the rich decorations with beautiful murals. The church must have been five or six hundred years old. I couldn't concentrate on art appreciation; I needed to get out of Bulgaria as fast as I could. The problem was that I had no papers or any other ID. Even if I'd had my Peter Wooten passport, I couldn't have used it without becoming an immediate guest of the Bulgarian prison system. Since I hadn't liked the Romanian prison, I was pretty sure I wouldn't like the one in Bulgaria.

When day broke, I ventured out. I was very close to the border crossing, but with the fences and the mean-looking dogs, I didn't think it was wise to attempt crossing there. I saw a sign for the train station. I walked to the small termi-nal and viewed the map. The next city in Serbia would be Dimitrovgrad. That should be my target. The posting indi-cated that the trains were drawn by a diesel locomotive and could get me to Nis, where all passengers traveling to other cities must change to electric trains. I could change there to the train for Belgrade. I went outside to the taxi station and got in a cab.

"Do you speak German?" I asked in that language, try-ing to find a common language denominator between us. He nodded.

"Good." I handed him a twenty-dollar bill, a fairly large amount in Bulgaria. "Take me for a ride." But there wasn't much to see. After an hour driving through the countryside, I was hungry and asked him to take me to a restaurant. He brought me to a grocery that had two tables to serve as a restaurant. I invited him to join me; he was surprised but agreed. I asked him about his family and did everything I could within reason to befriend him. Finally, when I thought the time was right, I asked the question.

"I need go to Serbia, but my passport was stolen in Sofia. The German embassy said it'd take a few days to issue me a new passport, but I can't wait. Do you think you could help me cross? I'll pay you handsomely."

He thought for a moment and said gingerly, "One hundred fifty euro, OK?"

I'd expected a much higher demand. I saw the tariff card on the taxicab station, which indicated a ninety-euro fare, so the 66 percent premium he wanted for crossing the border with an undocumented alien wasn't exorbitant.

"How do we cross?"

"I have a friend at the border crossing. He'll let me pass through."

"And me?" I was confused.

"Yes, but you'll have to give him something too."

"How much?"

"Maybe fifty euros." He looked at my face for a reaction.

"Fine," I said. "When?"

"I'll call his home to ask his wife if he is working now."

He came back ten minutes later. "Yes, he is working today. We can go now."

"Wait, what do I do on the Serbian side? They will ask for a passport as well."

"I don't know," he said. "I don't know anyone there." I had to decide whether to top the list of the risks I was already taking to include the risk of being refused entry to Serbia and turned back to Bulgaria. It might not be to my cabbie friend's booth, and that meant trouble on both ends. I decided to take the risk.

I gave him two hundred twenty-five euros and said, "Let's go."

Within five minutes we were in line. There was just one open checkpoint out of four, with a big line of cars and trucks waiting. My cabbie didn't hesitate; he headed for the fourth line, which appeared closed. He must have known where his friend was waiting for us. We stopped near the booth. My cabbie waived his hand and conspicuously gave the officer his passport. They exchanged a few words in Bulgarian, and my cabbie turned his head over and said, "He wants one hundred euros."

This wasn't the time or the place to bargain. I slipped the money to my cabbie, who paid the officer. The officer returned the passport to my cabbie and waived his hand. We crossed to the Serbian side. My cabbie suggested I pretend to be sleeping. Not a good tactic, I thought. What, the border guards would forgo inspecting me just because I was asleep?

We stopped near the Serbian checkpoint. A woman officer asked for my passport. I spoke German. "I'm sorry, I don't have my passport. I'm German. It was stolen in Sofia—you know how it is there," I said and rolled up my eyes. "The guards on the Bulgarian side let me pass."

"Why didn't you get a new passport at the German Consulate in Sofia?"

"I tried, but they said it'd be a week. I must get back to Germany. My daughter is about to give birth to my first grandchild, and I must be there. Now when Europe is one union, passports don't mean much for European citizens crossing borders within Europe, do they?"

I knew very well that was true only within the boundaries of the Schengen area, when traveling between Austria, Belgium, Denmark, Finland, France, Germany, Greece, Italy, Luxembourg, the Netherlands, Portugal, Spain or Sweden. However, there is a border control when you travel to and from Ireland and Great Britain and any of the twelve countries that have joined the EU since 2004: Bulgaria, Cyprus, the Czech Republic, Estonia, Hungary, Malta, Latvia, Lithuania, Poland, Romania, Slovakia, and Slovenia.

"We're outside the Schengen boundaries, and I need to see ID." Her expression was stern.

I shook my head, waiting for her verdict. I hoped Serbian prisons served better food than Romanian prisons did.

"Where are you off to now, if you need to be in Germany?" she asked.

"To Dimitrovgrad."

"It's far from Germany."

"I tried to board a plane in Sofia, but with the security restrictions I couldn't do it without a passport. I took a cab to the border hoping to catch the train to Nis, but missed it. I hope to catch that train when it gets to Dimitrovgrad, because I was told it takes ninety minutes to examine all passengers, so I could just make it." I sat there very slightly panicked, waiting for her next move.

The unbelievable happened; she smiled and signaled my cabbie to drive on. "Good luck with your grandson," I heard her say before my cabbie put the pedal to the metal. In twenty minutes, we were in Dimitrovgrad. I bought a train ticket to Belgrade. I waited on the platform for the train. It arrived and justified Gordon's Rule no. 7: no matter where you stand on the platform, the train will never stop with its doors close to you. I arrived in Belgrade in the afternoon.

I called Eric and asked him to get the embassy in Belgrade to issue me a new passport. "This time as Dan Gordon," I requested. "I've had enough of the European police—I want to go home quietly."

In two days I was back home. I knew, though, that my first day in the office would be "interesting." I thought of the curse attributed by some to the Chinese: "May you live in interesting times." I knew there'd be some pointed questions, including the usual *I told you so* from Eric. I had prepared answers, because I knew that teamwork allowed Eric to blame others for his own mistakes.

The meeting was held at the federal building at 26 Federal Plaza. Attending were the "usual suspects," or should I say "the usual accusers," ready to attack me.

Eric started with the onslaught. "I hope you have a good explanation for all of this."

"All of what? I got you first-rate intelligence on who killed Badescu and Dhimitër. You did get it, didn't you?"

"Yes, we did. It's garbage." His face showed disgust.

"Garbage? What do you mean? My asset photocopied the police files."

"They are a forgery. Not even a good one."

"Forgery?" I said faintly, remembering I'd suspected foul play with the coroner's toxicology report in the file.

"I took and sent you what she gave me. I couldn't read the Romanian, and rushed to scan and e-mail the documents."

"What did you do with the originals?" asked Eric.

"I shredded them and threw the confetti into the fireplace at the hotel."

"Why?" asked Bob.

"Because there were some signs of odd behavior demonstrated by my asset, and I didn't want to hang around with documents she'd obtained unofficially."

"Are you sure that's the real reason?" asked Bob in a worried voice.

"Of course it was. What other reason could there be?"

"Not wanting us to discover they were forged," suggested Eric.

"You received them scanned!" I was growing impatient.

"True, but our lab couldn't check the paper and the ink to conclusively determine they were forgeries." Eric's voice was cold.

"Look, I was right to suspect my asset, because as I returned to her room after sending you the scanned documents, the Bulgarian police came in. It's amazing how efficient the police in Eastern Europe are sometimes—they always appear at the right time to arrest me," I added. I was already seething at their line of questioning. "And besides, what's that bull about print and paper. The 'originals' were just photocopies. You guys are becoming ridiculous."

"Dan, this is serious," said Bob, and his voice reflected it. "Then there's the fact that the documents you said you recovered from Badescu's home were also forged."

"Am I dreaming here or what?" I almost yelled, "*Said* I recovered. *Forged?* By whom?"

"We don't know," said Eric calmly. "Perhaps you can help us identify them."

That was too much. "Are you accusing me of forging these documents, or at least knowing they were forged?"

Bob shook his head. "We should be very careful before we accuse you, but see for yourself. There are some unanswered questions, and we were hoping you could help us with some answers."

"Let's start with the Badescu documents," I said, trying to remain calm, but I was pumped up. I thought of the first day's lecture to my class at the Mossad Academy.

Intelligence war is dark. There are no embedded journalists in every combat unit. There are no tanks, or missiles. The war is waged using minds, not munitions and weapons. Deceit is our best weapon. You deceive, you cheat, you lie, and you conspire. While working against your enemy, there are no morals, rules, or manners. The last man standing is the winner in conventional wars. But in intelligence wars you don't see the color of your enemy's eyes or come close enough to drive a dagger into his heart. Only time will tell if your side won the battle and can stand up tall. Intelligence wars are dark also because its heroes remain in the dark, sometimes forever, six feet under without a headstone. The wars are dark because they are dirty; you betray all vows and promises, except for those you made to your country. Since you're alone in the field, your colleagues and supervisors must provide you with full support. Make sure you don't lose it. If they think you strayed, you may find that the solid ground you thought you were standing on was actually a trap collapsing under your weight.

"Wait a minute," I said, trying to regain my composure and understand what had just happened. "Why do you think Badescu's documents were forged?"

"Our analysts reviewed their content. They stand in contrast to information we have. They seem like an attempt to change descriptions of events, after the fact," said Eric.

"You got the documents I retrieved from Badescu's house in the original, right?" I asked Eric.

He nodded.

"They were not scanned documents. Were the paper and the ink authentic?"

"Yes."

"Did you check for prints?"

"Yes. Badescu's and yours."

"How do you know they were Badescu's?"

"Dan!" Bob said. "Really!"

"OK, have you considered the idea that Badescu, the black-propaganda expert, would keep documents that were forged? Maybe they were the products of his work?"

"We thought of that, and even assumed it. Therefore we never even mentioned it to you when you brought them from Romania. But now, when you'd e-mailed us another set of forged documents, we started wondering how it was that these forgeries follow you," said Bob. "And again, I'm careful not to accuse you. I just wonder."

"What were the documents I retrieved from Badescu's home trying to convey? I haven't read them thoroughly."

"That some of the attacks on civilian targets attributed

to Hezbollah were in fact carried out by unaligned smaller terrorist groups. That Hezbollah's leadership was just as surprised at the attacks as anyone else was, but chose not to distance itself from the acts when they saw accolades coming from their supporters and allies. Since no one else claimed responsibility, they just kept quiet when the U.S. accused them."

"And what about the Dhimitër documents I've just sent?"

Eric exchanged looks with Bob and Benny. They nodded.

"We were tipped off, in a way," he said cryptically.

"Give me the whole story," I said. "After the harsh words and the insinuations, I've earned the right to know."

"NSA has intercepted a communication from Romania criticizing some officers in SRI for their conduct regarding the arrest and recruitment of Peter Wooten."

"I assumed it happened when Bob gave me the letter from SRI releasing me from the contract."

"Right, but now we have the response of an unidentified police officer who claimed that the U.S. tricked Romania by asserting that Wooten wasn't a CIA operative but an innocent researcher. To prove his argument, the officer said that they investigated all contacts that you, as Wooten, had while in Romania, and they identified Mikaela, the prison's psychologist. Under their investigation she confessed to developing inappropriate contacts with you, and that your interests during your contacts went beyond curiosity about who killed Badescu."

Bob and Benny sent a look at me that said, "Women again, Dan?" I didn't know whether it was envy or criticism, but I didn't ask.

"If you mean did I have an affair with her, the answer is definitely not. Did I ever consider that? Yes. She is attractive and pleasant, and if I had to get into her pants to obtain the information I needed, I would have done it, and enjoyed it at the same time. I could never tell whether she was interested in me personally, or because she thought I could be a conduit for a better life for her and her son. Did you find out what she said?"

"In a way," said Bob. "We only know she agreed to cooperate."

"Aha!" I exclaimed. "I felt her behavior was odd."

"No so fast, buddy," said Benny. "There's more to it. We're not sure who her contact in the police was, and who was making the decisions there. The process seems odd, I must say."

"What process?"

"Our sources tell me that they suspect the authenticity of this intercepted communication."

"My God," I said. "Is there no end? Another forgery? Is anyone in this industry ever telling the truth? What do they say when they want to eat Chinese food? 'Order pizza'?"

"I suggest we leave it at that," said Eric, "since there are unsolved questions that can't be answered now. I think we should look forward and see how we can resurrect Operation Pinocchio."

As I was about to leave, Benny said quietly in a conciliatory tone, "Don't mind their nasty comments. I think they were trying to test you, but they were just shooting in the dark. There was nothing suspicious about your conduct, as far as I could tell from our discussions before you returned."

"Thanks, Benny," I said. I knew he meant it.

"Remember what they taught us at the Mossad Academy? 'Friends you make after work; here you deal with people. Just make sure your conduct is not threatening them.'"

"Our old sages taught us, 'A wise man needs only a hint,'" I agreed.

Benny smiled. "The proverb continues," he said, "'and the fool needs a punch.'"

As I was entering the elevator, I couldn't avoid the harsh

conclusion. We had been fooled by Hezbollah. They knew at any given time that the documents I'd allowed to be stolen in Istanbul were faked. They knew, although at a later stage, that Badescu had betrayed them and worked for a foreign-intelligence service. Did they also identify which service? I didn't know. Maybe they'd gotten through only to Badescu's purported and faked French connection, but in order to unveil the true Mossad tentacles, Hezbollah had to get to Mahmoud, and I knew he'd been pulled out by Benny. Then they let black-propaganda documents remain in Badescu's apartment, intending them to be "found" and considered genuine.

The grim conclusion was that they were ahead of us. Not a huge compliment. Were they also connected to my escapade in Bulgaria? I had no idea, but the bottom line was that I was left with a bitter taste in my mouth. Hezbollah had the upper hand, I was stepped on by my supervisors, and a woman I liked was difficult to decipher and probably conspiring against me. What else could go wrong?

I went home to walk Snap, my golden retriever, who was always happy to see me, no conditions attached. As I was walking him, staring ahead but not absorbing the street scenes, I became less convinced that Hezbollah was ahead of us. Perhaps I'd been too quick to give them that much credit. Something was missing—it just didn't sit well in my mind. My little devil told me to keep on looking. I revisited my earlier conclusion. We hadn't lost to Hezbollah yet; we'd simply had a temporary setback. Was that conclusion achieved by deceit, this time self-deceiving? I'd have to work hard to refute that.

I decided to call Mikaela, all inhibitions removed. I had to demonstrate concern for her. I couldn't reveal that I knew she hadn't been truthful with me. Well, since nobody's listening, let's downgrade it to say bluntly that she might have deceived me. I conveniently ignored the fact that I had also been untruthful with her.

I caught her at home. She answered as if nothing had happened.

"Hi, Peter. Where are you?"

"I'm OK," I answered, pretending she'd asked how I was. "I'm glad to see you're at home. Are you safe?"

"Yes. I had some trouble." She paused. "It started as a big trouble with the Bulgarian police, but after you ran away, they left as well without returning, and I was back in Bucharest the next day. That was odd."

"Just like that?" I asked.

"Yes. They yelled at you to stop, but when you didn't, they returned to the room, called someone on their mobile phone, and just left. The assistant manager apologized and told me that he had never seen such behavior."

While I was digesting what Mikaela was telling me, I asked, "Did you have any trouble at home? I mean, because you took the documents?"

"No, not at all. Surprising isn't it?" She was so calm and nonchalant about it, again I was uncomfortable. Only yesterday I'd heard that she had been interrogated and agreed to cooperate. Was she lying to me again?

"What do you mean, nothing? Didn't anyone from the prison or the police question you?"

"No. I just went on with my life. How did you get away?"

"I managed." I was at a loss for words. The things Mikaela had just told me knocked me off balance. If she was telling me the truth, then what happened at the Sheraton Sofia with the Bulgarian police wasn't just odd, it was utterly bizarre. They just let her go? And when she went home, nobody from the police or SRI was waiting with an arrest warrant?

Think outside the box, I could almost hear my Mossad instructor tell me, as if I weren't always doing it.

"Mikaela, let me ask you a question that has bothered me. Who is your friend at the police?"

"Why do you want to know?"

"Is he the same person that told you that the body in prison wasn't Enver?"

"Yes."

"And he gave you a copy of the police file, the one you gave me?"

"The same person," she said.

"Did you tell him why you needed the documents?"

"Yes. In fact, he was very helpful and even suggested I meet you in person to give you the documents. He was sympathetic to your ordeal."

"Did you tell him about our meeting in Sofia?"

"Sure. He even instructed me how to be careful, because he didn't want the leakage of the documents to lead to him."

"Have you known him for long?"

"Just for a few months. He is a new addition to that department of the police, and I met him when he had some business at the prison."

"Do you trust him?"

"Peter, I trusted you. . . ." She didn't continue, but I got the idea.

"Can you give me his name?"

She paused to think. "Sorry, I can't."

"Why?"

She gave a deep breath. "I'm afraid."

There was no point in pressuring her at this time. I could find out his identity on my own. I spent the next day occupying my mind and considering several ways to solve the mystery. Why was I locked into the idea that Hezbollah was behind all of that? This was a typical "inside the box" thinking. I knew where I'd erred, when I thought of one of the most important courses in the Mossad Academy dedicated to decision making in times of uncertainty. The lecturer, a distinguished university professor, had no idea he was talking to a group of Mossad cadets. The lecture was given at his university campus, and he was told that we were management trainees of a major bank.

"How do you reach a decision?" he asked us right at the beginning. Without waiting for our answers he said,

> Let me give you the basic pitfalls of decision making. People tend to collect facts they are already familiar with, that support a direction they have already decided upon. Therefore, they ignore facts that could change their decision. When we need to decide, we tend to give greater weight to events that occurred recently and less weight to things of the past. Some people tend to stop searching for answers once they identify the first plausible solution, and tend to stick to decisions made earlier even if circumstances change. And they tend to see problems in a brighter light than they are, hoping they can manage somehow. People tend to beautify the past, thereby distorting what really happened. When a group makes a decision independently or assisted by outsiders, we have a tendency to adopt the ideas of people who support us. Conformity is a human trait in which people side with the majority, even when it's clear that the majority is wrong. If it turns out that the decision was erroneous, they won't be individually held responsible, because the others supported it as well. Decision makers tend to believe that they can control future events. They disregard potential problems and uncertainty.

When I traced back my steps and assumptions in this case, I realized I should have listened to the professor's advice and prevented embarrassments, not to mention prison time.

I called Eric. "I think we have been subjected to a very clever sting operation."

"I'm listening."

"Please communicate with SRI. I think there's a mole

inside the Romanian police." I gave him the details about Mikaela's police contact. "I think he is the one who concocted the entire affair. He fooled the Romanian Police, SRI, and us. We thought Hezbollah was behind it. I doubt it now. I gave them too much credit."

"Who's he working for, then?" asked Eric.

"I'm working on it," I said, although I had no concrete plan yet.

"I'll get back to you," he said and hung up.

A few days went by and nothing happened. Then Bob called.

"What did you tell Eric?"

"That I suspected that a mole inside the Romanian police caused all that havoc. Why do you ask?"

"Because Eric has been running around, ignoring my phone calls, and is locked up in meetings all day."

"I have no idea what is happening," I said, and it was the truth.

Three days later Eric called me. Without a hi or hello, he went straight to the point. He demanded to know how I'd reached my conclusion.

"What conclusion?"

"That the Romanian police have a mole."

"I already told you in our conversation a few days ago. Since everything in this case was either fake or deceitful, I thought maybe the whole matter was a deceit as well. Look at the last episode with the Bulgarian police. I suspected they were not real police when they didn't guard the hotel room's door, when they had no walkie-talkies, but cell phones, when they were confused when I refused to go with them. Whoever instructed them did a poor job. And Mikaela confirmed that they left her room immediately after I escaped. Real cops would have arrested her.

"The conclusion: I was the target of an attempted kidnapping, Mikaela was the decoy, probably unwittingly. I don't believe SRI would have disputed the Romanian government's assurance to USG that my arrest and recruitment attempt was the unauthorized initiative of low-level agents. Next, who knew I was meeting Mikaela in Sofia? Only Mikaela, and she confirmed telling it to her source at the police. Therefore, the only plausible conclusion is that someone in the Romanian police went rogue and has an independent agenda. We need to look him up for some answers."

"Dan, you may have stumbled onto something, and if you have, we should be concerned," he said.

When I heard the words *may have*, I knew my hunch had merit. I knew why Eric was so concerned. We in fact were launching a counterintelligence effort to defuse any achievement of FOE. The problem was that we thought FOE—forces of evil—were Hezbollah retaliating against us for planting Badescu. My Mossad training has taught me that engaging double agents and provocateurs in a case such as ours may serve our objective to identify who belongs to FOE, their intelligence personnel, gathering methods, and their information requirements, so that we can feed them with false info. However, now we had an FOE enigma.

Eric continued. "We have intel from a different source that unidentified Islamic groups were attempting to infiltrate into Eastern European security forces. After the fall of Communism, many police forces were refreshing their rank and file, retiring old-guard men, and recruiting new people who were not educated and trained by the Communist regimes. Naturally, some of the new recruits were bad. Your suspicion led to further discoveries, and we're working together with SRI to identify his network."

"So you know who the mole is?" I asked.

"Yes," he answered.

"Is he in custody?"

"No. The Romanians don't want to scare him off."

"He should have already been alerted when the fake Bulgarian cops came back empty-handed, and when Mikaela was left intact without any Romanian police questioning," I said.

"We're aware of that, so we're working on a limited-scale operation to get to his network. He must be getting orders from somewhere."

I knew Eric. He wouldn't be telling me these things unless he wanted something. I was playing it cool, waiting for him to ask. I didn't have to wait for long.

"I want you to revisit all your activities in this case to see if you faced, or were faced with, radical operatives, Islamic or otherwise. We focused on Hezbollah, but perhaps we should have looked at a broader spectrum."

Eric admitted to making a mistake? Hello! Was the world listening?

"Fine, I'll do that."

I decided to reread the brief pages that I had on international Islamic militant organizations beyond Hezbollah, which is mostly but not exclusively Shiite. The identity of all opposition members we encountered thus far led me to start looking for Islamic operatives. I didn't rule out, though, any other terrorist organization with different identities and goals. Reading the brief again I agreed with the writer's conclusion that many but not all of these terrorist organizations are radical Islamic groups that attract young Muslims to help them reach their goal—the establishment of Islamist states. Other goals are defeating "non-Islamic regimes" and conquering Jerusalem. They don't see terror and killing of civilians as verboten, because they believe that Christians and Jews want to destroy Islam.

What is common to these organizations is that they have no shared or umbrella leadership issuing orders to carry out attacks. At the top there are only spiritual leaders issuing guidelines that provide the ideology, leaving the various groups the freedom to decide how to reach these coveted goals. That separate cell structure makes the fight against them more difficult. From an intelligence point of view, it's a nightmare. One group knows nothing about the other, no matter how strongly you shake them.

It was time to move. First, I went back to my reports and composed a list of names of people I'd had any contact with since Bob had assigned me to Operation Pinocchio. There were 289 such names. It was hopeless. How could I reconstruct every conversation I'd had with these people and extract their ulterior motives from external substance? There had to be a better way, but Eric didn't suggest any. The best way would be to analyze whether any of the people I'd met or spoken with had tried to steer me in a direction I wasn't originally aiming at, or suggested I do something I didn't think of independently. Otherwise, every gas-station attendant I'd spoken with or any receptionist at a hotel I'd stayed in could be put on the suspect list, and that was ridiculous.

Next, I thought of a better way. Perhaps I should list the people most likely to be terror-group operatives or sympathizers. Anyone in Paraguay? In Sierra Leone? Ireland? Turkey? Israel? Romania? Bulgaria? Did that person have to be a Muslim? Definitely not; there were terror attacks against Israel and the Israelis by Germans, Japanese, and other nationals recruited by Palestinian organizations. My head was spinning. Hitting a virtual brick wall may well cause you the same headache a physical collision would, except that it leaves no marks on your forehead.

A few hours later, my list was narrowed down to eighty-seven names, but no light at the end of the tunnel was seen.

After three beers, six teas, and one splitting headache I narrowed down the list to eleven names. I called Eric and discussed my concerns. "The best way to identify the MT, or master terrorist, is to go back to all the locations I visited, meet the same people again under some pretext, and listen to them. Maybe this time, when we know what we're looking for, we can identify him."

Eric didn't trash my idea on the spot, and that was encouraging, although it didn't promise approval. "I'll get back to you," he said, being, as usual, noncommittal but not dismissive.

When I thought of the pros, I didn't consider the cons. There were risks involved, unless I had a plausible and believable legend. There was no need to speculate now, not until Eric made a decision.

A week later, Paul called to discuss my idea. As always, his questions were slow to be made, carefully crafted, but accurately pinpointed. He should have been an engineer or a scientist, not a top-notch executive in a spy agency. At the end of our conversation, I was left wondering whether Paul was satisfied with my answers.

I called Eric two days later. "I went through all my contacts and ruled out all of them. I won't tire you with the list, but I don't believe any contact I had in this matter is more suspect now than he was when I first met him. I'm less sure, though, regarding the Shammas family in Paraguay and Sierra Leone. However, they made no secret of their support for Hezbollah, so what was I looking for in my contacts with them?"

"What our analysts are saying is that the recent events in Romania and Bulgaria are uncharacteristic of Hezbollah or Iran."

"In what way?"

"The intricacy and convoluted manner of their conduct is different. However, Iran and Hezbollah could also be taking a new approach: continue with terrorism to spread their ideology and influence, but hide and distance themselves from any acts that look repugnant to the Western world. Let the media and the governments speculate and search in the dark."

"Kitman," I said.

"Precisely," he agreed.

The Kitman doctrine has been applied by Shiites for generations: deny your views and acts, but continue to fight for them. Usually, what they say is not an outright lie; you should listen very carefully to the exact language used. Generally, statements laced with Kitman are not straightforward; there are always several ways to interpret them. When Iran denies it develops nuclear weapons, it says it follows the rule of Islam, which opens the door to all sorts of interpretations. President Carter misunderstood that Kitman was being used by Shiite leaders before the Islamic revolution in Iran, when Shiite leaders told the U.S. ambassador that when an Islamic government was instated, the good relationship with the U.S. would continue. But they had no intention of continuing the type of relationship the U.S. had with the Shah—rather, they would commence with *their* version of relationship. The purpose of Kitman here was to keep the U.S. from helping the Shah. Even nowadays, Ayatollah Sistani cooperates with U.S. forces in Iraq, helping the U.S. maintain control of the country. And when that is achieved, "*Allah Yerachamo*— God have mercy on the Sunnis, and also on the U.S., if it stands in our way."

"How many were there?" asked Eric.

"In Paraguay, there were Jacques Shammas, his wife, and two sons, Pierre and Abdul."

"Forget about the women. In that society I don't believe they play a leading role in such matters."

"In Sierra Leone, there were the two Shammas brothers: Ramzi, the older brother, and Abed. I also had limited social contact with Anthon, Ramzi's son."

"That leaves six on our list," said Eric. "If you had to suspect one of them right now, who'd you put on the top of the list?"

"Abed Shammas in Sierra Leone."

"Why?"

"I don't know—just a hunch, but don't count on it."

"I'll call you later. Send me a memo on these six," he said.

The next move was a meeting, joined by Erin. She was suntanned and all smiles. "What happened?" I asked. "Your expected marriage to your fiancé didn't work out, and you took a sunny vacation to get over him?" I joked.

"You guessed it right," she laughed, but when Eric, Paul, and Bob joined us, I thought I should have bought a lottery ticket, because my guess was accurate.

"The best way to solve that little, or big, mystery," said Eric, "is to return to the lion's den."

"Burst into their operation in Sierra Leone?" I asked.

"No. We'd like to sneak in, but not physically."

Following the briefing and a construction of a new plausible legend, I called Ramzi Shammas. After the necessary exchange of greetings, I asked how the diamond-prospecting project was progressing.

This was of course a verification process. We knew exactly what was going on, since the company selected by Ramzi to carry out the exploration had sent a team of twenty-four men to Sierra Leone, two of whom were CIA outside contractors. They were real engineers and diamond experts, but they also had a "side agreement" with the CIA to report on the Shammas brothers' activities. The comments Ramzi made were similar to the reports Langley had received from its men. CIA had also received indications that the Shammas brothers' contacts with Hezbollah were sporadic, always initiated by a Hezbollah operative who came to solicit money contributions.

"How's Anthon doing? I was sorry to hear that the relationship with Erin didn't work out. They seemed so happy together."

"I was also disappointed," said Ramzi. "But he is well."

"And how's your brother Abed?"

"He's very busy, and travels nonstop. He decided to develop other business areas, which I didn't join."

"Oh, in what areas?"

"International trade, with Eastern Europe. Their emerging economies after the collapse of Communism opened up many opportunities."

"That's very interesting," I said, hoping Ramzi would elaborate.

"Are you coming to visit us any time soon?" He masked his evasiveness with a polite talk.

"I wish I could. But since the passing away of my wife I have immersed myself in my work, and that leaves me with little spare time."

"I was sorry to hear about your wife. Anthon told us. Are you back in Dublin?"

"No, nothing was left for me there, with my wife dead and my children away. And with my work in remote areas of the world, I became homeless, so to speak. Any place I work becomes home until I move on. Come to think of it, how can I make contact with Abed? I've recently met an oil trader who was dealing in Russian and Romanian oil. I told him about my recent work in Sierra Leone, and he said he was interested in talking business with smart people with connections in the Sierra Leone Petroleum Refining Company. I think you and Abed fit the description."

"Thank you very much," said Ramzi, "but you should discuss these matters with Abed."

"I'd be glad to. Can I talk to him?"

"He's currently out of the country. Give me a number for him to call."

I gave him the CIA special number in the call center somewhere in the Midwest.

Several days later, Abed called. A conversation with him was never a pleasant matter.

"Hello, Mr. Mitchell," he said in a coarse voice.

"You can call me Patrick," I said, trying to make nice.

"*D'accord* . . . Patrick. I hear you have good business for me," he said in his French-Arab-accent mix.

"I don't know if it's good or bad," responded the cautious attorney in me, and proceeded to tell him about the business opportunity Langley had very cleverly designed. "The name of the individual is Helmut von Ditka, a German businessman. Since both of you travel extensively—"

Abed interrupted me and asked in a suspicious voice, "How do you know that I travel extensively?"

I ignored the hostility. "Ramzi told me. Anyway, let me have your availability dates, and I will try to coordinate a meeting between you two."

"Why? Just give me his number, I'll call him directly." Clearly, Abed had never graduated or even attended charm school.

"Sure," I said, happy that I wouldn't have to deal with him. I gave him yet another number of the CIA call center in the Midwest, but with a German country code. "Please wait a few more days; he is still in South America, where I met him. I think he said he'd be returning to Germany within the next few days." Meaning, "Let me have sufficient time to report this conversation and ask them to be ready to take your call."

CHAPTER FIFTEEN

Two weeks later, Eric notified us that contact had been established between Abed and a CIA operative. Eric didn't mention his name (need-to-know basis again?) but did say, "The first meeting went well, and the Agency is following up on the various leads developed during it and the subsequent communications." However, Eric instructed us to continue with our efforts of checking back all suspects on our respective lists.

While I was working on an approach plan to Jacques Shammas in Ciudad del Este, Paraguay, there were developments regarding Erin. What transpired during the coming days was the fruit of our joint innovative minds, as approved by Langley.

Dear Anthon,

I don't know how to start. I'm so ashamed and confused. I hope you're not mad at me and may even think of me at least half as much as I think of you. I made a terrible mistake. I know you're good-hearted and therefore I hope and pray that you will forgive me. When I returned to Ireland to care for my mother, I was worried and helpless. I had no one to turn to when I needed to calm down from my stress, and Owen, who was my boyfriend before I met you, was very kind and understanding. That continued also after my mother passed away. I made myself believe that he had changed, and that the reasons I'd left him wouldn't return. Therefore, I agreed to his marriage proposal and even followed him to London.

There, the old problems reemerged. He was a heavy drinker, spending his nights in bars with his drinking buddies. He used to beat me up and curse me. I realized I'd made a big mistake and left him. He begged me to return, but I told him I was through with him forever. I went on a short vacation to a sunny resort in southern Spain and couldn't stop thinking of you and how I much I missed you. Every dark-haired man reminded me of you, and that made me cry. If you think we can get together again and forget the immediate past, pretending it was just a nightmare, I will be here for you. I found a job in London, and I hope you will hold my hand again.

Love, Erin

A response came a day later.

Dear Erin,
I've just returned from a business trip and saw your e-mail. I'm glad that you realize that you made a mistake. At this time, I don't know how I feel or what to do. Give me a few days to think it over.
Yours, Anthon

"He is playing it cool," said Erin. "The proud macho won't just jump when I say hop. Let's give him more time. It will allow me another chance to get down on my knees and beg. He'll like that."

Dear Anthon,
I'm so glad you answered me, and that shows that at least you're not as angry with me as I feared you would be. We all make mistakes, and I'd be the first to admit that I made a huge mistake. I was so stupid not to compare you and Owen. You're a man of the world with manners and education. He is just a guy. You're a gentleman, and he is self-centered. You're kind, and he was crude. Need I say more? Need I spell out the words I love you? I'll whisper them in your ear when we meet, if you promise to hug me and never let me go.
With all my love, Erin

"If he won't fall for it, then he has a heart made of stone," said Bob, touching his mustache.

"He does," said Erin. "The guy is pretty tough."

"To me it sounds cheesy, like a two-bit screenplay that even a soap-opera director would reject," said Paul.

Would Anthon fall for it? I also was doubtful.

However, the response that came removed some but not all doubts. Too much high-intensity sweetener wasn't a problem for Anthon.

Dear Erin,
I thought it over. You were very direct and sincere in your
e-mails. That has surprised me, because in my society,
women don't open their hearts to men who are not their
husbands, but I know you meant well. I'm still not sure
what or how I feel. I'll be in London next week regarding
a business matter. If you wish, we can meet and talk.
Yours, Anthon

"We need to make arrangements," said Eric when he saw Anthon's response. "Erin, pack your bags."

Eric said nothing about me joining the trip to London, and I decided not to ask. A message that came in later on in the afternoon cleared the fog. I had to report to Global Response Center in London. My ticket and my Patrick Sean Mitchell passport and other documents arrived by messenger hours later. I flew to London and checked into the Cumberland Hotel opposite Marble Arch in West London, with its endlessly long corridors and colorful but stale carpets.

That evening we had a meeting in Erin's room to plan ahead. Eric, Paul, Bob, and another woman I didn't recognize rehearsed various possible scenarios with Erin. The woman, a blonde of indeterminate age, was classically and meticulously dressed, not forgetting the two-strand pearl necklace. As she saw my puzzled look, she introduced herself as Sheila Hanson. Sheila went over the Anthon meeting with Erin, suggesting body language and things to say.

"Don't act like you're programmed. Show Anthon that you have matured after your mother's death, and therefore the decisions you're making now are not capricious but are well thought out. Your e-mails sent him the core message, so there is no need to repeat what they said. We don't want to make you look pathetic."

Eric, who had been silent throughout the session, waited for Sheila to complete her instruction, and gave us the master plan, including Erin's legend for her new job.

* * *

Two days passed, and Anthon announced he'd be coming to London on the following day for a twelve-hour visit. "I can't stay longer," he wrote in his e-mail. "Meet me at Galvin at Windows on the twenty-eighth floor of the London Hilton on Park Lane, opposite Hyde Park."

"He's got class," said Sheila.

"No," said Erin. "Just money."

Eric returned with details. "Erin, wait for him at a table in the raised central area of the restaurant. That will ease some of the background noise from our mike."

"What do I do if he asks me to go to his room? That's definitely outside my job description. In Freetown I was never alone in the house with him," she said.

"If he asks, you go," said Eric. "If things become inappropriate, avoid him, for whatever reason. Alert us, if you find it necessary." He was impatient, which I thought wasn't appropriate under the circumstances. Eric continued, "The security backup will be in the next room on the other side. We'll wire his room."

It was a foggy Tuesday with limited visibility and spells of rain, as any season in London can be. Erin was dressed modestly. CIA did a nice job choosing her clothing. She looked like a country girl coming to town wearing her best dress, one that was a sensation out there in the countryside, but looked dowdy in the London of the rich. Thirty minutes ahead of time, Erin was sitting in Galvin at Windows checking the mike's reception, talking to us while holding her handkerchief to her mouth.

"We hear you loud and clear," said Eric.

Three floors below, with magnificent light emerging through the low clouds, we stretched out on the couches in an extended suite turned into a war room. Other than Eric, Paul, Bob, Sheila, and me, there were four technicians working on various electronics and computer monitors. One monitor showed the entrance to the twenty-eighth floor, another one was placed to show the hotel's main entrance, and a third video camera showed Erin from the back, sitting at the restaurant. A photo was taped on the top of a computer monitor.

"That's Anthon," said Eric when he saw Bob looking at the photo. The portrait taken by a professional showed Anthon looking much older than his midthirties age, maybe because of the sleeked dark and oily hair and narrowly trimmed mustache.

"How did you mount these cameras?" I asked the technician in appreciation, recognizing the hotel had twenty-four-hour traffic and heavy security.

"They are wireless, tiny, and are either pinned to a soft surface like a curtain, or with adhesive tape. None of them is bigger than a pinhead. It'd take an expert to spot them, provided he had the eyes of an owl in the dark or of an eagle in daytime."

"Here he is," said Bob as we watched the video on the monitor. Anthon, dressed in a smart, dark suit, walked toward Erin's table escorted by a waiter. He sat down and she bent over to kiss him, but he just offered his hand for a handshake.

"He's angry, or playing angry," said Sheila, recognizing his body language while taking notes. There was the usual exchange of greetings. We couldn't see Erin's face. It was more important to see Anthon's. After chatting for ten minutes and ordering drinks and appetizers, they continued talking about nothing. Erin was natural, trying to make Anthon comfortable. His body language broadcast that he wasn't relaxed. He glanced at his watch twice or three times, and his eyes shifted. Erin must have felt it and delayed moving the conversation toward their relationship.

What's the purpose of this? I asked myself, although Eric's briefing was clear—that we needed to revisit all contacts to identify who'd been instructing the mole in the Romanian police. That was crucial. Unless we solved the Badescu assassination mystery, we couldn't plant another operative in Hezbollah without risking that he and the operation would meet the same fate.

However, what were the chances that Anthon would invite Erin to return to Freetown or reveal to her anything about his or his family's affiliation to Islamic groups, when he'd never told her anything while she was living at his house and he was proposing marriage? Nonetheless, that meeting had to be arranged, I was certain of that, but only to keep that channel open, because nothing of substance would come to light during the dinner, and Erin wasn't going to return to Sierra Leone and face a likely marriage to Anthon.

On occasions, my little devil posed a question to me that I couldn't answer.

What if the Shammas brothers suspected Erin or me? Was there an explanation for the shooting incident in Sierra Leone's diamond region when I'd traveled there with Abed? Was he the intended target, or me? Was it anything more than attempted robbery or a tribal turf war? The problem with our profession is that in too many instances you never find out answers to important questions.

"He isn't acting naturally," said Sheila as she was watching the conversation Anthon and Erin were making about nothing.

"Something is going on, because nothing is going on in the conversation," agreed Paul. Eric relayed a short order to the security backup team. "Alert our men at the nearby table."

"What do you suspect?" asked Bob.

"To be on the safe side," said Eric. "His reactions could be dangerous, even though they are in a public area."

At a slow pace, Erin was diverting the conversation to personal matters. She told him about her devastation during her mom's death, and the difficult beginning in London, never mentioning the ex-fiancé. "Men don't like to hear about their spouse's ex, and Middle Eastern men in particular," Sheila had instructed. *Why only men?* I asked myself, remembering my meetings with my close friends, the world-famous medical professor and his wife of thirty years. Whenever he'd mentioned any of the many girlfriends he had dated before meeting and marrying her, his wife would bristle, referring to her as "Oh, that whore . . ."

"What about you?" we heard Erin ask.

"I'm fine."

"A new girlfriend?" she ventured.

"No. I'm too busy. I'm developing business out of the country."

"Doing what?"

"Import-export of hardware. I'm also a partner in an employment agency in Paris. We supply manpower to projects around the globe."

"That's exciting," said Erin. "Does it bring you to Paris frequently?"

"Yes, sort of . . . once a month or so."

"That's cool," said Erin. "We could see each other. London is not too far."

Sheila bit her lip. "*Cool* is an American expression, not Irish or English. Let's hope he is not that sophisticated to pay attention to linguistic nuances."

"What's the name of the Paris company?" Erin asked.

"Why do you want to know?"

"Oh, to look you up, maybe call you, if it's all right with you."

"World Jobs & Work."

The conversation continued over dinner, but it was clear that there wasn't going to be a renewal of the relationship, from Anthon's perspective. He was stiff, uneasy, but ultimately cordial. They finished dinner and parted with a handshake.

Eric spoke to Erin's earpiece when she was outside the restaurant. "Go down to the hotel's main entrance and take a black cab driven by a cabbie with a black barrette and yellow scarf. We'll meet you at the safe house." Eric didn't want to risk meeting Erin at the hotel, fearing she was being shadowed.

"Wait," I almost yelled at the technician before he turned off the video at the restaurant. "Look at that!"

Anthon signaled with his hand to two men who were sitting nearby. One was heavyset and very tall, approximately six feet six, with dark hair and eyeglasses, and the other was dark and medium built. Both were in their late twenties and wore dark suits. They got up from their table and headed to the exit.

"Unit One," barked Eric into the mouthpiece. "Two men were just sent by target, could be hostile, alert post at point R and double escort to Princess."

Communications gear and phones started buzzing. Video monitors were recording the sudden activity.

"Princess, do you read?" Eric was holding a mike hooked to the computer. There was no response. "Damn it," said Eric. "Erin may still be in the elevator—there's no reception."

Seconds later, we heard Erin's voice. "King, this is Princess."

"Where are you?

"In the elevator."

"Get off before you get to the lobby, I'm sending Unit One, once you tell me where you are."

"Roger," said Erin in a voice that reflected she was trained well and didn't waste time asking questions.

She came back on. "Second floor."

"Unit One on the way. Stay put."

"Roger."

Eric rushed out the door. We stayed behind watching the drama, but mostly listening in, where no video cameras were available.

In the monitor covering the hotel's entrance, we saw

Anthon's men looking around. When they couldn't see Erin, they reentered the hotel.

"King, this is Duke. The two have just reentered the lobby. Suggest you don't use main entrance," I said, taking the initiative.

"Roger," came Eric's voice.

"What the hell is going on?" asked Bob.

"I think Anthon suspected Erin and sent his men after her to see who she communicated with," I said. I was uncomfortable with the turn of events. Was Anthon a spurned boyfriend who wanted to know what his girlfriend was doing? But he had been the one to reject Erin's advances. . . . So why the commotion?

Five minutes later, we saw on the monitor how Anthon was emerging from the lobby to the hotel's entrance, looking around and returning to the lobby. I reported it to Eric.

I heard Eric's voice. "Unit Two, pick up target, but stay at a distance. I need to see what he's up to."

"Roger." I heard the voice of an unidentified man.

Eric returned to the suite-turned-control center. "There's no doubt we averted something," he said. "I don't know what. Anthon was up to something."

"From a docile man in love, he turned into an avenger, just because she left him for another man?" asked Paul.

"I think there's more to it. It's not personal," said Sheila.

"That means he suspects her professionally. Why?" asked Paul.

"We'll find out." Eric called Langley and gave out the name of Anthon's employment agency in Paris. "I need background ASAP."

"Where is Erin?" asked Bob.

"In her room," said Eric. "I didn't think it'd be prudent to sneak her out."

"What's next?" asked Paul.

"We wait for the dust to settle. I want to know what's going on here."

We just sat and waited. Eric called Erin occasionally to check on her.

"I don't need babysitting," we heard Erin say. "I have guys from Unit One here. That's more than enough."

An hour later, an encrypted message came from Langley. Eric read it quickly and passed it to us to read.

The message was concise.

> *World Jobs & Work is a French company incorporated in 2002. Both founders were known extremist Islamic operatives who were believed to be killed in Afghanistan. Others from the group took over. The company maintains a legitimate employment-agency business; however, there's growing evidence that under the guise of offering employment, the company recruits young Islamic men and sends them to Iraq and Afghanistan. We have asked the French internal security service, DST— Direction de la Surveillance du Territoire—to give us a broader report.*

Eric mailed back, "We need names of current owners and directors. Please expedite."

When no response came for two more hours, we called it a day and canceled the meeting planned at the safe house.

My bedside phone rang; it was Eric. I looked at the clock radio. It was three thirty-five A.M. It'd better be urgent.

"Erin disappeared from her room. We're meeting in her room, twenty-five eleven," Eric said and hung up.

I tried to understand the meaning of this. Hadn't Erin stayed in her room protected by our security detail? I jumped into a pair of jeans and a sweatshirt and rushed to the twenty-fifth floor. Bob and Paul arrived at the same time. Eric was on the phone. A clean-shaven, twentysomething man with a crew cut walked aimlessly around the room, looking embarrassed. A .38 was tucked in his waistband.

The atmosphere was strained. Eric had a serious look on his face. He hung up the phone.

"What happened?' asked Paul as we walked in.

"This is Cristian of Unit Two," said Eric, pointing at the young man. "He just called, telling me that Erin has disappeared. Cristian?" Eric signaled for him to continue.

"I was sleeping here." Cristian pointed to a brown couch in the corner. "I woke up with a terrible headache and went to the bathroom for a drink of water. When I returned I saw Erin's bed empty. She was gone. There were no signs of forced entry to the room."

"Was she in her bed when you got up to go to the bathroom?"

"I don't know. I didn't pay attention."

"Any thoughts?" asked Eric, looking at us.

"Cristian, did she say anything before you fell asleep?" asked Bob.

"No, nothing. We watched college sports on TV, and I think I fell asleep before she did."

"What was she wearing?"

"Last time I saw her she was wearing a white T-shirt and loose cotton lounge pants, pajamalike."

"Do you suspect foul play?" asked Bob.

"What else is there? Erin is a well-trained operative and would never do anything irresponsible."

"Cristian," said Bob suddenly. "Do you suffer from headaches frequently?"

"No, never. I felt dizzy and had a strange, sweet taste in my mouth. In fact, my tongue is sort of numb."

Eric approached him and sniffed Cristian's mouth. "Chloroform," he announced. Eric moved a chair and climbed to get closer to the air-conditioning air duct. "It didn't come from here," he said as he stepped down from the chair. He went to the doorstep and kneeled to smell the carpet. "Chloroform," he said again getting up. "It was forced into the room underneath the door, putting you to sleep. Then they entered the room and snatched Erin."

Eric dialed a number and alerted MI5, Britain's internal-security agency. Then he called GRC, or Global Response Center, the CIA watch center, which monitors worldwide operations, and finally the duty officer at the embassy, who transferred the call to the CIA station chief. Ten or fifteen minutes later, four plainclothesmen came over to the room. Eric gave them just the bare basics of the case, describing Erin as a dual Irish-American citizen. I realized that I didn't even know her real name.

The MI5 agents were discreet enough not to ask too many embarrassing questions. They didn't even ask Eric what his connection was to Erin or who the others in the room were. It appeared that the resident CIA chief of station at the embassy had already briefed them.

"Do you think it's a kidnapping for ransom?" asked an MI5 agent who seemed to be out of the loop.

Eric shook his head. "No. I think they want to question her on her relationship with her ex-boyfriend. She had dinner with him last night at the hotel's restaurant, and when she left, the boyfriend sent his men after her."

They didn't ask the obvious question—how Eric knew that.

When the MI5 agents left, Eric suggested we return to our operations room down the corridor. Two technicians were reinstalling the equipment.

"Check the feed," said Eric to a red-haired technician. He hooked up a few cables, and we saw on the monitor the restaurant being cleaned. "It kept recording for about three hours after Erin left," the technician said.

"That's great," said Paul. "Now run the video feed of the hotel's entrance."

"Give me a time frame," said the technician. "The traffic there is heavy."

Eric looked at his wristwatch and said, "Cristian called

me at approximately three twenty A.M., so look from midnight through three twenty A.M., and if we can't get any activity regarding Erin, then we'll go back in time. Anyway, at that late hour there wasn't much traffic, and you can fast-forward when no people are seen."

While the technician was working on the video feed, Paul asked, "How can you be sure they took her out of the hotel—and if they did, why through the main lobby where so many people could suspect irregular conduct?"

"I'm not sure at all," said Eric, "but we must cover all bases."

"We have to assume a worst-case scenario," I said. "We must regard this as a professional, not relationship-based, kidnapping."

"Hold your horses," said Paul. "Why the assumption that Anthon was involved?"

"Because the circumstances support it. We saw how he signaled his men at the restaurant to follow Erin. The proximity of time from their meeting to Erin's disappearance, the video showing his men, and later him, popping out of the main entrance of the hotel looking for something, when they couldn't find Erin. That could be enough even in a criminal case, under certain circumstances, and here we're not at a trial." I was being a lawyer again.

"Even if it was Anthon," said Paul defiantly, "how can we be sure that he didn't abduct her on a personal basis, as men in certain societies do?"

"Why should he do that?" asked Bob. "She practically threw herself at him, and he didn't even bend to pick her up."

"I think Dan is right," said Eric. "Worst-case-scenario thinking is helpful here, particularly when from Erin's perspective she is a victim, no matter what the motive was for her kidnapping. If she talks, there could be some serious consequences, beyond her personal safety."

I knew what Eric meant. The question wasn't *whether*

Erin talked, but *when*. Everybody talks in the end, particularly when your captors are not subject to hearings before Senate committees, to an independent counsel, or to investigative panels, which judge your conduct and ethics after the fact as if you were in a sterile lab, when in fact you were on a soiled battlefield fighting a lawless enemy.

Just sitting there waiting for things to happen wasn't my idea of saving Erin or running a rescue operation.

The redheaded technician interrupted our conversation. "I ran the video feed of the main entrance since the time that Anthon arrived at the hotel. I didn't see anything suspicious. I never saw Erin, and not even containers big enough to hold her."

"That means she's still in the hotel, or she was hauled out through a back entrance," concluded Eric.

"Call hotel security," I suggested. "They must have security cameras on each floor."

Eric gave me that look reserved for people telling him how to do his job, but putting pride aside, he called the MI5 detail that had been there earlier. They could get it from the hotel in no time. Ten minutes later, we met the MI5 lead agent, a stocky man you wouldn't start a fistfight with.

"I'm Tim Harrington," he said. He told us that the hotel's security officer was waiting for us in the hotel's control room. When we entered, the security officer told his man to run the video recording of our floor first.

"There it is," said Tim. We saw the two men we'd seen earlier at the restaurant walk toward Erin's room, looking around to see whether anyone was watching. The tall man pulled out a tube with a small plastic pump at the end and connected it to a thin pipe, which he inserted underneath her door, squeezing the pump. They were talking to each other, but the video recording had no sound. They retreated to a nearby service room, only to return eight minutes later, wearing masks on their faces. They inserted a key card into the door slot and pushed open the door.

"How the hell did they get a key?" I asked the security officer, who was dumbfounded at the sight. "And how did they know where Erin's room was to kidnap her? It seems like they had someone on the inside."

He didn't respond. He didn't explain how two men wearing masks could roam in the hallway without interruption. But there was no point in asking again. I saw the answer. I measured with my watch the frequency with which the displays on the multiple video monitors changed. There was a lull of eight minutes. Anthon's men must have been told how long they could be on the floor without being spotted. On a rewind we could see the events as they occurred, because the video cameras were recording nonstop. But someone must have tipped Anthon off on how frequently the images were displayed on the monitors in the control room.

Two minutes later, we saw the two men dragging Erin toward the elevator, an arm around each man's neck.

"They were trying to make it look like Erin was drunk, if they encountered anyone in the hallway," said Tim.

They stopped near the elevator door and pressed the button.

"Hold it there," said Eric. "Zoom in. I want to see if they pressed the up or down button."

"It's the up button," said the technician, after zooming in.

"Can the elevator command log show on which floor the elevator stopped?" asked Eric.

The security officer shook his head.

"How many floors are there above Erin's floor?"

"Three."

"OK, let's get the video feed for each of the upper floors."

Five minutes later, the technician raised his hand, keeping his eyes on the monitor. "Here they are, on the twenty-sixth floor." We saw the men walking Erin, who appeared semiconscious, toward a room at the end of the corridor.

"That's a suite," said the security officer.

"Keep the video running," said Eric. "I want to make sure they didn't remove her from that room."

The technician confirmed it. "No movements identified since they entered."

Tim radioed his coagents, and four men joined us in the control room. It was becoming cramped.

"We need police assistance to break in," said Tim, looking at Eric for approval.

"Not just yet," said Eric. "I want to make sure first that she is safe and that they have no weapons or explosives."

"All right, but my instructions are to alert the police regardless," Tim said, and talked to his men. A few minutes later we saw on the monitor how a plainclothesman was slowly approaching the suite's door, kneeling down, and unscrewing a metal plate. At a snail's pace, he then inserted a flexible plastic tube through the air inlet of the air-conditioning shaft next to the door frame. He held his hand to his ear, probably listening to communications over his earpiece, and pushed the tube in deeper. He turned his head to the end of the corridor, signaling with his hand to ask whether the tube was in position.

"This is a hi-tech camera using fiber optics. It'll give us video and audio," said Tim.

Immediately afterward we saw on a monitor the inside of the suite. Erin was tied to a chair with her hands behind her back, her mouth strapped with duct tape, her head tilted to the side. She appeared to be still under the influence of a sedative. The two men were speaking French. The security officer was translating. I decided not to intervene, although he made several translation errors, thinking I'd correct him only if the errors were seriously misleading.

"When will the bitch wake up?" asked the tall man.

"How the fuck should I know?" answered the other man. "You were the one to pump her with this shit. We're lucky it didn't hit us when we came into her room. Why did you give her that extra dose?"

"I thought she was about to wake up."

"Do you know who the other guy in her room was?"

"I don't know. He wasn't a boyfriend or something."

"How do you know?"

"When you have such a hot woman sleeping in your room, you don't sleep on the couch, you idiot."

They went on talking and smoking, but nothing of substance was said, except when the tall man used his cell phone.

"Yes, boss, I'll do that," he said after listening for about a minute, and hung up.

"Do you see any guns or weapons?" asked Eric.

Tim shook his head. "But they could be carrying." He turned to Eric. "I don't think we should wait for Erin to wake up."

"What do you suggest?" asked Eric.

"Tim, I see that your men are staking out the door from all sides of the hallway. I think we should call the room and demand their surrender and Erin's release," said Paul.

"That would turn the matter into a hostage situation," I said.

"Isn't it what we have now?" asked Paul.

"No," Tim retorted. "Because they don't seem to be pressed for time, and that keeps Erin out of imminent danger. However, if we call them, tension will rise and they'll use her as a hostage to gain safe departure." I looked at Eric, waiting for his input.

"I think Tim is right, for now. Let's wait for their next move," said Eric. "They aren't going anywhere. If we break in when Erin is still under the influence, she couldn't be cooperative, and that could endanger her."

Eric turned to the technician. "OK, once we have Erin's video in place, locate the boyfriend, Anthon Shammas. Run the feed on the restaurant's floor."

"Starting what time?" asked the technician.

I turned to the hotel's security officer. "Please call the restaurant to see at what time Anthon paid his bill. That should give us a time frame."

"They're closed now. I'll call reception—the information should already be on the computer," he replied.

A minute later, he gave us the answer. "Mr. Shammas paid the bill at nine forty-three P.M."

"Charged to a room?" I asked in hope.

"No," he answered. "In cash."

"See if he is a hotel guest," asked Eric.

"And the name is Mr. Anthon Shammas?" repeated the security officer, trying to make sure.

Eric nodded.

The security officer got off the phone. "No guest by that name. Any other names?"

"Can you check by nationality?" asked Paul.

"Yes."

"Try first all guests from Sierra Leone."

A minute later he said, "Sorry, no guests from that country."

"How about Lebanon?"

A few minutes later the answer came. "Seven guests. Three are women's names, one child under twelve, and three men."

"And their ages?"

"We don't know. We don't register our guests' ages, only if they are children that get a reduced rate."

He gave Eric the names of the three Lebanese men. Eric jotted them on a piece of paper and gave it to Paul, who went to the room's corner and read out the names to someone he called with his mobile phone.

"Let's find Anthon on the video, then," said Eric and directed the technician. A few minutes later, we saw on the monitor a full-body view of Anthon arriving at the restaurant. He was by himself. "Freeze it," said Eric when he saw a good shot of Anthon's face. "Can you print it?"

"Not here," said the technician. "But I can e-mail it to main security, and they can print it."

"Please do that," said Eric in a rare burst of politeness. "Ask them to print thirty copies."

The eight-by-fourteen photos were brought to the control room and given to the security officer, who handed them to Eric. Eric gave the technician a piece of paper with an e-mail address. "Please e-mail the photo to this address," he said.

"Done," the technician said a minute later.

Eric turned to the security officer. "Distribute the photos among security, reception, bellmen, and chambermaids, and ask if anyone has seen this person."

The security officer signaled one of his men and gave him the photos.

"Now, let's find out where Anthon went after he left the restaurant," said Eric. I liked the way he was prioritizing his orders. First locating Erin, and when he made sure she was alive, he turned to look for all others involved.

I glanced at my watch. It was four fifteen A.M. I looked at the monitor. Both men were just sitting in the room, waiting. Erin was still asleep.

"Here he is," said the technician, pointing at the monitor. We saw Anthon exit the elevator at the main lobby, walking toward the hotel's exit and entering a black car. The clock on the video feed showed nine fifty-one P.M.

"Can you get the license-plate number?" asked Eric.

"I'll try," the technician said.

A uniformed police officer came into the control room and received a quick briefing from Tim and Eric. There weren't any developments to report, though.

"Soon they'll be hungry," I said as I felt my stomach move, reminding me I had skipped dinner last night.

"If they order room service, it'll be our best bet yet," said Eric. "It doesn't seem they have realized that we know where they are with Erin. Maybe their alert level won't be high."

"I have a partial plate number," said the technician. "Just the first two letters and a number: XJ5. The rest I couldn't identify."

Tim radioed the partial numbers. "That's three out of the usual seven, but we'll try to match with the car model and color." He turned to the technician. "Please mail us the frame. Our lab might be more successful."

"Hold on," said the technician. "We have a movement." He pointed at the monitor showing the room where Erin was being held. Erin was raising her head, and dropped it again, mumbling. We couldn't comprehend it, as the audio wasn't clear. The tall man went to the bathroom and brought her a glass of water. He removed the duct tape from her mouth and said, "*Tais-toi*, shut up. Don't you dare make any noise!" Erin nodded and drank from the cup.

"Where am I?" she asked looking around. "And who are you?" Then, I saw an expression on Erin's face that showed that she knew who her captor was. She was a trained professional, though, and chose to conceal it.

"Shut up!" ordered the tall man. "I'll ask the questions, and you'll answer. Do you understand?" He spoke with a combination of Arab and French accents.

Erin answered faintly, "I understand."

"What's your name?" he asked.

"Erin Beth Mitchell."

"You're lying," he said, bringing his face close to hers. "You're a liar!"

Erin didn't answer and took a deep breath. "Is it money you want? I can ask my family to send you some, but we're not rich."

"What's your name?" he asked again.

"I've just told you, I'm Erin Beth Mitchell. Can you please tell me what this is all about?"

"Tell me how you met Monsieur Anthon Shammas."

"Did he send you? Is that it?" she asked. "I met him on the Internet. I answered his posting and we exchanged e-mails until I met him in Freetown."

"What was the name of the Web site where you met?"

"LebaneseDate."

"Are you Lebanese?"

"No, I'm Irish."

"So how come you ended up on that site?"

"My sister told me about it. She dated a Lebanese guy. I thought I'd try something different. I've always wanted to travel. I saw Anthon's posting and answered. What's wrong with that?"

"I'm telling you that it wasn't a coincidence at all. I want to know who told you to go to that site."

"I already told you it was my sister."

"What did you do in Israel?"

"I went on pilgrimage. I won my church's raffle."

"Did you meet or talk to anyone from the Israeli government?"

"I don't understand your question. I saw an immigration officer at the airport, and maybe other members of the government helping tourists, but other than that, nothing. I was in a church group touring religious sites with twenty-two other men and women. Will you tell me, what do you want and who are you?"

"Never mind, you just answer my questions. Who's your father?"

"Patrick Sean Mitchell."

"Where is he?"

"Right now?"

"Yes."

"I don't know exactly. He could be in China, if I remember correctly. He's a mining engineer and travels all the time in connection with his work."

"I think you're Israeli agents."

"Huh?"

"You're working for Israeli intelligence."

"Is that a joke? I'm Irish, and spent all my life in Dublin and worked in a grocery store after graduating school. What do I have to do with espionage? I swear, you're making a big mistake. Are you from the police? You can call our constable in Dublin—he'll vouch for me. Or you can also call my parish priest." Erin started crying, convincingly.

The tall man used his mobile phone, but we couldn't hear the conversation. He folded the phone and put it in his pocket.

The other man pulled a chair very close to Erin's face until I was sure she could smell his breath. "Mademoiselle, I don't want to hurt you"—he paused—"unless I have to." He gave her a sinister smile. "Now answer my questions, and I'll let you go, I promise."

"I don't know what answers you want." Erin was sobbing, but I could see she was faking; she's a tough cookie. Her captors didn't seem to be touched by her spectacle. "I'll first take off your blouse," said the man on the chair. "Then your pants"—he smiled again—"then your bra, then your panties. Then you'll talk, or we continue by peeling your skin off."

Eric turned to Tim. "I think you'd better tell your men to get ready, before it gets worse. Did your men get a floor map?"

"Of course," he answered. "Tell me when to give the word."

"I want that bastard to move away from Erin first. He's too close."

Tim radioed his men. We saw on the monitor a group of seven or eight men dressed in black gear and wearing peculiar-looking hats. Before I could ask Tim what they were, he addressed us. "Please be advised that once we break in, I'll be the only one to give orders. Also, remember that your visibility will be limited, so please be patient."

The man next to Erin got up from his chair and told the

tall man, "Get me some scissors. I'll cut her clothes off. Otherwise I'll have to release her hands and legs."

Eric said, "Go for it now."

Tim gave the order. Suddenly the monitor went pitch-black.

"What the hell," I muttered, but soon realized what had happened. The assault unit had cut off power to the suite in which Erin was being held. I expected the door to be burst open, but they used a key card and just opened it, and six or seven men bolted inside holding automatic weapons, blinding the captors with halogen flashlights mounted on their hats. So that was the strange getup on their hats. We heard "On the ground, on the ground" and "Don't move." Although the flashlights gave us a general idea what was happening, it seemed like a devil dance. We couldn't see any details, and most important, we didn't see Erin.

The power to the room was restored. Erin was sitting calmly in her chair next to two armed men. The two captors were on the floor, their hands cuffed behind their backs. A policewoman removed the duct tape from Erin's hands and legs and then helped her get up. She led her to the bathroom. It was noticeable that Erin had difficulty walking after being strapped to the chair for hours.

"Let's go," said Eric, and we followed him to Erin's room. When we got there, both men were sitting on the carpet with dazed looks on their faces. Erin was still in the bathroom. "She's OK," said the police officer as she exited the bathroom. "She's a bit shocked, but she doesn't seem to be hurt physically. Our doctor is here to check her out as soon as she leaves the bathroom."

"Good job," said Eric to the police officer and to Tim as they approached him. "A nice clean job!" They were the highest accolades I've ever heard Eric bestow on anyone.

"We'd like to talk to these punks," said Eric.

"Well, we need to talk to them first," said the police officer. "They are under British jurisdiction. You'll have to coordinate that through your embassy."

He was polite, but firm. There would be no exception to the rule.

I saw the disappointment on Eric's face. "Sure," he said reluctantly.

Eric turned to Paul, Bob, and me and said, "We need to continue looking for Anthon. It could be days before we get interrogation access to these assholes."

"Eric," I said. "My experience has shown me that even if we have face time with them, it won't do much. They are criminal suspects, so normal rules apply. Don't forget that the rules have changed." He knew what I meant. The UK used to apply the "five techniques" for interrogation: wall-standing, hooding, subjection to noise, deprivation of sleep, deprivation of food and drink. But the European Court of Human Rights ruled that the five techniques were a practice of inhuman and degrading treatment, in breach of the European Convention on Human Rights. So now an interrogation could be like a gentleman's conversation at the club.

"Let's find Anthon before the UK police gets to him."

"How?" asked Bob.

"Tim's men are getting us the registration of the car that took Anthon. We'll start from there," said Eric.

The bathroom opened and Erin came out guided by the policewoman, walking shakily, pale and disheveled after her ordeal. "Glad to see you guys," she said faintly.

"How are you?" we asked, almost simultaneously.

"I'm a bit dizzy," she said, holding the policewoman's shoulder.

I gave her a bar of chocolate I'd taken from the minibar. "Here, that'll help you get some strength."

"Thanks, Dad." She smiled at me. But before she managed to open the wrapper with her trembling hands, a doctor with two paramedics and a stretcher came into the room.

"That won't be necessary," she said when she saw the stretcher. "I can walk." She took one step toward him and collapsed. The doctor, who'd foreseen what was about to happen, caught her under her arm just as she was about to land on the carpet. "Please leave," the doctor said firmly, "while I treat her."

We left the room, leaving behind Erin, the doctor, and the two paramedics. We waited in the hallway. Ten or fifteen minutes later, the door opened, and the paramedics hauled Erin out on the stretcher. She was looking pale, with an oxygen mask on her face, and waved her hand at us.

"What's wrong?" Eric asked the doctor.

"She's weak and dehydrated. I didn't find anything serious, but we need to stabilize her, run some tests, and keep her for observation at the hospital for a day or so."

As we were about to leave, the two captors were led out, hand and legs shackled, surrounded by some twelve police.

"Let's caucus," said Eric. "My room in forty-five. But first I have to send an aardwolf." He walked away.

That was a rare moment when Eric told us of his plans. An aardwolf is a thorough written report and assessment generated by a senior CIA field operative to Agency management.

"He's probably suggesting bringing in CTC—the Counterterrorism Center," said Paul.

"It's about time," I said, realizing we finally had live FOE to interrogate.

I returned to my room to freshen up. It was just past eight. I ordered a continental breakfast and went into the shower. I really needed that hot, relaxing stream. It delivered negative ions to my system, producing a biochemical reaction that decreased my serotonin level and helped to relieve my stress. The negative ions in the shower can make people sing, but I just couldn't do it to innocent hotel guests within hearing distance. Instead, I opted for the negative ions' positive influence on my mind and the way I process information.

Standing under the shower, I digested the recent events. Based on the kidnappers' questioning of Erin, I was concerned that my and Erin's legend wasn't as airtight as we'd thought earlier. Their questions were nothing more than shots in the dark, but they reflected a suspicion that couldn't be ignored. The mere fact that they went to the trouble of kidnapping Erin and risking themselves had shown that their in-the-dark shooting was accurate at finding the general location of an assumed target. However, I could tell that they were just thugs and unsophisticated interrogators: in their questioning, they'd revealed what they suspected and what they assumed. I dressed and went to Eric's room. Minutes later the rest of our team joined us.

"I got a call from the hospital," said Eric. "They admitted Erin and will keep her for a few days. British police are guarding her room. If any of you were thinking of visiting her, I suggest you forget about it. The hospital might be under observation by the captors' cohorts."

"I can visit her," I said. "I'm her dad, remember?"

"I suggest you don't. We heard her saying you were in China, and we also heard they suspected you as well." Eric had a point.

"Tim called," Eric continued. "They have a positive ID on the car that took Anthon."

"And?" Paul and Bob asked at the same time.

"Reported stolen in London two days ago."

"Have they found the car, though? It could give us some forensics."

"Not yet."

"OK," I said, trying to put order to my thoughts and

maybe move our investigation forward. "We know there are at least four people here: the two captors, Anthon, and the driver of the car."

"Right," said Eric. "But where does that take us?"

"It's more reason to believe that the motive for the kidnapping wasn't personal. Anthon had an organization here. The captors are not British, they came here from somewhere, and they used chloroform, which requires a prescription. They came with duct tape, rented a room, bribed a hotel employee to give them a key to Erin's room and her room number, and most important, security information. That shows planning and experience. It sounds like the perpetrator was an organization, not a person."

"Why is that so important?" asked Paul.

"Because it shows a preconceived intent," said Eric. Right, and it could focus our investigation.

"We need your input regarding the supposed purpose of the kidnapping. I mean the ultimate one," said Paul.

"I think they didn't intend to hold Erin for ransom, money, or something else," I said, "because they knew that once Erin disappeared, people would be searching for her. If she were just a country girl as she told them she was, it would have taken a few days before people started looking for her. She e-mailed Anthon that she moved to London and found a job. Her father is in China, her mother died, her sister is in Dublin. On the other hand, were she an operative of a foreign-intelligence service, reaction time would be very short. And that's exactly what happened. So in fact, by rescuing Erin before they made a ransom demand or took any step that revealed she was in their possession, we confirmed she was more than a shop assistant in a Dublin grocery."

"We heard them accuse Erin of being an Israeli spy. Doesn't that make it totally obvious that the kidnap wasn't personal?" asked Bob.

"Maybe," said Eric. "But it doesn't mean that we have to

support their suspicion by moving in too soon, unless Erin is in imminent danger."

Bob smiled. "I never thought of it that way," he said. "Anyway, I think we should ask CIA chief of station in Sierra Leone to get from Sierratel, the Sierra Telecommunications Company, outgoing and incoming phone records of the Shammas brothers. I'm sure Anthon was in contact with the captors."

"I've already done that," said Eric. "I also asked for the same records regarding Jacques Shammas in Ciudad del Este."

"How long will it take?" asked Paul.

"Ages," sighed Eric. "They take their time."

"I have an idea," I said. "Let's try Helmut von Ditka, the German businessman we connected with Abed Shammas. We could use him as a conduit to Anthon."

Eric used his mobile phone and spoke for a few minutes. "I don't know if they only spoke on the phone or have already met," he said. "I think the agent we assigned to pose as Helmut von Ditka is on assignment in another location on a different case, but we'll see. I put a tracer on him."

Just then, his phone rang. Eric listened and waved his hand at us. "Thanks, Tim," he said. "We're on," Eric told us. "Scotland Yard agreed to let us interview the kidnappers."

"When?" asked Bob.

"Right now. Their car is on its way to pick us up."

An hour later, we were in an unmarked squad van. "They are being held at the West End Central Police Station in Savile Row," said the detective driving the van.

We entered the station and were led by the detective to an inner office, empty of furniture but for one table and a few chairs. The entire opposite wall was a thick glass. Probably a one-way mirror.

"How do I introduce you?" asked the detective.

Shit, did we need a "proper introduction," à la old British Empire?

"You don't," said Eric curtly. "I'll ask the questions, if you don't mind," he said, turning to us. "There are too many of us here. Please go to the other side and watch the interview through the mirror, and listen in through the speakers." Apparently, Eric had been informed of the arrangements. Bob, Paul, and I went to the other room.

"I've always wondered about those mirrors," said Bob, making conversation in the terse silence. "I know they don't see us, but why not?"

"It's mostly because of the lighting of the two rooms," said Paul, glad to finally have an opportunity to volunteer his engineering knowledge. "The glass has a reflective coating applied in a very thin, sparse layer called a half-silvered surface, because it has only half the coat needed to make the glass a regular mirror. The interrogation room is kept very brightly lit, and the light reflects back from the mirror's surface. Therefore it appears as a mirror. In this room, because it is kept dark, there is very little light to transmit through the glass, so we can see through it like a window. On the interrogation-room side, when you look at the mirror, you see your own reflection."

Through the mirror we saw the detained tall captor brought in handcuffed. He was told to sit down. The detective said, "My name is Detective McPherson, and I am going to ask you questions and take your testimony."

The detainee just looked at him.

McPherson continued. "We gave you your first caution when you were arrested, that you were not obliged to say anything unless you wished to do so, but what you say may be put in writing and used as evidence."

"Yes."

McPherson said, "It is my duty to give you a second caution, since I am informing you that you may be prosecuted for an offense. Do you wish to say anything? You don't have to, but whatever you do say may be taken down in writing and may be given in evidence. Do you understand?"

The suspect nodded.

"Speak up," the detective said strongly. He wanted the recording device to get the answer.

"Yes."

Hearing the exchange, I thought of the Sherlock Holmes story, "The Adventure of the Dancing Men," where Dr. Watson describes a suspect that was arrested and warned of his right to remain silent. Sir Arthur Conan Doyle subtly mocked the "magnificent fair play" of British criminal law: " 'It is my duty to warn you that it will be used against you,' cried the inspector." No wonder the suspect just shrugged his shoulders and said, "I'll chance that."

"What is your name?" asked McPherson.

"Felix Saaid."

"Age?"

"Twenty-nine."

"Nationality?"

"Lebanese."

"Address?"

"In the UK?"

"Yes."

"No address. I came for a visit."

"Your permanent address?"

He hesitated. "I don't have one. I travel."

"What were you doing on the twenty-sixth floor of the London Hilton hotel when arrested by the police?"

"I was guarding my friend's girlfriend."

"Who is your friend?"

"I forgot his name."

"Was it Anthon Shammas?"

"I don't remember." He looked around and said, "I want to smoke."

"No smoking here, sorry. House rules. Why did you have to guard her?"

"Who?"

"The woman."

"She was kidnapped. My friend rescued her, brought us to her room, and went to call the police. Then you came and arrested me. I didn't do anything wrong."

Paul, Bob, and I exchanged looks of amusement. When this guy's IQ reached fifty, he should sell.

"Look," said McPherson, "I think you should stop with this nonsense. Your friend rescued his girlfriend but didn't release her from the duct tape?"

"You should ask him," said Felix.

"Why didn't he use the phone in the room to call the police?"

"I don't know, ask him."

"I will. Where can I find him?"

"Who?"

"Your friend?"

"I don't know."

"Who kidnapped the woman?"

"I don't know."

How deep did McPherson have to dig before he realized it was a dry well? Eric seemed to agree. "I think we've heard enough," he said, and got up abruptly to join us.

"Dan, I want you to continue with tracking back your movements. Go back to Ciudad del Este and see whether we overlooked anything."

"What about Anthon and these assholes?" I asked. I didn't want to be separated from the crowd, not after what I'd been through.

"We'll manage. I think we need to prioritize. Go to Paraguay. While you're packing, I'll call the embassy to alert them to make your travel and other arrangements."

"I want to be clear on my instructions," I said. "What exactly are we looking for?"

"Who was instructing and probably financing the mole you suspect is in the Romanian police. We agree with your assumption that he is not a Hezbollah operative or affiliate. See if the clue is there."

"I don't even know the mole's name," I said lamely.

"Mihai Turcescu. I'll e-mail you more details. Go pack your bags."

CHAPTER SIXTEEN

Reluctantly, I left the police station. Was I imagining it or was a pair of eyes stuck to my back? I stopped near a tailor's shop window, one of those famous Savile Row suitmakers, and took special interest in the reflection. There was no doubt. Two Middle Eastern–looking men were trying to avoid my spotting them. But training and experience was everything—they hadn't succeeded. I went to a red telephone booth on the street corner and called Eric's mobile, pretending to use the pay phone, but in fact I was using my mobile through the speakerphone.

"I've just spotted company. We, or least I, have been identified." I gave him the details and description.

"Give these men the merry-go-round," he said. "But they could also be connected to Felix and comrades and were standing outside the police station, without knowing you were connected."

"I agree, but if they took my picture for future reference, I'm toast."

Eric thought for a minute. "Try to dry-clean them. If they are persistent, that means they're after you specifically. Wait inside a café once you've lost them. Call me and we'll send a car to get you to the airport. An agent will meet you there with your instructions."

During my Mossad training we spent two weeks learning how to make sure we were followed and then shake off, or "dry-clean," followers. This was another opportunity to use my training.

First, I left the telephone booth and crossed the street. Through the reflection of a store's window I saw one of the men enter the phone booth, probably trying to redial the number he thought I'd used. That confirmed that I was indeed being followed. Next, I stopped a man walking opposite me holding a briefcase and asked him for directions. When he politely explained, I asked him about a library nearby, and when he wanted to point in a direction with his free hand, I grabbed it to shake it, making it appear we knew each other. That would force my followers to decide whether to follow him as well, thereby making them split.

Next, I hailed a cab. I told the cabbie to take me on a tour of London, and to cross Hyde Park several times. The roads within the park are not as congested as city streets, making it easier to spot followers. After an hour, employing tactics that made my cabbie cheer me on—he believed I was trying to lose a detective hired by my wife to track a possible affair—I was fairly certain that either I'd lost them, or they were watching the police station for some other reason. There was the chance, one I didn't really consider, that I'd overreacted or behaved as a common paranoid—although even medically diagnosed paranoids sometimes have real enemies.

I reported to Eric. "To be on the safe side," he said, "don't return to the Hilton. Find another hotel."

I found a small hotel in a quiet area in Hampstead, where followers would have a difficult time because traffic was slow. In the morning, a car with my luggage and travel documents was waiting for me. I went to Heathrow, met an Agency representative who gave me an envelope, and proceeded to the business lounge. I opened my instruction envelope and quickly read my instruction, written in plain language without any revealing specifics. I knew that an encrypted e-mail would follow. I sent Jacques Shammas an e-mail using Patrick Sean Mitchell's Gmail account.

Dear Jacques,
I'm sorry for not getting in touch with you earlier. I was asked to return to Ciudad del Este to do some final tests on location. I'll be there for about ten days and hope to have dinner with you. This time, I'm treating! I'll be staying at the Casablanca Iguazu Falls Resort. See you.
Patrick S. Mitchell

I knew that if Jacques was a member of FOE, then I could be in serious trouble for giving him a head start on my arrival. But I took the risk. I boarded an Iberia Airlines flight to Asunción, Paraguay, continued on a one-hour connection with Aerolíneas Paraguayas to Ciudad del Este, and checked into Casablanca Iguazu Falls Resort.

"Welcome back," said an all-smiles pretty receptionist. I went to my room and collapsed on the bed, clothes and all.

The room was dark. A rustling noise woke me up. I turned on the light. A message envelope had been slipped underneath my door. I picked it up.

Dear Patrick,
I didn't want to wake you up. I'm glad to hear you're back in Ciudad del Este. Please call me.
Your friend,
Jacques Shammas

In the morning I sent a message to Eric, Bob, and Paul. "Arrived in location. Initial contact was made, and response was nonthreatening. Will follow up."

I went outside to sit on the metal chairs in the hotel's walkway overlooking the Paraná River, just a few feet from a sloping lawn that extended to the river. I saw a few coatis running around looking for food. The wind was pleasant and the sun was shining, but my head wasn't ready to enjoy the view or the relaxed atmosphere. I was planning my conversation with Jacques and wondered whether he was aware of the recent events in London involving Anthon. After allowing myself the thirty-minute luxury of basking in the sun, I went inside and called Jacques. He sounded pleased to talk to me, and we agreed to have lunch that day. True to my promise to my children to lose weight, I skipped breakfast.

Jacques' Mercedes, with a driver and another man sitting up front, picked me up at one o'clock, when I was hungry and, as a result, impatient. The driver headed toward Ciudad del Este and stopped near the Friendship Bridge. "Where are we going?" I asked.

"To a Brazilian *churrascaria*, a very good one," said the man sitting next to the driver. The two side doors were opened at the same time and two men entered the car, one from each side. I was stuck between them.

"Go," said the man on my left. He told the driver to move fast, a mission impossible in the congested traffic on the bridge.

"Where is Mr. Shammas?" I asked, starting to feel uncomfortable with the situation.

"He is waiting for us at the restaurant," said the driver. "Have you ever eaten in a *churrascaria*?"

"Yes, on several occasions in New York." I liked the Brazilian version of a rotisserie steak house. "Where is it? Far from here?"

"Just across the border," he said briskly. What? Jacques had never said anything about crossing to Brazil. When we approached the checkpoint, our driver just said something I couldn't hear to the officer, who just waved at us to continue. We were in Brazil now. "Maybe I'll have an opportunity to visit Iguaçu Falls while I'm here," I suggested. I made plans to bolt out of the car in the first traffic jam or red light, if we were to leave the center of town.

"We're very close," said the driver. He pulled into a single-story building and parked the car. The sign said CHURRASCARIA DO SOL.

My concerns were eased as I walked in and saw Jacques sitting next to a table with a white cloth, tasting wine.

He got up and embraced me. "I'm very glad to see you," he said. I sat across from him and the *passadors* (meat waiters) came to our table, each with a knife and a four-foot-long skewer holding a different kind of meat. On the table were small round cardboard coasters with a round NO ENTRY sign on one side and a green traffic light on the other. They were used to signal the *Passadors* to stop bringing more skewers or to keep them coming. The meal was delicious and the company friendly.

Jacques asked very little about the reason for my visit and never mentioned Anthon or Erin. He raised his glass. "This is to our friendship." He drank his glass down and I sipped mine. A moment later, I felt heat waves overcoming me. I was nauseated and felt like I was going to faint. That was the last thing I remembered.

As I came to, I felt my dry lips, my numb nose, and a terrible headache at the back of my head. I opened my eyes and closed them again. The light was too intense. I took a deep breath trying to remember what had happened to me and where I was. I heard voices, people talking in Spanish and some in Portuguese.

I opened my eyes again. I was in a room, lying on a bed. Two or three men were sitting on chairs against the wall. I raised myself a bit, but the headache was too intense. I let my head drop back on the bed.

"Where am I?" I asked. "What happened?"

"You passed out," said one of the men. "Too much to drink."

I wanted to say that I'd only had one glass of wine, but

stopped in midsentence. I felt my stomach turn, and the little suspicious devil in me told me to shut up, because I was in trouble. *The less you say, the better you are*, he advised. Interestingly, these were also my instructions during training at the Mossad. Another lesson I should have remembered: my little devil must have learned something as well. The second rule that he told me to pay attention to was the fact that we had moved from Paraguay to Brazil.

> *A last-minute or unscheduled change in the plans or in the place of a meeting is frequently ominous, particularly if you're meeting anyone other than your longtime personal friend or family. A member of FOE will always try to move your rendezvous to another location where you wouldn't have had time or opportunity to prepare defenses.*

It had been stupid of me to go alone to the meeting with Jacques without even a single backup, particularly when his cousin's son Anthon had proved to be vicious and unpredictable. I didn't know, though, if I was being held prisoner or was just being taken care of after a case of food allergy or poisoning. It took only a moment longer to figure out: my right hand was chained to the bed.

I raced to remember if I'd been carrying anything telling on my person. But routine habits forged during long years of experience assured me I was all right. Everything I was carrying identified me as Patrick Mitchell. There was nothing to connect me to any other alias I'd previously used, or to the U.S. government. What about the laptop computer I'd left in my hotel room? I wasn't too concerned. The hard drive was empty of any data, and to use the computer you needed a twelve-character password.

"Where am I?" I asked. "And why am I chained?"

A dark-faced man sitting next to the window answered in a thick Arabic accent. "Shut up."

Now, that was an unfriendly response. But after all, since I was drugged and chained, I probably shouldn't have expected the red-carpet treatment.

"Water," I croaked, my lips dry and my throat hurting. "Can I get some water?"

"Ooskoot ya Kalb," shouted the man. Why did he shout at me in Arabic? Did that mean he thought I could understand the rude Arabic words for "Shut the fuck up, you dog"? Couldn't he have used the more polite word, *ookhloos?* I'd have to lodge a complaint with his boss. I knew it wasn't a time for humor, but that was my way of calming down. First Erin was kidnapped, and now her "dad"? Were the events connected? Apparently.

I needed to choose a strategy, and fast. I had to assume that either my or Erin's legend had been breached. I feared thinking what would happen if both legends had been compromised.

I didn't get any water or explanation. I closed my eyes and listened to the occasional conversation. Maybe I'd learn something about what the hell I was doing here. The only thing I could gather was that the men were waiting for their boss to arrive.

An hour later, the door opened. All the men rose to their feet as a medium-built man in his early thirties with coarse black hair, a thick mustache, and sunglasses walked in. Classic, I thought, but he took the glasses off and signaled for the men to sit down.

"Señor Peter Wooten?" he asked as my heart palpitated. "Or maybe you prefer Patrick Mitchell?" He didn't wait for an answer and added, "I have just one name, Marwan."

I felt as if the ceiling were crushing me—or make that the entire sky. In one sentence, two of my legends were blown, and it would be very difficult to BS him without consequences. And more important, it probably wouldn't work. He had me as his prisoner, and that meant that I'd been had.

I didn't answer, mainly because I had no answer. I was glad, though, that he hadn't discovered half a dozen other aliases I'd used while on assignment for USG and previously for the Mossad, or my real name. I'd been stripped of all defenses; I didn't know what he knew and what he didn't. How many forms of *shit* did I know? It looked as if I'd need to use plenty of them. OK, so I knew I hadn't joined the Peace Corps—shit came with the territory with the CIA, even if you were just a transient. But why had I been getting truckloads of it lately?

"Tell me," said Marwan slowly and deliberately. "What were you trying to achieve?"

"You mean here? Get more sand samples for potential sites."

"Señor Wooten, do you think I'm stupid? You're insulting me. Give me an answer I can live with. What were you hoping to achieve here?"

"I gave you my best answer," I said and closed my eyes, because usually after I offered these kinds of answers, a blow to my face followed. But not this time.

"Señor Wooten, you underestimate us," he said quietly in a tone that shivered my spine. "Please don't make me force you to answer."

"Marwan . . . is it Mr. Marwan, or is it your first name?"

"Just call me Marwan."

"I'm embarrassed. You call me Señor Wooten, and I can't extend the same courtesy?"

"Just Marwan," he said firmly.

"I have another question. You said 'we.' Who is we? Are you from the Paraguayan government?"

"Señor Wooten, we heard that you were a smart-ass wise guy. Not here. I'll make you answer me. I have time, but you don't."

I didn't realize that my reputation traveled continents.

"You can kill me only once," I said, wondering whether that was an accurate statement.

"Maybe, but I can make you wish many times that I'd killed you. You can save yourself the trouble."

Before I could answer, he raised his eyebrows, signaling to a man standing behind me, and I felt a blow to the back of my head that shook me, darkened the room, and sent me to oblivion. I woke up hours later, judging by the darkness outside. I was alone in the room. I was still chained to the bed and could only turn halfway on the bed. I was thirsty, hungry, and aching. I raised my hand to see the type of chain they used. It was a U.S.-police style of handcuffs. I wished I could get my hands on a safety pin, paper clip, bobby pin, or piece of wire to shim open or pick the lock.

One cuff was holding my wrist, and the other end was locked around the bed frame. I rolled to my right to see the connection to the bed. The handcuffs allowed me to get off the bed, but I was too dizzy to try and fearful to attempt it before I could evaluate the time I had and the risk of my efforts being discovered. The bed frame was a standard metal frame used for queen-size beds with an additional center rail support. I rolled over, searching it with my left hand. I realized that they had chained me to the center crossrail. I sent my fingers to feel the frame and found a point where it was connected to the center bar with two bolts and nuts. I heard the noise of people talking and quickly assumed my martyr position: on my back with hands stretched to my sides. Marwan entered with another younger, muscular man dressed in shorts and a dirty T-shirt. He had dark eyes, and a scar was visible on his left arm and cheek. The scar on his cheek hadn't healed well, leaving a pulled-up left cheek and permanently exposing part of his upper jaw, giving him the look of a hungry piranha.

"Your friends in London captured Anthon Shammas," Marwan said in a disinterested tone. "I'm sure you know that unless they release him immediately, you are no more."

"Anthon? You mean that young man who was in contact with my daughter? Who got him and why?"

"Señor Wooten, unless you stop giving me attitude, I'll have to ask Joao here"—he pointed to the young man standing next to him—"to make you talk like a parrot."

I didn't answer.

Marwan flashed a small camcorder. "We'll make a short video. You will tell the CIA and MI5 that unless they release Anthon by noon tomorrow, you will die." He handed me a piece of paper. "This is what you'll say. Not even one more word."

I didn't answer.

"Are you ready?" he demanded.

I nodded. What other choice did I have? I sat up in bed stretching my chain to its maximum range. I held the paper with my left hand and read out the message: "I ask that Anthon Shammas be released immediately, or I will die. This is a serious matter. Please do as I ask, I beg of you. I don't want to die."

I felt ashamed and guilty, but I was sure they'd understand at home that I'd been coerced, particularly when they analyzed the audio to detect the hidden syllable I was trained to stress if I was under duress.

"Good," said Marwan, satisfied, and turned to Joao. "Give him some water."

I was very hungry, and felt dizzy. "Can I have some food as well?" I ventured. Marwan snapped something to Joao and both left the room. Twenty minutes later Joao brought me a plastic bottle of mineral water and a meat sandwich, which I devoured. I drank half the bottle and put it under the bed for later use.

Marwan returned to the room. "Now tell me everything about you. Start from the day the CIA recruited you."

"I have nothing to tell you about it. I'm a mining engineer and have never worked for the CIA."

"I'll ask only one more time before I call Joao."

I just lowered my head. Marwan went to the door and told a man guarding my room to call Joao, who came, unchained me from the bed frame, and hooked the handcuff to his left hand. He led me out the door to a narrow and dark corridor, down two flights of metal stairs, and into a windowless basement.

"Nobody will hear you cry," said Marwan who appeared out of nowhere. I looked around. It was a torture room. They tied me to a chair.

"See this?" asked Marwan, pointing at a bar of metal hooked with chains to the wall.

He didn't wait for my answer and continued, "The Brazilian police call it *pau de arara*, or parrot's perch. It's very effective." He showed me a photo clipped from a newspaper describing prisoners' torture in Brazil.

"Do you see how it works?" he asked in a teacherlike tone. Again he didn't wait for an answer. Joao stripped me naked and tied me to the bar, suspending me from the back of my knees, with my hands tied to my ankles.

"Soon you'll be like a parrot—and you'll talk like one, believe me," said Marwan laughing.

I closed my eyes. He continued, "I'm going to use this on you," and flashed just the bottom of a battery-operated stun gun from his pocket. "Do you know what a stun gun is?" he asked, as if we were walking in the park and he were trying to remember a name of a flower he'd seen.

Of course I knew. Stun guns are handheld devices that send, through two metal probes, a high-voltage, low-current electrical discharge to sensitive parts of the body. The low electric current is pushed by high voltage to overcome the electrical resistance of the human body. The resulting shock is caused by muscles twitching uncontrollably, appearing as muscle spasms. It makes people talk. I knew that after three or four jolts, I'd admit that I was Cain and that I'd killed Abel. After five or six, if I could still speak, I'd declare that I was Napoleon.

"Have you seen a fish out of the water? Now think of your muscular spasms when you get the shock. Did you write your will yet? I don't want to kill you yet, but there are cases of people who went into cardiac arrest after such a shock. I'm just wondering."

I didn't answer.

Without warning Marwan touched my rib cage with the stun gun. I felt deep pain, and became paralyzed.

"Here is another one," he said, and I blacked out.

It was obvious that he made every effort to make me suffer. In that respect, he did a fine job—I *was* suffering. He wasn't going to kill me, for now, since I'd become a subject of potential prisoner exchange. The good news was that Eric and MI5 had caught Anthon. Too bad I was the one to pay the price. They'd made the video before my visit to this torture chamber, before any torture wounds showed up on my flesh. I had to give them credit for advance planning.

Sending my photo without any visible sign of torture would signal to the Agency that there had been no need to torture me, because I must have spoken voluntarily.

"I'll give you until the morning to decide. If you still refuse to talk, we'll be back here," promised Marwan. He told Joao to bring me back to my room. Marwan left while Joao reconnected my handcuff to his hand. I was naked and held my clothes with my other hand. He told me to leave my shoes behind and directed me to the staircase. It was dark and I was dizzy, so I tripped and fell on the stairs, rolling backwards, dragging Joao with me. I fell on him—not a light punishment, as I was one hundred pounds heavier than him. This was a one-time opportunity. I quickly folded my knee to press his diaphragm, sucking the air out of his lungs, and clenched his jugular with my left hand. Remembering that there was an armed guard just one floor above us, I put my chained hand over Joao's mouth. He still managed to let out a weird sound that was muffled by my hand, and to make sure he'd go to a better world for the next hour or so, I suffocated him with my shirt, which I was still holding. Was falling on the stairs an accident? Just at the beginning it was, but I'd immediately seen the potential. Although Joao was much younger than I, he was a foot shorter and a good deal lighter. Sometimes an unwanted membership in the overweight club has its privileges.

With a sudden rush of adrenaline, my hands were trembling as I was searching his shorts for the handcuffs key. I retrieved the small key, but immediately dropped it in between the metal stairs. I heard it fall to the lower floor. I had no time to lose, and dragging Joao with me to the lower floor to search for the key in the darkness wasn't a practical idea. But I had to release myself from the handcuffs one way or the other.

Half a floor above us was a door. I put Joao on my shoulder, and panting and breathing hard, I gingerly opened the door. I saw a dark corridor with three offices. I was still naked as I walked to the first office's desk and searched, in the dark, for a paper clip. The first one I found was too big. I kept feeling the desk with my fingers and found a smaller paper clip. I put Joao down on a chair so that our hands would be on the same level. With a steady hand, I inserted the end of the paper clip into the handcuff lock and turned it. It clicked. I tried opening the handcuff, but it didn't work. I turned it again for a second click; it remained in place. I knew I had to be careful not to jam up the lock. For the third time I slowly inserted the clip and the wire went in deep enough. I turned it once and it clicked open. I took a deep breath.

I looked around. I had to prevent Joao from getting help when he woke up. I hoisted him back on my shoulder and slowly walked back to the staircase and down into the basement, and locked the open handcuff to the metal bar of the *pau de arara*. "Now, you'll be the parrot to sing," I told him, but he was still unconscious. Marwan had told me that nobody could hear my yell when I was tortured here. Joao would put it to the test.

I put on my shoes and climbed back to the office floor to

search for things I could use. I opened a few desk drawers looking for a gun, but couldn't find one. I did take a long metal letter opener, though. When no singing nightingale was to be found, a crow would also do. I saw a small refrigerator and took two small bottles of water. I peeped out—the corridor was empty and the building seemed to be quiet. The guard on the upper floor seemed not to have heard anything. For a minute, I thought of going upstairs and overpowering him for his gun, but I discarded the idea. I didn't know how many more people were around who could hear the struggle.

I walked out of the office to the hallway and found the door out. The building was built on a slope, and there was more than one exit. A gust of warm wind lifted my spirit. I was free. I had no idea where I was. I suspected I was still in Brazil, but couldn't be sure. I touched my pockets. They were empty. All I had were the bottles of water, the letter opener, and a strong sense of defiance and anger.

I went to a parking lot. Three cars were parked, all with Brazilian license plates. I tried to open the doors, but all were late-model, Japanese-made cars equipped with central locking systems. Fearing the cars were also protected by alarm systems, I decided against breaking a window to get inside. I looked around me. I was in a business area of offices and light industry. I used cross streets to get away from the building I'd been held in as quickly as I could, but remembered to memorize its address. I had to find a pay phone, but even after walking a mile, I couldn't find any. All the shops and restaurants were also closed. For lack of choice, I kept on walking and hiding each time I saw car lights coming my way. They could have been a search party.

From a distance, I saw the lights of a gas station. I walked there. It was closed, but they had a pay phone. I had no coin to dial. I couldn't understand the instruction label that not only was written in Portuguese, but was also half–scratched off. I pressed several buttons in despair and finally got to an operator. She didn't speak a word of English. I tried Spanish. That she understood. I didn't have the CIA's access number in Brazil that connected to Langley. I finally gave her the number for the duty officer at the DOJ main building and reversed charges. They accepted the call.

"This is Dan Gordon. I'm a senior investigative attorney at the Office of International Asset Recovery and Money Laundering. I'm in distress, probably in Brazil, but I'm not sure where. Please connect me with Eric Henderson." I gave him the number.

After a verification process, he said, "Please hold on." Three minutes later, which seemed like a century, because cars were passing by and I had no place to hide and couldn't disconnect the call, Eric came on.

"Hi, Dan. Where are you?"

"I don't know. I was drugged and kidnapped. I got away, and this is my first call. I'm in a gas station somewhere, probably in Brazil, but I'm not sure."

"Dan, are you still wearing your shoes?" came his calm— I'd say too calm—voice.

What an idiot, I muttered. Not Eric, but me. I'd completely forgotten that I was wearing shoes with a GPS device that should identify my location in no time.

"Yes, I have them on. Please identify my location and send for help. I have no money or documents."

"OK," he said. "Get yourself to an open-air shelter to avoid masking the signal, but in case we lose contact, can you give me any reference to where you are? A building, an address?"

"Hold on," I said. "I must be in Brazil, because all the signs are in Portuguese." I looked at the gas station sign. "I'm in Foz do Iguaçu. I see tall buildings in the distance, and the address on the door is Avenida Costa E. Silva, but I can't get a number."

"OK, stay put. It may take a few hours, though. You're in a remote area."

"Remote? Millions of tourists come to see the falls. Get someone here as fast as you can."

I didn't know if Eric heard my last sentence, because I had a dial tone telling me that the conversation had ended. I went behind the gas station and sat on a junked office chair, leaned my head against the wall, and fell asleep. I was tired after that long and busy night of torture.

I was awakened by the heat and the noise. Summer in Brazil is not a cool season. I'd left London in the rain with temperatures in the thirties, and now it was probably nine A.M. and hot. The street became busy. I stretched, and ventured to the front of the station. No cars were filling up, but the shop was open. I used their bathroom and washed up a bit. I looked in the mirror. I had a two-day beard, my eyes were red, and there was an ugly red mark on my face. I couldn't even remember how I'd got it, whether it was from Marwan or from the fall on the stairs. I was hungry but decided against moving too far to look for food. I told myself that this imposed diet would do me good, but the hunger made me restless.

Four or five hours passed and there was no sign of Eric's men. I thought of calling him again, but decided against it. I didn't want to be locked in a telephone booth clearly visible from every passing car. A man who was probably the gas-station manager came over and said something in Portuguese. I didn't understand the content, but the tone was hostile, and with his hands waving, I got the message that he wanted me off his property. I walked to the street looking for a better place to wait.

I should have known the peace wouldn't last. Not five minutes later, an old-model American-made car stopped right behind me. Three men grabbed me and tried to force me into the car. I saw Marwan slowly exiting the car on the driver's side, watching us. Amazingly, a group of young students who were walking on the sidewalk ran over to intervene. In the melee I broke loose and ran toward Marwan, who jumped back into the driver's seat. I opened his door, and without hesitation stabbed him with the letter opener in his rib cage, pushed him inside, jumped in, and drove away. Marwan looked at me in disbelief, trying to decide what hurt more, the letter opener in his ribs or the fact that I'd overpowered him. But he didn't give up and was trying to grab the wheel. I slowed down, and with my right hand, I pushed the letter opener deeper. A growing bloodstain was visible on his shirt.

I wasn't going to repeat my mistakes. "Sorry, Marwan," I said. "To err is human, but to forgive is against Company policy." To demonstrate the policy, I hit his jaw with my right hand. He stopped fighting. I parked the car on a side street and searched him. I grabbed his wallet, and his gun as he was trying to pull it out. I opened his door, pulled him out, and pushed him into the backseat, face down. I looked in his wallet. There was a lot of Brazilian and Paraguayan money, which I didn't count. I had to decide what to do.

I couldn't wait for Eric's men to come—it could be too dangerous. Marwan may have had a backup team, and the local police could intervene. Bottom line? Return to Ciudad de Este. That could be unwise, but since it would also be the conclusion of Marwan's men, who'd continue looking for me in Brazil, I chose that option. I followed the signs to the Friendship Bridge. This time the officer at the checkpoint asked for my papers. I answered in English that I didn't understand, that I needed to get my friend who was in the backseat to a doctor, because he wasn't feeling well, and I enhanced my request with a bunch of bills I took from Marwan's wallet. I was sure Marwan wouldn't mind.

We crossed the bridge. I couldn't return to the Casablanca hotel, not knowing what to expect. My laptop computer and personal belongings were there, but I decided to go there only escorted, in case we encountered members of FOE.

CHAPTER SEVENTEEN

I found a hotel that didn't even ask for any ID. I insisted on getting a ground-level room with access directly from the parking lot. "My uncle is in a wheelchair, and he'll be joining me soon." I even paid extra for an additional person in my room.

I moved Marwan—my uncle—into the room. It wasn't easy. I locked the door and walked a few steps to a pay phone near the laundry room. I called Eric and told him where I was, but didn't elaborate how I'd made it.

He was cool. "My men are already looking for you in Foz do Iguaçu, I'll let them know where you are now. We're making arrangements to return you home." I still had some unfinished business here before going home, but I didn't share that thought with Eric. I also had to remove the car from the parking lot, but couldn't leave Marwan unattended.

Next, I called Alberto, the jack-of-all-trades who'd sold me supplies when I first came to Ciudad de Este. "Get me a doctor—there's been an accident." I gave him the hotel's address, and an hour later, he came with another man.

"Dr. Gonzales," he introduced himself. I didn't let Alberto enter the room, but gave him enough money to keep his mouth shut. The money came, of course, from Marwan's wallet. "He isn't injured seriously," said the doctor, who pulled the letter opener from Marwan's ribs. "I don't see any internal bleeding, and he'll be all right."

"Why is he unconscious?" I asked the doctor at the door when I paid him, as usual, from Marwan's wallet.

"Unconscious? He is not."

"What do you mean? When I brought him in, he was unconscious. I had to drag him."

"Señor, he is very weak and needs resting, but he's fully alert."

I ran inside and caught Marwan by his shirt the minute he was getting ready to leave through the door leading to the parking lot. "Sorry, Marwan. You're not going anywhere." I pulled him back to the room and waved his gun in his face. "You're not going anywhere before we talk. And to make you talk, I won't need the *pau de arara*. I have better ways to persuade you."

He was very pale and breathing heavily. His black eyes were shifting from side to side. I didn't want to start interrogating him until Eric's men arrived with equipment. The things I wanted Marwan to tell me should be recorded. Therefore, I thought I'd take the friendly approach.

"What is your name. Is it really Marwan?"

"Yes, Marwan."

"And your last name?"

"No last name."

"OK," I said. I didn't want to be confrontational. At least not yet. I had his wallet with his driver's license.

"You're not a supporter of Hezbollah, are you?"

"All Muslims support Hezbollah."

"On religious grounds? Are you a Shiite?"

"No, on the basis of their struggle."

"Against whom?"

"The Christians, the Western civilization, the Israelis."

"Sounds more like Al-Qaeda."

"I support them as well," he said fiercely.

"This is a war you can't win," I said, hoping to get him started ideologically.

"You have no future, only present," he said contemptuously. "We're returning to center stage."

"That's nonsense. You're nothing but a bunch of criminals with a recently invented ideology. I bet that most of your followers are those that were refused a visa to the U.S." I couldn't think of a more incendiary speech to get him going.

"Criminals? Are you familiar with Salman Rushdie's book *The Moor's Last Sigh*? You'd better read it."

"Have you? He's your declared enemy, and you recommend his book?"

"He is, but you should read the book to understand our history, not to follow his infidel ideas."

"I will," I said, "I promise. But until then, tell me."

"The book will tell you who we are and how we're going to get our honor and lands back."

Of course, I knew about the Moors, the Muslims that had their own kingdom in Spain until Granada was conquered by Ferdinand and Isabella in 1492. Then they were forced to convert to Christianity. However, these converts didn't blend into society and were mocked as "Moriscos" until finally exiled at the beginning of the seventeenth century. Europe and Spain became Muslim free. But not for long.

"The last Moor to leave Europe looked back and sighed. We're not sighing anymore. We're back. Listen to Osama bin Laden's recent speech, calling for the return of Spain to Islam, turning it to a caliphate."

I found this conversation to be totally bizarre. Why was Marwan talking about Europe and Spain, when he was a Lebanese living in South America? Was he sending me a message?

"Do you think you can convert the Spanish people to Islam just because their ancestors fought your ancestors five centuries ago?" I asked.

"It is never too late to correct a wrong," he said. "Andalusia and Granada represented the glory of Islam, and they will be rebuilt as Islamic centers. This is rooted deep within every Muslim. Look at the palace of Bashar al-Assad, the Syrian president. The only painting displayed in the hall where he receives his guests describes Andalusia on fire. Have you seen the two-hundred-Syrian-pound banknote?"

I found this to be very showily educated for someone I thought to be just a random guy.

"No."

"It shows Salah ad-Din, who drove out all the Christians from Palestine. Do you know what is Assad's birthday?"

"No."

"Nine eleven."

"Are you telling me it has any significance beyond just being the day he was born?"

"Do the math: one plus one is two. He supports our cause by displaying the Andalusia-on-fire painting for his guests to see, and promotes the idea that a new Salah ad-Din will drive the infidels away. We gave him a birthday present soon after he became president."

"What's terrorism in the U.S. got to do with Muslims returning to Europe?"

"The Americans claim to be the leaders of the West. There's a price to pay for leadership into colonialism and imperialism on Arab lands. America is the head of a snake invading Islamic lands and culture."

"Go eight hundred years back and see the Christians invading as Crusaders to a land populated by Muslims. That was colonialism. But now do you call spread of democracy an invasion?" I asked.

"And as for your imperialist wars," he went on, "we don't want your values. You'll be driven out like the Crusaders."

"So? Do you hear Christians vowing to return and kill the Muslims by the sword?" I was still trying to provoke him.

"The Muslims want their right of return to Europe. See what happens. In a few years many European cities will have a Muslim population majority. The first will be Dutch cities. See how many new mosques are built in Europe."

"So are we having a religious war?"

"The Islamic world against the Christian world."

"There's no such thing as the 'Christian world,' in national terms. You can talk about Western civilization, or democracy and human rights."

"We'll win, because we're determined to win. Young Muslims by the thousands enlist to defend Muslim beliefs and fight for jihad."

Had I heard what he'd said correctly? There was more than a hint that he was a supporter of Al-Qaeda's preaching idea, of what Osama bin Laden was saying, and about Bashar al-Assad's support of the right of return of the Muslims to Spain. These were not Hezbollah's ideas, they were Al-Qaeda's, plain and simple. Were we dealing here with Al-Qaeda while we were chasing Hezbollah? Was Al-Qaeda the real FOE? Whatever the conclusions to be drawn from this conversation were, it opened a door to a completely new direction. Was this a mind game or a clue? Was Marwan the local boss of Al-Qaeda? I had been lured to meet Jacques Shammas, who I'd always believed was a Hezbollah supporter. So were Hezbollah and Al-Qaeda in rivalry or in cooperation? Were Marwan and the Shammas brothers my lead into the upper echelons of Al-Qaeda?

I heard knocking on the front and the back doors at the same time. I peeped through the door and I saw familiar faces. They were Eric's men. I opened both doors. Six men came in.

"I'm Tony," said the man who entered first. "Eric sent us." He gave me the password created for such cases: *sisterhood*. He then quickly passed a handheld scanner over my shirt. It beeped. The RFID tag had survived my ordeals.

"Glad to see you guys," I said.

"I see that you're OK." He looked at me.

"Right, I'm fine." It had taken them long enough.

Tony called Eric to report, while his men handcuffed Marwan.

"Good catch," said Tony, looking at Marwan's driver's license, which I had just given him. "Marwan al-Bakri? Bullshit. This is Khallad Derwish. We've been looking for him all over. We have his photo on our wall at the office, and not because we're his fans. He's a card-carrying member of Al-Qaeda, posing a clear and imminent danger to the United States."

"What are we going to do with him?" I asked, realizing Marwan was listening attentively. Tony looked at me with Marwan behind him, and winked.

"We can't take him back with us to the U.S., so we might as well whack him here."

"Good idea," I said, catching his drift. "He tortured and threatened to kill me."

I looked at Marwan, or Derwish. He was pale but calm.

Tony's handheld communication device vibrated. He looked at the minimonitor. A color photo of Derwish appeared.

Tony looked at Derwish and the photo. "It's the same guy, all right." He read the text and showed it to me. "Khallad Derwish, also known by several aliases, DOB 2/15/75 in Beirut, Lebanon. Known to have attended Al-Qaeda training camps at the Al Farooq complex in the mountains west of Kandahar, Afghanistan. Later, he traveled to Bosnia to help the Muslims. In 1997, he was jailed for extremist activities in Saudi Arabia. After an early release, he ended up in Ciudad del Este as the commander of Al-Qaeda operations in the Triple Frontier region of Paraguay, Argentina, and Brazil, a duty mostly involving recruiting volunteers and raising money."

"A big fish," I said quietly. I asked Tony to follow me to the hallway.

"Seriously, what are we going to do with him?"

"I'm waiting for instructions from the Company. Until then, we stay put. I think that the real interrogation of this asshole should be done at home. There isn't much we can do here without alerting the entire city's police force, who'd probably hear him cry if we used any special interrogation techniques."

"Do you have details regarding London?" I was anxious to find out. All I knew was that we'd gotten Anthon.

"Nothing," he said. "If the info isn't operational, I suggest you wait until we get back."

Tony's communication device vibrated again, and a message appeared. "We want him here. Get him ASAP. We'll clear it later with the Paraguayan government. Be at the airport's parking lot at ten A.M. tomorrow. Use caution, as suspect's men are looking for him."

Two of Tony's men left and took Marwan's car with them. "Dump it in the city somewhere," I said. They returned an hour later with a beat-up rented van and also brought pizza and soda. I went to the reception desk and rented three more rooms. "My uncle came with his family," I said. The receptionist couldn't have cared less, particularly when I paid in cash—from Marwan's wallet, of course.

I approached Derwish, aka Marwan. "Are they going to kill me?" he asked, trying to keep a straight face, but the tremble in his voice told me he was terrified.

"Only if you try to escape or attack any of us. If you make it in one piece to the U.S., you will be tried."

"For what? I was never in the U.S."

"Your presence in Al-Qaeda training camps, your recruitment of volunteers for jihad against the U.S, and your fundraising for them, will send you to prison for the rest of your miserable life. You provided material support to terrorists." I didn't mention a death penalty he could face, as I didn't want to tell him he had nothing to lose before we got to the U.S. "Now, let's not forget kidnapping me." I pointed at the agents. "They'll take no shit from you. If you try anything, each will shoot you just once, but there are six of them. That'll be enough to dispatch you directly into the receptive hands of Satan. I know he has plans for you at the furnace."

I went to speak with Tony. "I think we should search his premises before we take off. Derwish's driver's license and his business card list his address. Let's check it out."

Tony thought for a moment. "I'd advise you against it. We can't just go there and risk confrontation with his men without intel telling us what the risks are."

"I think I'm going to try it anyway," I said, trying to be pleasant, but in clear defiance. I wasn't taking orders from Tony. He was sent to bring me back home, not to be my babysitter. He was giving me all sorts of reasons why I shouldn't, and I had one good reason why I should: Derwish must have had relevant intel in his office, and the opportunity was there. It was night, and we had Derwish chained. There was another reason why Tony's arguments were met with my defiance: I don't give up. He grimaced, but knew there was nothing he could do. He finally relented, giving me an expression of someone badly constipated, and more arguments were the last thing he needed. He had to get me out of his sight.

"Can you at least send one of your men to protect my backside?"

"Well, OK, but it's against my better judgment." He addressed a young man in jeans who was chewing gum. "Josh, go with Dan as his security. Take your handheld with you."

"Thanks, Tony," I said. "Can we take the van?"

Tony nodded.

We drove to the center of town looking for Avenida Monseñor Rodriguez y Carlos Antonio López, which appeared on Khallad Derwish's business card under the business name Derwish & Co. Import-Export, SA. The address was of a three-story commercial building with a variety of colorful signs of different sizes. The street seemed to be a part of the city business center, but at this time of night, it was empty. We parked the car in front of the building and entered the staircase on its left side. It was dark. I found the light switch and turned it on. The staircase area was dirty with scattered pieces of paper, discarded cigarette boxes, and plastic cups. On the inside wall were ten or so mailboxes, all of them with broken doors showing a history of tenants coming and leaving. I found the box for Derwish & Co. Import-Export, SA. It contained a few bills and junk mail. I took the bills and put them in my pocket.

"It's on the third floor," said Josh after studying the building directory. He pressed the elevator button.

"I'm not taking that elevator," I said. "With the kind of maintenance of the building I see here, we could get stuck. Let's climb up. I need the exercise."

On the third floor was a long corridor. The Derwish & Co. Import-Export, SA office was the third one. It was dark, and the door was locked. "It's just a simple wooden door," I told Josh, "so let's break in."

"Tony told me to protect you. So do whatever you do, but I can't help you with it."

There was no point in arguing with him. But I needed tools. "At least go back to the van and get me the jack and a wrench."

Josh left without a word. Meanwhile, I walked along the corridor reading the signs on the doors, making sure they were dark.

Josh returned with the van's jack and a wrench. I put the jack on the door's left panel and cranked it against the door, and the door broke open. The noise was more than what I'd expected, and we quickly jumped into the office.

"You'd better stay outside and guard the entrance, in case anyone comes," I told him.

Derwish's office had one executive office, two back offices, and a reception area. I only turned on the light in the back office to prevent any light coming out of the windows of the reception area. The entire office was in complete disarray. Empty or half-empty boxes of textile goods, piles of shipping documents on the desks, full ashtrays, and dirty coffee cups. In the executive office I saw a photo of Al Aqsa Mosque in Jerusalem on the wall.

That must be Derwish's office.

I went to the back office, but it had nothing interesting. I turned off the light and entered the other back office. It was probably used by a bookkeeper, judging by the calculators with paper rolls. I couldn't find anything of interest. It seemed that Derwish was also running a legitimate business, in addition to his clandestine activity. I looked for his telephone directory on the receptionist's desk, but to no avail. I returned to Derwish's office and sat at his desk. I looked around and found a worn-out telephone directory. I turned on the computer, but it required a password. I turned it off and unplugged the power cord. I returned to the hallway.

"Josh," I asked, half whispering. "Is everything OK?"

"So far," he said.

I returned to Derwish's office and unscrewed his computer's cover. I located the hard drive, disconnected it from the cables, and put it in my pocket. As I turned around, the hard drive dropped on the floor next to the desk. I sat on Derwish's chair and picked it up. But I also saw something that made my pulse race. Underneath the desk was a small vault. I had to open it. A small amount of explosives could do it, but I had none. The vault, though small, was bolted to the floor, and there was no way I could carry it out. Bolts or no bolts, it still weighed at least two hundred and fifty pounds.

I looked at the combination lock in near despair. I had to find the combination. I searched Derwish's drawers, his desk, the receptionist's desk. . . . Nothing. My only alternative was to return to the hotel and make Derwish give me the combination. Before moving toward the door, I looked in Derwish's wallet again to find the note I'd seen yesterday when I searched it. In my haste to find cash, I'd flipped through papers that at the time looked meaningless. I was also too impatient to decipher the several Arabic notes it contained. I wasn't lazy now. I went over the three small notes handwritten in Arabic. The first note read

ثلاثه يسار اربعه يمين سته يسار واحد يمين

I thanked my Mossad instructors, who'd insisted that we get at least a basic command of Arabic. It took me years to appreciate it. I read the note twice. There was no question it was a combination: *three left four right six left one right*. I turned the dial, the vault clicked, and the door opened. Inside were six document files, checkbooks, cash, and a .38 gun. I collected the files and the gun and locked the vault. I needed a bag to carry out the files and the hard drive. The only thing I could find in the office was a women's plastic tote bag. I emptied its contents on the desk and stuffed it with the files and the hard drive. I examined the gun, pushed in the magazine, engaged the safety, and put it in my pocket. I now had two guns. I turned off the light and went to the hallway, also taking the jack and the wrench.

"Josh?" I called. There was no answer. I gingerly walked to the third-floor elevator door and looked down the staircase right next to it. I called Josh again, but he didn't answer. I put the bag on my shoulder and cocked the gun. I started descending the stairs very slowly without turning on the light. I finally made it to the ground floor, and peeked outside.

Josh was being hassled by two Spanish-speaking men,

probably Paraguayans. I heard them arguing, and soon they were pushing and shoving. I saw one of the men draw a knife. I put my stuff on the floor and drew the gun, aiming at them in case things got beyond words and pushing. However, I immediately discovered why the training course at the Farm took eighteen weeks. It must have included a good deal of martial arts classes. Josh, after they had pushed him two or three times, decided that enough was enough. With both hands, he grabbed their shirt collars and banged their heads together. That was just the appetizer. As I heard the cracking sound of the meeting of their heads, he added the main course—separating them again as his elbows struck at their lower chests. For dessert, he kicked their groins with a swing of his leg. They fell to the sidewalk panting and crying in pain. I ran toward him, thinking to get a piece of the action, but they were flat on the sidewalk, with no sign that they intended to get up. Josh said coolly, "Let's go."

"What happened?" I asked as we entered the van.

"I made a security tour while you were in the office and went downstairs to see that all was clear. I saw these punks hovering around our van. I approached them, and they tried to rob me. Well, you saw how it ended." He started the engine. "What do you have in the bag?" he asked.

"Stuff I found," I said. He didn't ask any more questions, and we returned to our hotel. I went straight to my room. My roommate for the night wasn't there yet. I sat on my bed, opened the bag, and retrieved the files. I just didn't know where to start. I was overjoyed. There were lists of donors, with names, addresses, and amount contributed. Next to each name was a marking in Arabic describing the donor's affiliation and willingness to contribute. Some markings said "willingly"; others said "needs persuasion." I had no doubt what kind of persuasion was needed. There were deposit slips for several bank accounts in Paraguay and Brazil. I also saw memos sent and received from individuals with Arabic names. Al-Qaeda was mentioned on multiple occasions, most of the time together with *jihad*. Altogether, I must have retrieved approximately one hundred documents.

I wanted to read more and celebrate the discovery, but I was so exhausted that I could barely keep my eyes open. *Let me sleep on it*, I thought, and lifted the mattress, shoved the files underneath, then went to sleep with one gun under my pillow and one gun in my hand. Just in case. I was sure, though, that when I gave Eric this treasure trove, he'd include himself in the list of people who wanted it to happen, mention Derwish and his men, who wondered what happened, but would forget me, who'd made it happen.

In the early morning, three agents quickly moved Khallad Derwish into the van, and I went with Tony in his car. A third car was behind us. I told Tony about the encounter Josh had had last night with the two men. "Yes, he already told me. I think they might have been guarding Derwish's office," said Tony.

"I think you're right," I said. "What's the plan?" I asked as we neared the airport.

"We'll wait here," he said. "I think we must be prepared. If the two men were Derwish's men, we'll soon see more of them. Ciudad del Este is not that big, and they could easily conclude that whoever broke into Derwish's office will leave through the airport."

We parked in the parking lot next to the service gate of Guarani International Airport northwest of Ciudad del Este. Tony ordered two of his men to cover us from a distance—a smart move, for soon after we arrived, three cars sped into the parking lot. The two agents Tony had placed on the two ends of the lot began firing their automatic weapons at the three cars. Two cars slowed down significantly when the bullets hit the drivers or the tires, but they slammed, albeit at reduced velocity, into the two cars of the agents. The third speeding car exploded thirty feet before it could slam into the cars. The CIA operatives jumped out from their badly dented cars with guns drawn, some of them bleeding, but the parking lot had already become eerily silent. The opposition who'd come to Derwish's rescue had been eliminated. It was nine fifty-five A.M., and Tony got the call, "You're cleared to go."

"Leave your cars behind," shouted Tony to his agents. "Get into the van!" With doors still open and everybody clinging for dear life, we sped across the one hundred yards to the open service gate and drove directly onto the tarmac. An unmarked Gulfstream V turbojet with tail number N379P was parked nearby with its engines shrieking. Eric emerged from the jet's door. "Move it, move it." We rushed to climb in, and in one or two minutes, which seemed like an eternity, we were airborne.

I looked outside through the window. The parking lot was still vacant of people, and only smoldering cars evidenced the short-lived action we had had there. Khallad Derwish was put in the back, placed in a "three-piece suit," which is a set of leg restraints, a belly chain, and a set of handcuffs looped through the belly chain so that the hands are restrained at the waist. He was then chained to a hook on the floor, while two gorilla-size men watched him. We were seated up front around Eric.

"Are we all here?" he asked Tony.

"Yes. Two of my men are slightly wounded from the collision. The rest are fine."

Eric asked the two injured agents whether they felt they should make the full flight. "We can land in Miami and get you medical help," he said.

They shook their heads, and one of them said, "We'll be fine."

Eric called the pilot through the intercom. "Ask for priority landing privileges, an ambulance for two injured agents, and security arrangements for a high-value detainee."

Eric looked at us and broke the news. "The president was briefed on our success in his PDB—president's daily brief on intelligence matters—and he sent his congratulations. We've also received confirmation that the Brazilian and Paraguayan governments gave their permission for the rendition of Derwish to the U.S."

"Of course they agreed," I said. "They don't need that scumbag in their territory. Anyway, I have a goody bag here," I told Eric and waved the ladies' tote bag.

"I wondered what you were doing with that bag." Eric was amused. "What's in there?"

I told him, and added, "I hope this time the documents are not forged."

"We'll see," said Eric, who didn't even get the undertone.

After a short refueling stop in Miami, we landed at Dulles Airport near Washington, DC, and drove to a safe house just off Dolley Madison Boulevard in McLean, Virginia. Derwish was brought inside. I was full of energy to participate in his interrogation.

"We're not going in," said Eric as he saw me getting ready to exit the car. "They need to process him first and get a doctor to check him over. We're not sure yet whether he'll be interrogated here, but anyway we can join the party after he's been interrogated for a few days, when most of the information juice has been extracted. Then we could do a follow-up."

I was surprised and frustrated, but what could I do?

I was drained from everything I'd been through, so I flew to New York and called my children. I went home to play with Snap, who was jumping and licking me as always. A week later, after some briefing and debriefing sessions, Eric called to arrange for our team's interrogation of Derwish.

I was met at the Williamsburg, Virginia, airport and was

driven to the Farm. "It's more convenient here," said Eric. "With in-house security of the best kind, we can focus on the agenda."

We parked next to a barrack in an isolated section of the Farm. Inside was a big room with a visible video camera, and some that I gathered were not visible. Two interrogators were waiting next to a long and narrow desk. Khallad Derwish was dressed in jeans and plaid shirt. He looked pale and tired.

Paul and I were given a thirty-page brief on Derwish's prior interrogation. After reading it, I wondered what was left to get out of him. He was like a skinny onion, after all its layers are peeled off. He admitted to being the head of Al-Qaeda in South America, recruiting volunteers, raising money, and participating in meetings that had led to major terrorist attacks.

"I think we should focus on Operation Pinocchio," said Eric. "How did they get to be ahead of us?"

I expected Derwish to look subdued after I read the confession CIA interrogators got from him. I don't know what tactics they used, and I didn't ask. But Derwish looked defiant.

"Derwish," I said. "Here we meet again. Maybe this time I can get some answers."

"I've already told them everything I know," he said wearily.

"Well, there are matters I want to clarify with you."

He didn't answer.

"When did you hear my name for the first time?"

"What name? You have plenty."

"Any of the names you mentioned."

"About six months ago."

"How?"

"I got a word from my comrades that the CIA was attempting to infiltrate our organization, and they said that a Peter Wooten would be coming to Ciudad del Este."

"Who is the person that gave you that information?"

"I don't remember."

"Try harder." I raised my voice.

"I think his name was Ali, but I'm not sure."

"How did he know about Peter Wooten's visit?"

"I really don't know; you should ask him."

"Do you have his last name?"

"No."

"How did he give you that information? By phone? Personally?"

"By phone."

"Had you ever talked to him prior to that conversation?"

"No."

"Then how did he know your name and number?"

"I don't know."

"You said that the CIA was attempting to infiltrate your organization. What organization did you mean?"

"Al-Qaeda."

"Do you know Jacques Shammas?"

"Yes."

"How?"

"We both came from Lebanon and worked in Ciudad del Este."

"Is he an Al-Qaeda supporter?"

"All Muslims support Al-Qaeda."

"But Shammas is a Maronite Christian," I said.

"Many of them support us as well."

"Did he make any money contribution to your organization?"

Derwish hesitated. We both knew that it was an important question, but for different reasons. Derwish didn't know we'd broken into his vault and retrieved his donor list; his answer to that question would tell me if he was telling me the truth.

"I think not."

"You don't know for sure? He's a prominent businessman that you personally know."

"Maybe he made small contributions."

"Any other help from him? Other than money?"

"No."

"Are you sure?"

He hesitated. "I think so."

"Well, Jacques Shammas is also in custody, and he tells me that you forced him to give Al-Qaeda not only money but also other assistance."

He turned pale. "I don't believe he told you that."

"Why not? Is he lying?"

"I never forced him to do anything. He helped us voluntarily."

"Well, he says that you're a bunch of thugs that threatened his family and business unless he helped you. That's why he agreed to lure me to a meeting so I could be kidnapped."

Derwish was moving in his chair. I continued to hammer him. Was Jacques Shammas in custody? Of course not, at least not yet. But Derwish, who'd been cut off from the world, couldn't know I was bluffing.

"I'm telling you that Shammas confessed that he gave you personally fifty thousand dollars in cash, in addition to the money you forced him to contribute to Al-Qaeda. He said that you used the money to buy drugs to smuggle to Brazil and distribute there."

Derwish's face became red. "That's a lie," he yelled. "He never gave me any money for my personal use. I don't know why he's inventing these things."

"Prove to me that he's wrong. We have a deal with him that if his confession is found to be truthful, he'll be released in one year, but if we catch him lying, he'll serve a life sentence. Can you prove he's lying?"

"How can I do that when I'm here?"

"Tell me what you need, and I'll get it for you."

Derwish looked at me, trying to see if I was joking.

"I'm not joking," I said. "What do you need?"

"In my office there are records of money contributed to Al-Qaeda. I could show you that Shammas only gave us five hundred dollars, not fifty thousand dollars."

"He said he gave it to you personally," I said.

"*Kalb*," he retorted in contempt, *dog* in Arabic. That was a good sign; I'd gotten him to warm up. Analysis of the file I'd taken from Derwish's office showed various small contributions from Jacques Shammas, but I was certain he could have helped Al-Qaeda in more ways than just by giving money.

"I can get the records you mentioned if you sign a letter to your people directing them to give us the documents."

He looked at me, startled. "There's no one who could get it but me."

"Let's talk about our first meeting. I had a scheduled lunch appointment with Jacques Shammas in Ciudad del Este, Paraguay, but ended up chained to a bed in Brazil as your guest. That puts you in bed with Shammas."

He bristled. "I never went to bed with him!"

"I meant figuratively," I said. "He cooperated with you. Why?"

"I told you, he supported our struggle."

"So he told you I was coming Ciudad del Este?"

Silence.

I repeated the question. He didn't answer.

"I'll have to turn you back to your previous interrogators to soften you up," I said. How had they gotten him to spill so much? And why was he a raging bear with me?

"There's no need to," he said and gave me a scared look. "Yes," he added faintly.

"Speak up!"

"Yes."

I wanted to make sure. "Shammas told you I was coming?"

"Yes."

"Did Shammas identify me as Peter Wooten?"

"Yes."

"What else did he tell you?"

"That you work for the CIA and that they are trying to sneak into Hezbollah."

"But you're Al-Qaeda. Why did he tell you that?"

"I already told you that. He supported us."

"Maybe he gave you that information because you threatened to kill his family and burn his business unless he helped you?"

"Did he tell you that?" he asked.

I nodded.

"It's true that I asked him to help us, but I never said I'd kill his family."

"So he cooperated with you all along?"

"Yes."

"Did you know about my movements in Ciudad del Este?"

"Yes, right from the beginning of your visit we recorded your conversations."

"You did?"

"No, Jacques did."

"Was I followed?"

"Yes, by us."

I decided to tighten the screws and became more aggressive in my interrogation. I pressed him regarding the identity of Ali.

"He is Palestinian," said Derwish finally after a lengthy back-and-forth. "I understood it from his accent."

"Why did he choose to call you?"

"Because people know I support Al-Qaeda, and he wanted to help."

"Did you ever call Ali?"

He hesitated.

"Derwish, don't lie to me!" I said in an ominous tone.

"I may have."

"Where can I find his number?"

He didn't answer.

"Was there more than one conversation between you and Ali?"

"Yes."

"How many?"

"Several."

"Did you talk about me?"

"Yes."

"Did you use a code name to identify me?"

"Yes."

"What was the code?"

"Tall snake."

I considered whether to pull out Derwish's telephone directory and ask him to show me Ali's number, but I decided against it, because Derwish could deduce that we'd retrieved additional, far more damaging documents from his office.

We took a break. I went outside and took a brisk walk. An hour later, Eric and Bob came over with gloomy faces. Eric handed me a folder. "This has come in from Paraguay."

Inside were sixty pages of phone records. "Derwish's?" I asked.

Eric nodded. "Our analysts identified all the numbers. I also just read the transcript of your interrogation of Derwish."

"And?" I knew from Eric's face that something bad had happened.

"Derwish wasn't lying when he said Ali was in contact."

"Are we talking about the same Ali? Benny's asset in Europe?"

"Yes, it's him," said Eric grimly. "Ali Bin Tulila, who was recruited by Mahmoud, Benny's case officer. Ali believed he was working for France, and now it seems that he had also another master—Al-Qaeda."

"That's what happens when an asset doesn't feel committed to anyone. Does Benny know?"

"Yes," said Eric. "I alerted him yesterday."

"What is he going to do?"

Eric gave me an amused look that extricated him from his mood. "You know what happens in cases like this."

"They need to find him first," I said.

"I understand that it's what they are doing. Ali will have to provide the Mossad with some good answers." We were silent for a moment. What else had been compromised? Eric went on. "In the meantime, I want you to continue with Derwish's interrogation."

After I was done with Derwish, I returned to New York with Eric and also Bob, who'd arrived in Washington earlier that day.

"It looks like he'll be declared an SDGT and be tried by a military tribunal," said Eric as we hit I-95 North. "He could get the injection."

"A military tribunal? It's very disconcerting. We did all this work, and these guys are going to come in and take it over," said Bob. Always with the turf battles.

"These matters are above our heads," said Eric. "In a military tribunal, the prosecution won't have to reveal the methods applied and the information obtained from its intelligence investigation. We can't allow that."

I thought about Derwish. When I was his prisoner, Derwish was boastful, displaying self-importance, a pathetic demonstration of an exaggerated sense of his power. The problem with his grandiosity was that although he'd behaved as if he were at the top of the world, he had a fear of heights. At the end of the day, he was a coward, a deflated balloon.

"It's all over," said Bob.

"Well, in that case I owe an explanation to Mikaela, the prison's psychologist."

"Dan, you owe her nothing. It was just a job. Nothing personal. Don't tell her who you are, unless you want the State Department to come knocking on my door. Again." Bob was serious.

It was more than a job, I wanted to tell him—she was there for me when you weren't. But again I managed to keep my mouth shut. I'd find a better way.

A few days later, I called Mikaela. I had to talk to her. As usual, she was happy to hear my voice. "Thank you very much for the beautiful track suits you sent my son. He wears them all the time."

I'd forgotten all about it. "I'm glad he likes them. Anyway, there's one thing I forgot to ask you. When you gave me the documents in Sofia, you said they were given to you by your friend at the police."

"Yes, but he's no longer there. I think he resigned or was fired."

"Did he also give you the coroner's report?"

"No. I took a copy from the prison's files. I thought you should have it as well."

"So he didn't know you gave me the autopsy report?"

"No. Is it important?"

"No, not anymore," I said. For a moment, I thought of defying Eric and Bob's instructions not to reveal my real identity to Mikaela, but realizing the potential dire consequences to the U.S.-Romanian relationship, I didn't.

"Anyway, the reason I called was to ask whether you'd be interested in applying for a fellowship position at John Jay College in New York, working toward a PhD degree. John Jay's reputation is in criminal justice. I hear they have a very good doctoral program in forensic psychology."

"Peter, thank you so much. I wish I could, but you know I can't do that on my meager government salary."

"Well, I made some phone calls, and it seems that if

they determine that you are qualified academically, you could get into their PhD program. You'll pay no tuition, get room and board, and even some money as well. The program takes three to five years, and at the end you'll get a doctorate."

"That's—that's fantastic. Where is John Jay?"

"In New York City. It is part of the City University of New York, a highly respected university."

"What do I need to do?"

"I'll send you the initial contact information, and you can take it from there."

"Peter, I can't thank you enough," she said, making me feel guilty. "If I come to New York, we could see each other more often."

If Mikaela could pass the hurdles and end up in New York, I'd think of some way to level with her, I consoled myself, not knowing if I ever could. Even if we couldn't develop a relationship, it was nevertheless more thrilling to be on the brink of love than in the trenches of a relationship that could fail. There was an ocean of different cultures dividing us, and so many lies.

Manhattan
August 15, 2007

Benny, Eric, Paul, and Erin were having a quiet conversation in the conference room when I walked in.

"Let's begin," said Benny, who unexpectedly wasn't looking angry or sad. He was all business. "Ali talked."

"Voluntarily?" asked Paul.

"At some stage, yes," answered Benny, leaving to our imagination what had caused Ali to cooperate.

"As I reported earlier, we caught Ali in Austria as he was about to board a plane to a Gulf state. He discovered that Derwish was captured, and he understood he'd be next unless he took off. We suspect it wasn't his final destination, and that he planned to hide in a different country. Ali denied it and claimed he wasn't running. He was perplexed, though, to realize that his captors were Israeli. We removed him to Israel, and we have been interrogating him for the past two weeks. We're far from done, because there are many questions we need answers for."

"Does he know he worked for the Mossad?"

"We're not sure. At the beginning, he protested his detention and claimed he was an Algerian citizen working for France. But at some point he may have understood he was actually working for us. However, we got some answers regarding Operation Pinocchio."

"Give us the basics that concern us," said Bob, who was noticeably impatient.

"OK," said Benny. "But first there's some necessary background. Ali was recruited in France by Mahmoud to work for us approximately two years ago."

"Was there a domino affect?" asked Eric. "Was Mahmoud rotten as well?"

Benny shook his head. "We checked Mahmoud in more than one manner, and he's clean. He's a proud Palestinian Arab that believes the Israeli-Arab conflict must be resolved peacefully, and vehemently opposes terrorism. His family has a strong history of loyalty to the state of Israel. When he targeted Ali, also a Palestinian Arab, their relationship looked natural to all concerned. Mahmoud told Ali he was working for France, and Ali agreed to collect intelligence in Europe among Palestinians. Verification techniques we applied sporadically to Ali never indicated any suspicious conduct. Ali was freely roaming Europe on an Algerian passport in a job that wasn't exactly nine-to-five, and was therefore hard to control. Twelve months ago, Ali met Al-Qaeda operatives that hooked him, or 'trapped' him, as he claims. As a result he was doubled by Al-Qaeda and told them everything he knew about Operation Pinocchio."

I looked at Eric. I was sure he thanked the Mossad in his heart that they'd kept Ali for themselves, thereby preventing CIA contamination outside Operation Pinocchio.

"Twelve months?" I said. "That means that when I met him in Paris, he was already working for Al-Qaeda."

"Even earlier," said Benny. "First he sold to Mahmoud the idea of infiltrating Hezbollah by installing an expert in a subject they needed. Then he pushed Badescu to the Shammas brothers for an introduction to Hezbollah."

"If he was working for Al-Qaeda, then why was he pushing Badescu toward Hezbollah?" asked Paul.

"A smart move," said Benny. "Ali presented the idea that Badescu would work for Hezbollah and get paid by the Shammas brothers. We liked the idea, because Badescu was expected to report to Ali, who in turn reported to Mahmoud, who was working for me. In reality, since Ali was Badescu's handler, he filtered the information Badescu gave him and blocked us from vital information Badescu gave him. Instead, he delivered it to Al-Qaeda. When we decided to send Dan to meet Badescu in Bucharest, Ali faced a problem. On the one hand, he had to comply with our instructions to arrange the meeting, but on the other hand, he feared that Dan's direct contact with Badescu could potentially reveal that Ali was betraying Mahmoud and the Mossad. That sealed Badescu's fate. He had to die."

"Did Ali kill him?" asked Paul.

"Yes. In a clever move, Ali and his Al-Qaeda comrades decided to kill several birds with one stone. Ali went to Badescu's house unannounced. Badescu knew him, of course, and let him into his study. Ali killed him and had a Romanian accomplice, who waited outside to call the police when he saw Dan enter, posing as a concerned neighbor. That framed Dan. When Dan managed to get away from Romania by pretending to agree to work for SRI, Ali and his Al-Qaeda comrades tipped the police that the assassin was Enver, who could easily be connected to Hezbollah, but they gave the description and address of Dhimitër Daci."

"Who was Daci?" asked Bob.

"A day laborer, a nincompoop convinced by Ali to admit to the murder he never committed. Ali gave him five hundred euros in cash and promised another ten thousand if he pulled off the ploy, and 'guaranteed' he'd be out of prison within a year. Ali and his partners gave Dhimitër the identity of Enver, a known Albanian Hezbollah operative. Then they had Dhimitër killed in prison to silence him forever, thereby cementing the blame for Badescu's murder on Hezbollah."

"How did Dhimitër die?"

"Al-Qaeda had a mole within the Romanian police, Mihai Turcescu, an ethnic Romanian-Albanian who was secretly supporting Al-Qaeda. He came to the prison 'for a visit,' entered Dhimitër's cell, and poisoned him. We think he gave him a small bottle of vodka laced with rat poison."

"Where is Turcescu now?" asked Paul.

"We don't know."

"Why the runaround between Enver and Daci? Couldn't they put the blame on Enver and kill him later on?" I asked.

"Ali confessed that they had a deal with Enver to spy on Hezbollah for Al-Qaeda and save his life."

"Why do they need to spy on each other?" asked Paul.

"The Shiite-dominated Hezbollah and the Sunni-led Al-Qaeda's silent struggle for supremacy and attention continues the centuries-old rivalry between Sunnis and Shiites," said Benny. "Iran, in an effort to expand its regional influence, pushes Hezbollah to become more active. And Al-Qaeda must remind the world that they, not Hezbollah, carry the torch for Islam. Therefore, although the two organizations could be cooperating, it's always on a local and temporary basis that does not change the rooted rivalry."

"Do you know where Enver is?" asked Bob.

"No," admitted Benny. "But we are looking."

"Did you ask Ali about the incident in Sofia?" I asked.

Benny said, "Indeed. Ali laughed when we asked him about it. He said it was a clumsy move perpetrated by Mihai Turcescu that backfired. The idea was to frame Hezbollah for Badescu's murder. But Turcescu had no control over the coroner and didn't realize Mikaela would take the initiative to add the autopsy report to the envelope she gave you in Sofia."

"Was the police report that Dan got from Mikaela forged, as Eric suspected?" asked Bob.

"Legally, yes," Benny chuckled. "It was a genuine report that was 'edited' by Turcescu to suit the particular needs of his ploy. But the body of the report was authentic."

"That's why our lab determined it to be a forgery," said Eric, without retracting his earlier insinuation that I knew the documents were a complete fake.

"What about me?" asked Erin, who had been quiet until then. "I'm still in the dark why Anthon kidnapped me."

"It's complicated," said Benny. "Ali told the Shammas brothers, and Anthon in particular, that Erin was a CIA agent."

"So far so good," said Erin.

"Ali taunted Anthon for letting himself fall for a CIA agent and told Anthon that he could get even by kidnapping Erin or risk the suspicion of the community that he was Erin's accomplice. Anthon fell for it. What Ali didn't tell the Shammas brothers or Anthon was that he knew Dan was also a plant and he wanted to get to him through Erin. Ali thought that the legend that Dan was Erin's father would continue to be played, and Dan would rush to rescue her and could be nabbed. But when Eric told Dan in the London police station to travel to Paraguay immediately,

Dan saw two men who were casing the station. He suspected them and shook them off and disappeared. They were later arrested by Scotland Yard. They carried Dan's photo, taken in Sierra Leone, and admitted they had plans to kidnap him."

"I've already had my share of kidnapping," I said.

"Did Ali talk about the documents Dan took from Badescu's house?" asked Bob.

"Yes—in fact, we owe Dan an apology. The documents were genuine, some collected and some prepared by Badescu under Ali's orders, to make Hezbollah look responsible for attacks that killed many civilians, but in fact were perpetrated by Al-Qaeda. Badescu, albeit working for Hezbollah, couldn't care less. He complied with Ali's instructions without questioning him about what the purpose was. Badescu was an outsider, and the organizations' rivalry was of no interest to him, as long as Ali kept paying him with the Shammas brothers' money."

I looked around, but no apology was forthcoming.

"Who was the threatening person on Badescu's answering machine?" Paul asked. "The threatening message made the assassination look like a criminal homicide resulting from a dispute over money."

"We're not sure. It could have been Turcescu, the policeman, but Badescu is dead and Turcescu has disappeared. SRI is looking for him."

"He could be somewhere under a rock in Afghanistan," I said.

"Probably," agreed Benny.

"What about the Shammas brothers? Were they in the loop?" asked Bob.

"No. Ali maneuvered them as well. Ali used a business contact he had with the Shammas brothers to mention their name to Mahmoud. Then Mahmoud suggested that we use them as conduits to infiltrate Hezbollah to safeguard French interests in Lebanon. Ali had also mentioned to Mahmoud at the beginning that the Shammas brothers had a cousin in Ciudad del Este, an area known to be a hub for Islamic extremists' activity. Therefore, when Anthon posted his message on LebaneseDate, it was a perfect way to make the initial contact with his family in Sierra Leone, and from there to another family member in Ciudad del Este. That route was very important, because it enabled Dan to appear recommended by locals, a must in this close-knit society traditionally suspicious of strangers."

"The only problem was," I said, "that I was a walking target. These recommendations placed me in the center of their sights." I gave Eric a sharp look. "You never told me you knew ahead of time about the Ciudad del Este contact of the Shammas brothers."

"I didn't?" asked Eric. "Maybe I forgot."

"Does that mean we were transparent to Al-Qaeda throughout Operation Pinocchio?" concluded Bob.

"Pretty much," conceded Benny. "But let's apply the 'last man standing' test. We jointly captured the leader of their South American operations. We have volumes of documents that are likely to lead us to more successes. We exposed a double agent who deceived us, and we most certainly prevented or at least hindered attacks on the U.S., because their operatives must be on the run, fearing they were exposed. They don't know how much we know about them after the break-in into the vault in Ciudad del Este and following the capture of Derwish and Ali."

"One thing you didn't mention," I said amusedly. "Now we can give Al-Qaeda and Hezbollah a real taste of black propaganda, this time well-founded by facts."

"How?" asked Paul.

"Pitting them again against each other. Al-Qaeda tried a dirty trick on Hezbollah that was nearly successful. Do you think Hezbollah will swallow its pride? Each day that passes without these groups cooperating serves the purpose. Let them fight."

"Not a bad idea," said Eric pensively. "Not at all."

A week later, I was called to a meeting in the main Justice building in Washington, DC. Eric met me at the entrance. "Let's go into the conference hall. You'll have a surprise," he said. It was the warmest I'd ever seen him.

Staggeringly, for someone who works in the shadows, it was a news conference, and at its head was the assistant attorney general for national security.

"United States law enforcement," he said, "has identified, investigated, and captured an Al-Qaeda-trained terrorist who headed their South American operations. The arrest sends a very important message: terrorism is real, and not just in the United States. Victories are won every day. Here and worldwide. These are victories in the war on terrorism. But individual glory is insignificant when compared to achieving victory as a team." He went on to praise the CIA, and the Department of State and Department of Justice. No names were mentioned. I was OK with it—one more mention of my name would send me back to a desk, and I'd joined to be a hunter. His personally addressed letter of appreciation arrived two days later.

I thought of my conversation with Khallad Derwish before he'd disappeared behind the door of the interrogation room, chained and shackled.

"Do you have any regrets?" I asked him.

"No. Jihad will release me."

"Only hellfire will set you loose. Remember our conversation about the Moor's last sigh? Well, you'll have the same fate, because Jihad will bring disaster to your followers. Sighs will be accompanied by tears."

"Muslim men never cry," he said defiantly.

"Let me tell you about Boabdil Abu-Abdallah, who was